# DEATH
# NOTICE

# DEATH
# NOTICE

TODD RITTER

Minotaur Books ☎ New York

This is a work of fiction. All of the characters, organizations, and events portrayed in this novel are either products of the author's imagination or are used fictitiously.

www.minotaurbooks.com

ISBN 978-0-312-62280-0

First Edition: October 2010

10  9  8  7  6  5  4  3  2  1

*To Mike, for everything*

# DEATH
# NOTICE

# PROLOGUE

The pain snapped him into consciousness. A sharp, steady throbbing, it began at his mouth and pulsed down his jaw and neck. He tried to moan—it was the kind of pain that made men moan—but couldn't. The pain flared so badly after each attempt that he stopped trying.

He stayed quiet, listening to the ragged streams of air rushing through his nostrils. When he opened his eyes, he saw only darkness as something brushed against his lashes.

Cloth. Heavy and rough.

He was blindfolded.

His face felt damp. He wasn't sure, but he thought it was blood, smeared across his chin. A thin line slipped down his cheek. The liquid was inside his mouth, too. On his tongue. Pooling in the crevices between his teeth.

Blood. He was certain now. He could taste it.

He lay flat on his back, his body stretched taut, arms at his sides. When he tried to move them, they wouldn't budge. Rope was wrapped across his arms, legs, torso, and head, binding him tight. The pressure flattened him, ironing out the stooped shoulders that fifty years on the farm had given him.

He began to panic, breathing faster through his nostrils, a locomotive picking up speed. He tried to yell for help, parting his lips to scream. But his mouth wouldn't open. His lips refused to separate, the pain there growing more extreme. He tried two more times, the hurt so bad it formed deep grunts in the back of his throat. Since the grunts had no way of escaping, he was forced to choke them back.

On his last attempt to scream, he realized what had happened. The pain brought clarity, sharpening his mind so that he understood the situation fully.

Someone had sealed his mouth shut.

He tried to scream once more, hoping the sheer strength of the sound would blast through the barrier his lips now created. The noise that emerged was familiar to him. He heard it all the time on the farm—the high-pitched squeal made just before the slaughter. Only this time the sound was coming from him.

He heard another noise, audible beneath his own desperate attempts to cry out.

Footsteps.

Someone else was there.

"It won't be as bad if you hold still," a voice in the darkness said.

The owner of the voice stood just behind his head. He felt warm breath on his ear. Fingers crawled along his chin and held his head in place.

Something pressed against his neck. Cold. Sharp. There was a moment of pressure, an unsettling suspense. Then the cold, sharp something pushed *through* his skin, entering his body, dividing flesh from flesh.

Blood poured out of him, spilling onto his shoulders, dampening his hair. He lay there helpless, feeling like a freshly gutted animal. Each beat of his heart sent another wave of blood coursing out of his body.

This time, the pain was unbearable. It wasn't just at his mouth anymore.

It was inside him.

It was everywhere.

He began to scream. Not out loud, but in his head, the desperate sirens of noise ricocheting off the inside of his skull. The cold, sharp something remained in his neck, wriggling. The pain was so overwhelming it erased his thoughts, his silent screams. It kept erasing until there was nothing left in his head but pain.

And fear.

And, finally, darkness.

# MARCH

# ONE

"Chief Campbell!"

Kat's name rattled up Main Street as soon as she set foot on the sidewalk. She had just stepped out of Big Joe's, a Starbucks wannabe, carrying an extra-large coffee, for which she had paid Starbucks' prices. Normally, the concept of four-dollar java would have annoyed her. But it was a gray and frigid morning, and she needed the heat and clarity that coffee provided. Unfortunately, the sound of her name, now being shouted a second time, prevented her from taking that first, precious sip.

"Hey, Chief!"

The source of the yell was Jasper Fox, owner of a flower shop burdened with the name Awesome Blossoms. Despite the cold, perspiration glistened on his face as he barreled up the sidewalk. Huffing and puffing, he waited until he reached Kat to finish his sentence.

"I've been robbed."

Kat, coffee cup suspended in front of her mouth, blinked with disbelief. In Perry Hollow, robberies happened about as often as solar eclipses. Its pine-dotted streets and exhaustingly quaint storefronts were mostly trouble-free.

"Robbed? Are you sure?"

Jasper had an absurd mustache that dripped from his face like two dirty icicles. Whenever Kat saw him, she thought of a walrus. That morning, the mustache drooped even lower than normal.

"I think I'd know," Jasper said.

His hangdog expression told her he had been expecting a different response. Something action-packed and decisive. Maybe Kat could have lived up to his expectations had she been given a chance to take a sip of her coffee. Instead, she could only lower the cup and watch Jasper as he watched her.

She knew what he was thinking. She read it in his eyes. He saw a woman five feet tall, ten pounds overweight, and six years shy of middle age. A woman who darkened her blond hair in order to be taken seriously. A woman who had bags under her eyes because the furnace was on the fritz and her son was up half the night with a cough. Most of all, he saw a woman—with a badge pinned to her uniform—idling on the sidewalk when she should have been investigating the town's first theft in more than a year.

Knowing all of this was going through Jasper's brain, Kat asked, "What was stolen?"

"I'll show you."

She followed him down Main Street, which was waking up faster than she was. She spotted Lisa Gunzelman unlocking her antiques store and Adrienne Wellington adjusting a floral-print frock in the window of her dress shop. Similar activity took place on the other side of the street as store owners got ready for another day of commerce in Perry Hollow, Pennsylvania.

Their efforts were in vain. The town had seen few visitors since the Christmas rush, simply because January and February were too cold for shopping. Now it was the middle of March, and although store windows showed off shorts, sunglasses, and tank tops, the scene outside was anything but springlike. Just two days earlier, a nor'easter had dumped six inches of snow on the roads. That was followed by an arctic chill that froze the plowed snow into miniature icebergs against the sidewalks. Kat stepped around one as she followed Jasper into his own store, two doors down from the dress shop.

Once inside Awesome Blossoms, Jasper made a beeline to the rear of the store and pushed open a door that led back outside. Kat followed him through it, finding herself in the center of a vacant parking lot covered with a thin sheet of ice. Only then did she begin to understand the situation. Jasper's delivery van—a ubiquitous white Ford with the store's name painted across its sides—had been taken during the night. The realization gave her an inappropriate kick. At last, something to investigate.

"Are you positive this is where you parked it last night?"

"Of course."

"I know you think I'm asking the obvious," Kat said. "But these are the things I need to know if you want me to find your van."

Jasper pointed to an empty patch of gravel. "I parked it right there."

"Are you the only person with a set of keys?"

"I keep a spare set in the glove compartment in case someone else needs to make a delivery."

"Let me guess. You leave the van's door unlocked, too."

Jasper didn't need to speak. His mustache did the talking for him. And when it sagged sadly, Kat knew the answer was yes.

As stupid as his actions sounded, Kat couldn't hold it against him. Perry Hollow *was* the kind of town where you could leave your car unlocked with the keys in the ignition and know it would be safe. Until now, apparently.

"Don't worry," she said. "We'll find the van. Everyone in town knows what it looks like. Some kids probably took it for a joyride and left it behind the Shop and Save."

Kat assumed this theory would relieve Jasper in some small way. Instead, the florist's face scrunched with worry.

"There was something else in that glove compartment, Chief."

"What?"

Jasper hesitated, just for a moment. "A pistol."

Kat groaned. It wasn't the best thing to do in front of Jasper, but it was better than her first instinct, which was to throttle him. How could he be so stupid as to leave his van unlocked with a gun in the glove compartment? And why did he have a gun in there to begin with?

"I had it for safety reasons," Jasper said, sensing the unspoken question that hung like a clothesline between them. "I had a permit for it and everything. I just kept it there in case I got carjacked."

Unless he made regular deliveries to West Philadelphia, Jasper had no reason to worry about a carjacking.

"Was it loaded?" Kat said.

A sad nod from the florist told her this was a bigger problem than she had first suspected. She needed to find that van. Pronto. And when she did, hopefully the gun would still be there.

Quickly, she made her way back through the store and onto Main Street. When she reached her black-and-white Crown Vic—still parked in front of Big Joe's, thank God—Kat heard Deputy Carl Bauersox trying to reach her on the radio.

"Chief?" his voice squawked as Kat slid behind the wheel. "You there?"

Carl, her sole deputy, worked the night shift. Kat was usually in the station by that hour to relieve him of duty. But she had been sidetracked by Jasper's van troubles, and now Carl was probably wondering when he could go home.

Kat grabbed the radio. "I'm on my way, Carl."

"We have a big problem, Chief."

Kat doubted that. Two crimes taking place on the same day would be some sort of record for Perry Hollow. It was probably more like a cat in a tree, which in Carl's world did amount to a big deal.

"What kind of problem?"

"A truck driver called. Said there's a wooden box sitting on the side of Old Mill Road."

As Carl spoke, Kat realized she was still carrying her neglected Big Joe's house blend. She raised the cup to her lips and, just before getting to that long-delayed first sip, said, "Why didn't you go out there and move it?"

"Because it's more than a box."

Kat stopped herself mid-sip. Again. "More than a box how?"

"Well, Chief, the trucker swears up and down that it's a coffin."

A coffin. On the side of the road. The idea was so preposterous Kat knew it couldn't be true. The truck driver was mistaken. It was simply a box. And now her job was to move it before some distracted driver smashed into it, possibly necessitating the use of a real coffin.

"I'll check it out," she said. "In the meantime, do me a favor and put out a countywide APB on Jasper Fox's delivery van. It was stolen last night."

She didn't mention the gun. It would have been a good idea with anyone but Carl, who flapped his gums faster than a hummingbird worked its wings. If he knew about the gun, the news would be all over Perry Hollow within an hour.

Carl signed off with a chipper "Righto, Chief," leaving Kat to reluctantly lower her coffee, start the Crown Vic, and head out to whatever awaited her on Old Mill Road.

When Kat found the box, it was indeed sitting on the side of the road, resting on a patch of frozen snow. Although the truck driver who spotted it called it a coffin, Kat, in true police chief fashion, refused to speculate on the matter. Squinting against the sun's reflection on the snow, she peered through the windshield at the box sitting a few yards away. Rectangular in shape, it looked to be made of untreated wood. Probably pine, if Kat cared to guess. Which she didn't.

She climbed out of the car, her breath forming a brief ghost of vapor that floated away in the frigid breeze. It was too damn cold for March, which Kat thought was bad news in several ways. For one, the prolonged winter depressed her. Second, the cold had kept the tourists away for too long. And most folks in Perry Hollow depended on them for their livelihoods.

Finally, the cold seemed to Kat a shivery warning of impending danger. It was too sharp, too unnatural.

When she finally got around to taking that first sip of coffee, it was in a vain attempt to steel herself against the chill. But the java itself had already succumbed to the cold, not helping her one bit. Kat instead had to rely on her parka, which she zipped up to her chin.

When she reached the box, Kat understood why someone passing by could think it was a coffin. It certainly looked casketlike. More than six feet long, three feet wide, and about two feet deep, it was definitely big enough to hold a body.

Kneeling next to it, she inspected the box for signs of where it had come from and, hopefully, where it was supposed to go. She looked for an invoice stapled to the side or a company's logo branded into the wood. She found neither. As she ran a hand across the box's top and along its sides, the rough wood scraped her palm. Whatever its intended use, the box was definitely homemade, most likely by an amateur. Any craftsman worth his salt would have subjected the wood to at least some form of sanding.

Leaning in close, Kat sniffed deeply, detecting a faint trace of pitch. Pine. Just as she had suspected.

She wanted to believe the box had simply landed there after falling off a truck, but instinct told her otherwise. It was in perfect condition. No scratches or scuff marks. No signs of impact with the road. The way it sat—on its back, stretched tidily across the ditch—also raised suspicion. No box tumbling from a truck could have landed so perfectly without some assistance.

Its location was no accident. Someone had placed it there. Someone had wanted it to be found.

Finished with her examination, Kat saw no point in delaying the inevitable. Coffin or not, the box needed to be opened. Tugging on the lid, she noticed it was nailed shut at the corners and at two points along each side. She marched back to her patrol car and grabbed a crowbar from the trunk before returning to the box. With the crowbar's help, the nails barely resisted when she pried the lid open and yanked it away.

The first thing she saw was a pair of wheat-colored work boots. Next was a pair of mud-streaked overalls that continued over a red flannel shirt. Finally, framed by the shirt's collar, was the face of a man in his late sixties.

The full picture sent Kat scrambling backward. Standing halfway between the box and her car, she turned away and clamped one hand over her mouth to calm her gasping. She pressed the other hand against her right side, where a sudden fear jabbed at her ribs.

When a minute passed, Kat willed herself to look at the coffin again. The second glance was accompanied by the sad, stomach-sinking realization that she knew who the corpse was.

His name was George Winnick, and until this morning he had been a farmer who tended fifty acres on the outskirts of Perry Hollow. Kat didn't know him well. Other than exchanging greetings at the Shop and Save or in passing on the street, they had barely spoken. But he was enough of a fixture in town for her to know he had been a decent man—hardworking and dependable. She also knew there was no reason he should be lying dead in a pine box on Old Mill Road.

"George," she whispered as she unsteadily approached the body again. "What happened to you?"

His corpse had been crammed inside the coffin like a doll stuffed into a shoe box. His arms were folded across his chest, each open hand resting against the opposite shoulder. The ashen shade of his hair matched the pale flesh on his hands, neck, and face.

Two polished pennies sat atop each of his eyes, hugged by bushy, gray-studded eyebrows. Both coins had been placed heads up, Abe Lincoln's profile glinting in Kat's direction. The effect was eerie, the pennies looking like eyes themselves—dead and unblinking.

A wound marred the right side of his neck, partially hidden by his shirt collar. Pushing the fabric out of the way, Kat examined the gash. About three inches long, it had been stitched shut with black thread. Beads of blood had frozen to the thread, like raindrops in a spiderweb.

Similar ice crystals could be seen on George's lips, which were coated with rust-colored flecks of dirt. That's when Kat realized it wasn't dirt she saw. It was dried blood. Lots of it, crusted around more black thread that crisscrossed his lips.

George Winnick's mouth had been sewn shut.

Kat gasped again as the pain in her ribs deepened. It was an overwhelming sensation—part nausea, part horror. Still, she managed to make it back to her patrol car and radio Carl.

"I need you to listen closely," she said. "Call the EMS squad. Tell them to get here immediately."

"There's someone inside the box?"

"Yes. George Winnick."

Carl reacted the way Kat had expected him to—he prayed.

She waited as he murmured a quick prayer for George's soul. After the amen, he asked, "How did he die?"

Kat told him she didn't know.

"What I do know is that you need to get on the horn and call the county sheriff. Tell him to bring the medical examiner. We're going to need some help, because this—"

She stopped speaking when she realized she had no idea what *this* was. Nor did she have the first clue how to handle it. All she knew was that she had been right about the relentless chill. The cold *was* a bad omen.

Very bad.

# TWO

It's called a death sentence—that single line in an obituary detailing who died, how, and when. Henry Goll, who wrote them on a daily basis, enjoyed the nickname. He liked its sly wordplay, its mordant wit. Plus, he appreciated how the name hinted at a deeper, darker truth just below its surface: from the moment we are born, we are sentenced to death.

Part of Henry's job was to make sure every obituary printed in the *Perry Hollow Gazette* contained a death sentence. For the most part, it was easy. A grieving family gave the information to the county's only funeral home, which in turn faxed it to Henry. Using that as a guide, he sat in his cupboard-sized office and wrote a respectful overview of the deceased's life. The death sentence always came first. It was the meat of the obituary, the only thing readers really wanted to know. The rest—family, work histories, achievements—were just side dishes to be consumed later.

Henry knew the obituary for George Winnick was a fake because it wasn't a complete death sentence. Other than a name and a time of death, it contained barely any information at all.

*George Winnick, 67, of Perry Hollow, Pa., died at 10:45 P.M. on March 14.*

Five years of being the obituary writer at the *Gazette* had made Henry an expert at spotting fakes, which arrived with alarming frequency. He had no idea how anyone could see humor in that kind of prank, but many did. The worst offenders were teenagers, who often sent in fake death notices of much-reviled teachers. Others were sent by the alleged corpse's friends, usually during a milestone birthday. Under Henry's watch, none had managed to sneak into the paper. Whenever he saw an obituary claiming someone had died on his fiftieth birthday, he automatically threw it away.

He was close to doing the same with George Winnick's, which had been sitting in the fax machine when he entered his office that morning. But because there was nothing suspicious about the age and date listed, he figured it was best to at least confirm it was a fake before relegating it to the trash.

Henry's first and only call was to the McNeil Funeral Home. Tucked away on the far end of Oak Street, McNeil was a father and son outfit that had a monopoly on Perry Hollow's dead. If someone in town passed away, the folks at McNeil knew about it.

Deana Swan, the funeral home's receptionist, answered the phone after a single ring.

"McNeil Funeral Home," she said in a bored voice. "This is Deana. How may I help you?"

Henry cleared his throat before speaking. "This is Henry Goll from the *Perry Hollow Gazette*."

Deana interrupted him with a pert "Hey, Henry."

"I have a question about a fax I received."

"Why don't you ever say hello to me?"

Taken aback, Henry replied with a confused "Pardon?"

"You call here, like, every day. And you just get straight to the point. No hello. No chitchat. Why is that?"

Henry was at a loss for words. "I don't know. Maybe I'm not that interesting."

Deana's response of "That's not what I heard" surprised him, mainly because she offered no follow-up. Henry didn't find himself interesting in the least, so he doubted Deana's mysterious source.

"Trust me," he said. "I'm not."

Henry wasn't lying. He might have been interesting once, but his life in the past five years was a strict schedule of work and solitude. Every morning he arrived at his third-floor office by nine. He worked until six, taking an hour to eat lunch at his desk. When he left for the day, it was via the back stairs, where he could bypass the prying eyes in the main newsroom. Once home, Henry exercised for precisely an hour. After that, he prepared dinner, watched an old movie on TV, then read a book until he grew tired. In the morning, he had breakfast, made his lunch, and repeated the routine.

His unbending schedule, coupled with the fact that he rarely showed his pale face in the newsroom, had earned him a nickname among the reporters—Henry Ghoul.

No one suspected Henry knew about the nickname. But he did. And he thought it amusingly appropriate, just like death sentence. He was the phantom of the newsroom, the odd duck writing about dead people. Sometimes he went out of his way to act accordingly, sweeping ghostlike up the back steps and making sure moody music emanated from his office under the eaves.

As for the other, crueler reason they called him Ghoul,

Henry tried not to think about it. He couldn't change the way he looked. Not now, anyway.

"Well, interesting or not, you should visit me sometime," Deana said. "We can go to lunch."

Her suggestion was the biggest surprise in a conversation filled with them.

"That's probably not a good idea," Henry said.

"Why? I don't even know what you look like."

Henry touched his face before he spoke, his fingertips running along the scar that started at his left ear, sliced through the corners of both lips, and ended in the center of his chin. Moving upward, his hand slid across the mottled skin above his left eye. Although he couldn't see it, he knew the large burn mark retained a dark redness against the white of his flesh. It was usually darker in the morning, only fading as the day progressed.

"We should get back to the fax," he said.

Deana didn't bother to hide the disappointment in her voice. "Of course. What's the name?"

"George Winnick. I can't tell if it's legitimate or not."

Henry heard the rustling of paper on Deana's desk, followed by a few taps on a keyboard.

"There's no sign of him in our records," she eventually said. "Did the fax come from us?"

Henry told her the fax didn't seem to have come from any funeral home—another sign of its impostor status. Having nothing else to add, he thanked Deana for her help and hung up before she had another chance to invite him to lunch. He then grabbed the obituary for George Winnick, crumpled it into a tight ball, and dropped it into the trash.

Henry spent the rest of the morning writing obituaries for people who actually were dead. There were four of them altogether, two coming from funeral homes outside of the county and two faxed to him by Deana Swan. On the second fax, just beneath the funeral home's letterhead, she had scrawled, "Sorry if I made you uncomfortable."

She had, mostly because Henry had been momentarily detoured from his usual routine.

He worked in the same manner he lived: without spontaneity. Everything in his impeccably organized office had its place and its purpose. The lamp on his desk illuminated the cramped and windowless room. The bookshelf bulged with reference materials. The fax machine, exactly an arm's length away, provided grist for the mill.

While writing, he played one of the many tragic operas downloaded onto his computer. That morning, he listened to Wagner's *Tristan and Isolde*. Instead of a distraction, the swelling music, soaring arias, and tale of doomed love served Henry well. It helped him concentrate, allowing him to sustain the somber mood necessary to write about those who had shuffled off this mortal coil. And by the time poor Isolde died of heartbreak, he had finished his work for the morning.

Lunchtime was promptly at noon. Henry ate the same meal every day—turkey on wheat, small salad, bottle of water. He brought everything from home except the water, which was purchased from the vending machine downstairs.

In the break room, a lone reporter stood in front of the snack machine, mulling over his options. He offered a forced smile, which Henry refused to return. Henry Ghoul didn't smile.

The reporter's name was Martin Swan. Blandly handsome, he had the look of a former football star going to seed in the working world. His white shirt fit tightly, and his silk tie trickled down a broad chest and the beginnings of a beer gut. Henry knew nothing about him other than the fact that he was Deana's brother. In a town as small as Perry Hollow, coincidences like that were common. Because of this tenuous link between them, Martin always felt compelled to talk to Henry, even though his voice was usually poised somewhere between sincerity and indifference. Today was no different.

"You'll be getting an obituary from my sister soon," Martin said flatly.

Henry stood at the machine next to him, fishing in his pocket for change. "What makes you think that?"

Martin's voice suddenly became animated. "You didn't hear the big news?"

"Hear what?"

"Someone was murdered this morning. Chief Campbell found him in a coffin on the side of Old Mill Road. It's creepy as hell. Poor George."

The name made Henry freeze. "George Winnick?"

Martin nodded. "Did you know him?"

A chill shot up Henry's spine. He felt surprise. And fear. The coincidence was too great to not cause at least some bit of fear.

"What time was he found?"

"I think eight or so," Martin said. "Have you heard something about it? I'm working the story, so tell me if you have."

Henry left the break room without saying another word. Taking the back steps two at a time, he rushed into his office, streaked to the garbage can, and rustled through its contents until he found the balled-up sheet of paper.

He smoothed the fax out on his desk, scanning the single sentence typed across the page.

*George Winnick, 67, of Perry Hollow, Pa., died at 10:45 P.M. on March 14.*

In the top left corner of the page was a series of small numbers printed in black. A time stamp of when the fax was sent. Henry read it three times, disbelief growing with each pass. Another chill galloped up his spine. Unlike the first, it stayed there, refusing to be thrown off even as he scooped up the fax, grabbed his coat, and sprinted out the door.

# THREE

The man sitting opposite Nick Donnelly was ugly. There was no doubt about it, no eye-of-the-beholder bullshit. He was ass-ugly, yet Nick couldn't stop looking at him. He was fascinated by the man's pockmarked cheeks, greasy hair, and teeth that resembled half-nibbled corn on the cob.

Nick bet it was torture to be that unattractive. Thank God he'd never know. The Donnellys were a good-looking, strong-bodied clan. Black Irish, with faces that could have been carved by Michelangelo himself. Add in the rogue's smile inherited from his father, and Nick knew he was one handsome devil.

But this other guy—this Edgar Sewell sitting a table's length away—he'd had a hard life. Nick was sure of it. Being taunted. Being called names. Heart sinking every time he looked in the mirror. It still didn't excuse what he did. Nothing could, no matter how ugly he was.

"So, Edgar," Nick said. "Why did you do it?"

Dressed in an orange jumpsuit, the man lowered his eyes to the handcuffs at his wrists and said uncomfortably, "I told you already."

Edgar's voice matched his looks—unbearable. High-pitched and wavering, it made Nick's ears hurt.

"Tell me again."

"Why do you need to hear it again?"

"Because I want to help you."

It was a lie. Edgar Sewell, the killer of three little girls, was a lost cause. He would spend the rest of his life in this shit-hole prison outside Philadelphia. Nick's true goal was to crawl inside his mind and figure out what drove him to commit his unspeakable acts. Understanding that could possibly help Nick stop the killers who were still out there, still preying on the innocent and unsuspecting. That's why Nick wanted to know.

"They told me to do it," Edgar said.

"Who?"

"The voices."

It was the old voices-in-my-head-made-me-kill excuse. Nick had interviewed four killers in the past week, and Edgar Sewell was the third person to use it. But it was a bullshit excuse, used to hide their true motivations. People like Edgar killed not at the behest of ominous voices. They killed because they wanted to.

"What did these voices sound like?"

"I can't remember."

Nick leaned back in his chair and crossed his arms. "That's interesting. If voices in my head told me to butcher little girls, I'd remember what they sounded like."

That made Edgar change his tune. "I do remember."

"Then tell me."

Edgar stalled by putting his left thumb to his lips and licking it, his tongue a flash of pink poking around the thumbnail. Nick had seen two other killers do the same thing. It was a trait that signaled maternal issues.

When Edgar became aware of Nick watching him, he jerked his thumb away and said, "Elvis."

Nick had to give Edgar credit for originality. The others had simply said Satan. But the lie also pissed him off. After an hour, he had learned nothing new about Edgar Sewell. But now it was time to put him on the spot and, hopefully, get some real answers out of him.

Nick reached down and opened the briefcase sitting next to his chair. He pulled out a manila folder that contained three photographs. The first one showed a brown-haired girl who smiled shyly for the camera. Nick slapped it onto the table and slid it toward Edgar.

"This is Lainie Hamilton. Do you remember her?"

Edgar refused to look at the photograph, turning his head until he faced the wall.

"I know you do," Nick said. "She was eight and lived downstairs from you. Her mother, Ronette, was a prostitute, just like yours was. And on June 1, 1980, you offered Ronette twenty dollars to have sex with you. Any of this ring a bell?"

Edgar popped his thumb into his mouth and shook his head.

"She refused, didn't she? She laughed at you. Maybe called you ugly. You went back upstairs to your apartment and stewed. Later that night, when Ronette was walking the street, you snuck downstairs, broke in, and killed Lainie."

The thumb popped out long enough for Edgar to say, "The voices told me to."

"There were no voices," Nick said, his own voice growing angry. "It was only you. And you killed little eight-year-old Lainie of your own free will. You even liked it so much that you did it again six months later to the daughter of another prostitute."

Nick tossed a second photo onto the table.

"Then you did it again."

A third photo. All three of Edgar Sewell's victims—the youngest six, the oldest eleven—looked up at their killer with innocent eyes.

Forced to face their stares, Edgar said, "They deserved it."

"Who? The girls?"

"The mothers. Those dirty, filthy whores. They thought they were better than me. They were rotten sluts who were mean to me and made fun of me and called me ugly, just like—"

Nick finished the confession for him. "Your mother?"

Edgar nodded so vigorously that Nick was afraid he'd bite off part of his thumb, which was shoved fully between his lips. Then, to Nick's surprise, Edgar Sewell did what none of the other killers he interviewed had done.

He cried.

The tears signaled that the interview was over. Nick knew he'd get no more information out of Edgar. Which meant it was on to the next prison—this one in Centre County—and maybe two more after that, if Nick had the time.

Before leaving, he stopped by the prison's public restroom, which was one step above a gas station's. One toilet. One urinal. Permanent grime coated the sink's basin. Nick tried not to touch it as he splashed cold water onto his face. In the mirror, a hollow-eyed man stared back at him.

Christ, he was exhausted. This was the start of his second week interviewing killers, and all that talk and travel had taken its toll. But it would be worth it in the end, he hoped.

After drying his face, Nick exited the bathroom and then the prison itself, relieved to be free of its walls, its bars, its unrelenting grimness. His mood brightened enough that he could muster a whistle. A little "Folsom Prison Blues" in honor of his location.

The good mood—and the whistling—lasted only until he reached the parking lot, where an unexpected visitor waited for him.

Captain Gloria Ambrose, his boss at the Pennsylvania State Police Bureau of Criminal Investigation, leaned against the unmarked car that had shuttled her there. She hugged herself for warmth until she caught sight of Nick. Then her arms dropped to her sides. The move was vintage Gloria—always trying to look tougher than she really was.

"How did you find me?"

"You made an official request to speak to a prisoner of the state," Gloria replied. "So finding you was easy. I should be asking you why you're interviewing prisoners when you're supposed to be on vacation."

Nick *was* on vacation. At least officially. And what he did during his time off was his own business.

"Just tell me what's going on," he said irritably. "I know there's a reason you're here."

Even more, he knew what that reason was. Gloria didn't even need to tell him. Her presence alone spoke volumes.

"He struck again."

"Where?"

"A town called Perry Hollow. It's about forty-five minutes from here. The rest of your team is already there."

"I assume you want me to join them," Nick said.

Gloria, who was done with being cold, opened the car's rear door and slipped inside. "That's entirely up to you," she said, sneaking a glance at the gray-walled prison rising behind Nick. "You *are* still on vacation."

She closed the door, leaving Nick alone in the frigid wind with one question still unspoken. He was about to rap on the car's window, but it lowered before he had the chance, revealing Gloria's stern gaze.

"And no," she said. "I won't tell anyone about your extra-curricular activities. But next time you say you're taking a vacation, do it. You can't keep pushing yourself like this, Donnelly. It's not healthy. You really need to learn how to let go."

Nick drove to Perry Hollow in the company of the Rolling Stones. Nothing was better for a road trip than Jagger's spastic voice and the band's relentless sound. Nick propelled himself along the highway to the strains of "(I Can't Get No) Satisfaction," "Gimme Shelter," and "Brown Sugar." By the time the band was showing some sympathy for the devil, he had reached Perry Hollow, where a devil of a different stripe had just claimed one of its residents.

He found the crime scene easily enough. On the outskirts of town, it was the place with the most people gathered there. The entire road was closed, forcing Nick to stop his car on the shoulder.

Sitting in his car, he surveyed the scene. On one side of the barricade was a crowd of curious onlookers. They craned their necks and talked among themselves, their faces all displaying the same shell-shocked look. On the other side of the police tape was a mix of sheriff's officers and state troopers. They, too, stood around and chatted while looking as stunned as the bystanders.

The only people in the crowd unfazed by the situation were the only three faces Nick recognized. And that was because they worked for him.

Tony Vasquez was the first to spot Nick as he flashed his credentials and ducked under the police tape.

"You made it," he said, lifting the brim of his campaign hat. A full-time state trooper and part-time bodybuilder, he was the only task force member who wore a uniform. It sure as hell made him look intimidating, which Nick knew Tony liked. But he also wore it with a certain amount of pride. Only 2 percent of the state's troopers were Hispanic. And Tony was one of the best. With stats like that, he had every reason to be proud.

"We placed bets on if you'd show up or not," he said. "I won."

"How much?"

"Twenty bucks from Cassie and the chance to bench-press Rudy."

"Well done, Vasquez."

Rudy Taylor, the bench pressee, was nearby, kneeling before a patch of ice on the side of the road.

"Is this where he was found?" Nick asked.

Rudy nodded. "But he didn't die here."

"How can you tell?"

"No blood. No struggle. Just the box he was dumped in."

Stump short and toothpick thin, Rudy Taylor was considered the odd duck of the team. His size didn't help. Neither did the bowl haircut that made him look like a grade-school science club president. But he was the best crime scene technician they had. Rudy could survey a scene for five minutes and find ten things a whole team had missed after looking for an hour.

"What about tire marks or footprints?" Nick asked.

Rudy stood and stomped the frozen ground for effect. "There's not too much of that on this ice. I did find something in the snow over there."

He pointed to a footprint a few feet away. It was marked with a yellow evidence tag.

"You wax it?" Nick was referring to impression wax. Sprayed from a can, it let them make impressions in the snow without destroying the footprint itself.

"Yeah," Rudy said. "It belongs to the first responder."

"Where's the body?"

"The medical examiner took it away fifteen minutes ago."

The answer came from the last member of Nick's team—Cassie Lieberfarb. She stood behind him, a state police baseball cap pressed onto her frizzy orange hair. On her feet were the bright green galoshes she always wore in the field. She called them her profiler boots.

"How was Florida?" she asked, her eyes zeroing in on Nick's face.

"Hot and sunny."

"Then where's your tan?"

Nick shrugged. "I used sunblock. Now back to the murder—who's the victim?"

"Caucasian male," Tony said. "Mid-sixties."

"Just what our guy likes," Cassie added.

"When is the autopsy?"

"At four."

Nick compiled a list of things that needed to be done that day. He and Cassie had to examine the corpse before the autopsy started. While they did that, Rudy would supervise the collection and examination of evidence. Tony would wrangle up the best sheriff's officers he could find and start the legwork. When they met up again eight hours later, they'd hopefully have a time of death, a cause, and enough evidence to point to a suspect. Only Nick and the rest of them already had an idea who the killer was. As for why he killed, none of them could begin to guess.

"Has the victim been identified?" he asked.

"The first responder did an ID," Tony said.

"Who was that?"

"The police chief."

"Let me talk to him."

Cassie pointed to the crowd, picking out a woman in uniform who was dwarfed by the other cops around her.

"*She* is right there," she said with sisterly pride. "Her name is Kat Campbell."

Nick took a moment to size up the chief. She looked exhausted. Her kind eyes were dimmed by the dark circles sagging beneath them, and she moved in the weary, slump-shouldered way of someone carrying a heavy load on her back. Discovering a murder in your own backyard would do that.

"Are you Chief Campbell?" Nick asked as he approached.

The chief nodded. "Are you in charge of the task force?"

"I am," he responded, shaking her hand. "Nick Donnelly. BCI, the Bureau of Criminal Investigations."

She eyed his civilian clothes, hoping in vain to find something that indicated his rank and position. Since there wasn't, Nick volunteered the information.

"I'm a lieutenant," he said. "But in rank only. In reality, I'm just part of a team trying to catch bad guys."

"We thank you for the help."

"Just so we're clear, the county sheriff has turned the case over to us. So the state police, specifically the BCI, is in charge of the investigation. I hope that sits well with you."

Kat responded tersely. "Understood."

"Good. I heard you were first on the scene."

The chief briefly described everything she had seen and done that morning. It was all by the book, from finding the box to forming a perimeter around the crime scene. That made Nick happy. Sometimes local cops did more harm than good.

"I was told you knew the victim."

"Only by sight. Perry Hollow's a small town. After a while, you know everyone."

Her voice caught on the last word, and for a second, Nick worried that the chief was going to start crying. But she swallowed hard and kept her emotions in check.

"I'm sorry," she said. "We've never had a murder before. So it's been a bad day."

Nick had no doubt. For Chief Campbell, it was probably the mother of all bad days. And she didn't know the half of it yet. Once she did, her day was going to go from bad to downright miserable.

# FOUR

Kat understood the situation perfectly.

She knew the limitations of Perry Hollow's police force. Between her and Carl, they barely had enough manpower to write speeding tickets, let alone investigate a homicide. She knew the chain of command in such a situation. If the local cops couldn't handle a case, jurisdiction moved to the county sheriff. And the sheriff, who was busy running for re-election in the fall, didn't want to get his hands dirty in a homicide that—if unsolved—could sully his reputation. So he had called in the big guns—the state police. They had the manpower and equipment and a special investigative task force led by lieutenant-in-rank-only Nick Donnelly. Most of all, Kat knew that she needed them more than they needed her, which is why she vowed to do anything that was asked of her.

So, when Nick asked if there was a place his team could work out of, she offered her office. When he wondered if they could make full use of her police force, she introduced him to Carl Bauersox, his eager baby face poking out of his too-tight jacket. And when Nick sought a private place where they could talk, she led him to her patrol car.

And there they sat, the heater cranked on high while the slowly fogging windshield painted the action outside a gauzy gray.

"So why do we need to speak in private?" Kat asked.

Nick answered with a question of his own. "Have you ever heard of the Betsy Ross Killer?"

"No. Interesting nickname, though."

"I hate it," Nick said. "But you can thank *The Philadelphia Inquirer* for it."

"Why do they call him that?"

"Because he's good with a needle and thread. His victims had their wounds sewn shut postmortem. Then they were dumped in a public place."

"How many victims are we talking about?"

"Three so far. The first was found in a park in Philadelphia last year. Another washed up on the shore of Lake Erie nine months ago. The third was found up north in November at World's End State Park."

"And you and your task force have been leading the investigation?"

"We have. Three murders. All across the state. And now it might be four."

It was obvious what Nick was implying, and the thought of it made Kat's spine stiffen.

"This Betsy Ross Killer—you think he's the one who murdered George?"

"Perhaps."

A strong, primal fear pinned Kat to her seat. A murder taking place in Perry Hollow was bad enough. But knowing it could be the work of a serial killer made it all the more horrible. What if he was still in her town? Or worse, what if he lived there, blending in with everyone else?

"Will you be able to confirm that?"

"I hope so," Nick said. "I need to examine the body. See if there's a similarity in the stitches and the wounds. Maybe my guys will be able to pick up something from the evidence. So far, Betsy Ross has been very stingy with the transfer."

"And what can I do?"

"Just sit tight," Nick told her. "If we find something, you'll be the first to hear about it."

Even as fear held her in place, Kat felt a new emotion tugging her body. It was the urge to protect, and it was stronger than fright.

"That's not good enough," she said. "I have to do more than sit tight."

Perry Hollow was her town. It was where she grew up. It was the town her father swore to protect and serve decades before Kat swore to do the same thing. And while she appreciated all the help she could get, she wasn't going to just stand by and hope others caught a killer for her.

"I understand your position," Nick said in a voice that veered perilously close to patronizing. "But you need to let us do what we're trained to do."

"This isn't a turf fight," Kat said. "Or some jurisdiction bullshit in which I can't get along with outside cops. Men care about that stuff. Women don't. We just want to get the job done."

She watched as Nick considered her policemen are from Mars, policewomen are from Venus argument. Eventually, he asked, "What did you have in mind?"

"George Winnick's wife, Alma, reported him missing this morning, at about the same time I found his body. Now, I know that when a married person is murdered, the spouse is automatically the main suspect. But Alma didn't do this. She's just not physically capable. But she might have heard something or seen something. And I'm the best person to talk to her. She's old-school. She won't trust you or someone from your team."

The man sitting next to Kat clasped his hands together, extended his index fingers, and placed them against his lips. Then he nodded.

"I like the way you think, Chief," he said.

Kat nodded back. She was still frightened. And still exhausted. But she was also pleased with herself. Because for the first time since meeting him, she had finally impressed Nick Donnelly.

When Kat entered the police station a half hour later, Louella van Sickle was waiting for her. Lou, who had been the department's dispatcher since before Kat's father was chief, was a grandmother of twelve and looked after Kat like she was one of her own.

"I got you lunch," she said, holding up a burger and fries from the Perry Hollow Diner. "You need to eat something."

Kat should have been starving. Other than her lone sip of coffee, she had consumed nothing all day. But eyeing the burger and fries, she knew she wouldn't be able to eat a thing. Seeing George Winnick's corpse hours earlier and then hearing about the Betsy Ross Killer's crimes left her stomach feeling nothing but queasy.

"I'm not hungry."

Lou gave her a disapproving look. "The crime scene diet never works."

"This is the overwhelmed single mother diet," Kat said. "I heard it works really well."

"Speaking of that," Lou said, biting into one of the rejected fries, "do you need me to pick James up from school?"

Kat, who had been steadily working her way to her office, froze in the hallway.

"What time is it?"

"Two thirty."

School let out at three, and no matter how hectic her day was, she made it a priority to be waiting at the curb when class was dismissed. It was her sole routine. If she didn't show up, it would throw her son's whole day out of whack.

"I'll get him," she said. "But it would be a huge help if you could call Mrs. Lefferts and see if Amber is able to watch James after school."

Lou cocked an eyebrow. "Amber Lefferts is still your baby-sitter?"

"I know what you're thinking," Kat said. "Trust me, I've thought it myself."

"At least you know what you're getting yourself into."

Kat reversed direction and headed back the way she came. As she neared the front door, she asked, "Is there anything else before I go?"

Lou's expression—a combination of knowledge and regret—told her there was.

"Someone from the *Gazette* is here," she announced. "I put him in the break room. He's been waiting for almost two hours. Says he needs to talk to you about George Winnick."

Kat sighed. "If it's Martin Swan, tell him I don't have time to make a statement. I'll give him something as soon as I get a chance."

"It's not Martin, Chief. It's Henry Goll. The obituary writer."

The name sounded familiar to Kat, although she couldn't come up with a face to match it, which bothered her. Perry Hollow was a small town, and although she didn't personally know all of its residents, she at least had an idea of what most of them looked like.

"He said it was important," Lou added.

Kat switched directions again and marched into the break room. Seeing her, Henry Goll stood rigidly, arms folded across his sizable chest.

"Henry? I'm Chief Campbell."

The reason Kat couldn't match Henry Goll's name with a face was because she had never laid eyes on him before. She would have remembered it if she had. He was tall—over six feet—and powerfully built. When he stepped toward her, his muscles moved smoothly beneath his khaki pants and black polo shirt.

His facial features were strong, too—square chin, Mediterranean nose, a thick head of black hair. He could have been a real looker, Kat thought, it if wasn't for the massive scar that sliced diagonally across the lower half of his face. The upper part was also marred, dominated by a large burn mark covering his left temple and most of his forehead. His skin was pale—startlingly so—making the defects stand out all the more.

Kat extended a hand. When Henry shook it, she willed herself to look him directly in the eye and act as if everything about him was normal. Because of James, she understood the importance of treating someone different just like everyone else.

She smiled when she spoke. "I hear you have something that might interest me."

Henry didn't smile back. "Is there someplace private we can talk?"

Kat glanced at her watch and saw that she had five minutes. She needed to keep the conversation short, but Henry Goll appeared to be in no rush.

"I apologize," she said, "but I need to run out for a little bit. Family matter. Could this wait until later?"

Henry pulled a creased sheet of paper from his pocket and thrust it into her hand. Kat scanned the page, seeing George Winnick's name and little else.

"Is this his obituary? It's pretty skimpy."

"It's a death notice," Henry said. "Not an obituary."

"What's the difference?"

"An obituary contains details—the person's family, his career, his hobbies. A death notice is exactly what it sounds like. It's a notification to the world that someone just died."

Kat glanced from the paper to Henry and back again. "So this is George's death notice. I'm still not sure what the issue is here."

"The issue," Henry said with maddening calmness, "is that it's a fake."

"How do you know that?"

"Just read it again."

Kat obliged, eyes sliding across the humble sentence. When she got to the mention of George's time of death, her heart skipped a beat.

"Now look at the top left corner," Henry instructed.

Her gaze drifted to the top of the page. There, she saw what Henry was referring to—a time and date printed in minuscule letters. She had discovered George's body at about eight that morning. The time printed on his death notice said he died at quarter of eleven the night before. Yet the time stamp on the fax indicated it had been sent at ten fifteen—thirty minutes before his death.

"This is impossible."

"I told you it was important."

Kat eyed her watch again. She needed to leave immediately, and there was only one solution she could think of.

"Do you feel like going for a drive?" she asked. "I need to pick my son up from school. On the way there, you can tell me everything you know."

# FIVE

Henry didn't know where to begin. It wasn't easy sounding sane while telling someone a killer faxed you his victim's death notice before the murder occurred. But he was determined to try.

He also didn't know what to make of the woman sitting next to him. Kat Campbell seemed to inject everything she did with relentless drive, whether it was marching out to her patrol car or buckling her seat belt. That quest for efficiency extended to her facial features. Her sharp chin jutted forward while her lips formed a grimace.

Yet Henry noticed small attempts at femininity peeking through her determined personality. Light pink gloss coated her lips. Tiny gold hoops hung from her ears. And some salon-produced highlights colored her obviously darkened hair. All that, coupled with shapely curves that couldn't be erased by a severely starched uniform, made her look both tough and vulnerable—a soccer mom heading into battle.

And she drove like a maniac. Careening out of the station's parking lot, they barely missed hitting a fire hydrant and had to swerve out of the way of an approaching car.

"First thing," Kat said, steering through an alley that would take them onto Main Street, "when did you receive the death notice?"

"It was sitting in the fax machine when I got to my office this morning."

"And what time was that?"

Henry clutched the dashboard as Kat jerked the steering wheel, making a sharp right onto Main Street. "Nine."

"I found the body just after eight. I'm certain word trickled out to enough people for someone to send it before you got to work."

"That doesn't explain the time stamp," Henry said. "And before you ask, yes, I already checked the fax machine to see if its date and time are set correctly. They are."

"What about the fax number it was sent from?"

Henry knew what she was talking about. On every fax, the sending number appeared next to the time stamp.

"I don't recognize it. Which means it wasn't sent by a funeral home I regularly deal with. Or even by a funeral home at all."

"So who do you think sent it?"

"If I had to guess," Henry said, "I'd say it was sent by whoever killed George Winnick."

On Main Street, traffic was plentiful. A UPS truck idled in the middle of the road, forcing all vehicles behind it to inch their way past. Kat huffed in frustration, her knuckles turning white as she tightened her grip on the steering wheel.

"Have you told anyone else about this?" she asked.

"No. I thought it was best to keep something like this quiet."

Kat no longer appeared to be listening. Instead, she glanced in her rearview mirror before snapping her head toward the window, her hair whipping across her cheek. With her jaw set and the nostrils of her pert nose flaring, she said, "Hold on."

She flicked on the car's lights and siren before swinging the vehicle around the car in front of them and into the left lane. Without slowing, she continued on the wrong side of the road until they were past the UPS truck.

"Did you get a look at that truck's plates?" she asked. "I should ticket him."

A shaken Henry, who figured Chief Campbell should ticket herself first, shook his head.

Kat shrugged and veered left, bouncing them through another alley until they were on Baker Street, home of the elementary school.

"Let's say the fax really was sent at ten fifteen last night," she said, resuming their conversation. "Now, assuming it is from the killer, that means he would have sent it almost immediately before George Winnick died. But why would he do that?"

"I have no idea," Henry said. "Maybe it was a warning."

Kat sighed. "Or else a taunt."

As she spoke, the school edged into view. Kat steered the patrol car into a line of sedans and SUVs waiting at the curb. She put the car in park just as the school's front doors flew open, depositing a wave of children onto the sidewalk.

"I have a favor to ask," Kat said, her eyes glued to the school doors. "Don't tell anyone about this. Not your editor. Not any of the reporters. Not even Martin Swan."

"Agreed."

The chief glanced away from the school long enough to flash him a look of pleased surprise.

"Not a very devoted employee, are you?"

"My loyalty lies with the people I write about," Henry said. "Nothing else is my concern, so I don't bother with it."

"That's a good attitude to have."

"I think so."

Among the last students out of the school were two boys. One of them was a small child with ebony skin, thin limbs, and a pair of glasses balanced on his nose. The other was larger but slower, and he broke into a smile when he saw the patrol car. From where he sat, Henry could tell that the boy had Down syndrome.

"Hey there, Little Bear," Kat said as she jumped out of the car and planted a sloppy kiss on the boy's cheek.

He ran the back of his hand across his face, wiping the kiss away. "Mom, not in front of Jeremy."

The boy's voice was thick and halting, though not as bad as most other cases of Down's that Henry had seen. The clothes he wore—jeans and an oversized Philadelphia Eagles jersey— made it clear Kat wanted him to be treated like any other boy.

"How's your cough?" she asked him. "Better?"

The boy nodded. "I only coughed eleven times today."

"Eleven? I guess that's better than twelve."

When the police chief smiled this time, Henry noted it wasn't a forced grin like the one she had offered him in the police station. It was natural and maternal, spreading across her face with unconscious joy. Much more attractive than the pinched expression she had worn during the drive there.

Kat opened the patrol car's back door to let both boys climb inside. When he saw Henry, the chief's son held out a pudgy hand.

"Hi. I'm James."

"My name's Henry."

The other boy crinkled his nose at Henry, a gesture that made his glasses rise and fall.

"What happened to your face?"

James swatted him lightly on the shoulder. "Don't be rude."

"I was just asking," the other boy said.

"This is Jeremy," James told Henry. "He's a stupid head."

Jeremy scowled. "You're a stupid head."

Kat slid behind the wheel and admonished the pair with a stern glance in the rearview mirror. "You're both stupid heads. End of discussion."

That sent the boys into hysterics.

"Mom called us stupid heads," James said through a torrent of giggles. "That's funny."

Henry should have found it funny, too. Yet the presence of the boys made him so uncomfortable it eclipsed all amusement. He wasn't good with kids. Not anymore. And although he could normally bear brief moments of contact with them, this was too much to handle. He had to get out of the car.

"I need to go," he mumbled.

"But we're not finished," Kat said, baffled by his sudden change in mood. "You need to come back to the station and make an official statement."

Henry shook his head, feeling tears form at the corners of his eyes. He didn't want anyone to see him crying. Henry Ghoul didn't cry. Especially in front of children.

"I can't right now," he said, opening the door and stepping out onto the street. "If you need me, you know where to find me."

Kat was left with no choice but to drive away. As the patrol car departed, James and Jeremy pressed their faces to the window and waved.

Henry mustered a small wave in return. Then, once they were gone, his anger and sorrow took over. These feelings were difficult to control, even after five years. Still, Henry tried. And as he breathed deeply, the rage flaring in his chest, only one tear leaked out. It caught on his scar and followed its path down the entire length of his face.

# SIX

Kat and James arrived home after school to find Amber Lefferts waiting on the front porch. She wasn't alone. A tall, young man with a shock of black hair and an intimidating build leaned against the railing next to her. One of his huge arms was propped over the babysitter's shoulders. He had the other wrapped around her waist, hand sneaking upward toward her right breast.

The youth immediately stopped pawing Amber when the patrol car turned into the driveway. Despite his speed, Kat saw it all. And when she got out of the car, the groper offered a sheepish grin.

Kat knew his name. Everyone in the county knew Troy Gunzelman, the star quarterback for the Perry Hollow Cougars. He was as good as any player his age in the state, and the town expected big things from him. There were rumors Penn State was trying to recruit him, a big deal for a place as small-time as Perry Hollow.

"Afternoon, Mrs. Campbell," Troy said in his best suck-up voice. "How are you today?"

"It's Chief Campbell. And I'm not married."

She eyed Troy warily. He wasn't merely good-looking. With his chiseled features, he was movie-star handsome. Kat didn't know exactly why he was hanging out with Amber, but she had a pretty good idea.

"Troy gave me a ride from school," the babysitter said. "He was just leaving."

That was news to Troy, who shot Amber a disappointed look. She apparently forgot to tell him about Kat's strict no-boys-allowed policy.

"Whatever," he said. "I've got to hit the gym anyway."

"See ya, Troy." Kat patted him on the back as he stomped down the porch steps. "Hit it hard."

She remembered Lou's earlier comment about Amber as she watched Troy cross the yard to his vintage green Mustang. Yes, she knew what she was getting herself into.

The babysitter came from one of the most respected families in town. Reverend Lefferts was pastor of the First Presbyterian Church. His wife volunteered with every organization in town, despite having to raise seven children, all of them blond, pale-skinned, and squeaky-clean. They were Perry Hollow's own von Trapp family, only without the lederhosen.

Except for Amber.

Barely fifteen, the youngest of the Lefferts children was by far the wildest. She smoked behind the high school, stayed out after curfew, and altered her clothing to reveal as much as she could get away with. In spite of the winter weather, that afternoon she sported a pink T-shirt, white Keds, and a denim skirt so short it might as well have been a belt. Despite being a natural blonde, she had put streaks in her hair that were practically white. Combined with her porcelain-doll skin tone, it almost made her look like an albino.

No one had high hopes for Amber, including Kat, but she was an angel with James. Unlike other sitters, Amber talked *to*

James and not at him. Since she showed no signs of being uncomfortable around him, James responded in kind. Amber was the only babysitter he looked forward to spending time with. For that reason, she was always the first person Kat called.

When he got out of the car, James bolted onto the porch and gave Amber a hug.

"Do you wanna play Wii with me?" he asked. "I got a new dog game."

"Sure," Amber said, shaking off the sting of Troy's abrupt departure. "We'll do whatever you want."

Kat opened her wallet and took out a twenty.

"This is for pizza. I have no idea what time I'll be home. If it's past ten, I'll pay you overtime."

Amber accepted the money with a shrug and tucked it into a fake Gucci purse slung over her shoulder. "It's cool."

Before leaving, Kat pulled James aside. Although she knew what his answer would be, she asked, "Are you going to behave for Amber?"

"Yes, Mom," he said, his voice tinged with the sarcasm he was just beginning to learn. For that, Kat blamed Jeremy.

"Now, on the hug scale, how much do you love me?"

When James wrapped his arms around her and squeezed, Kat felt overwhelmed with love. Moments like that made all the hard work it took to raise him worthwhile. Moments like that made Kat realize she would do anything for her son.

"Go have fun with Amber," she said, reluctant to let him go. "I'll be home as soon as I can."

James smiled and waved before running inside the house. Kat trudged back to the car, dreading the long evening ahead and wanting only to stay home with her son.

Ten years ago, while still a rookie officer with everything to prove, Kat never thought she would one day feel this way. At the time, she considered her pregnancy to be an unwanted burden.

So did the father.

His name was Jackson Moore—Jack, for short—formerly the other half of Perry Hollow's two-person police force. Back then, he and Kat considered themselves a couple, although not a serious one. Kat's focus was on her career, and she knew that when the time came to settle down, it wouldn't be with someone as undependable as Jack. Despite a killer smile, a quick wit, and being an animal in bed, he wasn't husband or father material.

Then Kat got pregnant, forcing both of them to make major decisions. The first was whether to keep the baby, a question Kat wrestled with more than she cared to admit. When she told Jack she'd decided to have his child, he did the honorable thing and proposed. Kat said yes, not because she wanted to be his wife but because she felt it was the right thing to do.

The wedding ceremony lasted ten minutes and was followed by beer, chips, and a cake Lou had baked the night before. Their honeymoon trip consisted of moving Kat's belongings from her mother's house to Jack's apartment. They pretended to be happy while waiting out the remainder of her pregnancy. But the fact Kat kept her maiden name should have been a signal to everyone that she assumed it wouldn't last.

When James was born with Down syndrome, Kat vowed to love and protect her son for the rest of her life. Jack assured her he was also up to the challenge of raising a child with special needs, and Kat wanted to believe him. But deep down, she couldn't. She expected the marriage to last at least a year. She got ten months.

Kat felt no anger when Jack filed for divorce, quit the force, and moved to Montana. Nor did she harbor any bitterness toward him after he abandoned all contact by the time James turned three. Jack was weak, and she forgave him for that. Besides, she knew her love for James would get them through whatever difficulties they faced.

That love, so strong it sometimes frightened her, prompted her to pursue the job of police chief when James was seven. As a mother, it was her duty to protect her child. And like her father before her, Kat thought protecting the entire town was the best way to go about it. If Perry Hollow remained safe, then so did James.

Other than a few adult variations of the Amber Lefferts model, Perry Hollow was a cinch to monitor. It was small, sleepy, dull.

Until today.

Driving up Main Street, Kat wondered how the town would handle something as disturbing as George Winnick's death. It left her rattled and uncertain. She assumed the town felt the same way.

Tucked among the mountains of southeastern Pennsylvania, the town bore the name of Mr. Irwin R. Perry, who had deemed the area a worthy enough place to build a lumber mill. Fueled by abundant forests of pine, the mill prospered and the town grew. Perry Hollow was never large; nor was it ever rich. But it was comfortable, which was good enough for the folks who lived there.

The whole town had revolved around Perry Mill, which stood at the far end of Lake Squall. Homes were built to house the mill's workers, who frequented stores that kept track of every mill payday. Even Kat was a product of the mill—her grandparents met while working there.

The first blow came in the sixties, when demand for lumber faltered. It only got worse in the ensuing decades. When the mill closed in 1990, Perry Hollow shuttered itself along with it. Residents left in droves, and a drive through town was a depressing tour of vacant storefronts and crumbling homes.

In 2000, when a restaurateur from New York City chose Perry Hollow as the location for a fancy French bistro, no one thought it would last very long. The food was so expensive that no one in town could actually afford to eat there. But out-of-towners could, and the restaurant thrived. "Destination dining" it was called, and it worked. For the first time in years, people actually stopped in Perry Hollow instead of cutting through it on their way to the Pennsylvania Turnpike.

Other businesses eventually followed. A gourmet bakery opened next to a bed-and-breakfast. An art gallery specializing in modern painting moved in, along with several upscale dress shops. Longtime residents such as Kat suddenly and surreally found themselves living in an arts community.

No one who lived there could have predicted that the town would experience such a rebirth. But whether one liked it or not—and Kat did—it looked like Perry Hollow was there to stay.

While she drove up Main Street, Kat scanned the thoroughfare. There was Big Joe's, doing steady business both day and night. Beyond it sat Awesome Blossoms, where Jasper Fox probably still waited in vain for his missing delivery van, Gunzelman Antiques, and Wellington's, the dress shop. The other side of the street boasted a bakery called Neverland Cakes and a store specializing in designer handbags.

Each storefront was decked out oh-so-tastefully for the upcoming Spring Fling, one of Perry Hollow's numerous festivals designed to bring in day-trippers from Philadelphia and New Jersey. The festivals worked. Last year's Spring Fling, with its flower sales and Ferris wheel, had drawn thousands of visitors. Attendance for that was surpassed only by July's Independence Day street fair, which advertised food, fun, and fireworks, and October's Halloween Festival, which lured tourists with the promise of fall foliage and hot apple cider.

How much of a draw the events would be now that Perry Hollow was the location of a brutal murder remained to be seen. As Kat drove, every pedestrian on Main Street glanced at the Crown Vic. When she looked into their eyes, Kat saw fear reflected back at her. Every man, woman, and child in town had by now heard about the murder. Kat was certain those staring bystanders on Main Street wondered where she was heading—all the while hoping it would be to catch a killer.

Only one person didn't pause when Kat passed. Dressed in a shirt and tie, he sprinted off the sidewalk and into the street in front of her so fast she had to slam on her brakes to avoid hitting him. The man hurried to the car and gestured for Kat to roll down her window.

"Afternoon, Martin," she said.

Like Kat herself, Martin Swan was one of those people who never got around to getting out of town. To his credit, Martin made it farther than Kat had, getting all the way to Temple University. Then his mother died, forcing him to come back home with only three years of journalism school under his belt. It was enough for the *Gazette,* which hired him as a reporter, and it seemed to be enough for Martin himself.

"You got a minute, Chief?" he asked. "I wanted to ask you a few questions about George Winnick."

"The investigation is still ongoing," Kat said. "So I don't have much information to give. When I have something, I'll tell you."

Her statement—or lack of one—didn't deter the reporter. Whipping a pen and small notebook out of his shirt pocket, he asked, "Was George murdered?"

The answer was yes. George didn't sew his own mouth shut before he died. Nor did he deposit his corpse on the side of the road. Yet she wasn't going to tell Martin that until there was an official cause of death.

"I don't know yet," she said. "We'll have a better picture after the autopsy is conducted."

"Is it true he was found in a homemade coffin?"

Unfortunately, Kat couldn't lie about that. A truck driver saw it. So did several dozen cops.

"It was a wooden box, not a coffin," she said, not even convincing herself.

She expected Martin to bring up the premature death notice that had been faxed to his own newsroom. When he didn't, Kat realized Henry Goll was telling the truth. He hadn't informed anyone at the *Gazette* about it.

Thinking about the obituary writer created a question of her own, which she immediately posed to Martin.

"How much do you know about Henry Goll?"

Martin gave her a sly smile. "You're the second person to ask me that today."

"Who was the first?"

"My sister," he replied. "She said he had a cute phone voice and wanted to know if the rest of him matched it."

"What did you tell her?"

"Yes, but only if his voice cracked."

Kat frowned at his cruel reference to Henry's scar. Martin noticed and quickly apologized.

"That was mean of me. The guy can't help how he looks."

"Do you know what happened to him?"

Martin shook his head. "No idea. Henry Goll is pretty much a closed book."

"I thought that was the case," Kat said. "Now, if you'll excuse me, I need to get moving."

She shifted the Crown Vic into gear and started to slowly pull away. Martin followed next to the open window, keeping pace with the car.

"Come on, Chief," he begged. "I have to file a story by seven and I have nothing to go on."

"I have nothing to tell you. I wish I knew more."

Martin had fallen behind. He was now beside the patrol

car's back window, but Kat could still hear him call out, "Are there any suspects?"

Kat called back: "We're looking at all possibilities."

Although the reporter tried, he couldn't keep up anymore. He stopped in the middle of the street and, with labored breath, yelled, "Tell me as soon as you find something!"

Kat stuck her arm out the still-open window and gave him a thumbs-up sign before speeding up the street. In the rear-view mirror, she watched his retreating figure return to the sidewalk, shoulders slumped in disappointment.

At the end of Main Street, Kat turned onto Old Mill Road, which ran as far as Lake Squall. Perry Mill still stood there, now only a shadow of its former glory. Despite the town's revitalization, no one had thought to restore the one thing that had led to its formation in the first place. So the mill was left in ruins. Its crumbling outbuildings had collapsed into piles of rotted wood. Its roads became pockmarked with gullies and potholes. Its long dormant railroad tracks vanished into the weeds.

All that remained of the compound was the mill building itself, a formidable structure that measured seven stories from base to rooftop. It hovered over the trees in the distance, the muted sun slipping behind its angled roof. At one point, hundreds of people worked there. Now it was a ghost from the past, shrouded in the fog that rose off the lake.

Although Kat had never stepped foot inside the mill, it had haunted her imagination ever since she was a little girl. When she was growing up, her father would occasionally come home and announce that another accident had happened there. He never filled in the grisly details, which made Kat's imagination spin madly. Late at night, hunkered down beneath her covers, she pictured a mill full of deformed men working the same saws that had snatched their limbs.

She had quickly grown out of that phase, thank God. But

now the horrors of her youthful imagination had come to life in adulthood. Only George Winnick's murder was more disturbing than anything she could have come up with as a girl.

Kat shuddered as she drove past the area where she had found George's body, still marked by a banner of police tape. Although the coffin and its grisly contents had been hauled away, she could still see them there, lying in the snow. She hoped the image would fade with time and that eventually she could drive Old Mill Road in peace. Yet she suspected the image would be like Perry Mill—always present, unchanging, and waiting to be revisited.

# SEVEN

That afternoon, Nick drove to the county morgue. Cassie Lieberfarb rode with him, fiddling with the radio. Flitting from station to station, she found nothing to satisfy either of them.

"We've got country, country, Muzak, and more country."

"No classic rock?" Nick asked.

"No, but if you'd like, I could sing 'Stairway to Heaven.' I learned it in the girls chorus at Temple Beth El."

"As tempting as that sounds, I'll pass."

"Then instead of singing," Cassie said, "how about you tell me why you lied about going to Florida on vacation."

She was using her analyst's voice, which contained no judgment, no amusement. It was a flat, neutral tone that Nick had heard hundreds of times. Although normally when he heard it, the voice was directed at suspects, not him.

"I didn't lie," Nick said.

"Did you go to Florida?"

Eventually he shook his head.

"And was it really a vacation?"

Another more reluctant shake.

"See," Cassie said, "that means it's a lie."

Caught in her inquisitive gaze, Nick felt like a specimen beneath a microscope, wriggling and defenseless. He straightened his spine in a show of strength. It didn't work.

"I was interviewing killers," he said.

"Who?"

"Edgar Sewell. Mitchell Ramsey. Frank Paul Steel."

Cassie processed the names a moment, matching them to the unspeakable crimes they had committed.

"Those cases are thirty years old," she said. "Why were you talking to them?"

But she knew the answer. And Nick knew that she knew. But Cassie wasn't going to let him off the hook. She thought it helped to talk about his past, that it was therapeutic. Nick disagreed, so he said nothing.

After a full minute of silent détente, Cassie declared defeat.

"We won't talk about it anymore," she said. "But you know how I feel about this. I understand it's hard for you to deal with, but digging into your past like that won't—"

Nick stopped her with an upraised hand. "I thought we weren't talking about it."

"We're not," Cassie said with a shrug. "We're traveling in silence."

Fortunately for Nick, they didn't have to travel much farther. They had reached their destination.

Once they were parked, it took them no time to find the medical examiner. He was a squat and gray-faced man, having a cigarette outside the equally squat and gray-faced county morgue.

"Lieutenant Donnelly?" he asked, eyeing Nick through a haze of smoke.

"In the flesh."

The medical examiner extended the hand that didn't contain a Pall Mall. "I'm Wallace Noble. Any trouble getting here?"

Instead of waiting for an answer, Wallace Noble let out a hacking cough that emerged from deep within his chest.

"Goddamn these cigarettes," he muttered before taking a hearty drag. "Things are going to kill me soon."

"Why don't you quit?" Cassie asked.

Wallace exhaled twin streams of smoke through his nostrils, like an angry bull in a Bugs Bunny cartoon. "I've spent almost forty years looking at dead folks and determining their cause of death. Frankly, it gives me comfort already knowing the cause of mine."

With a half cough, half chuckle, he dropped the cigarette and ground it into the sidewalk with the toe of a wingtip.

"Now let's go take a look at poor George."

Nick and Cassie followed him inside, where they passed a small waiting area before entering a long hallway painted the same color as pea soup. At the end of the hall, they made a right and stopped at the door to the autopsy suite. There they wrangled into autopsy gowns and slipped shoe covers over their feet. Then it was into the autopsy suite itself.

George Winnick's corpse was already out and lying uncovered on a stainless steel table in the center of the room. The halogen lamp hanging over it cast a wide halo of light onto the skin, turning it a shade of white so bright Nick had to look away until his eyes adjusted.

"Is there an obvious cause of death?" he asked.

"Nothing jumped out at me so far," Wallace said. "When I cleaned him up a bit, I found marks on his arms, legs, and forehead."

"What kind of marks?"

Wallace shrugged. "Off the top of my head, I'd say they were rope burns."

Nick shot a sidelong glance to Cassie, who was already taking notes. Since killers who bind their victims are usually smart and organized, the rope burns suggested a high level of planning. Right away, both of them knew this murder wasn't a spontaneous act.

"As for what killed George," Wallace continued, "I don't think we'll know that until we open him up."

He handed Nick and Cassie latex gloves before snapping a pair onto his own hands. "What are you guys looking for anyway?"

"The stitches," Nick said as he put on the gloves and approached the table. "We need to see if it resembles the handiwork of another killer who sews up his victims."

"The Betsy Ross Killer, right?"

"He's the one."

"Why does he sew them up?" Wallace asked, both fascinated and repelled at the same time.

"I'll get back to you after I catch him and ask him."

Wallace and Cassie joined him at the examination table.

"I only found stitches on two places," the medical examiner said. "One's at the neck. The other spot was the lips."

Nick saw both areas. The lips had been sewn shut in a wide cross-stitch pattern. On the neck, the stitches were close together, sealing up a small gash.

"What do you think?" he asked Cassie.

She gingerly placed a finger at the wound and ran it along the thread.

"At first glance, it certainly looks like the work of our guy," she said. "But the lips—that's unusual."

The Betsy Ross Killer had never gone for them before. Until Mr. Winnick, he had stayed away from the face entirely.

Nick reached into his jacket and removed a small digital camera. When he bought it, the clerk at Radio Shack told him about all the "awesome" vacation photos he'd be able to take with it. That was a year ago, and so far, corpses were the only things the camera's lens had seen.

Leaning over George's body, he took a picture of the lips, the flash from the camera filling the room in a quick burst. Nick took five more shots from various angles, as the medical examiner watched. Each flash of the camera caused him to flinch.

"What happened to his eyes?" Cassie asked.

Nick stopped taking pictures long enough to look at George Winnick's eyes, where a small line of red circled each socket.

"That's where the pennies were," Wallace said. "Placed right over the eyes."

"But why the red marks?"

"The coins were frozen to the skin. I had to use hot water to pry them off."

"Do you still have them?" Cassie asked.

The medical examiner nodded. "They're in my office. Tagged and bagged and ready to be examined."

Nick raised his camera again and moved on to the neck. He crouched down next to the table and snapped off another five shots.

"I need you to remove the thread," he told Wallace. "And save it. We'll need to examine that, too."

Wallace obliged by picking up a pair of suture scissors and carefully slicing through the thread, one stitch at a time. The gash widened, although no blood dripped out of it. The blood had all settled by that point.

"Here you go," Wallace said, tugging the thread from the skin and dropping it into an evidence bag that Cassie had waiting for him.

He then moved out of the way, letting Nick and his partner get an unobstructed view of the wound. It was a clean cut, smooth along the edges. There was no hesitation involved. The killer had done it in one careful slice.

"I'm thinking scalpel," Cassie said. "That incision is too clean for a knife, no matter how sharp it is."

"That's a change," Nick added. "The Betsy Ross victims had ragged wounds."

Cassie nodded in agreement. "That's because there was rage involved. He was angry when he did the cutting. But this wound is different. It's clinical. Detached."

Nick had a better word to describe the wound. *Precise.* Whoever had caused it chose that spot for a reason.

Free of the stitches, the incision widened like a toothless smile. Nick raised his camera and fired off a few shots. He zoomed in. On the camera's display screen, the depths of the wound came into sudden, startling focus. Nick saw an artery— most likely the carotid—bulging just beyond the parted curtain of flesh and fat. Colored a pale purple, it was marred by tiny lines of black.

Nick lowered the camera.

"I think there's more stitches."

He backed away as Wallace Noble swooped in. Using a small hook, the medical examiner gently tugged the artery until it emerged from the open wound. In the harsh light of the examination room, it was clear that Nick was right. The artery had been sliced open as cleanly as George Winnick's neck had been. And just like the neck, the wound had been sewn shut with tight loops of black thread.

"I'll be damned," Wallace said, shock setting off his smoker's cough. "Now I know what killed poor old George."

# EIGHT

"George wasn't a great man. But he was a good one. And he did right by me."

Alma Winnick, a potato sack of a woman in a powder blue housedress, gave her stunted eulogy from an armchair covered in cat fur. Kat knew it was an act and that Alma mourned her husband. But the widow refused to show her grief while a stranger was in the house.

"I think he knew death was coming for him," she said flatly.

"How so?"

"My brother died last month. Car accident. You probably read about it in the paper."

"My condolences," Kat said, feeling even more sorry for the woman sitting across from her. So much loss in such a short period. Kat's own family had spread it out. Her father died suddenly when she was eighteen, killed by a heart attack. Her mother stuck around for two more decades, succumbing to cancer the previous summer. Losing them separately had been hard enough. Losing them both within a month of each other would have been too much to bear.

"At my brother's funeral, George was the first person to sign the condolence book. As he wrote his name down, he said, 'Alma, dying is a terrible thing.' He never talked that way before. Never mentioned death. That's what makes me think he knew his time had come."

Kat, who didn't put much faith in premonitions, doubted George Winnick knew he was about to die. If he did, his death surely ended up being far worse than he ever imagined.

"I told him not to worry," Alma continued, eyes cast down. At her feet lay a calico with a milky eye and only three legs, and Kat couldn't tell if the widow was addressing her or the calico. "He was strong. And tall. Do you know how tall he was?"

"No idea."

"Six feet, two inches." Alma said it with a mixture of admiration and awe that made Kat's heart break just a little. "I come from a short family. So when I first laid eyes on George, he looked like the tallest man in the world."

"Do you know of anyone who might have wanted to harm your husband? Any enemies? Grudges?"

Alma shook her head at each suggestion Kat threw out.

"I don't understand why someone would want to hurt my George. He was a good man. People liked him. He worked this land a long time. His folks were here before the mill. That's a good number of years, and people respected that. Even the boys he had out here in the summer respected that."

Kat's ears perked up. "Boys?"

"Every summer, George would hire a couple boys from the junior high to help out on the farm. It took some of the load off his back and it did the boys some good, too. Taught them the value of hard work."

Kat asked Alma if she remembered the names of some of the summer employees.

"Troy Gunzelman," she said. "Him, I remember."

That was no surprise. Troy's notoriety extended beyond Perry Hollow and into the next county. Even a woman as sheltered as Alma would know about his exploits on the field.

"Any others?"

Alma shrugged. It was obvious she was getting tired of being peppered with questions. Kat was tired of doing the peppering. But both of them had to continue.

"When was the last time you saw your husband?" Kat asked.

"Last night. I thought he would have come to bed after checking out the noise, so I went to sleep. When I woke up, his side of the bed was untouched."

"Is his truck missing?"

"No," Alma said. "It's parked in the same place it was last night, so I assume he didn't drive it."

"You mentioned a noise. What did it sound like?"

"Animals."

Alma turned to look out the window next to her chair. Kat followed her gaze across the snow-covered yard and past a John Deere tractor old enough to be in a museum. Beyond it was the barn, where several more cats and a handful of chickens loitered outside. Kat heard the whinny of horses from within, followed by the sharp bark of a dog.

"It was a racket," the widow said. "They were making noise something fierce. George thought it might be a bear or a mountain lion. They're rare, but they're still out there, believe you me. Saw a bear out on Old Mill Road once. Scared the Lord out of me."

Kat saw Alma's dead husband on Old Mill Road, and it scared the Lord out of *her*.

"What time did the noise start?"

"About ten thirty."

A cold bomb of fear exploded in Kat's chest. If Alma was correct, then the fake obituary had indeed been sent *before* George Winnick died.

"You're certain of that?"

"Fairly sure," Alma said. "I remember looking at the clock when George left to go check on the barn."

Kat jerked her head in the direction of the barnyard. "Do you mind if I poke around out there a bit?"

When Alma shrugged again, the hopeless lift of her shoulders said, *Sure, go out there. Find your clues. But it won't bring my husband back. He's gone forever.*

After thanking Mrs. Winnick for her time and patience, and after offering her condolences once again, Kat left.

Outside, she tramped across the yard toward the barn. The sun was still out, thanks to daylight saving time, which had gone into effect the previous morning. The newfound brightness allowed her to look for footprints in the snow. She saw dozens of them—from Alma, from George, even from the stray cats that seemed to roam everywhere. If the killer had crept through the yard the night before, it would be impossible to trace his steps.

Inside the barn, Kat found herself confronted by a surly Rottweiler chained in a far corner. It barked ferociously as soon as she entered. When it lunged in her direction, the chain hooked to its collar stretched so tight she thought the animal was going to choke itself to death.

The noise from the dog set off the horses housed in stalls along the barn's right wall. There were three of them in total, their heads shaking in agitation at the presence of a stranger. The only animal not perturbed was a black cat sleeping in a square of fading sunlight that slanted in through a cracked window. Unlike the other animals, it didn't move a muscle.

Kat surveyed the cluttered barn, the scent of hay and manure stinging her nostrils. In addition to the animals, the barn housed a tractor, a riding mower, and a plow. A pyramid of hay bales sat near the horse stalls.

This was where the farmer first encountered his killer. She was certain of it.

The killer had most likely entered the barn not long after faxing the death notice to Henry Goll. His presence there had irritated the animals, which in turn roused George.

Kat put herself in the place of George Winnick, standing in front of the open barn door in about the same spot where he would have entered. She saw what he would have seen—a barn full of shadows.

She took a few steps forward. Cautious ones. Like what George might have taken.

Because there were no signs of a struggle in the barn, her assumption was that the farmer didn't notice his stalker until it was too late. Perhaps he didn't see him at all. The killer could have snuck up on George, creeping up quietly behind him.

Looking around for hiding places, Kat saw the possibilities were endless. Behind the barn door, for one, or in the shadow of the tractor. Near the sleeping cat was a small alcove, no larger than a broom closet. The killer easily could have hidden there, eyes adjusting to the darkness as he waited for his victim.

Kat crossed the barn and peeked inside the alcove. She saw a modest nook consisting of a clean concrete floor and plank walls. Her view from the threshold gave her no reason to enter the alcove outright. Besides, if George's killer hid there the night before, then a tech team needed to do a thorough scan of it. Maybe it would turn up something. A footprint. A stray fiber. Perhaps a hair. Anything would help because at this point they had nothing but a corpse, two pennies, and a wooden box.

Leaving the alcove, she gazed at the cat lying a few feet away. It hadn't moved the entire time she was there. Not once. She watched for the tiniest of movements—an ear wiggle, the idle sway of a tail—but saw nothing.

Approaching the animal, Kat nudged it with the toe of her boot. It was as still as a brick and just as heavy.

The cat was dead.

Kat bent down to examine the animal further, noticing a small pile of sawdust around its hind legs. When she nudged it again, more sawdust trickled from a gash in the animal's stomach.

The cat had been cut open, a long incision across its stomach showing where the knife had sliced. In place of its organs, someone had filled it with sawdust, which explained the heaviness. An unruly pattern of fur-obscured thread crisscrossed the incision. Stitches, used to sew the cat back up.

Kat inched away from the dead animal. What it meant to the case, she didn't know. But staring at the poor creature sprawled on the ground, she clearly understood that despite her theories and best guesses, she didn't have a handle on the situation at all.

Tony Vasquez was the first member of Nick Donnelly's team to reach the barn. With him were a half dozen other state troopers. Tony stretched police tape across the gaping barn door. He then ordered two troopers to go on the other side of it and stand guard while the rest went to work.

Not wanting to get in the way—and not wanting to destroy any evidence in the process—Kat retreated to an empty corner of the barn and parked herself on a bale of hay. From her itchy perch, she watched as Rudy Taylor arrived, armed with enough evidence bags to seal up every strand of hay she sat upon.

Nick Donnelly and Cassie Lieberfarb showed up five minutes later. While Cassie joined her coworkers, Nick made a beeline to the bale of hay.

"I need to talk to you," he said.

"That's good," Kat replied, "because I have to talk to you."

Nick plopped down on the bale next to her. "You first."

Kat took a deep breath and began. She told Nick about the death notice faxed to the *Gazette* newsroom before George Winnick died. She then moved on to what Alma Winnick had said about George investigating noises coming from the barn. That led to the search of the barn itself, where she found the dead cat stuffed with sawdust.

"That confirms my theory," Nick said, once she had finished.

"And what's that?"

"That it might not be the Betsy Ross Killer we're dealing with."

It wasn't what Kat wanted to hear. Strange as it seemed, she had been hoping that all of this was the work of Betsy Ross. It's easier to face the devil you know than the devil you don't. And whoever killed George Winnick was one sick devil.

"All of this—the fax, the dead animal—sounds far different from what Betsy Ross does," Nick said. "Serial killers like him do sometimes change their MO, but not as extreme as this. And George's wounds were different from the ones on the Betsy Ross victims."

"How did he die?"

"He bled to death."

"From the cut on his neck? That was barely three inches long."

"Three and one-fifth inches long," Nick clarified. "Wallace Noble measured it. And it was more than just the cut that caused him to bleed out."

"I don't understand."

Nick leaned forward. "Do you know what the carotid artery is?"

"Sure. It's where the nurse checks your neck for a pulse. What does this have to do with George Winnick?"

"His right carotid was sliced open," Nick said. "It's difficult but doable. Whoever did this most likely reached through the cut in his neck and pulled the artery out of the body. One careful incision later and you have a blood geyser on your hands."

Kat felt a stress headache coming on, signaling her brain was getting overloaded. The slight pain began just behind her eyes, ready to spread to her temples. Considering the circumstances, she was surprised the headache had taken so long to arrive.

"It's a horrible way to die," Nick said.

Kat couldn't agree more. Perry Hollow had experienced its share of tragic deaths. Accidents. Brutal falls. But what Nick described seemed so cruel and hateful that she couldn't quite believe it. Making someone bleed to death implied premeditation and planning. You needed to be prepared to do it.

"It gets worse," Nick warned. "Do you want me to go on?"

Kat didn't, but it was her job to say yes.

"The killer did more to George after he was dead."

"The lips," Kat said. "They were sewn shut."

"That's not what I was talking about."

"What do you mean?"

"When you cut open a corpse, there's very little bleeding because circulation has stopped and most of the blood has settled. There's some leakage, but it's minor. Wallace said there was an unusually large amount of blood on George Winnick's lips."

"There was," Kat replied. If she closed her eyes, she could easily picture the reddish ice crystals that had coated his lips. It was the first time she had ever seen frozen blood, and she hoped to God she'd never see it again.

"That means," Nick said, "that George was still alive when his lips were sewn shut."

Kat's mind whirled, imagining what such an act sounded like to the victim. Was it silent? Or could George hear the thread slipping through his skin, his flesh pulling together as it did so? If Kat concentrated, she could hear it, something not unlike the sound of a shoelace passing through the eyelet of a sneaker.

Trying to force the sound from her head, she asked, "Then what was the time of death?"

"That's the problem. Wallace couldn't tell for certain. It was definitely within twelve hours before you found him, but he couldn't pinpoint it more than that."

"Why not?"

"After George bled out," Nick said, "the killer pumped liquid into his body."

"Jesus," Kat muttered. "What kind?"

"Part water, part formaldehyde."

"Formaldehyde? Are you sure?"

"His body was filled with it. That's why Wallace can't pinpoint an exact time of death. The mixture killed off the microorganisms that cause decomposition. It slowed down rigor mortis. The right carotid was engorged, although that could have been from the tube."

Kat's voice rose with disbelief. "There was a tube?"

"Not when you found him, but the incision in the artery had been widened by something. The assumption is that the killer inserted a tube into it. That's how he was able to get the formaldehyde and water mixture into the circulatory system. It got the job done, but it was pretty rough. Not at all like the professionals."

"Professional who?"

"Morticians," Nick said. "After George Winnick bled to death, the killer tried to embalm him."

# NINE

Henry lay on his weight bench, grunting against the 250-pound barbell he pushed away from his chest. The muscles in his arms tightened as he held the weight aloft for three seconds. When he lowered it, the tension eased, flooding his muscles with a satisfying warmth.

"One," he said.

He raised the barbell again. He paused three more seconds. He lowered it.

"Two."

Henry's routine included a workout in a corner of his apartment filled with exercise equipment. One hour of each day was devoted to honing his body to its full potential. Although pushing forty, he possessed the strength and agility of a much younger man.

"Three."

With his face looking the way it did, Henry knew peak physical prowess was the only thing that kept people from pitying him completely.

"Four."

And he didn't want pity.

"Five."

He wanted to be left alone.

While he worked out, music blasted from a CD player against the wall. Puccini's *Tosca,* one of his favorites. Opera was still relatively new to Henry. It was only in the past five years that he had become obsessed with it. Now it was the only music he listened to. Especially the tragedies. What he heard in the music, other people missed. The tales of doomed love, mistaken identity, and broken hearts of epic proportions were melodramatic, yes. But they were also true. You *could* love someone so much you would kill for them. Your love could be so strong that if they died, a large part of you died with them. Opera was tragic. So was life.

Finishing another set of reps, Henry lowered the weights and—breath heavy, heart thumping—paused to listen to the music. It was "E lucevan le stelle," Cavaradossi's third-act aria in which the doomed painter recalled memories of his lover, Tosca. The aria was sung in Italian, and Henry knew every word. He was fluent in Italian, having learned it in his old life. Before the accident. Before Henry Ghoul.

*E lucevan le stelle.*

Henry repeated it in English, like a prayer. "How the stars seemed to shimmer."

Closing his eyes, he focused on the music, on the lyrics, on the perfect voice singing them. It reminded him of Gia. Sweet Gia. His Italian rose. The aria could have been written about her.

*Entrava ella, fragrante.*

"How she then entered, so fragrant, and then fell into my arms."

Usually, he would have been enthralled, swept up in the aria's embrace. But that day was different. The aria—and thoughts of Gia—put him in a dark mood, which was accompanied by an itching restlessness.

*L'ora è fuggita . . . e muoio disperato.*

"My last hour has flown and I die hopeless."

*E non ho amato mai tanto la vita.*

"And never have I loved life more."

Henry left the room without bothering to turn off the CD player. His apartment, located above a used-book store on the end of Main Street, was large by modern standards. But that evening, the place felt absolutely tiny. As he roamed restlessly inside it, the walls seemed to constrict around him.

He had to get out. Just for a little bit.

His steps quickened in the hallway as he headed for the front door. By the time he was outside, he was at a full jog—legs churning, arms pumping. He picked up speed to tackle the slight incline of north Main Street. When it flattened out at the end of the street, he kept the same pace, streaking over the sidewalk.

The stares of strangers confronted him as he passed. Blurs

of faces trying to get a good look at him. Henry ignored them, soon becoming unaware of how many people he flew by or if they were staring. He also ignored the cold, which his flimsy workout clothes did nothing to ward off. He focused only on the steady exhalation of his breath and the rhythmic slapping of his feet on the pavement.

The sadness that overcame him in his apartment dissipated outdoors. He knew the melancholy would wash over him again at some point. No matter how fast he ran, Henry knew he couldn't outrun his pain.

After he had sprinted at full speed for about fifteen minutes, a cramp stabbed his midsection. He slowed himself, legs winding down until eventually he came to a stop at the corner of Maple and Oak streets. Bent forward in exhaustion, palms resting on his knees, he noticed a large Victorian mansion dominating the corner.

McNeil Funeral Home.

Henry had never been inside, but the exterior impressed the hell out of him. Three stories tall with white siding, it boasted a green gabled roof, wraparound front porch, and Tiffany accents in the tall windows. Pretty fancy for a stopping place on the way to the afterlife.

Once he regained control of his breathing, Henry stepped onto the walkway that cut through the property's expansive front yard. Without fully comprehending what he was doing, he trotted toward the front door. Not hesitating, he pushed inside, entering a tastefully appointed room dominated by a large mahogany desk. An attractive young woman sat behind it. She smiled at him when he entered.

"Hello, Henry," she said.

He halted in the doorway. "How did you know it was me?"

"Because you look uncertain."

Henry imagined he looked more than uncertain. He probably looked ghastly in his sweat-drenched T-shirt and running shorts, his flushed face making its flaws stand out even more.

Deana Swan, however, looked better than expected. Years of speaking to her on the phone had created a mental picture that wasn't flattering. In Henry's imagination, she was a female version of her brother, with chipmunk cheeks and oversized sweaters. *That* was the type of woman who spent her whole day in a funeral home.

The real Deana couldn't have been further from the image created in his head. In her early thirties, she was slim, well proportioned, and modestly stylish in a black skirt and lavender blouse. She wore her strawberry blond hair pulled back, revealing razor-thin cheekbones, and startling, sparkling blue eyes.

"What brings you here today?" she asked.

Henry didn't know, which was made obvious by his refusal to take one more step inside.

"I was jogging," he said.

Deana ran her gaze up and down his body, lingering on his chest, his stomach, his crotch. The boldness of her stare made Henry pulse with excitement, as did the sultry tone of her voice when she said, "I can see that."

"When I passed by, I thought I would stop in and say hello. Since you've told me I never do that."

"You don't," Deana said. "And thanks. That was sweet of you."

Oddly, Henry felt more awkward chatting with Deana than he did telling Chief Campbell about George Winnick's death notice. That was being helpful, a good citizen. This was something entirely different. This was, Henry guessed, flirting.

"I just want you to know," Deana said, her smile radiating a kind patience, "that my offer is still on the table."

"What offer?"

"Lunch. I think it might be fun, since we're coworkers in a weird way."

That was true. Henry talked to Deana more than anyone at the *Gazette*. And she seemed friendly enough, with no hidden agenda except to get to know him better. Plus, he thought it would be nice just once to break out of his safe routine.

"A great sushi place just opened up on Main," Deana said. "We could try it out one day."

Henry was on the verge of saying yes. He felt the muscles in the back of his neck loosen, preparing for the nod to follow. But then something on the wall caught his eye. It was a mirror—large and gilded—and framed in its center was his reflection.

Staring at his own image, Henry suddenly felt foolish. He was in excellent shape, yes. But his face—that was unacceptable. And the more that Deana smiled benevolently at him, the more Henry became convinced that her motives were suspect. She wasn't interested in him. Just like the patrons of a freak show, she was interested in his face. Its lines and scars and deformities.

"I don't think that's a good idea," Henry said, breaking his gaze from the mirror. "But thank you for the invitation."

He regretted stepping foot into the funeral home. It was a bad idea, he realized. And now he was eager to leave.

He turned and reached for the door, surprised to see it was already halfway open. Someone was on the other side, pushing the door so forcefully Henry had to hop backward to avoid being struck by it. That's when Kat Campbell burst inside, riding a gust of frigid air.

With her was a man Henry had never seen before. Although he was dressed in civilian clothes, Henry assumed he was a cop of some sort. He and the chief shared identical scowls as they passed, barely noticing his presence.

Henry nodded a wordless greeting and exited the funeral

home. Crossing the front porch, he heard Kat through the open door ask, "Are Art and Bob here?"

"Arthur is," Deana told her. "Is something wrong?"

Henry paused at the top of the porch steps, waiting for the chief's response. When it came, he was surprised, intrigued, and more than a little fearful.

"I need to know," Kat said, "how to go about embalming someone."

# TEN

In Kat's mind, few places on earth were as depressing as McNeil Funeral Home. Arthur McNeil, the owner, tried hard to make it as calm and comforting as possible. Beige walls, classic furnishings, fresh flowers on a side table by the front door. Yet the sterile perfection of the place always unsettled Kat. The décor felt to her just like the corpses on display there—posed, painted, lifeless.

Her opinion of the place was colored by the terrible hours spent there during her parents' funerals. Too uncomfortable to take a seat, she waited with Nick just inside the door. The position gave her a glimpse into the empty viewing room where her mother's body was laid out eight months earlier. Memories of that time rushed into her head. Seeing James cry. Weeping herself. Sitting next to her mother's casket, trying not to break down completely. The recollections were so painful that Kat sighed with relief when Art McNeil finally appeared.

"I'm sorry to keep you waiting," he said, taking one of Kat's hands in both of his. "Deana told me it sounded important."

He was dressed in light blue scrubs, with a paper cap on

his head and a surgical mask lowered to beneath his chin. Even out of street clothes, Art projected a benevolent calmness that was one of the tools of his trade.

When Kat introduced Nick Donnelly, Art flashed him the smile of a favorite uncle.

"It's wonderful to meet you, Lieutenant Donnelly."

"We hate to bother you like this," Nick said. "But there are some things we need to learn in order to investigate a recent crime."

Art shook his head sadly. "Let me guess—George Winnick. Wallace Noble told me everything when I made arrangements to pick the body up from the morgue."

On the one hand, Kat was annoyed that Wallace felt free to talk so openly about the case. But on the other, she was glad Art already knew the gory details of the situation. Since she still barely comprehended it herself, she had no idea how to go about explaining it to someone else.

"As you know," she said, "whoever killed George also tried to embalm him. In order to understand how and why, we need to see the whole embalming process. From start to finish."

She knew it was an odd request. So odd, in fact, she wouldn't have been surprised if Art flatly refused. But he seemed to understand the strangeness of the situation. Without thinking it over, he said, "Certainly."

He led them to the funeral home's basement, guiding them to a small changing room under the steps. Kat went first, stripping down to her T-shirt and trousers and slipping on surgical scrubs that matched Art's own. She topped off the absurd outfit with a blue cap over her hair and paper booties on her shoes.

As Kat left the changing area open for Nick, Art called to her from the embalming room, which sat to her immediate left.

"Come right on in."

Kat wanted to leave the embalming room as soon as she entered it. The white-tiled space was cold, for one thing, the chill instantly forming goose bumps on her arms. It also was eerily immaculate, as clean and sterile as an operating room. As she looked around, the scent of ammonia and formaldehyde tickled her nose and stuck to the back of her throat.

In the center of the room was a body lying on a stainless steel table. Large lights hung over the corpse, casting a brutal, white glow onto it. Beneath the table, the concrete floor gently slanted to a conspicuous drain.

"This is where we do it," Art said, standing next to the table.

Kat couldn't take her eyes off the body. It belonged to an elderly woman with a white sheet draped over everything but her head and bare feet. It took Kat a moment to realize she knew the woman, causing her to gasp when recognition hit.

"That's Barbara Hanover."

Art confirmed it with a solemn nod. "She died in her sleep during the night."

As a little girl, Kat had purchased candy from Mrs. Hanover every Saturday at the store she ran with her husband. She had been a jovial woman, quick with a smile and a free Jolly Rancher. Standing in the same room as her corpse, Kat felt like she was violating the woman in unspeakable ways.

She was grateful when Nick finally entered the embalming room. His new uniform of crisp scrubs gave her something other than Mrs. Hanover's body to look at.

"I'm assuming both of you know very little about the embalming process," Art said.

"Nothing at all," Nick said, answering for both of them. "But I understand it's very important."

The mortician beamed. "Oh, it is. The most important aspect of my job is creating a memory picture for the family of the deceased to take with them. They find it helps with the grieving process."

Kat recalled the way both her mother and father had looked in their caskets. Contrary to what Arthur McNeil thought, it didn't help her one bit. The images were something she wished she could forget.

The door to the embalming room opened and Art's son, Robert, emerged, also dressed in scrubs. Unlike the rest of them, he wore a rubber apron tight around his torso.

"What are they doing here?" he asked, his voice harsh in the hushed atmosphere of the embalming room.

Kat graduated high school a class behind Bob, and the intervening years hadn't changed him one bit. The polar opposite of his father, he was without manners of any stripe. Kat knew part of Bob's rudeness stemmed from his lifelong outcast status. He was an ungainly, unattractive boy, whose social life didn't benefit any from living above a funeral home.

Things only got worse for Bob when he turned ten, the year his mother, no longer able to live among the dead, decided to become one of them. Wearing three layers of heavy clothes, a brick shoved into every pocket, she threw herself into Lake Squall, the water quickly consuming her.

Leota McNeil stayed underwater for three days. When she finally floated to the surface, Kat's father was unlucky enough to find her.

Kat vividly remembered the conversation that took place that night at the dinner table. Her father doled out details to her mother, who clucked with sympathy. He then turned to Kat and said, "Be nice to Robert McNeil the next time you see him at school. Give him a little smile in the halls."

The next day, to everyone's surprise, Bob showed up at school, thudding through the halls with the same old chip on his shoulder. When he neared her, Kat recalled her father's words and forced a smile. Bob ignored it, giving her a withering glance as he barreled on by.

It surprised no one when he went into the family business after high school. The general thinking was that Bob McNeil had to work with the dead because he didn't know how to act among the living. They also suspected that he continued to reside with his father because Art was the only person who could tolerate him.

"Chief Campbell and Lieutenant Donnelly are here to observe the embalming process," Art said, as his son moved deeper into the embalming room. "You will extend them every courtesy, understand?"

He then turned to Kat. "Despite his ornery mood, I know Robert will be a huge help. He always is. I've found that children of single parents are especially attuned to the needs of the remaining parent. Like your son, for instance. How *is* James?"

"He's doing great," Kat said.

Art seemed pleased by the news. "I'm happy to hear that. James is such a good boy. Very special. You should be proud of him."

She assured him she was, which satisfied Art. With a smile and a wave, he said, "It was a pleasure seeing you again, Kat. And very nice meeting you, Lieutenant. Be sure to ask Robert any question you want."

"You're leaving?"

The nervousness in Kat's voice was obvious to both father and son, but she couldn't help it. Bob McNeil was the last person she wanted to be with in an embalming room.

"Unfortunately, yes," Art said. "I work days. Robert works nights. But truth be told, he's a better embalmer than I've ever been. You're in good hands."

Arthur departed, leaving Kat and Nick alone with one corpse and one mortician. It was like school all over again, with the mere presence of Bob McNeil creeping her out.

"How have you been, Bob?" she asked, trying to make an effort to sound casual and friendly.

The mortician wasn't buying any of it. Slipping a surgical mask over his nose and mouth, he said, "You ready?"

With the mask and cap on, the only part of Bob's face still visible were his too-large eyes. They were exaggerated further by the pair of Coke-bottle glasses he was forced to wear beginning in junior high. The lenses caused his eyes to look positively huge, which always made Kat think of a deranged Muppet.

"I guess we are," she said. "How long do you think this will take?"

"Not long. This one should be pretty easy. She's in good shape. Bodies that are really banged up or autopsied like George take much longer."

Bob whipped off the white sheet, leaving the body of Barbara Hanover fully exposed, with every wrinkle and sag on her chalk-colored skin visible. Nearby sat a stainless steel tray on wheeled legs, which he pulled to his side. Arranged on the tray were plastic bottles, a few folded towels, and medical instruments of various shapes and sizes. Within seconds, Bob was dipping a sponge attached to a wooden stick into a sudsy fluid. He then used it to swab the body.

"What are you doing?" Kat asked, oddly fascinated by the way Bob efficiently wiped down the body.

"Cleaning her," he replied, the sponge sliding over the corpse's drooping breasts. "I'm using a germicide. Kills off bacteria."

When he finished with the skin, Bob dipped a smaller sponge attached to a longer stick into the cleaning solution. This he used to swab first inside the corpse's mouth and then in each nostril.

With the cleaning over, he began to knead the body, his hands working down its arms and legs.

"This loosens things up," he said, moving to the shoulders. "Rigor mortis makes the corpse tight."

"Is this done to all the bodies?" Nick asked.

"For the most part. Some are in better shape than others, but all need a little work."

He rubbed a greasy, butter-colored lotion onto the corpse's hands, massaging it into the skin at the knuckles and on the surface of the palms. He then did the same thing to the face, rubbing the lotion deep into the wrinkles on Mrs. Hanover's cheeks and forehead.

"Moisturizer," he said. "Keeps things soft."

"When does the actual embalming begin?" Nick asked.

"In a minute. I need to set the features first."

"What does that involve?"

"Arranging the face to prepare it for viewing."

As he spoke, Bob shoved a clot of cotton into Barbara Hanover's nostrils. He then took a large clump of it and, holding the mouth open, placed it deep in the back of her throat.

"The cotton blocks any leakage," he said. "That's the first step. The eyes are next."

From the tray, he picked up a concave disc made of white plastic. One side of it was smooth, the other studded with small V-shaped hooks.

"This is an eye cap. Sometimes the eyes don't stay closed. Because the last thing you want is a corpse's eyes coming open during the viewing, we have to force them shut. In the old days, they used—"

"Coins," Kat said, unable to keep her brain from conjuring up the image of twin Honest Abes covering George Winnick's eyes.

Working on the left one first, Bob pulled the eyelid away and slipped the cap smooth-side down onto the eye itself. He let the eyelid drop onto the studded side, where it stuck to the cap, staying permanently closed. He then repeated the process with the right eyelid.

"Are the lips next?" Nick asked.

Bob looked at him, grudgingly impressed. "Yes, they are."

"Is it true that you sew them shut?"

"We do the entire mouth, at the jaw. George's lips were sewn shut, right?"

Kat replied with a weak nod, recalling the horrible pattern of thread that had overlapped George's blood-flecked lips.

"Why do you think the killer did that?"

"We don't know," Kat said. "We don't know why he did any of this. But we intend to find out."

"I'll show you how the pros do it."

Bob's voice was filled with a cold braggadocio that unnerved her. He actually *enjoyed* doing this, she realized with a chill. His tone made that abundantly clear.

She also suspected he was trying to show off in a warped attempt to impress them. His hands worked rapidly, with a flourish common to magicians and blackjack dealers. He wanted them to notice the nimbleness of his fingers. It was impossible not to. Despite all of his flaws, Bob McNeil was an expert at his job.

Next, he removed a needle from the tray. It was long—almost six inches—and curved slightly at the end.

"Watch this," he said, threading it with heavy suture string.

Kat winced as Bob parted the lips then poked the needle through the lower gums of the corpse's mouth. With his fingers inside the mouth, he shoved the needle through the upper jaw and into the right nostril, pulling the thread through. He next thrust the needle through the nose's septum and pushed it down through the left nostril. After taking the needle through the upper jaw again and back to the bottom gums, he tugged, pulling both sets of jaws tightly together.

"That's how it's done."

Pleased with his work, Bob picked up a crescent-shaped device made of transparent plastic. Just like the eye caps, one side contained small ridges designed to hold flesh in place.

"This is the mouth form," he said, as he parted Mrs. Hanover's lips to place the device over her teeth. Lowering the lips onto it, he delicately shaped them until they lay flat against each other.

Finished, he clapped his hands together and announced, "Now, we embalm."

A second wheeled tray stood in the corner. On top of it sat a chunky, box-shaped appliance with two knobs flanking a half-circle meter. A rubber hose, yellowed by age and chemicals, stuck out of the side. Sitting on top was a rectangular basin capped with a stainless steel lid.

"Is that the embalming machine?" Kat asked, slightly horrified by the antique look of it.

"It is."

Bob retreated to a cabinet along the wall, removing several bottles of liquid, all marked with the jagged symbol designating them as hazardous materials. Slipping on heavy-duty latex gloves, he turned to them and said, "Put your masks on. Take shallow breaths. And for God's sake, stand back."

Both of them took the warning seriously, moving backward in large steps until their spines touched the wall. When Bob opened one of the bottles, Kat slipped the mask over her nose and mouth before covering them with both hands.

Bob spent a few moments measuring and pouring liquids into the cylinder. Every so often, he glanced at the body, deciding how much he would need and of what kind. He was unfazed by the chemicals, although they were so strong Kat smelled them through both the mask and her laced fingers.

Voice muffled by the double barrier, she asked, "What are you mixing?"

"Arterial fluid, coinjection fluid, and just plain water."

Nick gave the next question. "What's coinjection fluid?"

"Just something that hydrates the tissue."

"You don't use formaldehyde?"

"It's in there," Bob said. "That's what the arterial fluid is—lots of formaldehyde."

"Is it easy to buy?" Kat asked.

Bob scoffed, as if her lack of knowledge insulted him. "Not the amount you'd need to embalm someone. It's toxic, not to mention highly flammable."

That bit of information surprised Kat. Her experience with formaldehyde ended at seventh-grade science class, when she had been forced to dissect a frog soaked in it.

"Flammable?"

"Yep," Bob said. "If this place caught fire, you'd have a mighty big explosion on your hands."

"If it's so dangerous," Nick said, "how do *you* get it?"

"Through a licensed supplier, who checks to make sure we're a legitimate funeral home. Dad's been buying it from the same place for decades."

Nick continued his questioning. "Is there a black market for it?"

"I suppose," Bob said. "There's a black market for everything, when you come right down to it. Sex. Body parts. Sex *with* body parts."

Although Bob's surgical mask covered his mouth, Kat could tell he was grinning. He thought he was being shocking. She thought he was just being a prick.

"So if I wanted to buy some of this stuff," she said, "I should check the Internet?"

"Either that or rob a funeral home."

This prospect seemed to intrigue Nick, who asked, "Could someone rob you?"

Bob jerked his head toward the cabinets along the wall. "Those are locked. And this room is locked. And then the entire house is locked and guarded by a security system. I doubt it's possible."

"That's good to hear," Nick said dryly. "Glad to know your formaldehyde is safe."

Bob finished filling the basin, replaced its lid, then capped the bottles. Kat removed her hands from over her mouth but kept the mask on. Even with the bottles closed, the air was rife with the scent of chemicals.

"How do you know how much fluid to use?"

"The rule of thumb is a gallon for every fifty pounds of body weight," Bob said. "Since Barbara here looks to be about a hundred and fifty, three gallons should do it."

"Now are you going to put the liquid in the body?"

"I am."

Settling onto a stool next to Mrs. Hanover's right side, Bob grabbed a scalpel and carefully cut a small slit down her neck.

"The killer used the right side, too," Nick told him.

"Then he sure knows something about how this is done."

Kat pushed away from the wall, taking cautious steps toward the body to get a closer view. The gash in Barbara's neck didn't bleed. Instead, it was blue-tinted and slightly puckered.

"Why the right side?" she asked.

"Because that's where a mortician's two best friends are hiding. The carotid and the jugular. Side by side."

Nick had told Kat the carotid was where the killer cut George Winnick open, causing him to bleed to death.

"What's the jugular used for?" she asked.

"Drainage. The blood flows out of the jugular; the fluid flows into the carotid."

"The killer used the carotid to do both," Nick said.

Bob looked away from the corpse long enough to yank down his surgical mask and flash them a yellow-toothed smile. "That's why I'm better at this than he is."

"How did you get so good?"

"Dear old Dad," Bob said, replacing the mask. "Taught me everything I know, whether I wanted to learn it or not."

He picked up a plastic tool that tapered into a thin hook. Slipping the hook into the cut on the neck, he probed inside Barbara Hanover's body.

"What are you using?" Kat asked.

"Aneurysm hook."

The hook emerged from the gash, pulling a pinkish tube out of the body and into the light. When Kat realized it was an artery, the sight made her feel faint.

"Which artery is that?"

"Carotid."

Bob dipped the hook back into the cut, pulling out seconds later with another, slightly thicker vein.

"And now the jugular."

With both blood vessels exposed outside the skin, he made small incisions in each of them, careful not to slice all the way through. Quickly, he added stitches to the edges of both cuts in both vessels.

"You have to stitch the cuts so the tubes don't slip," he said.

Kat was ready to ask about the tubes, but Bob beat her to it. Holding up something that resembled a miniature faucet, he said, "This is the arterial tube."

Attached to one end was a length of thin rubber hose that led to the embalming machine. Bob carefully slipped the tube's opposite end directly into the carotid artery.

Next, he displayed a longer tube that reminded Kat of the flute she had played in junior high band. It was of similar length and width as the arterial tube but with a valve in its center and a rounded knob at its end.

"This is the jugular tube," Bob told her.

As he slid the jugular tube into its corresponding vein, Kat noticed the valve was also attached to a rubber hose. Instead of being hooked up to the embalming machine, the hose slithered to a drain in the floor.

"Where's that one going to go?" Nick asked.

"It stays where it is."

"What comes out of it?"

"Blood."

"Where does the drain go?"

"Right to the sewer."

Bob didn't explain further, which was good, because Kat didn't want him to. She simply vowed never to descend into Perry Hollow's sewage system as Bob switched on the embalming machine. It rumbled to life, surprisingly loud, as the liquid inside the basin began to move. While Bob toyed with the knobs on the machine, embalming fluid rushed through the rubber hose into the body. Occasionally, he would pull the knob to open the valve on the jugular tube, sending a jet of blood spiraling down to the drain near his feet.

"Could someone do this by hand?" Nick asked, raising his voice over the whir of the embalming machine. In addition to the machine itself, a gurgling noise came from the tubes, sounding to Kat like a clogged coffeemaker.

"The results wouldn't be very good," Bob said, voice also raised. "But I guess it could be done with a funnel and some rubber tubing."

"That would be messy, right?"

"Definitely. You'd need a big place. Somewhere with good

ventilation or you'd asphyxiate on the formaldehyde. And drainage. Lots of drainage."

"So someone's basement is out of the question."

"That depends on the size. Whoever killed George probably had lots of room to work with."

He opened the valve on the jugular tube again, letting out another squirt of blood. After a few more releases, the blood was replaced by excess embalming fluid, which had pumped its way through the body.

"We're done," Bob announced, shutting off the embalming machine.

Kat couldn't keep a hopeful tone from creeping into her voice as she asked, "Completely done?"

"With the first phase."

Bob removed the tubes from both blood vessels and stitched them shut before tucking them back into the neck. After that, he sewed the cut in the neck closed.

"The second phase," he said, "is cavity treatment."

From the tray, he lifted a third metal tube. This one had a knifelike blade at its end, which glistened in the white glow of the overhead lamp. Kat thought the object looked like something more appropriate for torture than embalming.

"This is a trocar," Bob said. "Do you want to know what I do with it?"

Kat didn't. Nor was she going to stick around to find out. She had seen plenty for one day, and she had an uneasy feeling she'd be seeing it again in her nightmares for weeks to come.

After quickly thanking Bob McNeil for his time and expertise, she grabbed Nick by his scrubs and pulled him out of the embalming room. They got as far as the changing area under the stairs before Bob called for their return.

"Hey, Kat," he said when she poked her head back inside the embalming room. "From what you've told me, the guy who killed George sounds like he knows a lot about embalming."

"He does," Kat said. "Too much."

"But that's the thing. He doesn't know enough. If I were you, I'd look for someone who knows how this stuff works but not how to actually do it properly."

"Any ideas where we should start?"

"That's easy," Bob said. "Mortuary schools."

# ELEVEN

Sitting on the funeral home's front steps, Nick Donnelly shoved his cell phone deep into his coat pocket. He had called Rudy to check on his progress in the Winnick barn. He had told Cassie she'd need to have a profile by the morning. And he had ordered Tony to request enrollment records for every mortuary school in the state. Now he just wanted a moment away from autopsies and embalming and his state-sanctioned BlackBerry.

Turning to Chief Campbell, he asked, "Where can a guy get a good cup of coffee in this town?"

"I know just the place," Kat said. "You up for a stroll?"

Nick pulled his weary body off the steps and followed the chief. The night was clear, with no clouds blocking the stars and the waning moon. It was also as cold as a witch's tit. When Chief Campbell spoke, a cloud of vapor billowed from her mouth, making it look like she was exhaling cigar smoke.

"Big Joe's is this way," she said, pointing to a side road just off the funeral home's parking lot. She moved fast, pumping her short legs so rapidly Nick had to work overtime to keep up with her. Apparently, when Kat Campbell said stroll, she meant power walk.

"Did they find anything worthwhile in the barn?" she asked.

"Nothing but the cat. They're doing an autopsy to see when it was killed and how. A cat autopsy. Fucking unbelievable."

"What about the faxed death notice?"

"They're trying to get a trace on the number it was sent from. Also, Rudy checked it out and saw right away that the font is Times New Roman."

"Which is part of every word processing program in America."

"It is," Nick said. "And because it's a fax, there's no way to trace the things we normally look for. The ink, for example, or the type of printer used. Because the killer never touched the page in our possession, we can't look for fingerprints or transfer evidence or even what kind of paper it is. The fax machine was like a pair of gloves. It wiped everything clean."

They had reached the town's main thoroughfare, where most of the businesses were shuttered for the night. Only one remained open—a square of light and noise on an otherwise dark and quiet street. Kat propelled them toward it.

A hush fell over the coffee shop when they entered, and all eyes followed them to the counter. As Kat ordered two large coffees, Nick studied the room, trying to gauge its mood. He came up with: Surprised. Curious. And scared shitless.

"Hi, everyone," Nick told the room.

No one responded.

Carrying their two coffees, Kat brushed past him on her way out the door. Nick had no choice but to follow.

"I apologize on behalf of Perry Hollow," she said, once they were back on the street. "People are usually friendlier than that."

"Then what's their problem?"

"They're scared. By this point, the word is out. They know who you are and why you're here."

"But I'm trying to help."

"They know that," Kat said. "It still doesn't make them any less frightened."

They came to a stop in a tidy town square decorated with ornate lampposts and a few wooden benches inside a small gazebo painted as white as a picket fence. Nick plopped down on a bench. Chief Campbell continued to move. Walking the circumference of the gazebo, she had the jittery air of someone who knew she was in way over her head. It could have been the caffeine, but Nick doubted it.

"No clues," she said. "No motive. No suspect. I've never investigated a homicide before, but shouldn't we have something to work with by now?"

She was right. In most homicides, it became clear early on who did it. There's either an obvious clue—a shoe print, a hair follicle, a bloody glove—or an obvious suspect—an abusive boyfriend, a bitter ex-wife, an old enemy holding a grudge. But so far the Winnick murder contained neither, and it frustrated the hell out of him.

"Rudy has all the evidence at the state police lab," he said. "If there's something to find, he'll find it. Cassie is working on a profile. And Vasquez is as determined as they come. He's probably raiding mortuary schools as we speak."

"I didn't mean to sound like an ingrate," Kat said, finally plopping onto a bench. "I appreciate your help. You have no idea how much. But this is Perry Hollow's first murder. Ever. And it's still sinking in."

Every town had a dark side. It didn't matter if it was big or small, rich or poor. It had one. Nick was certain of it. And it was always revealed eventually.

For Holcomb, Kansas, that moment was the day two

punks killed a farmhouse full of people and inspired Truman Capote to write *In Cold Blood*. In Westfield, New Jersey, it was when John List murdered his mother, his wife, and his three children. And for Newton, Ohio, it was the day his sister—

Nick forced himself to not think about it. It had taken years of practice, but now he had it down to an art form. Whenever Sarah popped into his mind, he immediately came up with something else to think about. A Beatles tune. "Eleanor Rigby," perhaps. Anything but what happened to his sister and what it did to the rest of his family.

That night he focused on Kat Campbell, a one-woman representation of Perry Hollow itself. It was clear neither she nor the town had known about its dark side. But now they were being forced to accept it.

"I never thought it would happen here," she said. "Mostly because I have no idea how someone could do such a horrible thing to another human being."

"Cassie's profile should explain some of that," Nick said. "But whoever it is, he probably has some kind of trauma in his past, most likely something to do with death or funerals. Sexual abuse as a child could also be likely. We've found that serial killers are often created after suffering at the hands of another person."

Kat's mouth opened, her lips forming a circle of surprise.

"Serial killer? You think whoever killed George is planning to do it again?"

"Possibly. The faxed death notice, for one thing. The manner in which he killed George. The desecration of the body. All of it points to someone who is very clever and very prepared. Even the pennies on the eyes are textbook serial killer. It's a calling card. He wants people to know the death was his handiwork."

"What if you're wrong?" Kat asked. "I'm not saying you

are. But maybe someone with an overactive imagination had a beef with George Winnick and decided to kill him in the most elaborate way possible. That could be the case, right?"

It could, Nick knew. But it wasn't.

"Crimes as elaborate as this murder don't just happen once," he said. "It took too much planning on the killer's part to be only a one-shot deal."

With most of her coffee gone, Kat shook the cup, trying to find more to suck out. When she couldn't, Nick handed her his cup.

"What about the dead cat? Is that another calling card?"

"Before they move on to humans, many budding killers start with animals. Maybe this guy still enjoys the thrill, so he keeps doing it. I already told Deputy Bauersox to check your town's police records for the past twenty years and see if any kids from Perry Hollow were charged with cruelty to animals. I hope you don't think I'm stepping on your toes."

"If it helps, then step away," Kat said. "Anything else?"

"Just a question. This guy who discovered the faxed death notice—"

"Henry Goll."

"What do you know about him?"

Kat shrugged. "Very little. I only met him for the first time today. He seems to be a mystery to most people around here."

"Think he's capable of murdering someone?"

"No," she said, bristling at the very suggestion. "He's physically capable, yes. But I don't think he's the killing type. He's the one who alerted me about the fake death notice."

"Maybe that was so you wouldn't suspect him. Who's to say he didn't fax the obituary to his own office before going out to the Winnick farm and killing George. It's definitely one hell of a way to throw you off the trail."

"No way," Kat said with a finality that made it clear the subject was now closed. "I'm sure Henry Goll is one of the good guys."

"And sometimes," Nick countered, "the good guys are actually the bad guys."

A loud bang from a few blocks away prevented the chief from responding. The sound echoed through the chilly night, blasting toward them multiple times. But Nick only needed to hear it once to know what it was—a gunshot.

Kat recognized it, too, and was out of the gazebo within seconds. Nick followed, sprinting out of the square and down two blocks until they were at a street smattered with modest houses. Nervous residents peered out the windows of every home but one. Standing on the porch of that house was a man holding a shotgun, which he stared at with a mixture of surprise and pleasure.

The gun's presence didn't slow Chief Campbell, who marched up the porch steps and started berating the man.

"Lucas, what the hell is going on?"

"The safety was on," the man said. "I swear to Christ, it was. Or at least I thought it was."

A hollow ring in his voice instantly told Nick that he was lying. From the amused way he looked at the shotgun, Nick surmised the man had fired it just to see what would happen. The result was a hole in the porch roof the size of a dinner plate. Chunks of plaster surrounded the man's feet, and his entire top half was dusted with disintegrated drywall.

Kat brushed some of it off the man's shoulder before saying, "I see they let you out of jail."

"I served my time." He gave her a crooked, leering smile. "Now I'm a free man."

Nick focused not on the shotgun but on the man holding

it. Massive in both height and girth, he had the ferocious look of a pit bull. Shaved head. Neanderthal brow. A bump in his nose signified it had been broken at least once.

His appearance was so distinctive it initially masked the birthmark on his face. When Nick eventually did notice it, he found it hard to look away. As large and unruly as the man himself, it covered most of the right side of his face, its pigmentation twice as dark as the rest of his skin. It looked like a handprint, as if someone had slapped his face so hard it left a permanent mark.

Nick would have dismissed the man as a typical thug if it hadn't been for his dancing eyes and shit-eating grin. He may have been a thug, but he was a highly intelligent one.

"Who *is* that?" Nick whispered to Kat once she returned from the porch.

"Lucas Hatcher," she said. "Our local bad egg. This could take a while."

Nick understood. He was only in charge of the murder investigation. Dealing with public menaces wasn't part of his job. So he wished Kat well and called it a night. Walking away, he heard the chief ask, "Why the hell are you out here with a gun, Lucas?"

"Protection," the human pit bull said, again unconvincingly. "I'm not going to let what happened to George Winnick happen to me."

The only lodging Nick had been able to find in town was a bed-and-breakfast annoyingly called the Sleepy Hollow Inn. It was a nice place, if you liked floral prints and lace doilies. Nick did not. But it was better than some of the other hotels he had seen in recent days, so he didn't mind. Besides, he was too exhausted to be bothered by the décor.

Or so he thought.

Lying in bed, crushed beneath the weight of a rose-dotted comforter, he couldn't sleep. His mind refused to wind down for the night, and that evening's caffeine still made his limbs restless. When he closed his eyes, he still pictured George Winnick's corpse glowing beneath the autopsy room's lights. When he opened them, all he saw was a too-cute Norman Rockwell print hanging on the wall.

After fifteen minutes of alternating between those two views, Nick crawled out of bed and moved to his suitcase. It took a moment of rooting, but he found what he was looking for—a leather-bound photo album.

Sitting on the edge of the bed, he opened the album to a picture of a girl with brown hair and a welcoming smile. Sarah's school portrait, taken when she was fifteen. Nick had studied the photo so many times it was permanently seared into his memory, yet he got choked up every time he saw it. That night was no different. Looking at the decades-old image of his big sister, that familiar sense of grief rushed into Nick's heart.

"I haven't forgotten you," he told the photograph. "You know I haven't, right?"

He flipped through the rest of the album, reading newspaper headlines he knew by heart.

NEWTON TEEN MISSING. That one—dated January 7, 1980—was illustrated with the same photo from the front of the album.

NO CLUES IN DISAPPEARANCE. January 8, the same year.

POLICE STILL SEARCH FOR GIRL. The day after.

Nick skipped to the back page. It contained a headline from March 1980. Thirty years earlier. Thirty to the day.

CORPSE BELIEVED TO BE MISSING TEEN.

Nick read the headline a second time. Then a third. And a fourth. When he couldn't take it anymore, he slammed the album shut and tossed it into the suitcase. He then lay down on the bed, hugged himself tightly, and waited for sleep to come.

# TWELVE

*"Christ, Henry, look out!"*

Henry saw the truck, jackknifed across the road ahead of him. It emerged suddenly, bursting through the curtain of rain that draped itself over his windshield. The truck driver was there, too, running into the road, arms waving for him to stop. The glow of the car's headlights caused his shadow to loom large on the truck behind him.

He braked, feeling the tires lock as the car skidded. It seemed to pick up speed, sliding closer, closer, closer to the truck driver, who couldn't get out of the way.

Upon impact, the trucker flipped onto the hood, his face smacking against the windshield. His eyes bulged in terror while his nose formed a pale, flat triangle against the glass. Then he vanished, bouncing up over the car, a single smear of blood on the windshield the only sign he had been there at all.

While this was happening, Henry tried to steer away from the impending accident. He yanked on the steering wheel that refused to budge as the car barreled toward the truck, smoothly, swiftly, inexorably . . .

Henry screamed, the sound of it yanking him out of his nightmare. Lifting his head, he saw he was on the sofa in his living room. A book lay spread open on his stomach, and he examined the spine for its title. *The Man in the Iron Mask.* Definitely a sign he had been in a self-pitying mood.

His left arm dangled off the sofa, hand brushing the floor.

When his fingernails knocked against glass, Henry glanced down and saw a wine bottle. Empty, of course. He must have started hitting the bottle as soon as he got back from the funeral home. Frankly, he couldn't remember.

When he stood, his back and shoulders cracked loose after so much time spent crammed onto the sofa. He waddled down the hall to the bathroom and took a gratifying long piss. At the sink, he paused at the mirror long enough to stare at his reflection.

"*Mio viso*," he said. "*Mio viso è ripugnante.*"

After that, he lurched into his bedroom and flopped onto his bed, exhausted. Yet his eyes stayed open, fixed on his digital clock, which stared right back. Ten past five. Too early to get up. Too late to go back to sleep. The nightmare seemed to be aware of this.

It usually occurred once a week and was always the same, right down to the terrified scream that always started it off.

"*Christ, Henry, look out!*"

Despite its frequency, the nightmare's intensity never dulled from repetition. That night's appearance was so forceful that Henry was still shaken five minutes after waking. So instead of futilely trying to get more sleep, he opted to roll out of bed and start his day.

The hangover started to fade once he lurched into the shower. The nightmare, however, lingered. Deep down, he harbored hope it might one day go away. Not that he thought it would. Henry suspected the nightmare—that persistent replay of his past—would stay with him for the rest of his life.

Fifteen minutes in the shower left him feeling awake enough to function normally. And that meant returning to his morning routine. He toweled himself dry before swiping a circle of reflection in the steam-covered bathroom mirror. He then shaved, being careful to get the stubborn whiskers that sprouted along his scar.

He dressed quickly and went to the kitchen to down his usual breakfast of two eggs, one banana, and a glass of orange juice. After the last bite and a final swallow, Henry made and packed his lunch.

And that was that. His routine was over. It was time to go to work.

Opening the front door to his apartment, he saw the *Perry Hollow Gazette* lying at his feet. The top headline stared at him in big, black letters.

FARMER FOUND DEAD.

He didn't want to read the accompanying article. He knew the way newspapers worked. They loved stories that elicited the three emotions guaranteed to boost circulation—sadness, thankfulness, and fear. Readers were sad it happened in the first place, thankful it didn't happen to them, and fearful it eventually could.

The Winnick murder had all three, and Henry assumed the *Gazette* exploited them to their full potential. Martin Swan's article no doubt had the typical quotes of shock from residents, the various no comments from police, maybe even some editorializing about the sad state of humanity.

What it didn't have—and Henry had made sure of this— was any mention of the death notice faxed to him before the murder occurred. He had promised Chief Campbell to keep it under wraps. And he always kept his promises.

Henry was about to kick the newspaper into the apartment when something nearby caught his eye. It was a cardboard box, unmarked, and sitting about two feet away from his door. His was one of two apartments on that floor. Since the other was located on the opposite side of the hallway, Henry could only assume that the box was intended for him.

Kneeling, he studied it a moment. The box contained no address or postage, meaning it couldn't have been mailed. This had been delivered by hand.

The top was sealed only by a wide swath of masking tape, which peeled off easily. When it was all gone, Henry counted to three, opened the box, then looked inside.

What he found there was strangely unexpected but not completely surprising. He should have known finding the Winnick death notice wouldn't be his only involvement in the crime. Now there was this sudden gift to contend with. The meaning behind both items was a mystery, but their purpose was clear.

Henry was being pulled deeper into a twisted game thought up by an even more twisted mind.

"The cat's neck was snapped. Probably the day before George Winnick was killed."

The way Rudy Taylor gave his update—back ramrod straight, notes held tight in front of his face—reminded Kat of a nervous schoolboy giving a book report in front of the class. But despite his looks, Rudy was no schoolboy. And a book report would have been more detailed. So far, Kat had heard nothing but bad news. No prints. No transfer. No DNA. No suspect.

"It was gutted," Rudy continued. "Then filled with sawdust and put back in the barn, where Mr. Winnick most likely saw it right before he was abducted."

"Is that your theory?" Nick Donnelly asked. "That the dead cat was intended to catch him off guard?"

He had been forced to lean against Kat's desk, her office having only enough seating space for three. The other chairs were taken up by Kat herself, Rudy, and Cassie Lieberfarb. It was a tight fit, even with Rudy's small stature.

"That's my best guess," Rudy said. "If it had some special meaning, it probably would have been left with the body."

"What about the thread?"

"The thread found on both the cat and George Winnick was a cotton-polyester blend. It's manufactured by Coats and Clark in Charlotte, North Carolina."

"Is it rare?"

"No. I'm sure you can buy it in six stores in Perry Hollow alone," Kat said. "I probably have some in my sewing kit at home."

Nick frowned at the answer. "So I guess it can't be traced."

"But we did find another thread," Rudy said. "On Mr. Winnick's collar. It's white. One hundred percent cotton."

"Do you think it was transferred from the killer?"

"It had to be," Rudy said. "Unless Mr. Winnick normally wore something dipped in chloroform."

"Chloroform?"

"That's correct. The lab is positive of that one."

The dour expression on Nick's face transformed into something resembling a smile.

"A handkerchief," he said. "Doused in chloroform. Anyone else think that's how the killer was able to overtake George without a struggle?"

"It fits the profile," Cassie added. "The cut on George's neck was clean, suggesting practice and premeditation. This killer is methodical and knows what he's doing. The stitchwork was a little rough, suggesting a male—most likely between the ages of twenty-five and fifty."

Kat, for one, was impressed. "You got all that from one wound?"

"Not quite. I use statistics and data from past cases to help me. For instance, I know that the killer drives a pickup truck."

"How?"

"Statistics show most violent criminals in rural areas prefer them. We don't know why. But there's also the fact that he needed something to transport a body with a coffin in it."

Kat thought about Perry Hollow and its cluster of citizens. Quite a few were men in their thirties and forties. Most of them drove pickups.

"Cassie, you've just made half the town a suspect."

"About the town," Nick said, "we need to figure out how much of this information gets out. What should we tell the press?"

That morning's edition of the *Perry Hollow Gazette* sat on Kat's desk. The newspaper had devoted its entire front page to the Winnick murder, mentioning every detail she had released. The official line was that George had bled to death, which was true. No one needed to know about the rest—dead cat, embalming, and faxed death notice included.

Because the truck driver had seen the coffin on the road, that aspect of the case was released to the public. Martin Swan, of course, played it up in his main article. The paper even included a photo of the spot where the coffin had been found.

The coffin was the part that made the death so fascinating. It was strange, creepy, intriguing. The news stations out of Philadelphia led with it during the morning broadcast. An hour later, it had made its way onto CNN's Web site. By noon, Kat suspected it would be spread across the country. Just the kind of publicity Perry Hollow didn't need.

"We shouldn't release any of it," she said. "All it will do is stir up the media wolves. And this town doesn't need more of that."

With that, the meeting was over. Rudy and Cassie left, giving Kat's office some much-needed breathing room. Then Tony Vasquez arrived, taking up the recently vacated space. Held in his capable arms was a stack of paper that he dropped onto her desk with a resounding thud.

"What's all this?" Kat asked.

"Enrollment records from mortuary schools. Four of them. The closest is in Halliesburg. Thirty minutes away. All four were nice enough to fax a list of their students for the past twenty years."

The stack was large—at least two reams of paper. When Kat flipped through it, dozens of names, addresses, and phone numbers passed before her eyes.

"This would be helpful," she said, "if we had a name. Or something to suggest the killer was enrolled at any of them."

"We have a name," Tony said. "We were able to trace the fax number."

"This is good news, right? We should be happy."

"Do I look happy?" Tony asked.

Scanning the trooper's dark eyes and downturned mouth, Kat decided he wasn't.

"What's wrong with the name?"

It was Nick, who idly flipped through the stack of pages that Kat had just abandoned.

"It's a fake. At least, that's what it seems like."

Tony told them that the fax number had been activated two days before George Winnick's murder. It was registered to someone named Meg Parrier. According to company records, the number was used only once—to send a fax to the *Perry Hollow Gazette*'s obituary department.

"That's dead end number one," Tony said.

The number was paid for with a money order, also in Miss Parrier's name. The transaction for the money order took place at a Mexican convenience store in a bad part of Philadelphia. The nervous owner, most likely suspecting trouble with the INS, told the state police he couldn't remember anything about the transaction.

"Dead end *numero dos*."

The bill for the number was sent to a post office box, also in a bad part of Philadelphia and again under the name Meg Parrier. A search of the name itself came up with two hits in Pennsylvania. One Meg Parrier was an octogenarian in Erie. The other was a kindergarten student in Wilkes-Barre.

"And there we have dead end number three," Tony concluded. "So no smiles today."

"I'd still like to find this Meg Parrier—whoever she is," Nick said. "We now know the killer had help, whether it was willing or not. What about formaldehyde?"

"Because Bob McNeil said one way to get your hands on a large amount would be to steal it, I issued an APB across the state about funeral home break-ins."

"Any hits?"

"One. In a town called Shamokin."

"I guess all their formaldehyde is intact."

"Bingo," Tony said. "Only cash was taken."

Kat thought back to their funeral home visit the night before and how Bob McNeil had said there was a black market for everything. His suggestion had been to search the Internet.

"What if," she said, "the formaldehyde was bought through normal methods."

"Like the kind of licensed dealer Bob mentioned?" Nick asked. "Don't you have to be a registered funeral home to get it?"

"Yes, if you're getting large amounts. Maybe it's easier to buy it in small ones."

"And the killer then stockpiled it," Tony said, catching on.

Kat turned to her computer. "Let's check our old friend Google."

Nick and Tony watched over her shoulder as she typed "formaldehyde suppliers" into the online search engine. One click later, dozens of results appeared, boasting names such as

Blain Chemical Co. and M. L. International. Their locations were literally all over the map. Some were as close as Delaware; others as far away as Iceland.

Tony let out a low whistle. "Who knew the world needed this much formaldehyde? We chose the wrong career."

Kat clicked on one of the listings—a company called Science Lab Supplies Inc. Its homepage, which looked professional and legitimate, announced that the company specialized in supplies used for educational dissections in classrooms. For a reasonable price, Kat could buy a petri dish, dissection tools, and even bullfrogs preserved and ready to be sliced open.

She scrolled through the options until she came to a listing for chloroform.

"Look at this," she said. "One-stop shopping."

A few lines below the chloroform was a listing for formaldehyde. Kat clicked once more and was offered a plethora of amounts, ranging from ten milliliters to one liter.

"One or two orders from a site like that and you could amass a pretty good supply," she said. "Not to mention picking up some chloroform on the side."

"Especially," Tony added, "if you're ordering from different places at the same time."

"Contact these companies," Nick said. "All of them. Subpoena their records. Get their order information. If anyone sent anything to Perry Hollow, I want to know about it."

"Do you think it'll help?" Kat asked.

A voice from the doorway piped up. "I think I can be of help."

All three of them turned from Kat's computer to the office door, where Henry Goll stood. A cardboard box filled his arms.

"I found this outside my door this morning," he said. "It's from whoever murdered George Winnick."

"How do you know?" Kat asked.

Entering the office, Henry placed the box on her desk before thrusting his hands deep inside it. When he pulled them out, Kat saw that he was holding the smallest fax machine she had ever seen.

Henry placed the fax machine gently on the chief's desk. Removed from its box, it resembled a regular fax machine, only flatter, more narrow, and with a futuristic sheen. A panel of buttons ran along the front and a slot at the top allowed the faxes to roll out. A small tray for paper sat at the bottom.

"Where's the cord?" Kat asked.

"It's portable," Henry said. "And wireless. It works like a cell phone. You can send a fax from anywhere to anywhere, no cords required."

The three other people in the room looked at him quizzically, wondering how he knew this. The reason was simple—he had read about the device in *The New York Times* a month earlier. It was one of those puff pieces—half article, half advertisement—that every newspaper had been reduced to. People who owned one gushed about how fantastic it was to send and receive actual paper faxes on the beach in the Seychelles and in the far reaches of the Andes.

The machine fascinated Chief Campbell, who knelt until she was eye level with the front panel.

"I had no idea they made these. Technology sure is something."

"I think it's a little excessive."

That was spoken by the man standing next to Kat. Henry recognized him from the previous night at the funeral home.

"Nick," Kat told the stranger, "this is Henry Goll. He's the one who found George Winnick's death notice. And Henry, this is Nick Donnelly. He's with—"

"The state police," Henry said.

Nick Donnelly tried to laugh it off but failed. "Is it really that obvious?"

"And this," Kat said, "is Trooper Tony Vasquez."

Henry shook the hand of Trooper Vasquez, whose muscles were as large as his own. Gesturing to his uniform, the trooper said, "I really am that obvious."

As they spoke, Nick produced a handkerchief and used it to lift the fax machine. Tilting it gently, he examined the sides and the bottom.

"There used to be a serial number on it," he said. "Someone did a good job of removing it."

He let everyone see the oblong metal tag attached to the bottom of the machine. Of the dozen numbers printed on it, only the outer two were visible. The rest had been scratched out.

Placing the machine on the desk again, Nick turned it on. It started quickly and silently, so unlike the fax machine Henry used at work. Still using the handkerchief, Nick slid the empty paper tray out of the bottom.

"I need some paper," he said. "Let's see if it really was delivered by a killer."

Kat handed him a blank sheet, which Nick deposited into the tray. The chief then grabbed a folder off her desk and pulled out another piece of paper. Henry saw a single sentence neatly typed across its length. A few glimpsed key words—George Winnick, Perry Hollow, March 14—told him all he needed to know. Kat was holding the death notice Henry had discovered the day before.

All of them trailed her out of her office and to the dispatcher's desk at the end of the hall.

"I need your help, Lou," Kat said. "You're better at faxing than I am."

The dispatcher shuffled to a fax machine in the corner. It was much larger than the one sitting on the chief's desk and at least a decade older. When the machine was turned on, it responded with an elderly hum.

Kat handed Lou the paper and pointed to the upper left corner. "Send it to that number."

"Where will it go?"

"Hopefully," Kat said, "to my office."

A nervous hush fell over the group as the dispatcher punched in the number and pressed send.

Five seconds passed.

Then ten.

Finally, they heard it—a subtle whirring that emanated from Kat's office. It was followed by a click as paper was moved into place. After that came more whirring as the fax was being printed.

Henry led the pack back to the office and was first to the door. He immediately looked to the desk, where the fax machine sat. And sliding out of it was a lone page that bore a lone sentence.

*George Winnick, 67, of Perry Hollow, Pa., died at 10:45 P.M. on March 14.*

Confirming the origins of the fax machine set off a flurry of activity that Henry observed from the doorway. Nick Donnelly immediately picked up the machine, put it back in its box, and thrust the whole package into Trooper Vasquez's open arms.

"Take this to Rudy," he ordered. "Tell him to dust it, scan it, and find out where the hell it came from."

As the trooper fled the room, Nick and Kat turned to Henry. The lieutenant's gaze was especially intense, zeroing in on Henry's scar and tracing its path across his face.

"Where did you find this again?" he asked.

"I already told you," Henry said. "Outside my door. This morning."

"Does anyone else know about it?" It was Chief Campbell this time, matching Nick in intensity.

"No. I brought it directly here."

"Why do you think the killer would give it to you?" Nick asked.

Henry shrugged. "For the same reason he faxed me a death notice—he's playing a game."

"Do you know much about that?"

"I used to be a reporter," Henry said. "I've seen my share of crime. And I've heard all the legends about killers sending things to newspapers. Son of Sam. The Zodiac Killer."

"And you think George Winnick's killer is following suit?"

"That's my best guess."

"But he didn't send this fax machine to the newspaper," Kat said. "He sent it to you, Henry. Right to your doorstep. Which means—"

The killer knew where he lived. Henry had already come up with that chilling thought on his own.

"And the death notice," Kat continued. "That wasn't sent to the newsroom. It was faxed to your office."

Henry knew what was coming next, and he didn't want to hear it.

Kat said it anyway. "Maybe police protection is in order. I'm concerned about your safety."

"I'm not," Henry said.

He was a private man. He didn't want that privacy shattered by a bunch of cops, even if they were trying to keep him safe. Yes, the events of the past two days left him feeling scared. But the idea of constantly being watched and monitored frightened him even more.

"There's nothing to suggest I'm being targeted," he said. "It's not like I was sent a death notice with my name on it."

"Not yet," Kat replied.

"Even if that happens, I can take care of myself."

Henry sensed a presence at his back as he spoke. At first, he thought it was his imagination running at full gallop. All of Kat's talk about madmen and unseen threats would make anyone paranoid. But when he turned around, he saw there was indeed someone standing just behind him. It was a deputy, his pudgy frame slumped with exhaustion.

"Sorry to interrupt, Chief," he said.

Henry was grateful for it, especially since Kat's attention turned from him to the deputy in her doorway.

"What is it, Carl?"

"I found something in those old police records."

"What?"

"A fourteen-year-old was charged with animal cruelty twenty years ago. Apparently, he killed two cats with a baseball bat before skinning them."

"Sounds like a swell kid," Kat said, her face blanching. "Does he still live here?"

The deputy nodded.

"Then what's his name?"

"Chief," he said, "it's Lucas Hatcher."

# THIRTEEN

If Perry Hollow had possessed tracks, Lucas Hatcher would have lived on the wrong side of them. The Hatcher residence, like every house on the block, was a reminder of the town's not-too-distant past. Gentrification had yet to reach the neighborhood. All the homes remained the way they had been after Perry Mill's closure—a shambles.

Stepping onto the front porch, Kat saw the shotgun hole was still there, offering a glimpse of rotting plywood beyond it. Knowing the Hatchers as well as she did, Kat suspected years would pass before it was patched.

Lucas's mother met her at the door. A reed-thin woman in a flannel nightgown, she rolled her bloodshot eyes when she saw Kat's uniform.

"Is this about the shotgun?" she asked. "He was only out here 'cause I told him to be."

Kat assured Mrs. Hatcher that wasn't the reason for the visit. "Is Lucas home now?"

"He's at work."

That surprised Kat. Lucas never struck her as the type of guy who would be gainfully employed.

"And where's that?"

"Oak Knoll Cemetery."

"Thanks," she said. "I'll look for him there."

Located on the western end of town, the cemetery was as old as Perry Hollow itself and served as the final resting place for most of its residents. If you spent your life in town, chances were you'd spend death there as well. Kat's parents were buried there, as well as her grandparents. And she suspected that when the time came, it would be her resting place, too.

As she steered the Crown Vic into the cemetery's gravel parking lot, Nick eyed the wrought-iron gate that loomed over the entrance

"This is where Lucas Hatcher works?"

"So his mother tells me."

The cemetery was abandoned at that hour. No other vehicles were in the parking lot, and when passing through the gate, Kat saw no one, heard no one. The only noise was the crunch of their footsteps and the wind-rattled branches of the trees that gave the cemetery its name. But when she and Nick reached the center of the graveyard, another sound emerged—a muted rumble that came from a distant corner.

"I suspect that's him," Kat said.

After rounding a marble crypt, she caught sight of Lucas Hatcher. He was manning a small excavator, which dug up ragged chunks of brown snow. Seeing Kat, he stopped digging and hopped off the machine.

"You again," he said.

"Yep. Me again."

Before the previous night, the last time Kat and Lucas had talked was during his arrest for armed robbery three years earlier. His target was the town's only liquor store, and he had done everything right. Sunglasses, hat, and wig to disguise his appearance. Platform boots to disguise his height. He dismantled the surveillance cameras, avoided the obviously marked large bills, and made sure the owner didn't have a gun of his own. He would have made a clean getaway if it hadn't been for his mother. In an act of ironic timing, she entered the store during the holdup to buy a six-pack and recognized his voice.

"I see you're gainfully employed," Kat said. "How'd you land this gig?"

"The warden put in a good word."

"That was nice of him. Guess you made a big impression. How's the pay?"

In truth, Kat was asking if he made enough money that he could avoid committing armed robbery again. Lucas knew it, too, and sneered his answer.

"I do well enough."

Despite the cold, his face was flushed, making his massive

birthmark less visible. But Kat could still see it, a large blob on the right side of his face.

"Who's the suit?" he asked, looking past Kat to Nick Donnelly.

"A colleague. He's going to observe while I talk to you."

"About what?"

"George Winnick. Did you know him?"

Lucas shook his head.

"Did you know where he lived?" Kat persisted.

"No. But I know where he'll be living soon."

Lucas gestured to the hole he was creating. Since her arrival, Kat hadn't thought about why he was in the cemetery that morning. But now the answer was clear. He was digging George Winnick's grave.

"Where were you between ten and eleven Sunday night?"

"You don't think I killed him, do you?"

Kat truly didn't know what to think. She stared at Lucas's eyes, at his hands, at the conspicuous birthmark. He fit the rough profile Cassie Lieberfarb had come up with. He was strong enough. He was mean enough. But was he capable of murder?

"Maybe," she said. "I won't know until you tell me where you were."

"I was at the Jigsaw. I'm there every night."

The Jigsaw, a bar on the lower end of Main Street, was a remnant from the days of the Perry Mill. Workers used to crowd the place after their shifts, drinking beer and complaining about their bosses. Now it was home to most of the town's drunks. Kat easily pictured Lucas sitting at the bar, downing a mug of beer the size of a football while glaring at all who entered.

"Can anyone else confirm that?"

"The bartender. He could tell you."

Kat had already decided to ask him. And until she did,

there was nothing left to ask Lucas. She edged away from the fresh grave, gesturing for Nick to follow. But before she left, she offered a few words of advice to Lucas Hatcher.

"You'll be seeing me again real soon. Until then, don't try to pull anything like you did last night."

"What if I do?"

"Trust me, Lucas," Kat said. "You don't want to piss me off."

From the outside, the Jigsaw looked like a dingy hole-in-the-wall. The only color on its exterior came from a neon sign hanging above the door. In the shape of a circular saw, its lights blinked to make it look like it was in motion.

"Do you buy Lucas's story?" Nick asked as they passed beneath the sign.

"Chuck will tell us soon enough."

"Do you think he would cover for Lucas?"

Kat shook her head. "He's not that type."

When she entered the bar, a bell over the door started to chime. That was soon joined by another ring, but of the cell phone variety. Nick touched his jacket, feeling the vibration of the phone inside it.

"It's probably Rudy or Vasquez," he said, stepping back outside. "I'll be there in a minute."

Kat headed inside, where the bar's interior failed to be much of an improvement over the exterior. Sepia-toned photographs of Perry Mill and its blank-faced workers covered the walls. The other patrons at the bar—all two of them—looked just as weary and lost. They could have stepped directly out of one of the photographs.

A bartender waited to hit them up with another round. His name was Chuck Budman, and his barrel gut and tattooed forearms made him look like one tough customer. But Kat, who had known him all her life, frequently saw his soft side. He ran a toy drive every Christmas and volunteered monthly with Meals on Wheels. A Vietnam veteran, he rode his Harley to Washington, D.C., every Memorial Day.

When he saw Kat, a friendly smile appeared above his ZZ Top beard.

"A bit early to be drinking, ain't it, Chief?"

"Even though I could use one, that's not what I'm here for."

"It's about George, isn't it?"

"It is," Kat said. "And about one of your regulars."

"You think someone from Perry Hollow had something to do with his murder?"

"Maybe. That someone would be Lucas Hatcher. He said he was here the night George was killed. Is that true?"

On the bar behind Chuck was a small television turned to CNN, where a perky anchorwoman talked away. Kat normally would have ignored it, but that day she heard something that caught her attention—her own name.

"Chuck, turn that up."

The bartender raised the volume, catching the anchorwoman in mid-spiel.

"Chief Campbell confirmed the presence of the coffin, but declined to give any more details."

"Smack me with a chainsaw," Chuck said. "Your name was just on TV."

As was news of George Winnick's murder. On national television. Kat checked the clock over the bar—a slab of pine outfitted with hands and numbers—and saw it was eleven. Her prediction of national exposure was an hour early.

"Now what about Lucas?" Chuck Budman asked after lowering the TV's volume.

"Was he here Sunday night?"

The bartender chewed over the question like a cow did cud. "He was here. He's here every night."

So Lucas wasn't lying about that, which was good for him, bad for Kat and the investigation. Still, his presence alone didn't guarantee innocence. There was still the matter of when he was at the bar. According to Alma Winnick, George checked the barn at about ten thirty. He was probably abducted soon after that. The fax sent to Henry claimed George would be dead by ten forty-five. That meant Lucas could have done all that and still made it to the bar a little after eleven.

"Do you remember when he showed up?" Kat asked.

"Actually, I do," Chuck said. "I was looking at the clock when the bell over the door rang. It was about ten thirty."

"Are you sure?"

Chuck pointed to the clock. "That's what the clock said. The clock don't lie and neither do I."

His extended index finger guided Kat's gaze to the saw clock, which declared the time was five minutes after eleven. Her eyes then moved to the TV, where the time next to the CNN logo said it was five after noon. Finally, Kat checked her own watch, which verified the television's time.

"Chuck, did you change your clock Saturday night?"

The bartender scratched at his beard. "What do you mean?"

"Daylight saving time went into effect then. You were supposed to set your clock an hour forward. You know, spring ahead and all that crap."

From the way Chuck scrambled for the clock, it was clear he hadn't. The time in the Jigsaw had been wrong for more than two days. Which meant that Lucas Hatcher hadn't shown up at ten thirty the night George was killed. He actually arrived at eleven thirty. And that meant only one thing—Lucas Hatcher had no alibi.

Kat thanked Chuck before heading for the door. Her plan was to tell Nick the news and then return to the cemetery to bring Lucas in for official questioning. Hopefully, he'd sense the seriousness of the situation and fess up.

Outside the Jigsaw, Nick was ending his call. He tucked his phone into his jacket and turned to Kat, looking slightly dazed.

"That was Vasquez, just like I thought."

"Did they find something?"

"They did," Nick said. "A half hour ago, a man was arrested in upstate New York. He was speeding, probably making a run for the Canadian border. In his car, they found a fake passport, needles, and black thread. That's when he confessed."

"To what?"

"Being the Betsy Ross Killer."

The news was as surprising—and as jarring—as a bullet to the chest.

"They caught him?"

"Apparently," Nick said, disbelief never leaving his voice. "He confessed to killing four people. And one of them, believe it or not, was George Winnick."

# JULY

# FOURTEEN

The man was plain-looking and soft-spoken. His eyes were brown. So was his hair, albeit in a lighter shade and receding a bit. He was neither large nor small, handsome nor ugly. He was the type of person you wouldn't remember two minutes after meeting him.

His name was Ken Miller, but to the rest of the world, he was known as the Betsy Ross Killer. And finally, after four months of silence and four months of waiting, Nick Donnelly was about to talk to him.

"Good afternoon," Ken Miller said. "Thank you for agreeing to come today."

"Thanks for finally talking."

The man nodded, as if Nick had actually been trying to be complimentary. "I figured it was about time."

After his very chatty arrest, in which he confessed to killing four, Ken didn't speak another word. It was like a radio that had suddenly gone silent during the final minute of a tied football game. Everyone wanted to know the score, but there was no voice telling them the final outcome.

They tried to get him to talk, of course, doing everything the law would let them get away with. But Ken Miller remained silent as days, then weeks, then months passed. Finally, a guard delivering his dinner was greeted with four words. "I'm ready to talk." He followed that with a date—"Fourth of July."

That was two days earlier. Now it was just he and Nick alone in a heavily secured room at a federal prison outside Binghamton. Nick sat at one end of a steel table. Ken Miller sat at the other, hands and wrists cuffed. Beyond the door was an armed guard. Beyond him were two more.

"Why did you pick today to talk?" Nick asked.

"I thought it would be appropriate," the Betsy Ross Killer said. "Considering the nickname I was given."

"How do you feel about the name?"

Nick normally carried a pen when he interviewed a killer. A notebook, too. But since no one knew exactly what Ken Miller was capable of, no one wanted to take any chances. That meant no pens. No notebooks. Nick was forced to stash Ken's response—"Ambivalent"—in a corner of his brain reserved only for the Betsy Ross Killer.

"You do know why you received that name, don't you?"

"Of course," Ken said. "My sewing skills."

"Who taught you how to stitch so well? Your mother?"

Ken put his hands on the table in front of him, the tips of his fingers pressed together and forming a pyramid. "My father."

Nick knew it had to have been one or the other. No matter what kind of sick shit people did, it usually all went back to the parents. Edgar Sewell was one example. Now Ken Miller was another.

"Where was your mother in all this?"

"Gone. Ran off with a family friend to live in sin. That left just me and Papa. I was twelve."

"Did he abuse you?" Nick asked.

"You'd like that, wouldn't you? That way you'd have an easy answer to explain what I've done. But it isn't that easy, Lieutenant. Not everything can be sewn up so tidily. Pun intended."

"Is your father still alive?"

Ken shook his head quickly. "I killed him on my eighteenth birthday. Stabbed him three times. Before burying him in the backyard, I sewed the wounds shut, to show him just how much I had learned."

This brought the Betsy Ross Killer's total to five. Nick filed the number away, right alongside "Ambivalent."

"So he was your first victim?"

"Yes. Then there was the one in Philadelphia. After that was the friendly gentleman in Lake Erie. And then that camper."

Every murder and location he mentioned coincided completely. It might have taken him four months, but Ken Miller was now confirming his kills.

"And that brings us to Perry Hollow," Nick said.

The pyramid of fingers Ken had kept aloft suddenly collapsed in a jumble of overlapped knuckles on the table.

"I'm afraid I don't recall that town."

"Your final victim," Nick prompted. "George Winnick. You stitched his mouth shut."

"Oh, that." Ken swatted at the air, dismissing the crime as casually as if it were a dropped nickel or an unmissed lover. "I heard about that on the radio as I was driving to Canada."

A knot formed in Nick's stomach. "*Heard* about it?"

"That was the guy in the coffin, right? It was so inventive I remember wishing I had come up with it myself. So I told the police I did that one, too. For shits and giggles, as they say."

The knot in Nick's gut tightened, twisting hard enough to force him to clutch at his abdomen. His heart hammered deep in his chest, an insistent pounding that echoed all the way up to his brain.

"You didn't kill George Winnick?"

"No," Ken said. "Sorry to say, I didn't."

Nick felt sick. Sick that the man sitting across from him was sorry he didn't commit a fifth murder. Sick that although

George Winnick's death clearly didn't match the ones Ken Miller committed, everyone had been fooled into believing otherwise. And, most of all, sick that George's true killer was still out there, somewhere, most likely waiting for the perfect moment to strike again.

From where she was sitting, Kat had a clear view of Main Street. Instead of cars, the thoroughfare was packed with hundreds of pedestrians braving the July heat. They roamed the street, stopping at the craft tables and food stands that lined it. Many people were gathered in front of the bandstand erected just outside Big Joe's, where a fife and drum corps played patriotic tunes. The music floated up the street, creating a soundtrack for the festivities taking place there.

The only downside to Kat's view was that she was looking at it from inside the PTA's dunk tank. She had never been to a PTA meeting—she didn't have the time—but because she was the police chief, the supermoms that ran it had made her an honorary member. Apparently, the honor was being forced to spend the final half hour of the Fourth of July street fair inside the booth's chicken-wire cage, perched on a plank over several gallons of water.

Wearing denim cutoffs over a modest bathing suit, Kat peered out of her watery prison at Lisa Gunzelman, the PTA president, who stood on the other side of the chicken wire. Lisa sported a stars and stripes T-shirt that matched the sun visor pressed into her hair. Because she was president, Lisa didn't have to serve time inside the dunk tank, which made Kat resent her just a little. The matching outfit didn't help. Nor did the zeal Lisa displayed when trying to lure potential customers.

"Dunk the police chief!" she yelled, while holding up the baseballs that could send Kat plummeting into the water. "Only one dollar a toss!"

First up was Jasper Fox, who handed Lisa three dollars. He threw his pitches with a ruthless gleam in his eyes, which Kat suspected came from the fact that she had never found his stolen delivery van. It was long gone, probably taken out of the county and sold for scrap. Jasper had purchased a new one in April, the Awesome Blossoms logo as prominent as ever. As for the gun he had kept in the old van's glove compartment, Kat hoped it never returned to Perry Hollow.

Despite being cheered on by Lisa Gunzelman, Jasper's first attempt missed the dunk tank's target by several feet. His second and third tries also fell short, prompting a disappointed groan from the growing crowd.

The scene was a far cry from the last time the town had gathered together. That was in March, for George Winnick's funeral. Most of Perry Hollow had shown up, forming a black-clad wall of support around his widow. Lisa Gunzelman was there, accompanied by her son, Troy, who was the lead pallbearer. So were Deana Swan and her brother, who wrote about it for the *Gazette*. Amber Lefferts's father said a prayer and Art and Bob McNeil directed everything with the utmost precision. Even the freshly exonerated Lucas Hatcher showed up, although it was only to roll away the plastic grass that surrounded the lip of the grave.

Standing among the mourners that frigid day, Kat couldn't have predicted such a spirited atmosphere would exist four months later. But George's murder had only rattled the town temporarily. Now, everything was mostly back to normal.

A serial killer's confession had that kind of effect.

"Come on, folks," Lisa Gunzelman called, raising her voice and hefting the baseballs. "Step right up and dunk the chief!"

A few more people lined up to have a go, but none of them hit the target. When only five minutes remained of her tour of duty, Kat began to think she would escape unscathed. After that, she would meet up with James, who was swimming at Jeremy's house, have a hamburger dinner, and watch the town's fireworks. All in all, it would be a great day. If she managed to stay dry, of course.

Kat glanced down at the tank's unchlorinated water twelve inches beneath her sandals. It was dank and murky, like tub water after a bath. And although it was still hot as blazes, she didn't want to be cooled off in that swill.

"How's it going in there?"

Kat lifted her head to see Deputy Carl Bauersox. "Aren't you supposed to be working crowd control?"

"I am," he said. "The crowd is right here."

He was right. The majority of the street fair's attendees were now gathered around the tank, just waiting to see her get soaked. Sensing an opportunity, Lisa thrust three balls at the deputy.

"Would you care to try?"

"I can't," Carl said.

Lisa sweetened the deal. "It's on the house."

The deputy looked to Kat, who told him he would be forgiven in the unlikely event he managed to dunk her. After more coaxing from Lisa, Carl relented, pitching exactly the way you'd expect from a squat, sunburnt cop—badly. The first ball was way off the mark, not even coming within striking distance of the target.

"I was just warming up," he explained feebly.

Kat laughed. "Sure you were."

Her laughter stopped when Carl's second pitch actually hit the target, producing an excited cheer from the bystanders. Fortunately for Kat, the throw wasn't hard enough, and the ball bounced off the target's edge.

Inspired by the near miss, Carl raised his right arm. He

pulled back. He released the final ball. The crowd cheered as the baseball made a beeline toward the target, smacking it perfectly in the bull's-eye. The impact created a whacking sound that echoed up the street. The target lurched backward.

Beneath Kat, something clicked. It was the platform, flying out from under her.

Then, before she could even squeal with surprise, Kat dropped into the water.

On what was supposed to be a quiet day at the office, Henry found himself surrounded by noise. As usual, there was opera. His selection was Wagner, with all its accompanying bombast. But interrupting the music was another sound—firecrackers. A group of kids had gathered in the parking lot next to the newsroom and were now setting them off in an unceasing series of bangs. Humming beneath it all was the constant murmur of the crowd on Main Street enjoying the Fourth of July street fair. All three noises merged into a cacophony that gave Henry a mild headache. And just when he thought it couldn't get any noisier, his phone rang.

Henry turned off the music and waited for a break in the firecrackers before answering.

"Obituary department."

"Henry?"

The caller was Deana Swan, who sounded more than a little surprised to be talking to him.

"I didn't think you'd be working today," she said.

"I had to."

That was a lie. Henry could have taken the day off along with most of the other *Gazette* staff. But he opted to work, frankly because he had nothing better to do with his day.

"I guess you're on the clock, too," he said.

"Not for long. I'm leaving in a minute. I just called to say we have no more obituaries coming today."

Henry thanked her. "That means I can leave, too."

"Glad I could be the bearer of good news. Are you going to watch the fireworks tonight?"

"No. I have other plans."

That, too, was a lie. Sort of. He did have plans, although they consisted of going back to his apartment, opening a bottle of Syrah, and reading some John Updike.

"That's too bad," Deana said. "I was about to ask if you wanted to join me."

It was an invitation Henry had been dreading for the past four months. Every time he spoke to Deana, he thought of the evening in the funeral home when he had quickly rejected her offer of a date. And during every phone call, he expected her to bring it up again. She hadn't, until now.

"Thank you for the offer," he told her. "I'd take you up on it if I didn't have those other plans."

Henry knew she saw through the lie completely. And when Deana hung up, he felt guilty about turning her down again. But it really was for the best. He didn't want to cause her—or himself—any more pain than necessary.

Instead of leaving immediately, he lingered in his office. The firecracker gang had dispersed, providing enough quiet to let Henry listen to his opera in peace. Dimming the office lights, he cranked up the volume on his computer. Then he leaned back in his chair and listened to the music sweep over him.

He remained that way for a good ten minutes, stirring only when he heard a slight click from the fax machine. Turning toward it, he spotted a single white page purring out of the machine.

A late obituary. Deana had been mistaken.

Sighing, Henry turned the music off once again. He flicked on the lamp at his desk, grabbed the still-warm fax, and read it.

*Troy Gunzelman, 17, of Perry Hollow, Pa., died at 6:30 P.M. on July 4.*

Henry checked his watch and saw it was exactly six o'clock. Cold dread seeped into his body so quickly it felt like he was being dipped into icy water. He had hoped to never see a fax like that again. And after four months, he had come to believe he wouldn't.

But now a second one had arrived. Gripping it, Henry read it again and again, searching for some way in which it was different from the one sent for George Winnick. He found nothing. It was written in the same style. Exactly the same.

It was happening again.

Henry reached for the phone and furiously dialed the police station. When Louella van Sickle answered, he cut right to the chase.

"This is Henry Goll at the *Gazette*. I need to talk to Chief Campbell immediately."

"She's at the street fair, Henry," the dispatcher said. "I think she still might be in the PTA's dunk tank. I can leave a message."

If Kat was at the festival, that meant she'd be on Main Street. Henry would rather take his chances looking for her himself than leaving a message that might not be returned for hours.

"No," Henry said. "I'll find her."

He hung up, snatched the fax on his way out of the office, and ran down the back stairs. Soon he was pushing through the door, bursting outside onto a Main Street filled with people. They laughed and shopped and ate, completely unaware of what was about to happen.

But Henry knew. And he had to make sure Kat knew, too. He scanned the street until he saw the dunk tank a block away. If Lou van Sickle was correct, the chief would be there. And, with any luck, Henry wouldn't be too late.

# FIFTEEN

Emerging from the water, Kat saw Henry Goll running up Main Street. He stopped in front of the dunk tank, catching his breath next to Carl. It was the first time Kat had seen him since March, and his presence immediately worried her.

"Henry?" she said, standing waist-deep in the tepid water. "What are you doing here?"

That's when Kat saw the piece of paper folded in his hand. It told her everything she needed to know about his sudden appearance on Main Street. The only thing she didn't know was whose name the page contained.

The dunk tank was still surrounded by people. The crowd had grown right before her dip into the water, and they pushed closer after she emerged, eager to see her sopping wet and humiliated. So far, none of them had noticed the paper in Henry's hand. Before any of them got the chance, she gestured for him to leave the area immediately.

Carl caught on and pulled Henry away from the crowd while Kat scrambled up the ladder leading out of the tank. Once she was free of the water, she grabbed a towel and hopped out of the booth.

"Chief," Carl called. "Over here!"

Water still pouring off her body, Kat allowed herself a moment of silence. It was brief—an indulgent second of calm before the storm about to take place. When the second passed, she sprang into action.

"Who's it for?" she asked as she approached Henry.

"Someone named Troy Gunzelman."

Kat inhaled sharply. Troy's mother stood on the other side of the booth, probably within earshot. This was bad. Horribly so.

"Are you sure?"

She desperately wanted it to be a hoax. It was possible, after all. Maybe word had leaked out about George Winnick's faxed death notice and one of Troy's friends was trying to put one over on the police. Hell, maybe it was Troy himself.

Henry held out the page and Kat snatched it without a word. The moisture from her fingers seeped into the paper as she read the lone sentence typed across it.

*Troy Gunzelman, 17, of Perry Hollow, Pa., died at 6:30 P.M. on July 4.*

The death notice wasn't a copycat. It was worded exactly like the one for George Winnick. Eyes moving to the time stamp in the upper left-hand corner, Kat saw the fax had been sent at six. Five minutes ago.

"His mother is right over there," Kat said. "We need to ask her where Troy is."

It wasn't a great plan, but it was the only one she could think of. Besides, maybe Lisa would tell them that Troy wasn't alone or that he was in a public place. Hopefully, he was on Main Street at that very minute, lost in a crowd of people so heavy that the killer couldn't reach him.

Trying to keep things calm and inconspicuous, Kat tapped Lisa Gunzelman on the shoulder and led her behind the dunk tank.

"Do you know where Troy is right now?"

Lisa's eyes widened slightly as they swept over Kat, Henry, and Carl. Being a mother herself, Kat knew that if she had been asked such a question, the first thing she'd do was offer one of her own. Mrs. Gunzelman was no different.

"Is something wrong?"

Not wanting to lie, Kat evaded the question. "We just need to locate him."

"Is he in trouble?"

*He might be,* Kat thought. *He might be dead. Or dying. Or having his lips sewn together at this very moment.* Instead, she said, "It's very important that we talk to him."

"He's at the high school," Lisa said. "He went there to lift weights."

"Even in the summer?"

"Every day. Coach's orders. He has his own keys so he can go and get in shape for the fall."

"Does Troy have a cell phone?"

Lisa nodded and recited the number. Carl whipped out his own phone, dialing furiously. Pressing the cell to his ear, he waited.

"There's no answer."

"Keep calling," Kat ordered. "If he answers, tell him to lock himself inside until I get there."

She sprinted the two blocks to the station, water still trailing after her. She had just reached the Crown Vic when she heard a voice behind her.

"I'm going with you."

It was Henry Goll, momentarily forgotten in the chaos of the past five minutes.

"I can't let you do that," Kat said before climbing into the car.

Henry responded by getting inside with her and buckling his seat belt, showing he had no intention of leaving.

"I'm grateful for what you've done," Kat said. "You've been a huge help. But this is an official police matter. I won't let you be a part of it."

"I *am* a part of this. Whether I want to be or not, I'm involved."

"It's too dangerous."

"You think I'm already in danger," Henry said. "Or don't you remember the little present that was sent to me back in March?"

He had her there. The killer clearly had chosen him alone to be the recipient of the death notices. Kat didn't know why, but there was no denying Henry had been made a part of the crimes.

Without saying a word, Kat got out, rushed to the trunk, and removed a black vest from its depths. Sliding behind the wheel again, she tossed the vest onto Henry's lap.

"You can go if you wear this."

Henry lifted the vest to his chest. "What is it?"

"Kevlar. It's bulletproof. And it better be on you by the time we get to the high school."

"What about you? What do you have for protection?"

Kat showed him the Glock she had also removed from the trunk. "Don't worry about me. I've got this."

As Henry put on the vest, she peeled the Crown Vic out of the parking lot. She had wasted too much time arguing with him. Now she had to get to the school as fast as possible. The obituary said Troy would die at six thirty. It was now quarter after, and the math was clear.

Troy Gunzelman had only fifteen minutes to live.

Through a combination of driving skills, blind luck, and a disregard for traffic laws that only a police chief could get away with, Kat got them to the high school in five minutes. Henry admired her speed, even when she veered into the parking lot so hard it made his stomach lurch. If every second counted, then Kat's NASCAR-worthy driving saved them minutes.

During the frantic drive, Henry also impressed himself by getting the bulletproof vest on just as they reached the school's main entrance. The Kevlar was heavier than it looked. More solid, too. He felt guilty for being so armored when the chief was wearing nothing but a T-shirt over a sopping bathing suit. Her still-wet hair was stuck to her cheeks, sending rivulets of water running down her neck. But it didn't slow her down. As they barreled toward the school, she grabbed the radio.

"Carl? Did you reach him yet?"

The deputy's voice erupted with a crackle. "No. I'm only getting voice mail. Are you at the school yet?"

"We're here," Kat said. "We're about to go in."

The patrol car's tires squealed as she steered it into the heart of the school's parking lot. Rows of vacant spots slipped past the window. The entire lot was empty, except for a battered Mustang in the distance.

"That's it!" Kat yelled when she saw it. "That's Troy's car. He still might be here."

She swerved the patrol car past the Mustang on her way to the school itself. Once there, she brought her car to a gut-tugging halt.

"Ready?" she asked.

Henry nodded. As ready as he could be.

Kat was first out of the car, whipping out her Glock as she sprinted to a side entrance. She tried the door. It was unlocked. Before going inside, she hissed instructions at Henry.

"Stick behind me. Don't touch anything. Don't try to be a hero. And if something happens to me, run back to the patrol car and drive to the station as fast as you can."

She pushed through the door, Henry right behind her. Just inside the school was a darkened gymnasium. Henry saw a polished floor, basketball hoops, and bleachers along the wall. What he didn't see in the gym was a sign that anyone else was there. No one stirred in the corner shadows. No sound rose to the rafters.

The weight room's entrance was on the other side of the gymnasium. Instead of crossing the open gym floor, Kat opted for the cover of the bleachers. Stumbling in the darkness, she and Henry dodged the metal grid work under the stands until they were on the other side, right next to the weight room.

Its door was open, and both Kat and Henry peered inside. The lights were off. The room was empty.

The door next to the weight room led to the lockers. If Kat felt any hesitation about entering a place marked BOYS ONLY, she didn't show it. She burst through the locker room door and immediately pivoted on her heels to see if anyone was behind it.

No one was.

"Clear," she whispered.

Henry moved into the locker room, buffeted by the smell of steam, sweat, and urine. A small office sat to his right, its door closed and its lights off. The rest of the place was aglow, lit by fluorescent bulbs buzzing overhead.

Kat tried the door to the office. "It's locked. Go check the shower."

Henry crossed the room, running past rows of lockers until he reached the communal shower. It was empty, but remnants of steam warmed his face.

"Someone was just here," he said.

Kat turned from the office's front window, where her face had been pressed against the glass.

"But if it was Troy, where did he go?"

Henry didn't have an answer. Troy Gunzelman's car sat in the parking lot, but there was no sign of him inside. Not good odds for the quarterback.

While Kat poked through a closet filled with sporting equipment, Henry checked each row of lockers, looking for something amiss. He found it in the second to last row, where the door of one locker was ajar. A crumpled towel lay on the floor in front of it.

Henry moved to the locker, dropped to his knees, and touched the towel. It was still damp. Rising to his feet, he looked inside the locker.

A squirrel peered back at him.

The animal was dead. Motionless, it lay on a sweat-drenched T-shirt, its beady eyes pointed directly at him.

"I found something!"

"What is it?"

"You need to come see for yourself."

Joining him, Kat looked in the locker and cursed. She grabbed the squirrel and examined its stomach. A thin line scarred the gray fur, closed up by a series of stitches. Kat drilled an index finger between two of the sutures. When she removed it, the tip was coated with a beige powder that emitted a slight pine scent.

"Sawdust," she said. "The thing has been stuffed."

Just like the cat in George Winnick's barn. Henry knew with certainty that whoever abducted George had just done the same thing with Perry Hollow's star quarterback, in the exact same manner. Which meant that not only was Troy Gunzelman missing. He was also most likely a dead man.

# SIXTEEN

The first wave of backup, courtesy of the county sheriff, arrived at six forty-five. State troopers showed up five minutes after that. Together, they helped Kat seal up the locker room. Then the gymnasium. Then the school itself.

At seven, Kat contacted Carl and told him to remain at the station. They had enough manpower for the time being and she wanted someone there in case Troy turned up alive and well.

"Has word on the street leaked out yet?" she asked.

"Not yet, but Lisa Gunzelman's been calling nonstop. I told her you'd tell her what's going on."

Kat did, at seven thirty. She was brief, telling Lisa only that Troy was missing, police were looking for him, and that she needed to stay home by the phone in case he called. She didn't mention the death notice. Or George Winnick. Or how the town wasn't as safe as she thought.

After that, Kat called Lou van Sickle and asked her to pick up James from Jeremy's house and babysit until she got home. Dinner and fireworks were no longer on her schedule.

"Just tell him I have to work," Kat said. "Feed him. Take him to the fireworks. Then tuck him in and tell him I love him."

The first member of Nick Donnelly's task force arrived just after eight. It was Tony Vasquez, who greeted Kat in the school's parking lot with a fist bump. Upon seeing Henry Goll, he said, "You again. Are you a cop or a reporter?"

"Neither," Henry said.

"Then what are you doing here?"

In truth, Henry was stuck with Kat for the moment. She

didn't want to let him out of her sight, not with a killer still at large. The obituary writer might not have wanted police protection, but he needed it. And for the moment, being in the same spot with her was the best protection Kat could give.

"He's with me," she said.

The answer was good enough for Trooper Vasquez, who said, "I called Nick and told him what happened. He's trying to get here now."

"Where is he?"

"Upstate New York. With the Betsy Ross Killer."

The Betsy Ross Killer, who, it turned out, wasn't Perry Hollow's killer, despite his confession. Kat should have been angry at Lieutenant Donnelly and his team for not knowing that sooner. But she didn't have time for anger. Another resident of her town was missing and she needed to find him.

"What can I do to help?" Tony asked.

"Start a search party."

"Where should we look?"

Kat had no idea. If Troy was still alive—which seemed less likely with each passing minute—then he was probably in the same place where the killer had dispatched George Winnick. If he was dead, then his body could be anywhere, perhaps even the exact spot where she had found George.

"Old Mill Road," Kat said. "See if you can set up a checkpoint there, too. Tell them to stop every pickup truck they see."

Soon after Tony left to round up volunteers, Rudy Taylor showed up to take his place. Dressed in a tuxedo, he looked like a high school freshman arriving for his first prom.

"I'm a backup violinist for the Philadelphia Orchestra," he said, explaining the outfit. "We had an Independence Day concert at the art museum."

Kat didn't care where Rudy had come from or what he

was wearing. She just needed someone with a mind as keen as his examining the crime scene.

Inside the locker room, she led him to Troy's locker. The dead squirrel was still inside.

"We found this. Stuffed. Just like the cat."

Rudy loosened his bow tie and looked around the locker room. "There's a mess of DNA in here. Sweat. Pubic hair. A thousand prints on every conceivable surface. This won't be easy."

As Rudy went to work, Kat retreated outside, where Henry still waited. He sat on the sidewalk, back pressed against the side of the school. The Kevlar vest had been removed and now sat next to him in a heap.

"I think I have time to take you home now," Kat said. "So get in the car before I change my mind."

Henry grabbed the vest and got to his feet without speaking. He climbed into the passenger seat of the Crown Vic. Kat slid behind the wheel. As soon as she started the car, Carl Bauersox's voice squawked from the radio.

"Chief? You there?"

"I'm here," Kat said. "What's happening?"

"Bad news. I just got a call from someone out on Squall Lane."

The lane was a pine-shaded road that ran parallel to Lake Squall's western shore. A few million-dollar vacation homes dotted the area, built by wealthy Philadelphians looking for a taste of rustic living.

"What did he want?"

"He said he just saw a coffin floating in the middle of the lake."

Kat noted the caller's choice of words. Not box. *Coffin.* Just like the trucker who first spotted George Winnick.

"I'll be right there. Meet me by the boat launch as soon as you can."

Kat and Henry beat the deputy to the police department's boat by a minute. Once Carl arrived, the three of them hopped into the ancient ten-footer that was kept handy for the occasional water rescue. Despite its age, the boat got the job done, cutting quickly across the lake's glassy surface.

Kat sat next to Henry at the front of the boat, their eyes scanning separate sides of the horizon.

"See anything?"

Henry shook his head. "Nothing."

The night boasted a half-moon, which made Kat grateful. Low in the sky, it cast a glow over the water so bright they barely needed to use the spotlight mounted on the bow of the boat. On the shore, narrow beams of light bounced through the trees next to the water. Flashlights, no doubt manned by volunteer state troopers. Tony Vasquez's search party was already under way.

Turning to Carl, who manned the motor in the back, Kat asked, "This guy who called, where does he live?"

Carl pointed across the lake to a massive, lodge-style house pressed against the water's edge. A solitary figure stood on its wide deck, backlit by the home's interior lights as he watched the boat pass. When Kat waved, the figure waved back, arm arcing widely in the moonlight. She wondered who the mystery resident was and how he knew it was a coffin floating in the lake.

Overhead, a bottle rocket sliced the sky. A second later, a boom erupted through the clouds. It was followed by a red glow that briefly shimmered in the sky. Next came two more booms and two more flares of color, this time green and yellow.

Fireworks. They were being set off right on schedule.

Kat looked in their direction, seeing the shimmering colors just above the tree line at the lake's far shore. The more powerful ones cleared the trees entirely, rising high before exploding into blooms of fire that reflected off the water's surface.

Next to her, Henry rose to his feet.

"I think I see it."

Kat's gaze swept away from the sky and across the lake, stopping at a dark rectangle bobbing a few yards from shore. Following her orders, Carl steered the boat in the object's direction. He cut the engine when they drew close, letting the boat drift the rest of the way.

As the fireworks continued overhead, Kat swiveled the boat's light toward the rectangle. Illuminated, it looked like an exact copy of the coffin George Winnick was found in. Untreated wood. No visible markings. Obviously handmade.

Reaching beneath her seat, Kat grabbed a retractable pole with a large metal hook attached to the end. Extending the pole to its full length, she swung it out over the water. The hook caught a corner of the coffin, and with Henry's help, she pulled it toward them.

The coffin hit the side of the boat with a jarring thud. Something was inside it, that much was certain. A hollow box couldn't have caused that much of an impact.

Once again, the coffin's lid had been nailed shut, although Kat had cracked it when she hit it with the pole. That corner was slightly askew, creating an opening large enough for her to slide her fingers inside. With Henry leaning over the side of the boat to steady the coffin, Kat pried the lid up, easing a nail out of the wood. She did the same to each subsequent nail, working diligently until she had one side loose. A grunt and a tug took care of the rest.

Troy Gunzelman lay inside. He was naked, his skin damp from the few inches of water that had leaked into the coffin. The liquid sloshed around his body, a small tide rising and falling against his chalky flesh.

Kat reached into the coffin and pressed two fingers against the inside of Troy's wrist, hoping to feel the faint bump of a pulse. There wasn't one.

"He's dead," she said.

In the back of the boat, Carl's voice rose in prayer.

"Our Father, who art in heaven, hallowed be thy name. Thy kingdom come, thy will be done . . ."

The prayer continued as Kat examined the body. Blood was smeared across Troy's mouth and chin. Underneath it lay a pattern of thread pinning his lips together. The same thread was on his neck, sewing up the gash where the killer had tried to play mortician.

"Lead us not into temptation, but deliver us from evil."

Troy's eyes were covered by two pennies. In the darkness of the coffin, they resembled empty sockets instead of coins, giving the impression that Troy's eyes had been removed. Kat aimed the light into the coffin. The beam exposed the blood on Troy's face, brightening it into crimson Technicolor, and glinted off the two pennies.

"For thine is the kingdom, and the power, and the glory, forever and ever. Amen."

"Amen," Kat repeated.

Her voice was drowned out by the thunder of fireworks. Apparently, the display's grand finale was taking place because the sky was aglow with multicolored lights. The rest of the town was clustered under that glow, oblivious to the grim discovery on the lake.

Kat envied their ignorance. They didn't know another murder had taken place in Perry Hollow, in exactly the same way as the first. Yet the shock of the situation didn't the murder the second time. It was worse. Much worse. This time she knew the murder was coming, yet she hadn't been able to stop it.

She also knew that Nick Donnelly had been right about the situation from the very start. The killer had a taste for it now. He had a routine. And he wouldn't stop. Not unless Kat stopped him first.

# SEVENTEEN

Henry lay in bed, unable to stop thinking about Troy Gunzelman. It was hours after they had found his body in the lake, but the image refused to leave his head. Every time he closed his eyes, he pictured Troy's lifeless eyes, hidden under the two pennies. The image was unsettling, and it kept sleep from approaching.

Guilt also kept Henry awake. It wasn't his fault Troy was dead. The blame for that rested squarely with whoever had killed him. But it *was* his fault that Troy hadn't been saved.

Tossing and turning beneath the covers, Henry thought of all the scenarios in which the quarterback might have lived. If only he had grabbed the fax sooner. If only he had sprinted faster on Main Street. If only he hadn't argued with Kat before she let him tag along.

Had they happened, those events could have rescued Troy Gunzelman from the clutches of a killer.

If only.

Henry was accustomed to such thinking. It was a constant in the past five years. If only he had consumed one less beer. If only they had waited out the storm instead of plunging into the thick of it. If only they hadn't left the house in the first place.

But it was too late to go back and reverse all that, just as he couldn't relive that night's events and try harder. What's done is done, and Henry had to live with the repercussions.

Flopping onto his side, he checked the clock on the night-stand. It was just past midnight. Many hours of sleeplessness lay between him and dawn. It was going to be a long night.

When the doorbell rang five minutes later, Henry thought it was Kat Campbell. She probably had the same thoughts of regret he did. Padding out of his bedroom and down the hall, he suspected she wanted to commiserate. Human nature made us want to wallow in bad thoughts with those who shared them.

But instead of Chief Campbell, Henry opened the door and saw Deana Swan. There was sympathy in her eyes as she said, "I heard about Troy."

"Word travels fast."

"Martin told me," she said. "He said he'll probably be up all night working on the story."

Despite that fact, Henry imagined Martin Swan was having a field day with the news. A town's football star was murdered. A killer thought to be behind bars actually wasn't. Another grisly murder had rocked a place more quiet than Mayberry. This was the kind of story most reporters dreamed about.

"I also heard you were involved. I thought you might like to talk about it."

"That's very kind of you," Henry said, "but there's nothing to say."

"That's not what your eyes are telling me."

Henry tried—and failed—to understand what made Deana tick. She barely knew him, yet she had the bravery to show up at his apartment at midnight checking to see if he was okay. The violation of his privacy should have made him angry. But it didn't. He really did need some company, and he was touched that Deana hadn't been afraid to approach him about the murder.

"So are you up for a walk?" she asked. "The heat's died down."

"Actually," Henry said, "I could use a drink."

Exiting his building, they walked down a deserted Main Street to the Jigsaw. It, too, was empty, yet still open. The bartender poured their drinks with a minimum of small talk and told them to sit anywhere they liked. They went to a corner booth far away from the bar.

Once seated, Deana raised her glass of red wine, clinking it lightly against Henry's scotch. "A toast."

"What are we toasting?"

"Your heroism. You tried to help save someone's life. That was very brave."

"Even if I failed?"

"Yes. Even if you failed."

Henry took a gulp of scotch, feeling its burn deep in his chest. Deana took a gentle sip of her wine.

"So what's your story?" she asked. "I know you have one."

"Maybe I want to know yours. There must be a good reason why you work in a funeral home."

"I suspect it's the same reason you write obituaries."

Henry cocked an eyebrow. "Morbid curiosity?"

"Far from it," Deana said. "My mother worked there for ages. She was the receptionist for the McNeils, just like I am now. But she did more than that. Because there was no woman in the house to take care of them, she sometimes cooked dinner and offered to clean the living areas. I spent a lot of time there as a girl. In a way, I sort of grew up there."

There was sadness in her voice, as if she wanted to talk more but was afraid to. Henry could relate. There was so much he could have told her. He just chose not to.

"My father died when I was ten and Martin was twelve,"

she continued. "He worked at the mill, like everyone in this town, I suppose. One day there was an accident—his second. The first one only left a scar. The second one did a whole lot more damage. I don't know all the details. Honestly, I don't want to. I just know that he left for the mill one morning and never came home. It was devastating to all three of us. Martin took it really hard. So did I. I was Daddy's little girl."

Henry didn't offer his condolences. He had heard too many in his lifetime to know they were meaningless. Having someone tell you they were sorry did nothing to ease your pain. So he said nothing, letting Deana talk uninterrupted.

"Then my mother died a month after I graduated high school. Art McNeil was wonderful about everything. Because my mother had been so devoted to him, he covered the funeral expenses, which helped out a lot. A week after she was buried, he offered me her old job."

"That was very kind of him," Henry said. "But it sounds to me like you didn't choose your job. It chose you."

"I suppose. It's just like life, I guess. What we plan to happen and what actually happens never seem to coincide. For example, ever since I was a little girl, I always wanted to live in Paris. I even took French in high school to prepare for my new life there. But after my mother died, I realized very quickly that living in Paris would probably never happen."

"For me, it was Italy."

Henry tried to stop himself, surprised by how easy it was to reveal such information to Deana. But the combination of scotch and exhaustion urged him to reveal more.

"I was going to live there. Milan. I became fluent in Italian. Studied the food, the wine, the music. I even had an apartment all picked out."

"Why didn't you go?"

This time Henry was able to stop himself. Some things

were too hard to say, even with the help of booze and sleep deprivation.

"Something happened," he said.

Deana's gaze flitted to the burn mark and scar. It was quick—a mere glance—but Henry noticed it.

"Is that when you became an obituary writer? Martin told me you were once a really good reporter."

Emphasis on *once*. Now Henry was just a humble obituary writer, and it suited him fine.

But a long time ago—a lifetime ago, actually—he had been a great reporter. At the *Pittsburgh Post-Gazette,* the police beat was one of the paper's most coveted jobs. And Henry had loved it. He was good at it. He was a star in the newsroom, earning praise and awards in equal measure.

Then everything changed. His face. His life. His whole reason for living. It all vanished in a split second one night on Interstate 279.

After the accident, Henry quit his job and moved to Perry Hollow. It wasn't Milan by any means. But it was remote, which helped when you didn't want to be found. Plus, it was on the opposite side of the state, where no memories of Gia existed.

But once he settled in his new town, he discovered that memories of Gia were just as prevalent there as they were in Pittsburgh. That's when Henry realized thoughts of her would follow him no matter how far he roamed.

"Now I'm a good obituary writer," he said. "For most of these people, I'm the author of the last thing to ever be written about them. That's an important task. I take it seriously, and I try to do it with respect and honesty."

"You make it sound so noble."

"It is. People are too quick to forget the dead. This society encourages it. You're supposed to mourn for a bit and then move on. What I do preserves them. Their lives are printed right there on a piece of paper, for anyone to see at any time. I help them not be forgotten."

"People don't forget," Deana said. "They go about their lives because they need to. They have to work and raise their kids and meet new people. It's called life, and it doesn't stop when someone dies. It goes on. Just because you go on doesn't mean you've forgotten those in the past. But at some point you need to let them go."

She stared directly into Henry's eyes, making him wonder if she knew more about his past than she let on. As far as Henry knew, no one in Perry Hollow was aware of what happened to him before he arrived. They only saw the present Henry—dour, dark, disfigured. That's all he wanted them to see, which is why he remained in the shadows.

"I like you, Henry," Deana said quietly. "You seem like a good man, and there aren't too many of them in this town. Trust me, I've looked."

She edged toward him, drawing so close that the light, sweet scent of her perfume danced in his nostrils. She was going to kiss him. And Henry, astonishingly, wanted her to.

The kiss, when it arrived, was a peck on the cheek. Deana then slid her lips down to his own. As they made contact, a jolt of electricity exploded in his brain before zipping directly to his groin. Deana kissed differently than Gia, with more brash fervor than he was accustomed to. Her tongue caressed his own before slipping out of his mouth and running across his upper lip. When it reached his scar, all the excitement Henry felt immediately ceased.

"We need to stop," he said as he gently pushed her away.

The look in Deana's eyes shifted from arousal to confusion to hurt. "What's wrong?"

"You're a wonderful girl. But I'm not ready for this yet."

A slight pain pulsed at Henry's temple. The burn mark, no doubt flushed and flaring. He touched the scar on his face, fingertips tripping over the spot Deana had just kissed.

"It was only a kiss," she said. "It's not a big deal."

"That's the problem. To me, it's a very big deal."

After quickly walking Deana home, Henry returned to his apartment and tried to sleep. But the abrupt—and awkward—end to the night made that difficult. He pictured Troy Gunzelman in the floating casket. He thought of the sad expression on Deana's face as he broke off their kiss. And he had the dream—not as a whole but in fragments, as if his brain was a television being controlled by an impatient remote.

When morning arrived, he was just as exhausted as when he had gone to bed. But it was another workday, and he suspected writing Troy's obituary would be at the top of his agenda.

Groggily, he got out of bed and followed his morning routine. When he opened the front door to leave, the *Perry Hollow Gazette* was waiting for him.

GRIM REAPER STRIKES AGAIN, the headline screamed. Below that, in only slightly smaller letters, it read, FOOTBALL STANDOUT MURDERED, FOUND IN COFFIN.

The byline belonged to Martin Swan. Back in his reporting days, Henry would have felt a twinge of jealousy about that. But not now. Now, Martin could have all the attention-grabbing stories he wanted. Henry didn't care.

He scooped up the paper and tossed it into the trash can next to the door. When he turned around to leave, he noticed something else in the hallway. Something he hadn't seen since March.

There was no box this time. No attempt to disguise what it was. Instead, the portable fax machine sat out in the open, the buttons on its front panel making it look like a face. It was smiling at Henry, he was sure of it. Smiling and beckoning him to join the next round of whatever game it was that they were playing.

# EIGHTEEN

Had she been given the choice, Kat would have picked getting a root canal over holding a press conference. She couldn't stand the thought of facing all those reporters and their questions. If she could have avoided holding one, she would have. But that wasn't possible. A son of Perry Hollow was dead—a beloved one at that. When a town's football hero gets slaughtered, it's owed a press conference.

After a meeting with the mayor, the county sheriff, the prosecutor's office, and the state police, it was decided that Kat should do the talking. She was the face of Perry Hollow, they said, and she knew the most about the case. But Kat couldn't help feeling like a sacrificial lamb. All of them had thought George Winnick's killer was behind bars, and no one wanted to break the bad news that he wasn't. That left Kat to do their dirty work.

So at 9:00 A.M. sharp, she stood outside the police station and confronted a gauntlet of reporters. It wasn't just the *Gazette* that was interested anymore. Media outlets from far outside the county now wanted a piece of the action. As she gave her opening remarks, she saw reporters from *The Philadelphia Inquirer*, *The New York Times*, and practically every TV station in the state.

"I'll first go over the details of the case," she said, "then I'll open it up to questions."

Taking a deep breath, she began.

"Troy Gunzelman was found dead at approximately nine thirty last night."

She read her statement from a sheet of paper Lou had typed a half hour earlier, after Kat heard back from Wallace Noble.

The autopsy results were similar to George Winnick's, with a few variations. Instead of merely slicing the carotid artery, the killer had cut the jugular open as well. It was exactly like Bob McNeil had demonstrated—one to let the blood out, one to let the embalming fluid in. The killer again used a mixture of formaldehyde and water, although the solution hadn't entirely filled Troy's circulatory system. Apparently, he had been in a hurry.

"His body was discovered in a homemade coffin floating on Lake Squall. Cause of death was loss of blood. The exact time of death has yet to be determined."

Kat scanned the crowd as she spoke, immediately picking out Martin Swan. After that morning's edition, he and the rest of the *Gazette* staff were firmly on her shit list. Martin had decided to give the killer a nickname in that day's paper, dubbing him the Grim Reaper.

Quick to know a good sound bite when they heard one, the television news stations picked it up immediately, using the nickname throughout their morning broadcasts. And as Kat opened the press conference up to questions, she prepared to be bombarded with references to it.

Several dozen hands shot into the air, attached to reporters already calling out queries. Martin's was among the highest. Normally, Kat would have picked him first, giving him a home team advantage. But since she was still angry, she pointed to a woman who identified herself as a correspondent from a Philadelphia TV station.

"Do you think the Grim Reaper is responsible for the deaths of both Troy Gunzelman and George Winnick?"

Kat nodded solemnly. "There is reason to believe the perpetrator of this crime is the same person responsible for killing George Winnick earlier this year. Both victims died in similar manners."

Martin raised his hand higher, stretching it like a brainy third-grader. Kat picked the reporter next to him, a well-scrubbed fellow from CNN.

"Other than the manner of death," he said, "is there any link between Troy and George?"

"Troy spent a summer working on George Winnick's farm. Besides that, we have no reason to believe they were linked in any other way."

Mr. CNN had a follow-up. "Then why these two people?"

"That's a good question," Kat said. "I wish I had an answer."

She saw movement at the back of the crowd. Nudging his way between two reporters was a pale-faced man who stood a head taller than everyone else. It was Henry, arriving late to the media circus.

He had brought a second portable fax machine to the station early that morning. Unlike the first, there was no need to see if it was the same one used to send Troy's death notice. Clearly, it was. It was the same make and model as the first, and once again, the serial number on the bottom had been scraped away.

Why the killer was leaving them on Henry's doorstep was a mystery. And while Henry still didn't seem concerned about it, Kat definitely was. The killer was embroiling Henry in the crimes as much as possible, and she wanted to know why.

Standing at the podium, she caught Henry's eye. He gave her a nod of encouragement.

"Is it true you received advance warning about both murders?"

The question came from the opposite end of the throng,

near the front. Kat didn't need to see who asked it. Hearing the familiar voice was enough.

"Where did you hear that, Martin?"

Martin Swan grinned like the cat that ate the proverbial canary. "Is it true?"

Kat had no idea how he had found that out. Not that it mattered. She was cornered and Martin knew it. There was nothing left to do but answer truthfully.

"Yes," she said. "A fake death notice faxed to your newsroom. Both times, it was received by Henry Goll, the obituary writer, whose cooperation in this matter has been invaluable."

The revelation turned out to be a double-edged sword. Hearing that it had happened in his own newsroom shut Martin up, which was a plus. But it motivated the other reporters, who riddled the podium with questions.

"Do you believe Troy Gunzelman was dead by the time the fax was found?"

Kat shook her head. "No, I do not."

A wave of shock coursed through the crowd.

"Are you saying there was a window of opportunity in which he could have been saved?"

"That's correct."

The tone of the reporters' questions shifted quickly. They had suddenly moved from mere information-gathering to trying to pin the blame on someone. Trapped in the glare of their cameras, Kat knew that particular someone was her.

"Was an attempt made to save Troy's life?" one reporter shouted.

"Of course," Kat said, straining to keep her composure. "As soon as the death notice was discovered, we did everything in our power to locate him. Unfortunately, when we did find him, it was too late."

The reporters now tasted blood. They edged closer to her, a hungry glint in their eyes. Their proximity made Kat even more nervous. Her mouth suddenly grew dry, and a thin sheen of perspiration formed on her face. She was about to lose it up there, ready to fall apart in the glare of a hundred cameras. She couldn't let that happen. She had to fight back.

"Do you think the Grim Reaper will strike again?" another reporter yelled.

"First," Kat said, gaining control of her voice, "I don't appreciate or condone that nickname. Giving a killer a name like that only manages to provide him with validation while showing extreme disrespect to the victims' families."

Kat glared at Martin, who suddenly found the ground at his feet far more interesting.

"Now to answer your question—I don't know."

The reporter persisted. "What will you do if he does?"

"We'll do what we did last night. We'll try to stop him."

"What if you can't?"

It was Martin. He had raised his eyes to her again, staring defiantly. "What are you doing to keep the rest of the town safe?"

In the back, Kat saw Henry walk away. He had had enough. Kat had, too. But everyone was waiting for her answer. All of them no doubt assumed the Grim Reaper would keep on killing and that she would be powerless to stop it.

"We have scores of people helping with the investigation, from the county sheriff's office to the state police. And I have made it known to all of them that the safety of Perry Hollow's residents and its visitors are my top priority."

The only good part about holding a press conference was that Kat got to have the last word. She made sure she took advantage of it, saying, "To that end, I call upon everyone in Perry Hollow to stay calm while we investigate these crimes fully. I also ask that if you see something suspicious, report it. If you have any information about these murders, tell us. This is a good town. Folks here look after one another, and I encourage you to remain concerned about your fellow neighbors."

With that, the press conference was over, although its end didn't deter the reporters. Trying to squeeze out a few last drops of information, they crushed behind Kat as she turned away from them. She ignored them and hurried toward the station, where Lou and Carl waited by the door, holding it open so she could make a quick escape.

Once inside, she started designating tasks. "Lou, you should start manning the phones. I have a feeling those tips I asked for will be coming in any second now."

As if on cue, the phone on Lou's desk rang. She answered it, raised an index finger and whispered to Kat, "Tip number one."

Kat next turned to Carl. "Track down Lucas Hatcher for me. Find out where he was last night. But don't ask him. Ask his mother. She turned him in once accidentally. Maybe she'll do it a second time."

"Sure thing, Chief."

Kat reached her office and found Nick Donnelly and Cassie Lieberfarb waiting inside. In each of Nick's hands was a steaming cup of Big Joe's coffee.

"Good to see you again, Chief," he said. "You want leaded or unleaded?"

"Leaded." Kat grabbed the cup Nick held out for her. "Better yet, high-octane."

A pang of guilt hung in Nick's chest as he watched Kat try to fend off her exhaustion with caffeine. This was his fault. He had seen the stitches on George Winnick. He knew they weren't the work of the Betsy Ross Killer. Yet he and everyone else had been so eager to close the case. So Nick bought Ken Miller's confession, despite what his gut had told him. Knowing he had done so now made his gut queasy.

"I'm sorry," he said. "I was wrong."

"We all were wrong," Cassie added. "The profile was right. We just didn't trust it enough."

Kat emptied the coffee cup, swishing the last drops around in her mouth. Upon swallowing, she said, "First, don't apologize anymore. Second, since the profile is still right, tell me what kind of person we're looking for. Because there's a lot that I don't understand."

"Such as?"

"Why now? George was killed in March. Why wait until the Fourth of July to kill Troy?"

"There are two types of serial killers," Nick said, "each with their own distinct traits. Disorganized, asocial offenders and organized, nonsocial offenders."

"What's the difference?"

Nick let Cassie take over. Understanding killers was her specialty. Catching them was his.

"Disorganized, asocial offenders generally have IQs below ninety and avoid most human contact," she said. "They have trouble fighting their urges, sometimes killing impetuously with no attempt to cover their tracks. When finished with their crimes, they are capable of blocking out the experience entirely."

"I'm guessing that's not the kind of killer we're looking for," Kat said.

Cassie shook her head. "He's an organized one. They're the exact opposite. Highly intelligent, they're equally as cunning. And they love to plan. Sometimes, plotting the hunt is more thrilling than the hunt itself."

"It excites him," Nick said. "Thinking about killing someone, planning out exactly how to do it. It's foreplay to him. So that explains the time gap between kills."

Her first question answered, Kat asked another. "What about the abductions? We know George was taken from his barn. And we know Troy was taken from the locker room. But they weren't killed there and they weren't found there."

It was another trait of the organized killer. They favored abduction over killing on the spot. With them, it was a given that where a victim was found wasn't the same place as where he was killed.

When Cassie explained this, Kat said, "And that begs the question, where were they killed? And how did they get there?"

"Last night, Rudy found some transfer on the coffin from the lake," Nick replied. "It was a flower petal. Off a carnation, to be precise. Once pink, now wilted."

"Where does he think it came from?"

"He has two guesses. One is that it was floating in the lake and stuck to the coffin. The other is—"

Kat could guess the rest. "The murder site."

"Exactly," Nick said. "So I'm thinking a basement of some kind. Perhaps a greenhouse or an arboretum."

"As for transporting the body, we still stand by the pickup truck theory," Cassie said. "It's the most logical way for him to transport the bodies and coffins."

"You keep referring to the killer as he. Do you think it could be a woman? Remember, the first fax number was registered to someone named Meg Parrier."

While Nick had no idea how Miss Parrier was involved, he knew she wasn't the one doing the killing.

"The killer is a man," he said. "I'm sure of that."

Cassie agreed. "Female serial killers are usually caregivers or prostitutes or, in the case of some of the Manson clan, brainwashed. They mostly use guns or poison, leaving the knives, rope, and mutilation to the big boys."

"Fair enough. But how do you explain this?" Kat moved

to her desk, where another portable fax machine sat. "Henry Goll found it this morning."

Nick eyed the machine. It was just like the first one Henry had brought in, gleaming and new.

"Perhaps the killer is gloating," Cassie suggested. "He's showing that he's smarter than us. It's the same reason he's faxing the death notices in the first place. Organized killers love their mind games. It's why they send letters to newspapers. It's why they leave cryptic clues behind. The theory being that they subconsciously want to get caught."

"And," Nick added, "our job is make sure that happens. So this fax machine needs to go to Rudy."

Cassie volunteered. "I'll take it to him."

That settled, Nick turned to Kat. "Looks like you're stuck with me. What's next on the agenda?"

"We need to pay a visit to someone named Caleb Fisher."

"Who's he?"

"The man who reported seeing the coffin in Lake Squall," Kat said, elbowing Nick in the ribs as they left the office. "You can drive."

# NINETEEN

Nick drove fast, with the windows down and the music playing loud. It was Creedence Clearwater Revival. A little "Bad Moon Rising." A little "Fortunate Son." Even a little "Proud Mary," although he preferred the Ike and Tina version.

"I've been thinking a lot about the victims," Kat said, trying to be heard over the wind and the music. "Why Troy? And why

George? There's no connection other than the fact that Troy worked on the farm for one lousy summer."

"There's a connection," Nick said. "Even if we can't see it. Organized serial killers don't do things without a reason. There's a meaning behind the pennies over the eyes. A meaning behind the stitches and the embalming and the coffin. Just as there's a reason why George Winnick was his first victim and Troy Gunzelman was his second."

"So that means the killer knew both of them."

"Not necessarily. He could have just spotted them on the street."

Kat turned down the music. "Are you serious? He might have seen them walking around town and decided they were the ones who were going to die?"

Nick nodded. "It really could have been that simple."

And that scary. A killer could pass a hundred people on the street and not look twice. Then he could see one person that stands out, for reasons sometimes unknown even to him. And that's the person he's compelled to kill.

"But why?" she asked.

"It depends on the killer and the psychosis. Some only target girls who wear pink. Or little boys in Mickey Mouse T-shirts. Or redheads. Or blondes."

Or brunettes. He couldn't forget about that.

"But he always has to see them, right? He wouldn't pick out someone sight unseen?"

"Never," Nick said. "There always has to be that visual connection first. Have you ever heard of Floyd Beem?"

Kat told him she hadn't.

"They called him the Drugstore Killer. He was a traveling salesman on a route through the Midwest. At each town he stopped in, he'd go to the local drugstore. If the salesclerk was a man or an older woman, he'd leave them alone. If it was a young woman with brown hair, he'd sit in his car and wait until they got off work."

He didn't know why he was telling her this. It didn't have anything to do with the Perry Hollow murders. But, he knew, it had everything to do with him and what made him tick. So he kept talking, trying not to let a bitter edge seep into his voice.

"He'd then jump them and strangle them. After that, he threw them in his trunk and later left them on the side of the road. He killed six women that way during the course of two years."

"And that's all it took?" Kat asked. "Brown hair?"

"That's all. He killed them because they had brown hair and maybe because they were nice to the bastard."

He stopped talking, but it was too late. His anger was unmistakable. He saw Kat glance his way, noticing his clenched jaw, his fiery eyes. She knew this was personal.

"I'm hoping he was caught," she said quietly.

"He was."

"How?"

"The easy way. One of the drugstore managers saw the last clerk Floyd killed get into his car. He told the police, who caught him red-handed. He then confessed to the other crimes. Except one. That was never solved."

He was relieved to see the lake slide into view. It meant a change of subject, which he welcomed.

"Turn right," Kat said. "Onto Squall Lane."

Nick turned onto a dirt road. Rising to their left was a hillside studded with old-growth trees. To their right was a smattering of lodgelike homes on sprawling parcels of land. All of them boasted winding driveways and private docks that jutted out into the lake.

Caleb Fisher's house sat large and heavy amid a cluster of

pines and oaks. Three white-tailed deer nibbled the foliage next to the driveway. They bolted at the sound of the car, sprinting away so fast Nick had to slam on the brakes to avoid clipping them. He watched them spring across the road and vanish into the woods.

"That's something I don't see very often."

"Welcome to rural Pennsylvania," Kat said. "There are so many deer here I'm surprised they don't have voting rights."

Not wanting to hit a potential straggler, Nick pulled slowly into the driveway and parked next to a large red pickup truck. As he shut off the engine, someone emerged from the house to greet them. A grizzly bear of a man, he wore jeans and a gray T-shirt that strained to contain his barrel chest. A wild beard the same sandy color as his curly hair obscured his chin.

"Can I help you?" he asked.

His large hands were closed into fists as he approached the car. Nick wasn't sure, but it looked like the man was carrying a large marble in each of them. Strange, but not completely unheard of.

"Are you Caleb Fisher?" Kat asked as she got out of the car.

The man took a quick look at her uniform. "Is this about the coffin in the water?"

"It is," she said. "Mind if we ask you a few questions?"

"Sure. Come on in."

Caleb Fisher gestured to the house, opening his hands in the process. When Nick saw what was in them, he did a double take. Mr. Fisher wasn't carrying marbles.

Instead, nestled in each palm, was an eye.

Kat saw the eyes as soon as Nick did. And since he also had two eyes in his head, Caleb Fisher noticed their reactions.

"It's not what you think," he said, smiling cryptically. "They're made of glass."

One of them had to ask, so Kat did the honors. "What are you doing with them?"

"Come on in, and you'll see."

He led them across the lawn to the front door. When he opened it, a trio of beagles burst outside. They first made a beeline to Kat, running circles around her legs. When they lost interest in her, they moved on to Nick, who knelt to pet them.

"Don't mind them," Caleb said. "They love visitors, which makes them lousy watchdogs. An intruder would more likely be licked to death than attacked."

He whistled and all three beagles trotted back inside. Kat and Nick followed.

Stepping inside, Kat saw that Caleb Fisher's house could only be described as a hunting lodge designed by Frank Lloyd Wright. The décor left a lot to be desired. The furniture—plump chairs and sofas covered by quilts—was rustically threadbare. Hanging from the walls were the heads of practically every wild animal native to the continental United States. Several deer. An elk. A bear. All of them stuffed and thrown onto the wall like diplomas in a doctor's office.

The home was still gorgeous, in spite of the dead animals. Angular and vast, it was the kind of house seen in architectural magazines. Designed to highlight the land on which it sat, it boasted a wall of windows providing a panoramic view of the lake.

Caleb led them to a wide deck just beyond the windows. There, Kat caught glimpses of neighboring houses, all equally as opulent. Like the pricey shops on Main Street, these rustic retreats for the wealthy were recent additions to Perry Hollow. Ten years earlier, the land along Squall Lane had been home to dense forest. Kat had played there as a little girl, catching frogs and turtles as the whir of the mill's saws echoed across the lake.

"I was right here when I saw it," Caleb said, crossing the

deck to stand at the railing, the lake sparkling before him. "It's my nightly ritual—stepping outside for a cigar and a drink. It's the thing I miss most when I leave."

"Where do you live the rest of the year?" Nick asked.

"Philadelphia. I'm an investment banker, semiretired."

"How much time do you spend here?"

"About five or six months out of the year. Usually spring and summer, leaving sometime in the fall."

"About the coffin," Kat said, attempting to steer the conversation back to the original purpose of their visit. "When did you see it?"

"A little after eight thirty."

That meant Troy was in the water at least an hour before they found him.

"When you spoke with my deputy, you said it was a coffin. How did you know?"

"I didn't at first," Caleb said. "It was pretty far away."

Kat joined him at the railing. She gazed across the lake to a pair of ducks swimming near the spot where the coffin was found. She could see what kind of birds they were but was too far away to make out any other details.

"Then how could you tell?"

"My first thought was that it was a piece of wood or a raft," Caleb said. "Like maybe a boat had taken on water and someone might be floating with it. So I dug out my binoculars to get a better look. That's when I knew. It looked so much like a coffin that in my mind it couldn't have been anything else."

"Can you recall if there were any boats out on the lake before you saw it?"

Caleb didn't need to think about it. "None. Yours was the only one I saw all night."

"Was there anything else suspicious you might have seen? Any people walking around? Any vehicles?"

"A car," he said. "I didn't see it, but I heard it go down the road, past the house."

"Why is that unusual?" Nick asked.

"Because this is the last house on Squall Lane. Everything beyond here is woods."

Kat turned away from the water. "What time did the car pass by?"

"A little after six thirty," Caleb said. "That was the only time I heard it. So wherever it was going to or coming from, I missed it when it drove by again. I was probably in the basement working."

"But you told us you were semiretired."

Caleb Fisher held up the glass eyes he still carried. "It's a different kind of work."

Kat and Nick followed him back indoors and down a set of stairs to the basement. When they reached the bottom step, Kat froze in her tracks.

The basement had been converted into an animal's worst nightmare. Dead animals were everywhere, stuffed and mounted in a variety of shapes and positions. Kat took in the deer heads burdened with imposing antlers, the raccoon affixed to a piece of wood, and the waterfowl frozen in midflight.

The only area not covered by dead things housed a work space instead. Caleb moved toward it as he said, "Welcome to my workshop."

Nick, who covered his surprise much better than Kat, crossed the room to examine an elk head mounted onto the wall. "You do all this yourself?"

"I did." Caleb dropped the glass eyes into a drawer full of them. "I know taxidermy is a strange hobby, but it relaxes me."

"I'm impressed," Nick said. "How do you go about doing it?"

"I use molds mostly."

Mr. Fisher pointed to the far end of his work space, which contained a salmon-colored piece of foam in the shape of a deer's head.

"I slide the skin over the mold and work from there. Helps keep the shape."

"And all this time I thought taxidermists used sawdust."

Kat remained stone-faced, even though she knew the direction Nick was going with his questioning. They had two dead animals left at the crimes scenes, with no explanation as to why they were there. Now, they suddenly found themselves in taxidermy central, and Caleb Fisher had a lot of explaining to do.

"Once upon a time, they did," he said, turning away from the mold. "Taxidermists used whatever was available. Straw. Old rags. And sawdust. But that's mostly only done now by purists."

"No matter what materials are used," Kat said, "why stuff them in the first place?"

"There are many different reasons for taxidermy."

"Such as?"

"Most taxidermists consider it an art form. They pride themselves on creating a close facsimile of how animals look in the natural world."

Kat approached the raccoon display, which sat on an end table, like a lamp. The animal had been posed with one paw slightly raised, as if it was about to take a step. It looked so lifelike that Kat wouldn't have been surprised to see it trot off the base and scurry away.

"Is that why you do it?"

"That's part of it," Caleb said. "But there's also a bit of showing off involved. I hunt a lot, and I like to display the animals I've killed. It's a way of preservation."

Preservation. The word sent shivers through Kat's entire body. George Winnick had been preserved. Troy Gunzelman, too. What the Grim Reaper was doing to his victims was exactly like what Caleb Fisher did to his.

As they left the basement, Kat thanked Caleb for his time while Nick gave the dogs a good-bye pet. Then it was out of the house and back to the car.

"So," Kat said once they were alone again, "should we consider Caleb Fisher our prime suspect now or later?"

"We'll do a background check. See if his story holds up. Also, since he said he spends only part of his time here, we should see if he was in town during the Winnick murder."

Kat agreed. If Caleb had been elsewhere in March, then he had nothing to worry about. If he had been in Perry Hollow, however, then he fully earned his place on the suspect list.

"I still can't believe that basement," she said. "All those animals."

"I'm still thinking about its size. Lots of space. Lots of privacy."

"You noticed that, too?"

"Of course." Nick started the car, gunning the engine ever so slightly. "Caleb Fisher's basement would be the perfect place to kill someone."

Back at the station, Lou van Sickle was exactly where Kat had last seen her—at her desk, on the phone. As Kat passed, Lou thrust a piece of paper at her. It was a message from Jeremy's mother, reminding Kat that he was supposed to come to her house that night for a playdate with James.

Kat thanked Lou for the memo, although she didn't need it. James had reminded her that morning, bringing it up until she promised that his best friend could come over, despite all that was going on in the town. And since Amber Lefferts was too upset over Troy's death to pull babysitting duty, that meant Kat had to be home to make sure James got his wish. After being forced to neglect him the previous night, she owed it to him.

Next up was Carl, who intercepted Kat and Nick in the hallway.

"I tracked down Lucas Hatcher's mother," he said.

"Does he have an alibi?"

Carl shook his head. "She said she has no idea where he was last night. Her best guess is the street fair."

"What about Lucas himself?"

"I couldn't find him," Carl said. "I went to the cemetery, but he wasn't there."

Kat made a mental note to track down Lucas herself the next free moment she got. But when she turned into her office and saw Tony Vasquez and Rudy Taylor inside, she knew that would be a while.

"I traced the fax number from the latest death notice," Tony said. "Wanna guess who it's registered to?"

Kat and Nick responded in unison. "Meg Parrier."

"Yup. The mailing address was again a post office box in Philadelphia, only a different one than the last time. The number was activated three days ago and paid for with a money order from the same convenience store. It was used only once, to send the death notice to the *Gazette*."

Behind Tony, Rudy stood next to Kat's desk, which once again boasted a portable fax machine. Sitting beside it was a handheld ultraviolet light.

"Is that the new fax machine or the old one?" Nick asked.

"It's the one found this morning," Rudy said. "And there's something you should see."

He flipped the fax machine on its back. "Turn out the lights."

Kat closed the blinds on the window and switched off the lights. A moment later, a beam of ultraviolet light broke through the darkness. About twelve inches in length, it cast a bluish glow over the desk.

"I was doing a routine scan," Rudy said. "And I found this."

He passed the light over the fax machine's surface, moving it to where the serial number had been scratched off the bottom. Below it was a blank metallic strip. When the light hit it, a row of numbers appeared.

"Is that what I think it is?" Kat asked.

"If you think it's the serial number, then yes," Rudy said. "It's not uncommon for expensive electronic equipment like this to have it in more than one place."

"So you can trace where it was purchased?"

This time, Tony answered. "Yes. In fact, we already did."

Kat rushed to the wall and turned on the lights. "Where?"

"It was bought in February at a Best Buy in King of Prussia."

Kat knew the town well. A wealthy suburb of Philadelphia, it had a fancy mall and every big-box store known to man. She took James there every August to buy him back-to-school clothes.

"That's about thirty minutes away," she said. "Did the store confirm this?"

"The manager did after checking inventory records."

Her head spinning with all this new information, Kat took a seat behind her desk. Nick remained standing.

"We should request the security footage," he said. "See if this guy was caught on camera."

"I already did," Tony told him. "And it's too late. The store only keeps the footage a month before erasing it. It's long gone."

"Just our luck," Kat said. "Could the manager tell you anything else? What the guy looked like? What else he bought?"

"He told us that it wasn't a guy. It was a woman. But the cashier who rang her up couldn't remember any physical details."

Kat straightened in her chair. A woman bought the fax machine. Could it have been the same mysterious Meg Parrier who registered the number? Kat wasn't a gambler, but she'd wager a thousand bucks that it was. What she really wanted to know was Miss Parrier's true identity and why she was buying equipment that was being used in murders.

"Please tell me she used a credit card," Nick said.

Tony frowned. "She paid with cash. A lot of it."

"How much?"

"The total bill was close to four thousand dollars."

Kat's eyes widened at the amount. That was the equivalent of four mortgage payments. "One fax machine costs that much?"

"Not quite. The bill was so much because the customer bought more than one."

"How many did she buy?"

"Brace yourself," Tony said. "She bought four of them."

# TWENTY

Henry feared the fax machine.

He knew it was ridiculous to be afraid of an inanimate object. Yet he was terrified of it. And knowing he was being foolish didn't diminish his fear. Twice, bad things had come out of it, signaling the deaths of two people. And he was afraid it was only a matter of time before a third bad thing came his way.

Returning to his office after watching Kat's press conference, he found it difficult to follow his usual routine. Not with the fax machine by his side. Not with the possibility it could deliver another bit of bad news.

He tried to focus, attempting to ease his mind with one of his favorite operas. But it was useless. After an hour of nothing but jitters, he faced the fax machine. Its front panel contained a single green light—an unblinking eye, staring back at him.

Gazing at the light, not blinking himself, Henry realized the machine was a physical representation of dread. It was the anticipation that unnerved him, not the machine itself. He would receive another death notice from the Grim Reaper. He was sure of it. What remained frustratingly vague was when it would arrive. And whose name it would contain.

The fax machine suddenly hummed to life. The green light finally blinked—slowly, steadily. A signal something was about to be sent.

Unlike the pulsing green light, Henry didn't dare blink. He kept his eyes wide open as the fax machine purred. A soft click emanated from its depths. A sheet of paper being lifted into place. That was followed by a muffled whir as ink spilled across the page. Then, as swift as an arrow to the heart, the fresh fax slid facedown out of the machine.

Henry reached for it, then hesitated. Hand hovering over the paper, he remembered how blithely he had grabbed the death notices for George Winnick and Troy Gunzelman. Both times, he hadn't known he was reaching into a trap.

Now he did.

Now, every fax the machine spat out was a potential spider bite, sharp and venomous.

Yet the caution made him feel foolish. Not everything he received was dangerous. It could be an innocent fax, most likely from Deana and the McNeil Funeral Home.

He was right on one count. When Henry finally picked up the fax to read it, he saw it *was* from Deana, although not associated with the funeral home. It was a handwritten message thanking him for the previous night.

Henry fell back into his chair, feeling relief and confusion. He was relieved that the fax wasn't from the killer, but he was confused that Deana would thank him for such a miserable time. During their brief date, he had debated the grieving process before running away mid-kiss. Some great time he was. Deana Swan would be better off directing her affection toward someone else.

He tore up the fax. As he scattered the pieces into the trash, he heard another member of the Swan family.

"Hiding another secret? It seems you have a lot of them, Henry Goll."

Henry's back stiffened. "Can I help you with something, Martin?"

Martin Swan didn't answer, instead saying, "That was one hell of a press conference. Chief Campbell looked like a deer caught in headlights. But it was nice of her to give you a shout-out like that. Almost as nice as you helping the police all this time without telling me."

He stepped into the tight office, forcing Henry to back up against his desk to make room for him. It also kept him in his chair, an obvious tactical move on Martin's part. For once, Martin Swan could be taller than Henry.

"It was police business. I wasn't allowed to tell you."

"Just how much do you know about these murders?"

"Not much at all," Henry said. "I got a death notice. I gave it to the police. When I got another one, I did the same thing."

He decided not to mention all the other bits and pieces he knew, including the fax machines left at his door.

The reporter stared at the palm of his left hand, tracing its creases with the index finger of his right. His gaze was so intent that at first Henry thought Martin had blocked him out entirely. But when he spoke again, it was clear that was far from the case.

"You could have told me off the record. I thought we were friends, Henry. I mean, you did go on a date with my sister."

"It was hardly a date," Henry said, a little too defensively.

"She told me you kissed her."

Actually, Deana had kissed him. But Henry saw no point in arguing that with Martin.

"Is that a problem?" he asked.

"Yes and no. Deana really likes you. And that's under-standable. You're smart, athletic, *handsome*."

He drew out the word until it was almost a hiss. The sound of it made Henry flinch. Martin noticed and smiled.

"If you don't want me to date your sister, just say so," Henry said, unable to tamp down the irritation rising in his voice.

"You can date her," Martin said. "I wish you both all the happiness in the world. But Deana's been through a lot. I don't want to see her get hurt. So you'd better be honest with her."

"About what?"

Martin continued to fidget, this time rubbing the skin at the bumps of his knuckles.

"Do you ever miss being a reporter?" he asked.

"Not really."

"That's surprising. I did a little research. Looked up some of your old investigative pieces. You were good, Henry. Amazing, actually. You would have done great work writing about these murders."

"I'm an obituary writer. Not a reporter."

"But if you decided to go back to reporting, this would be the perfect time to do it," Martin said. "Especially since you know more about these murders than you're letting on."

Henry at last understood why Martin had invaded his of-fice. As the reporter covering the murders, he was naturally jealous of anyone who had more information than he did. Henry had been the same way when he was a reporter. The fear of being scooped, even by an obituary writer, was a powerful motivator.

"I'm helping them as much as I can," Henry said, adding, "Which isn't much."

"Do you know if the police have any suspects?"

Henry did, but he wasn't about to mention Lucas Hatcher. The last thing Chief Campbell needed was Martin tipping off her primary suspect.

"I have no idea."

"When you get an idea, tell me."

Martin moved out of the office, giving Henry more breathing room. But he didn't leave. Not by any means.

"For that matter," he said through the open doorway, "tell me if you hear anything valuable. It's really in your best interests if you do."

"And why is that?"

"Because I might have to tell Deana about your wife," he replied. "I think she'd be interested to know that you killed her."

Pleased with himself, Martin walked away. Henry stayed motionless, listening to the reporter's fading footsteps in the stairwell. When they vanished completely, he collapsed back into his chair.

Martin Swan knew the truth. Soon Deana would, too. And then everyone would.

His secret would be out.

Too rattled to stay at work and too reluctant to go home, Henry took to the streets. He walked quickly, trying to shake away his problems. That didn't happen. Instead, his mind was crammed with thoughts battling for prominence. Martin's sly threat and Troy Gunzelman's death jostled with thoughts of Gia and Henry's intense attraction to Deana.

All of it, the whole damn headache-inducing mess, was so great Henry thought he'd go mad. He knew about madness. It was a staple of most of his favorite operas. Yet they never addressed his type of situation. In the operas, characters went insane held captive by one great obsession, usually love. They weren't encumbered by several of them, all of them equally heavy. That left Henry with no frame of reference, no idea how to tame the intensifying vortex in his head.

So he walked, his pace never wavering as he moved locomotivelike across the sidewalks of Perry Hollow. First, it was Main Street, which was quickly clearing out as evening approached. Next, it was across the town square, equally as empty. It wasn't until he hit the side streets that Henry realized someone was watching him.

He knew because of a strange sensation he couldn't explain, let alone describe. It was a warmth at his back, as if a laser had been pointed there. When he turned around, he saw the shape of a man walking about a hundred yards behind him. The same man had been behind him on Main Street and in the square. Henry had just been too preoccupied to notice it.

But now he couldn't help but notice.

He was being followed.

Immediately, he thought of the two fax machines dumped outside his apartment. Kat had been worried about that. Henry wasn't.

Until now.

Now, he wondered if the man following him was the same person who had made those deliveries. And if so, Henry didn't want to find out what was now on his agenda.

He glanced back again. The sun was positioned behind the man, so all Henry could see was a silhouette. If he wanted to get a good look at his tracker, he'd have to be blunt about it.

Turning around, Henry started running toward him. The man didn't stop walking. He kept moving forward until Henry could make out a pink face, a police uniform, a cross affixed to the fabric.

It was Deputy Carl Bauersox, who nodded and said, "Evening, Mr. Goll."

He pronounced it *ghoul*, although Henry knew it wasn't intentional. That rudeness was a product of the *Gazette* staff alone.

"Are you following me?"

The deputy's face turned a darker shade of pink. "Sorry about that. Was just wondering where you were off to."

"Why?"

"Chief's orders."

Henry should have known. Kat's concerned thoughts had turned into concerned actions. Now she had the police tailing him.

"How long were you going to follow me?"

"Until you got home safely."

"And then?"

"Then I was told to hang around a bit and see if you left your apartment. If you did, I was supposed to make sure you made it safely to wherever you were going."

"Why don't you just give me a police escort?"

His sarcasm flew right over the head of Carl, who said, "I'll ask the chief about it."

"Instead, tell Chief Campbell I can take care of myself," Henry replied. "Better yet, I'll tell her myself. Point me in the right direction."

Carl did, telling him where Kat lived. When Henry resumed walking, he heard Carl take two footsteps behind him.

"Don't follow me, Carl."

The deputy backed off and reluctantly switched direction, trudging toward Main Street. Henry moved forward, crossing several more blocks until he reached a two-story house with a patrol car parked in the driveway. Just past the car was something else unusual—a girl.

She was difficult to spot, hiding in the shade of a maple tree in Kat's front yard. Standing with her arms at her sides, she stared at the grass at her feet. She seemed to Henry like someone hypnotized—silent, motionless, the living dead.

Henry stopped and called to her.

"Hey, are you okay?"

The girl didn't answer, which caused more alarm than if she had.

He approached her cautiously. Creeping into the yard, he said, "Hello? Can you hear me?"

It wasn't until Henry actually touched her that the girl responded. He tapped her on the shoulder and she spun around, terrified. Henry took in her tear-smeared raccoon eyes, her too-skimpy clothes. Her skin was porcelain pale, just like his. Going by skin tone alone, they could have been brother and sister.

"Is something wrong?"

The girl's white face moved up and down in a tentative nod. She then twisted her neck to glance toward Kat's house again.

"Do you know Chief Campbell?"

The girl nodded again.

"Do you need help?"

This time she started to shake her head. But she changed her mind halfway through it, and the shake transformed into another nod.

"Troy," she said. "It's about Troy."

"Troy Gunzelman?"

"I think—" Sobs interrupted her words, releasing the sentence in fits and starts. "I-I think I-I know who killed him."

# TWENTY-ONE

After the bad news about the fax machine, Nick Donnelly volunteered to make dinner, an offer Kat couldn't refuse, even though she knew there would be two additional mouths to feed. But when he arrived and found out her son and his best friend would be joining them, he took the news in stride, saying, "Good thing I brought a ton of food."

His good nature continued throughout the evening, entertaining James and Jeremy with jokes and stories while he made eggplant parmesan. The boys loved the food, grateful not to be subjected to the Hamburger Helper and tater tots that Kat had been planning. After dinner, Nick even offered to do the dishes, which Kat politely—and regretfully—turned down.

"You have a lovely home," Nick said as he cleared the table and brought the dishes to the sink. "And your son is great."

He was just being polite. Kat's house was modest at best. On both floors, the singular design scheme was organized chaos. Worn sofas sat next to antiques inherited from her mother. The walls held a mixture of family photos, mass-produced prints picked up at Walmart and James's artwork from school. And there was clutter everywhere—old newspapers, James's toys, a week's worth of clean laundry she hadn't had time to fold. The place was a mess, but to her and James it was home.

As for her son, Kat appreciated the compliment. It was hard raising a son with special needs, especially without a father figure around to help. She had to act as both mother and father, nurturing one moment, stern the next. After ten years of trial and error, Kat felt she had reached the right balance, although getting to that point had been exhausting.

James welcomed Nick with unbridled enthusiasm and not the suspicion he presented to most strangers. And Nick treated James like he was an average ten-year-old boy, asking him about sports, dogs, girls. Both he and Jeremy hovered around Nick as he helped clear the table, bombarding him with questions.

"Come on, guys," Kat said. "Go upstairs and play. It's time to give Lieutenant Donnelly some peace and quiet."

Both boys groaned as they trudged upstairs to James's bedroom.

"They're good kids," Nick said.

"I can only take credit for one of them. But thank you. And dinner was delicious, by the way. Where did you learn to cook like that?"

"My grandmother taught me. She made sure I knew my way around a kitchen."

"I barely know where mine is."

"You have other things to worry about."

Although he was talking about the murders, Kat projected his words onto her personal life until they took on another meaning. She had James to worry about, and spending so much time working and trying to provide for him took away from the things other, better moms did. Like cook decent meals and follow through on promises to watch the fireworks.

"It's hard," she said. "This balance of work and motherhood."

"It probably helps to have a husband," Nick said. "That is, assuming you don't have a Mr. Campbell stashed around here somewhere."

"Nope." Kat wriggled her unadorned ring finger. "He's in Montana. I'm here. And I sold the ring for cash during a trip to

Atlantic City. I was happy to have the thing off me. It had started to feel like—"

"A weight?"

Kat nodded. "Exactly."

As she stood at the sink, the urge to change the subject overwhelmed her. She focused on the dishes, plunging them into the sudsy water until Nick got the hint. When he did speak again, it was about the investigation.

"I know you're worried," he said. "About the other fax machines."

Kat grabbed a sponge and started scrubbing a plate. She *was* worried, and she took it out on the tomato sauce dried onto the dish.

"Four machines," she said. "One of them used before George's murder. Another before Troy's. That means he's planning two more."

"We don't know that for sure."

The flatness of Nick's voice indicated that even he didn't believe this.

"On a lighter note," Kat said, "we had almost twenty tips from concerned citizens."

"And I bet all of them are completely useful and totally accurate."

Kat recapped the messages Lou had taken. A dozen callers suspected their neighbors. Five more suspected their own spouses, which didn't bode well for Perry Hollow's divorce rate. Adrienne Wellington called to suspect Jasper Fox. Jasper Fox called to suspect Adrienne Wellington.

"And the last caller," Kat said, "claimed it to be the work of aliens. But I suspect that might have been a crank call."

"Did anyone say anything about Caleb Fisher?"

"Nope."

"That doesn't surprise me. I had a trooper check into

his past. He's clean. Divorced. No kids. Works hard half the year. Relaxes the other half. And when George Winnick was killed, he was apparently attending a financial conference in London."

"So the suspect list grows smaller," Kat said.

She had just started to wash another dish when the doorbell rang. The noise sent James shooting out of his bedroom and down the stairs. Nick's visit had wound him up, and the anticipatory clatter of his footsteps made it clear he was hoping for more excitement from another unexpected visitor.

From the kitchen, she heard him open the front door. That was followed by a deep, quiet voice asking, "Is your mother home?"

"Mom," James called. "It's the man who was in the car with us."

Kat experienced a pang of panic when she entered the living room and saw Henry Goll standing at the door. Every time he appeared, bad news tagged along with him.

"I'm sorry to bother you like this," he said. "But I think this is important."

"What's wrong?"

Henry stepped aside, revealing Amber Lefferts. She was crying, the tears mixing with her mascara to create black streaks on her cheeks.

"I have information about Troy's killer," she said.

Kat pulled her inside and shooed James upstairs. In the kitchen, she sat Amber down and made her a cup of tea. The babysitter's crying had subsided, but so had her voice. While Kat tried to coax information out of her, Amber stared into her teacup, as if the answer to all of life's most important questions rested at its bottom.

"Do you think you're ready to talk?" Kat asked.

Amber's reply was meek. "Yes."

"Good. Now tell us why you think you know who killed Troy."

A lightning bolt of fear flashed in the girl's red-ringed eyes. "You have to promise not to tell my parents."

"This is just between us," Kat said, gesturing across the table to where Henry and Nick sat. "We're all friends here. You can trust us."

Amber remained adamant. "You need to promise."

"I promise. Now tell us why."

"Because," she began, on the brink of tears again, "I met him."

"Where did you meet him, honey?" Kat put an arm over the girl's shoulder. When Amber sniffed, Kat offered her a napkin to use as a tissue.

"I don't want to say," Amber said as she wiped her nose. "I'll get in trouble."

"I've already promised I wouldn't tell anyone. If this is the man who killed Troy, then you're doing the right thing by talking. Now, please, tell us what happened."

Amber had calmed down enough to speak a full sentence without sobbing. Even so, Kat handed her another napkin in case she started up again.

"I knew Troy," Amber said. "We were—"

"Friends," Kat volunteered when she struggled to come up with a proper word to describe their relationship.

Amber seemed okay with that description. "We were parked in his car the other night."

Kat didn't ask what they were doing in Troy's Mustang. She could figure it out without Amber's help. She had been a teenager once. She knew what parked cars were for.

"We were off Old Mill Road, close to where Mr. Winnick was found. That started Troy talking about how Mr. Winnick was killed. You know, in the coffin."

Kat certainly remembered. The image was etched on her brain like a fresh tattoo, bright and blood-specked.

"Both of us wondered if he was still alive when he was put in there," Amber continued. "I mentioned how awful that would feel, to be buried alive. Troy told me he knew how it felt. He asked me if I wanted to find out, too."

"How would you be able to find out?"

"He told me he knew a guy."

"What kind of guy?"

"One who buried people. Just for a little bit. They pay him and he puts them in a coffin and buries them so they get the full experience."

Other than being a hit man, Kat couldn't think of a worse way to make money. Even prostitution was more respectable than burying people alive. The fact that it was going on in her town mortified her.

"You didn't do this, did you?" she asked, unable to keep herself from sounding judgmental.

When Amber started crying again, Kat knew the answer was yes.

"Please, please, please don't tell my parents. You can't."

"I won't," Kat said. "You can trust me. Now tell me where it happened."

"Oak Knoll Cemetery."

"In the cemetery itself?"

"Yes," Amber said. "There was a hole in the ground. And a coffin. I thought it would be easy, but it was dark. So dark. And cramped. I lasted, like, five seconds before screaming. I couldn't help it. I was so scared. I started screaming and they got me out of the coffin. Then I ran home."

Her sobs were so hard they shook the entire table. "It was the last time I ever saw Troy."

Kat hugged her, stroking her hair and whispering that

everything would be all right. But the assurances came out sounding fake and hollow. She didn't know if everything would be all right. So instead of lying, she simply stopped talking.

Nick then spoke up, asking the one question that needed to be answered.

"The man in the cemetery. What was his name?"

"Lucas," Amber said. "Lucas Hatcher."

Ten minutes later, Amber was in the living room, pretending to be entertained by James and Jeremy. In the kitchen, Kat conferred with Nick.

"What do you think we should do?"

"Go to that cemetery right now and haul him in," Nick said.

"But what Amber told us isn't enough justification," Kat said. "Besides, I promised her I wouldn't get her involved in any of this."

"Then we'll catch him in the act."

"When he's burying someone?"

"Sure. We fix someone up with a wire, get him to hire Lucas, and then bust him when the burying starts. Certainly that's grounds for hauling him in and asking a few questions. It's just like a drug sting, only without the narcotics."

There was no doubt Nick was serious, but logistics weren't on their side. The police department didn't have enough equipment required. In fact, it didn't have any.

"Where are we going to get a wire?" Kat asked.

"I have one in the trunk of my car," Nick said. "We'll use that."

"Second question: Who's going to wear it? Carl and I can't because Lucas knows who we are. He'll realize something is up the moment he sees us."

Nick shrugged. "I'll wear it."

"He knows you, too," Kat reminded him. "He saw you in the cemetery after George was killed."

"Then what's your suggestion? Rudy and Cassie would never go for it, but maybe Tony would."

A third voice erupted in the kitchen. "I'll do it."

It was Henry, who had been forgotten during their conversation.

"I'll do it," he repeated. "If it helps you catch this guy, then count me in."

Kat's response was instantaneous. "No. It's too dangerous."

"But I'm volunteering," Henry said. "I want to help."

"It doesn't matter. I'm responsible for the safety of everyone in Perry Hollow. Including you. And I refuse to put a civilian in harm's way. I shouldn't have done it yesterday, but you forced me into it."

Nick rose and placed both hands palms down on the table. "I don't think we have any other choice."

"Thank you for agreeing with me," Kat said, nodding. But when Nick bit his bottom lip, she realized he wasn't agreeing with her. He was siding with Henry.

"Come on, Kat. You want to see what this Hatcher guy is up to, right?"

"Yes, but something bad could happen."

"Like what?"

"Like Henry dying, for instance," she said. It was harsh, but since a simple no didn't do anything to sway Henry, maybe the worst-case scenario would.

It didn't.

"I'm fully aware of the risks," Henry said. "And I'm still willing to do it."

Both men stared expectantly at Kat, who refused to budge.

"No," she said. "And that's the last I'll say on the matter."

# TWENTY-TWO

Pissed off.

That's how Nick felt. Pissed off and taking names.

It was a common state police phrase used to describe a trooper's desire to catch a bad guy. It also summed up Nick's mood. So did angry. And exasperated. And most maddening of all, disappointed. After having virtually no real leads and no tips, a juicy one just dropped in their laps, yet Kat seemed content to do nothing about it.

Nick knew she was different from the other law enforcement yokels he had met. He also knew she wanted to lock the killer up as much as he did. That's what made her refusal to go along with the sting so frustrating. Unlike the Grim Reaper, she still planned on playing by the rules. But rules only got you so far. In order to win, you sometimes had to cheat a little.

He was back at the Sleepy Hollow Inn, and it was just like his first stay—a swirl of pastels and potpourri. The only difference was the Norman Rockwell print that normally hung on the wall opposite the bed was gone. Nick had taken it down, replacing it with newspaper clippings, photos, and his own handwritten notes about the case. He assumed whoever cleaned his room in the morning would think he was crazy. Or the killer. Either way, the display had the look of insanity.

He paced back and forth in front of the wall, scanning articles from the *Perry Hollow Gazette*, snapshots of evidence, and his own barely legible musings scrawled in blue ink. Because the collage faced the bed, it would be the last thing Nick saw before going to sleep. He hoped that by looking at it, the case would stay in his consciousness, working through his brain during the night and giving him new insight in the morning.

Only he had all the insight he could hope for. Lucas Hatcher, their prime suspect, was burying people for cash in the town graveyard. What he really needed was someone with enough balls to help him catch Lucas in the act.

Nick stopped pacing when he heard a rap on the door. He froze, suddenly aware that his footsteps could probably be heard throughout the entire bed-and-breakfast. Someone somewhere had just been roused from their sleep. And now they, too, were pissed off and taking names.

He crossed the room on tiptoes. Opening the door, he saw not an angry guest but an obituary writer.

"I hope I'm not disturbing you," Henry Goll said.

"You're not. Come on in."

Henry remained in the hall. "After you left, I tried to convince Kat to let me help in the sting."

"I guess she didn't change her mind."

"No. She didn't. And I haven't changed mine."

It dawned on Nick that Henry was there for a very good reason. He was volunteering for the sting, even though the chief had told him not to. His respect for the obituary writer instantly increased tenfold.

"I want you to know," he said, "that Kat was right. There is some danger involved. So, are you certain you want to go ahead with this?"

"Of course."

Although Henry didn't smile, Nick's grin was wide enough for both of them.

"Then let's get over to that cemetery and do it."

By the time Henry entered Oak Knoll Cemetery, a fog had descended on the town. It hung over the graveyard in a haze of swirling opaqueness, causing him to bump into the crooked headstones. Occasional statues broke up the monotony of the modest tombstones, marble angels and virgins lurching out of the mist.

Moving through the graveyard, Henry listened for signs of a human presence other than his own. He didn't hear much—a car rumbling in the distance, the forlorn hoot of an owl, the murmur of leaves in the trees.

Then a different sound sliced through the fog. Whistling. Someone else was in the cemetery. Henry headed toward the noise, trudging between the graves. In the distance, the fog changed color and brightened, casting a yellowish glow on the horizon.

The whistling grew louder as Henry got closer. He even recognized the song—"(Don't Fear) the Reaper" by Blue Öyster Cult. It was a surreal sound, the eerie tune emerging from the fog and echoing off the marble slabs dotting the cemetery.

Before approaching any further, Henry plunged a hand into the waistband of his khakis and switched on the transmitter taped precariously close to his crotch. Attached to it was a thin black wire that ran up the inside of his shirt to the microphone positioned near his collar. Turning away from the whistling and the brightened haze, he lowered his chin and spoke into the microphone.

"Testing. One. Two. Three."

He scanned the lengthy swath of cemetery he had just passed through until the beam of a flashlight blinked twice in the fog. A signal from Nick Donnelly. Everything was in working order.

He spoke into the microphone again. "I'm going in."

Resuming his walk through the graveyard, Henry struggled to comprehend the events that brought him there. A few months ago he was Henry Ghoul, content in his solitude. Now everything was different, unexpectedly so. In February, if some-one told him he'd be marching through a cemetery trying to help the state police catch a serial killer, he would have had them committed. But there he was, doing exactly that.

He followed the light until he was able to see its source through the fog—a lantern sitting on a headstone. Leaning against an adjacent grave was a bulky man in a dirt-smeared denim jacket. He stopped whistling when he spotted Henry.

"Who are you?"

Henry cleared his throat and spoke loudly, making sure the microphone picked up every word. "Are you Lucas Hatcher?"

"That depends," the man said. "You with the police?"

"Of course not."

"Step into the light."

Henry moved forward until he felt the lantern's warmth on his face. Lucas approached, eyeing him with suspicion.

"What do you want?"

"I hear you provide a service. I want to hire you."

Lucas's eyes drifted to the right. Henry's gaze followed, stopping a few yards away at a heap of dirt next to a canvas tarp thrown on the ground. Henry didn't need Lucas to tell him that beneath it was a hole roughly the size of a grave.

"Where'd you hear about this?" Lucas asked.

"Does it matter? I still want to hire you. Now tell me how much."

"One hundred. Cash. Nonrefundable. If you wimp out, you're not getting your money back."

"Do a lot of people wimp out?"

Lucas let out a ruthless chuckle. "Most of them. A few days ago, I had some little bitch start screaming after ten seconds in the coffin. It was her boyfriend who had ponied up the cash, too. Bet he was pissed."

"How long can I stay down there?" Henry asked. "If I don't chicken out?"

"I'm not answering anything else until I get paid."

Henry reached for his wallet. The cash was Nick's, extracted from an ATM on their way to the cemetery. Henry hoped the lieutenant wouldn't later regret the expense.

Lucas quickly counted the money before shoving it into his back pocket. "That'll do it."

Henry's response was intended solely for Nick. "Good," he said, lowering his chin closer to the microphone. "I'm ready if you are."

Lucas yanked away the tarp, revealing the ragged hole beneath it. A dirt-smeared casket rested at the bottom of it. Dark gray with a gently rounded lid, it reminded Henry of a submarine—heavy, strong, impenetrable.

"Where did you get that?"

"That's my little secret."

Lowering himself onto his stomach, Lucas eased over the hole and opened both halves of the coffin lid, top one first. He gestured to Henry and said, "Go on. Hop right in."

Staring at the coffin, it dawned on Henry that he actually had to do this. He had to be inside it, for an undetermined length of time. He approached the hole and inspected the inside of the coffin. All of it—bottom, sides, inside the curved lid—was lined with white satin, which in spots had turned a sour yellow. A small pillow, also made of satin, sat at the head of the coffin.

"Has it been used?"

"You asking if there was a dead guy in there at one point?"

Henry nodded. That's exactly what he was asking.

This time Lucas's chuckle was accented by a slight ratlike hiss. Hearing it made Henry almost as uncomfortable as the sight of the coffin.

"Nah. Only used for the living—as far as I know."

Taking a deep breath, Henry stepped into the coffin. After another breath, he sat down inside it.

"Now lay down," Lucas said.

Henry leaned back. Even with the satin lining, the coffin wasn't comfortable. Head resting on the pillow, he was barely able to cram the entire length of his body inside. The soles of his shoes pressed against the bottom edge of the coffin, and the hair on his head brushed the top. It was also too narrow for his frame. He had to wedge himself inside, his shoulders straining against the walls.

The confinement made Henry's heart beat faster. His arms felt constricted and his legs began to twitch. His whole body urged him to get out.

Lucas knelt beside the coffin and peered down at him. "Ready?"

Henry forced himself to nod.

Lucas reached into his jacket and pulled out a black pager, which he thrust into Henry's hand. "You'll need this. Use it when you want to come out. It's set to beep me, so all you need to do is press the button."

Holding the pager close to his face, Henry saw the flat plastic button Lucas was talking about. He pressed it. Seconds later, a series of high-pitched beeps emanated from the grave digger's jacket.

"See." Lucas pulled out a matching pager that emitted a blinking green glow. "It works."

"Do you really think this is necessary?"

Lucas switched off his pager, the insistent beeps cutting off and bringing silence back to the cemetery.

"You'll want to come up at some point," he said.

"How long can I stay down here?"

"You'll start to run out of air after about fifteen minutes. Not that anyone's lasted that long."

Lucas meant it as a taunt. He was daring Henry to tempt fate by staying down that long. Henry wasn't going to bite. He intended to be out of the coffin in less than a minute.

"If you have a watch, you might want to set it," Lucas told him. "In case you fall asleep or something."

Henry doubted he'd fall asleep. The discomfort he felt jammed into the coffin wouldn't allow it. Besides, he wouldn't be down there long enough to sleep. But he set his watch anyway, mostly to call Lucas's bluff. After programming the alarm to go off in fifteen minutes, he looked up at the grave digger and said, "I'm ready."

Lucas closed the bottom half of the coffin lid, trapping Henry inside from the waist down. He swallowed hard, resisting the urge to kick himself free. After two more swallows and some deep breaths, the sensation subsided, leaving him feeling slightly more calm but no less constricted. Lucas next stretched over his head and started to close the top lid.

"Have fun down there," he said. "I'll wait right here until you page me."

With one last hissing snicker, he shut the coffin lid, letting it fall over Henry's face with a deadened thud.

The first thing Henry noticed was that being in a closed coffin was entirely different from lying in it with the lid up. He immediately went from feeling merely constricted to downright claustrophobic. His body writhed in agitation, surrounded on all sides by mildewed satin and coffin walls.

It was also dark, alarmingly so. The blackness was so dense that Henry felt like he had gone blind, cursed to never see the light again. Pushing aside the sensation of helplessness the dark and claustrophobia produced, Henry dipped his chin toward the microphone at his collar.

"I'm completely inside," he said. "I hope you can still hear me."

He heard a sudden noise inches from his face. A dull thumping sound, it was followed by a slight skittering against the outside of the coffin. It wasn't until he heard the noise again that Henry understood what it was—dirt.

Lucas Hatcher was doing exactly what Henry had paid him to do. He was shoveling dirt onto the coffin lid. He was, Henry realized with growing terror, literally burying him alive.

# TWENTY-THREE

Nick crouched behind a marble crypt, surrounded by the humid mist that filled the cemetery. It was uncomfortable against the tomb, and his aching body wanted to be anywhere but there. Yet in this matter, as in most, Nick's brain won out. His desire to catch Lucas Hatcher was so strong that he was willing to spend the whole night in the cemetery if necessary.

His ears were covered by a headset, which allowed him to listen to Henry's conversation with the grave digger. In his lap was a digital recorder, which had preserved every word.

Only there were no longer any words to preserve.

*"I'm ready."*

That sentence, spoken minutes earlier, was the last Nick had heard from Henry. After that, a sharp hiss of static interrupted the transmission. Nick strained to hear more, but the static had taken over, sizzling in his ear. Then the transmission cut off, leaving an abrupt silence.

Nick waited breathlessly to hear something else. But no more noise came out of the headset, no words whispered into his ear.

The transmission was dead.

He tapped the recorder, hoping it would be enough to wake it up and get it functioning again. It wasn't. Nothing came out of the headset but silence.

He assumed Henry had said more. How much, he couldn't begin to guess. Was Henry now in the grave, being buried like Lucas promised? Or was he still aboveground, asking the grave digger more questions?

It was easy to find out. Nick could haul ass across the cemetery to the spot where Lucas plied his morbid trade. It's what was going on there that was the problem. If Lucas was in the process of shoveling dirt over a coffin that contained Henry, everything would be fine. Nick would have ample grounds to arrest him.

But if Henry still stood beside the grave, the game would be over. Lucas would know the score and Nick would have nothing to use against him. All their effort would be for nothing.

Which is why Nick stayed put. He didn't dare risk ruining everything. Not yet. Checking his watch, he vowed to wait five more minutes. That would be enough time. If Henry wasn't in the ground by that point, then he'd never be.

And if he was, well, Nick hoped Henry Goll wasn't now regretting his decision to come along.

Listening to the dirt being heaped onto the coffin's lid, Henry tried not to worry. He wouldn't be there long. There was plenty of air available if he kept his breathing steady. All he needed to do was remain calm.

But that was easier said than done, especially with dirt piling on top of him. Each shovelful rattled the coffin, jostling him with it and causing his teeth to clatter against each other.

After only a minute in the coffin, his lungs were already

aching for fresh air. Feeling tight, they urged him to gulp down all available oxygen. Henry resisted, opting instead for short, shallow breaths through his nose.

He took a breath and counted to three while holding it in. Then he exhaled, slowly and deliberately, the air scraping his nostrils.

He inhaled again. Mentally, he counted.

*One . . . two . . . three.*

He exhaled.

By that time, the coffin settled into place and the sound of dirt being thrown over it grew more distant. Soon, he couldn't hear anything other than his own breath.

Inhale.

*One . . . two . . . three.*

Exhale.

The darkness heightened his other senses. His nose picked up unpleasant smells he hadn't noticed at first—the tang of stale sweat mixed with mildew and the musky odor of dirt. Wiggling his fingers, he felt the cold smoothness of the satin, interrupted by the occasional snag in the fabric. And although his ears no longer detected the sound of the mounting dirt, he heard other noises. The scrape of his shoulders against the coffin's sides. His stomach, untouched by food since lunch, grumbling lightly. The steady ticking of his watch.

He tried counting the ticks, gauging when a minute passed. He didn't know how long he had been down there. Not long. Maybe two minutes. Two minutes more and he'd certainly be out, taking in fresh air while watching Lieutenant Donnelly cuff Lucas Hatcher.

After thirty seconds, Henry realized counting the ticks had disrupted the steadiness of his inhalations, throwing him off his breathing plan. He suddenly found himself with his mouth open, swallowing up precious air.

He clamped his mouth shut. Inhaling through his nose again, he counted.

*One . . . two . . . three.*

A strange noise appeared as he exhaled, one not made by his movements. Henry stopped breathing, trying to make out what it was.

He heard the noise again, coming from the top right corner of the coffin. The third time it happened, the sound lasted for a while, drawing itself out until Henry became certain of what it was.

Creaking.

Near his head, the lid of the coffin was creaking under the weight of the dirt being dumped on top of it.

Henry set his jaw, determined not to worry. Of course there was creaking. Everything creaked when you put some weight on it. Beds. Chairs. Even his own joints when he got up in the morning. The creaking was natural. It didn't mean the lid would collapse and rain dirt onto him.

Yet the noise made Henry twitch. It kept him from relaxing, the sound of it reminding his body of how cramped it was inside the coffin. Unfortunately, there was no room to move, no way to ease his body's impatience. With his arms against his sides, he was able to raise his hands but not much else. When he tried to lift them any higher, his knuckles scraped the lining of the coffin lid.

He attempted to focus his thoughts, reminding himself there was no reason to panic. He'd be out in a minute. Two, tops.

He inhaled.

He counted. *One . . . two . . . three.*

He exhaled.

The creaking moved to the other side of the coffin, making him grip the pager tight in his hand, his thumb sliding across the button in its center. His desire to push it was overwhelming.

But he couldn't do it. Not yet. He needed to give Nick time to arrest Lucas. That meant he had to lie still, start breathing regularly again, and wait.

But several minutes had already passed. Five, at least. Lucas told him there was only fifteen minutes of air available. That meant he'd start to run out in ten.

The number lodged itself in Henry's brain, and he was unable to shake it out.

Ten minutes.

Not a lot of time, really. Not long at all. Once Nick arrested Lucas, he would need to dig the coffin up again. Certainly that would take a while. Digging a hole took longer than shoveling one in. Even if Nick was cuffing Lucas at that very moment, it would take him five minutes to clear enough dirt away from the coffin lid to let him out.

Henry forced himself to stop thinking that way. Nick knew he was down there. He wouldn't leave him. So it would take him a little longer than expected. He still had ten minutes of air, which was plenty. He just needed to calm himself. He needed to inhale, count, exhale.

It didn't work. His thoughts turned to Gia, as they often did. She, too, was in a coffin. Probably similar to the one Henry now occupied. The only difference was the amount of time they spent in it. For Gia, it was five years and counting. Hopefully, for Henry it would be less than ten minutes.

He hadn't attended Gia's funeral. He wasn't able to. She was buried without him, planted somewhere east of Pittsburgh in a plot of ground he had never seen.

During the years since her death, he had never thought about visiting her grave. Seeing it didn't serve any purpose. Standing at her grave, knowing she was there under a layer of dirt and grass, would only make him feel his loss all over again.

A sobering thought popped into Henry's head. That exact moment, several feet below the ground, was the closest he had been to her in five years. Although many miles apart, they were in a sense together, sharing the same earth. It was a horrible thought, and just like visiting her grave, it served no purpose. Yet it fascinated him, making him temporarily forget his confinement, forget the diminishing air, forget the creaking.

Unable to move, his watch ticking madly, Henry felt Gia's presence. He could reach her if he really tried. If he punched through the side of the coffin, freeing his trapped arms, he could push his hands through the dirt and reach her.

"That's sick," he said aloud, his thin voice breaking the stale silence of the coffin. "You're sick, Henry."

It was difficult to speak. The air inside the coffin felt heavy and thick, like sludge in his lungs. Had it always been that way and he was just noticing it for the first time? Or was it getting progressively worse? If so, he couldn't waste any more.

He stopped speaking. He breathed. He counted.

Despite his attempts to relax, tightness crept into Henry's chest, pushing against his rib cage. It caused his breathing to become agitated and desperate. He no longer bothered with the counting. Instead, he gritted his teeth and breathed as fast as he could, air flaring out of his nostrils. The sound of it filled the coffin—a frantic wheezing taking over.

A long time had passed. That was undeniable. He estimated he had five minutes of breathable air left. Maybe less, if the warm thickness of it was any indication.

For the first time, it occurred to Henry that he could die there. He had been nervous from the start. But it wasn't a real nervous. Not a jab-in-your-guts-until-you-puked nervous. It had been tingly, almost enjoyable, like watching a horror movie.

But now real anxiety seized him, grabbing him by the neck

and refusing to let go. He was running out of air. There was no doubt about it. And it was messing up his head, making him crazy, making him think about reaching out to his dead wife.

He had to get out of the coffin. He didn't care if it botched the arrest, which should have taken place by that point.

He lowered his thumb, the pager smooth against it.

He opened his mouth, inhaling a deep gulp of air.

Then, as panic took control of his body, Henry pressed the button.

Nick stared at his watch impatiently. When five minutes passed, he knew he couldn't wait any longer. It was now or never.

Stuffing the recorder and headset in his back pocket, he moved through the fog-shrouded cemetery, stepping around oak trees and edging past headstones. When he saw the glow of Lucas's lantern in the mist, he swerved left, sweeping in a wide arc around the grave and keeping himself just out of the light's reach.

Unholstering his Glock, he kept low to ground, approaching the light in a predatory crouch. He moved in fits and starts, hurrying behind one headstone, pausing, then proceeding to the next.

As he got closer, he saw Lucas silhouetted against the lantern light. The grave digger held a shovel, heaving as he threw a clump of dirt into the hole at his feet. When he turned to get another scoop, Nick sprang from the fog.

"Lucas Hatcher, this is the state police! Put your hands up!"

It took a moment for Lucas to understand what was happening. When he did, the grave digger froze, still gripping the shovel.

"This doesn't have to be difficult," Nick said. "Just drop the shovel, put your hands in the air, and I'll be a happy man."

Lucas considered it, his eyes shifting back and forth while he pondered his options. To Nick, it was a no-brainer—drop the shovel or get shot.

The grave digger thought otherwise. He released the shovel, letting it fall into the dirt. Then he began to shuffle backward.

"Stop right there!"

Lucas ignored the order. He kept going backward, twisting his body as he moved. Once his back was turned toward Nick, he broke into a full-out run.

Nick ran, too, barreling toward Lucas and tackling him. Lucas howled, madly trying to push him away. Nick refused to let go, rolling until he was on top of Lucas.

"I asked you to make this easy," Nick said, flipping Lucas onto his stomach and cuffing his hands behind his back. "Why couldn't you just listen?"

Clicking the handcuffs tight, Nick saw a pager hooked onto the belt loop of Lucas's jeans. Pulsing steadily, it glowed an urgent green.

Nick hadn't forgotten about Henry. Running ceaselessly in the back of his mind was the knowledge that he had to get him out of the coffin as soon as possible. Only soon hadn't come as fast as it should have, and poor Henry was still trapped.

He reached for the shovel, which in hindsight was a bad move. Lucas realized he had one last chance at freedom, and he took it.

Rolling onto his stomach, he used both legs to kick at Nick's back. When Nick toppled forward, Lucas moved into a kneeling position. Two seconds later, he was on his feet, scrambling away.

Nick was up in a flash, sprinting toward the grave digger. When he was close enough, he made a rough leap and tackled Lucas once more. Arms and legs tangled in battle, they seemed to linger in midair a moment. When they fell, it was hard and fast, the two of them crashing down into the dirt-covered grave.

Inside the coffin, it sounded like a car crash right above Henry's head. He heard the groan of metal caving in, giving way.

Then the coffin lid crumpled in front of him. He couldn't see it, but he felt it lurching suddenly closer, stopping in front of his nose.

Something light and gritty slid onto his cheek. Startled, Henry yelped, allowing some of it to slip into his mouth. It softened on his tongue, forming a foul-tasting paste.

Dirt. It spilled into the coffin, onto his face, into his mouth.

Henry tried to spit it out, but more fell in. A steady line of it trickled in from above, unceasing. He turned his head to the left to keep any more from getting into his nose and mouth. The stream of dirt landed on his cheek and slid onto his right ear. Henry felt it gather in his earlobe. When it overflowed, it slid *into* his ear, tumbling inside, covering his eardrum until everything sounded distant and muffled.

He rolled his head in the other direction, trying to shake out the dirt. It was useless. The dirt was everywhere, falling over his entire face. The sound of it was a sickly, slithery noise that reminded Henry of bugs and snakes and other things he didn't want to be reminded of.

It sounded, he realized, like something was trying to get into the coffin with him. A hand. Dead and rotting. Reaching for him.

He imagined Gia's hands—those supple hands that used to slide across his bare skin—pushing through the dirt, busting through the coffin and grasping for his own. Now that he was in the ground with her, she didn't want him to leave.

The dirt's slithery tumble seemed to mutate into a hiss, like someone was calling for him.

*Stay,* it hissed. *Stay.*

It was Gia. He knew it. She was trying to speak to him, trying to get him to—

*Stay.*

Henry heard something else, something more horrifying than the sound of falling dirt. It was a beep, high-pitched and steady, loud even in his dirt-jammed ears.

The alarm on his watch. It was going off.

Fifteen minutes had passed since the coffin lid closed.

The seriousness of the situation stopped Henry from thinking about anything else. Gia vanished from his thoughts, as did the dirt still raining on his face. He couldn't even hear the creaking that had earlier seemed to surround him.

He was only aware of how he had been belowground for fifteen minutes. That was the limit Lucas dared him to push. Now the seconds were ticking beyond that limit, taking him over it.

And soon, very soon, he was going to run out of air.

Reminding him of that fact was his watch, which wouldn't stop beeping. He tried to turn it off, stretching his arm across his chest in an attempt to silence it, but he couldn't reach. There wasn't enough room. The beeping continued, drowning out all other noise, the incessant sound indicating that death would be coming soon.

Struggling to reach the watch, he noticed it had become much harder to breathe. He gasped for air, struggling to swallow some into his aching lungs.

He needed to breathe. He needed to get out, get away from the beeping, from the dirt, from Gia's voice that hissed in his brain, begging him to *stay.*

He scrunched down as far as space would allow, head sliding off the poor excuse for a pillow. Lifting his legs until his knees touched the lid, he shoved his feet against the bottom of the coffin, hoping it would—do what? He didn't know. He wasn't thinking straight. There was no time for rational thought. He was trapped in a life-or-death situation. He had no choice but to act.

He kicked a second time, a third time. The force of his feet jarred more dirt into the coffin. It poured onto his forehead— pebble-specked grit bouncing off his skull. Lifting his hands, he clawed at the lid, fingernails catching on the satin lining and tearing into it.

His lungs felt like they were about to explode. They needed more air than what was available. It didn't help that he was exerting himself, working himself into a state of breathless panic.

But he didn't stop. He couldn't.

He kept on kicking and shredding while trying to block out the beeping of his watch and Gia's voice, which was getting louder in his head.

He heard her clearly, pleading with him. *Stay.*

But Henry didn't want to stay. He wanted to live.

He increased his kicking and his desperate shredding. His hands burst through the lining and clawed at the underside of the lid, fingernails screeching along the impenetrable steel.

Then he no longer felt it. The lid moved away from his touch. Light shot into the coffin, a thin yellow line of it that rapidly expanded. Henry saw Nick kneeling over him. He opened his mouth and took in air the way a thirsty man did water. It tasted like water, too, cold and refreshing.

With Nick's help, he lifted himself out of the coffin and onto the ground, gasping.

He was alive. He was safe.

# TWENTY-FOUR

Kat sat on the edge of James's bed, trying to get him to fall asleep. It was long after they had taken Jeremy home. After Amber's tearful intrusion. After Nick and Henry both left in a huff.

It had been a strange night for James, full of new people and adult situations he couldn't comprehend. And although he looked ready for sleep, with a blanket pulled up to his chin and his ragged stuffed dog wrapped in his arms, he was full of questions.

"Mommy, is Lieutenant Nick your boyfriend?"

Kat laughed. "What gave you that idea?"

James's shoulders poked up from beneath the covers in a muffled shrug. "Jeremy's mom has a boyfriend."

"Lieutenant Donnelly is just helping me for the time being," Kat said. "He's a coworker, not a boyfriend."

"Do you want a boyfriend?"

Coming from a boy on the edge of sleep, it was a surprisingly complex question. Kat had moments when she wished there was a man around the house, able to do things she didn't have time to take care of. And there were lonely nights when she missed the feel of a man's arms, the sensation of his skin upon hers. But she was a realist. She knew her son and her job prevented an active social life. Besides, she had James, who was the love of her life.

"I'm happy with things the way they are," she said. "Are you?"

"I'd be happier if we got a dog."

James's desire for a dog was well documented in the Campbell household. Pictures of dogs plastered his bedroom walls. Every school art project he brought home contained some canine-related theme. And each Christmas, getting a dog sat at the top of his wish list. But owning one was a huge responsibility that neither of them was ready for.

"We'll get one someday, Little Bear. I promise."

James held up his stuffed dog. "One like Scooby?"

"Sure. Just like him."

When James rolled onto his side, hugging Scooby even tighter, Kat thought he was ready to sleep. But his eyes remained open as he asked, "Why was Amber crying?"

"Because she was sad."

"Because her friend is gone?"

A tingle of anxiety swept over Kat. She had no idea how much James knew about what was happening in Perry Hollow. She had hoped he was oblivious to everything, even despite the presence of a state police investigator in their home. But that wasn't the case. James apparently knew a lot.

"Yes," she said. "She's sad because of her friend."

"Jeremy told me the bogeyman killed him."

Under her breath, Kat cursed his talkative best friend. Compared to Jeremy, the thought of getting a dog sounded better and better. At least a dog couldn't fill his head with unhelpful ideas.

"Jeremy's wrong," she said, not bothering to elaborate.

"Is there a bogeyman?"

Kat wanted to tell him no, that bogeymen were harmless myths little boys talked about to scare each other. But she couldn't lie to James. Bogeymen existed. One stalked Perry Hollow, possibly using that very moment to pick the next person to kill. Knowing that terrified Kat, but she vowed to never let James see her fear.

"It's time for you to sleep," she said.

"Will the bogeyman come after me?"

Kat hugged James as tight as she could, wishing hugs were all it took to make his bad thoughts go away.

"Never," she assured him. "Mommy's the police chief, remember. I'll protect you. Nothing bad will ever happen."

Once James fell asleep, Kat crept downstairs and locked every door and window. It had become her nightly routine ever since March, when Nick Donnelly first shared his serial killer theory. Knowing he had been right only heightened her vigilance. There was a madman out there, and Kat was going to do everything she could to keep him from getting inside.

She had just locked the back door when the phone rang. Worried the sound might wake James, she lunged for it, answering with a harried "Chief Campbell."

"Chief? It's Carl."

Deputy Bauersox was working the overnight shift at the station. Hearing his voice sent Kat into a minor panic.

"What's going on?" she asked. "Has there been another death notice?"

"No," he said. "Nothing like that. But Lisa Gunzelman was just here."

Kat checked her watch. It was almost eleven. Why Mrs. Gunzelman would stop by the station at that hour was beyond her. But she didn't have a chance to ask Carl because the doorbell chimed.

"Carl, I need to run."

"But, Chief, there's something you should know—"

The doorbell rang again, and Kat pictured James being roused from his sleep, thinking it was the bogeyman coming for him.

"I'll call you back," she told Carl before hanging up and hurrying into the living room. She unlocked the front door and opened it, just as Lisa Gunzelman was ready to ring the bell a third time.

The smell of alcohol swirled around Lisa, and she swayed unevenly on the front porch. Grass stains on her jeans indicating she had taken a tumble on her way across the front yard.

"Hello, Kat."

The slur in Lisa's voice was noticeable after only two words.

"Lisa? What are you doing here?"

Kat briefly glanced into the living room behind her, hoping curiosity hadn't led James downstairs. This was something he didn't need to see. Lisa was so drunk she could barely stand on her own. She staggered backward across the porch, almost tumbling over. Luckily, the railing blocked her fall. She remained against it, the railing the only thing keeping her upright.

"Is it true?" she asked.

"Is what true?"

"That you caught Troy's killer?"

Kat wanted to chalk up Lisa's nonsense to drunkenness. But she remembered what Carl was trying to tell her on the phone. *But, Chief,* he had said, *there's something you should know.* Apparently, it was something Mrs. Gunzelman had already found out.

"Where did you hear that?"

"I want to know if he killed my Troy."

"I'll find out," Kat said. "I promise."

Once she found out what was going on at the station, of course. Had the Grim Reaper turned himself in? Barring that unlikely scenario, Kat had no idea what else could have happened.

"I want to ask him myself," Lisa said. "Right now."

When Kat told her she couldn't, Lisa looked crestfallen. "You have a child, don't you?" she asked.

"Yes. A son."

Mrs. Gunzelman's eyes moved away from Kat, turning instead to the darkened yard.

"I hope you don't ever lose him."

*So do I,* Kat thought. There had been many times since James's birth when she wondered what it would feel like to lose him. Thankfully, the thoughts never lasted long. Having to go on living without James was inconceivable. She imagined she would die the moment he did.

"Losing your only child is a strange feeling," Lisa continued. "I'm not myself anymore. I see myself in a mirror and I look the same as I always have. But I'm not. I'm not the same woman who nursed Troy and raised him. I became completely different when he died. I'm just a shell."

Kat's heart ached for Lisa Gunzelman. She tried to understand what she was going through but couldn't. Loss that great had to be experienced to be understood.

"You should come inside," Kat said. "I can make you some coffee."

Lisa shook her head, grateful but adamant. "I'm sorry for bothering you. I shouldn't have come."

She teetered at the top of the porch steps. Kat reached out to steady her but missed. Lisa slid down them, somehow managing to remain on her feet. Staggering across the driveway, she turned to Kat and said, "Promise me something."

"Anything."

"If this man is the killer, punish him." Lisa Gunzelman's face twisted into a grimace of fury. "Punish him, Kat. Make him pay."

Deana Swan's house was dark when Henry trudged across her front yard. It remained that way after he rang the doorbell. He knew she was probably sound asleep, oblivious to the noise, but he wanted to see her. He needed to.

After the events in the cemetery, he didn't want to be alone. Coming that close to death filled him with an urge to connect with someone. And that person was Deana.

He rang the bell again, keeping his finger pressed against it until he heard movement just beyond the door. When Deana opened it, her surprise was obvious.

"Henry?" she said, sleep making her voice husky. "What are you doing here?"

Henry didn't respond. He was too tired to speak, too exhausted from his ordeal in the grave. He couldn't articulate why he was there. The reason for his visit was too complex for mere words.

He stepped through the door silently. Deana gasped when she saw his soiled clothes and dirt-caked face.

"What happened to you? Are you hurt?"

Henry shook his head weakly.

"Let's get you cleaned up."

Taking his hand, Deana led him through a tidy living room full of bookshelves and houseplants. They headed upstairs to her bedroom, which was a soft oasis of lilac-colored walls and white furniture. Adjoining it was a small bathroom—their final stop. Henry stood by the door while Deana turned on the water in the shower.

Placing a towel next to the sink, she said, "Take as long as you need."

Once Deana left the bathroom, Henry began to undress. The dried dirt on his clothes made them stiff and difficult to remove. He tried to do it without causing a mess, but specks of grime flaked onto the floor and stuck to his bare feet.

In the shower, the steam softened his dirt-roughened skin and soothed his scarred lungs. He inhaled deeply, letting the steam heat the back of his throat. The water quickly washed away most of the dirt. Rivulets of brown liquid ran off his body and formed a muddy swirl around the drain.

Henry grabbed a bar of soap and began the task of scrubbing away the more stubborn spots of dirt. Lathering up, he felt a brief draft as the shower door opened. Wordlessly, Deana stepped inside.

Her pert nipples pressed against his back as she embraced him from behind. Kissing the nape of his neck, she ran her hands over his chest, soaping him up. Her fingers moved down his stomach, following the trail of hair that led to his crotch. Using the lather as a lubricant, she began to stroke him and he responded, growing hard in her hands.

"Deana—" he began to say, but she shushed him.

Henry swiveled to face her. She looked stunning naked, her breasts firm and full, her skin turning rosy from the steam. When they kissed, the force of it surprised him. It was hungry and lustful, their lips smashing into each other, their tongues probing.

Deana wrapped her arms around his neck and he lifted her easily. Soon he was inside her, thrusting with unquenchable fury as she moaned. He moaned, too, the sound of their passion getting louder as their lovemaking grew more intense. They climaxed together, Henry pulling Deana down onto him and holding her there as their bodies shook with spasms of pleasure.

When it was over, Deana shyly edged out of the shower, vanishing in a swirl of steam. Henry followed soon after, turning off the water and moving into the darkened bedroom.

He found Deana curled up in bed, warm beneath a heavy white comforter. He slid in beside her and wrapped his arms around her still-naked body.

Entwined with Deana, the feel of her bare flesh warming his own, he finally spoke.

"I was married once," he said quietly. "She died five years ago."

Deana rolled over to face him, pressing an index finger against his lips.

"You don't need to tell me anything."

"You deserve to know," Henry said. "You were right the other night when you said I needed to start letting go. I do."

Deana laid her head on his chest and draped an arm across his stomach. Sleep was settling over her, expressing itself in a tiny, catlike yawn and a fluttering of eyelids.

"Silly Henry," she said. "You already have let go."

# TWENTY-FIVE

"What the hell were you thinking?"

Nick blinked against the hot, angry breath blasting onto his face. It was the next morning. Six A.M. And Kat Campbell was ripping him a new one right in the middle of the police station's parking lot.

"Answer me, Nick," she demanded, getting into his face even more.

Nick expected some flak for disobeying her. But he had hoped to explain his reasons for doing so rationally, without shouting. He had even brought a cup of extra-strength coffee to get back into Kat's good graces. It was now splattered in the parking lot after she swatted it out of his hands.

"I was doing what I get paid to do," he said as the discarded coffee pooled around his shoes. "Catching bad guys."

"Even though I told you to wait?"

"You can't tell me to do anything. You don't have authority over the state police."

Nick felt lucky that looks couldn't kill. If they had that power, Kat's angry glare would have cut him down in a second.

"But I do have authority over this town," she said. "And the people who live here, which includes Henry Goll. I'm trying to protect him, not shove him further into harm's way. What if he had died down there?"

Nick sniffed. "He didn't."

"Sounds to me like he was pretty damn close."

"Henry wanted to help," Nick retorted. "He knew Lucas Hatcher was up to something, and he wanted to find out what."

"I did, too."

Kat backed away, looking spent. Her anger couldn't mask her sheer exhaustion. Nick doubted she had slept a wink, which probably accounted for her pissed-off mood. Well, Nick hadn't slept much, either, and he was also pissed off. Pissed off and taking names.

"Not enough, apparently," he said.

"What is that supposed to mean?"

Nick's anger was coming to a boil. According to an anger management class that Gloria Ambrose had forced on him, this was a deciding moment. He could stop himself, back off, and cool down before continuing. Or he could let the anger take control, making him say things he knew he'd regret.

Nick chose to let his anger loose.

"There's a difference between wanting to catch a killer and actually doing it," he said. "You talk about how concerned you are, how much you want to stop what's going on in this town. But when it came time to actually do something, you backed off. Jesus, Kat, you're just like them."

The word shot out of Nick's mouth before he could stop

it. Kat picked up on it. He could tell from the way she stepped away, narrowing her eyes in confusion.

"*Them?*"

Standing in the parking lot, feeling the spilled coffee seep into his shoes, Nick Donnelly realized the anger management class was right. His rage had taken control. And he regretted it. Now he would have to explain everything.

"The police," he muttered. "In Newton, Ohio. And other towns. About other cases. That's who I mean."

Kat's mood softened considerably. She tilted her head while contemplating Nick, no doubt wondering what went on in that crime-obsessed mind of his.

"You're not talking about the Grim Reaper, are you?"

He wasn't. Having no choice, Nick confessed he was talking about his sister. Pretty Sarah Donnelly. One day when he was ten, the sweet-faced fifteen-year-old had gone to work at Alexander's Drugstore on Hamilton Street.

She never came back.

"For months, my family lived in agony," he said. "There was no sign of her. No clue what had happened. Nothing."

Since Nick and his family didn't know if Sarah was dead or alive, they didn't know how to act. They couldn't grieve and begin to move on. They couldn't hold out hope, either. So they did nothing. His family barely spoke, barely moved. They only waited.

"They found her in March."

Nick paused. This was rough. After thirty years, just talking about it still ripped him to shreds. But he needed to go on. He needed Kat to understand why he behaved the way he did.

"They found her in a forest twenty miles out of town," he said.

Kat was a smart cookie. She remembered one of their earlier conversations and put it all together.

"Floyd Beem."

"No one could ever link him to it," Nick said. "The police promised to do their best. The FBI, too. But I didn't believe them. The Drugstore Killer was in jail. He confessed to five murders. They didn't care that one was still unsolved. That one family from a small town in Ohio would never know who killed their daughter."

"Is Floyd still alive?" Kat asked. "Could you talk to him?"

Nick shook his head. Floyd Beem had been dead for twenty-five years. There was no way to ever find out if he killed Sarah. His parents had gone to the grave not knowing. As would Nick.

"That's why I went to the cemetery," he said. "That's why I will do anything to stop this bastard."

Kat's anger was gone by that point. All the red had drained from her face, Nick noticed, except for her bloodshot eyes, which welled with tears.

"I'm so sorry," she said.

The apology was sincere, but Nick didn't need condolences. He needed to catch the Grim Reaper. He needed to make sure those who loved George Winnick and Troy Gunzelman didn't go through what his family had endured. And the first step would be interrogating Lucas Hatcher and finding out everything he knew.

Five minutes later, Kat pulled Lucas Hatcher from his holding cell and led him to the police station's break room. Its stainless steel table and folding chairs made it the only place suitable for an interrogation. Pushing him into the chair, Kat cuffed one of his ankles to a table leg. Next, she cuffed his wrists and had him place them on the table.

"Don't try anything stupid, Lucas," she said. "You're in enough trouble as it is."

After hearing his sad story in the parking lot, Kat told Nick he could do the bulk of the questioning. That was fine by Nick, who had planned to do it anyway.

When he entered the break room, he moved to the two vending machines buzzing against the wall. Without a word, he purchased a Coke, an orange juice, and a coffee. He then placed all three on the table in front of Lucas, just beyond the reach of his cuffed hands.

"Thirsty?" he asked.

Lucas responded with a sullen nod. "Parched."

"Carl didn't give you anything to drink last night?"

This time Lucas shook his head.

"Man," Nick said, taking a seat at the other end of the table, "your mouth must be as dry as Death Valley."

"Sure as hell is."

Nick framed the beverages on the table with his hands. "You've got plenty of choices here. Pick your poison."

"Coffee."

"Good old java." Nick looked to Kat, who leaned against the wall. "How do you drink your coffee, Chief?"

"Strong," she said.

Using an index finger, Nick slid the coffee cup an inch forward. Lucas grabbed for it but was still too far away to reach.

"Push it closer," he urged.

"I will," Nick said. "Once you tell me why you killed George Winnick and Troy Gunzelman."

Lucas scrunched his face, making him look more idiotic than he normally did. "Killed who?"

"You know their names. You used them in their obituaries."

"I didn't kill no one."

Nick feigned deafness. "I'm sorry. I don't think I heard you."

"I told you, I didn't kill those people."

With a flick of his fingers, Nick knocked over the coffee.

The cup's contents spilled onto the table and rushed in Lucas's direction, forcing him to scoot backward in his chair. When the cuff around his ankle halted his retreat, the table jerked forward, pushing the coffee off the surface in a steaming trickle.

Lucas watched with despair as the coffee spilled onto the floor. "What the hell did you do that for?"

"What's your second pick?" Nick asked brightly. "Soda or juice?"

Lucas hesitated before pointing to the can of orange juice. Opening it, Nick nudged it forward, but again not close enough.

"Just give me a sip," Lucas said. "I'm dying of thirst here."

"You can have it once you start telling the truth."

"I am."

"But you just told me you have no idea who George and Troy are. I find that hard to believe. If I took two people, sent their obituaries to the newspaper, abducted them, and then killed them, I'd remember their names."

"I know who they are," Lucas said. "They were the two guys that got murdered. I read it in the *Gazette*. But I didn't do it."

Nick ignored him, asking, "Where did you learn about embalming?"

"What?"

"They teach you that in prison?"

"Man, I don't know what you're talking about."

Nick swatted the juice off the table. Lucas made a fumbling attempt to catch it, arms stretching out uselessly as the handcuffs clattered together. The can hit the floor spinning, burping out juice in an expanding puddle.

"You have to give me something to drink," Lucas said. "I know my rights."

"Speaking of rights," Nick said, opening the Coke. "Do you have an attorney? If not, you might want to get one. A good one."

He lifted the can of Coke to his mouth and took a long, slow swallow. Lucas licked his cracked lips, an expression of longing in his eyes.

"Tastes good," Nick said. "You can have the rest after you tell me why you chose those two people. Was there some sort of logic to it? Some special meaning?"

"I didn't do it, man. I don't know how many times I can tell you."

"Who's next on your list? That's what we really want to know."

Lucas shook his head. "What list? I don't know what you're talking about."

In a flash, the Coke joined the orange juice on the floor. As the two liquids mixed to form a fizzing brown swill on the linoleum, Nick pushed himself up from the table.

He crossed the room to the vending machine and purchased two cans of orange juice. Opening one, he handed it to Lucas, who chugged it like an alcoholic in a beer commercial. He placed the other can in front of him before sitting down again.

"Now that you've whet your whistle, maybe you can start talking."

Lucas downed the first can and started to work on the second. Between sips, he said, "I didn't kill those guys. You gotta believe me."

"I called the state penitentiary in Camp Hill this morning," Nick said. "You familiar with it?"

Lucas belched in Nick's direction. It was a weak attempt to prove that he was still a badass. Nick ignored it.

"I know you were at Camp Hill, Lucas," he continued. "I spoke to the warden. Want to know what he told me?"

"That I served my time without a problem."

"Actually, he did. He also said you helped in the prison morgue. Is that true?"

Lucas's silence all but confirmed that he had.

"What did you learn there?" Nick asked. "Embalming?"

"A little."

"Did you learn the difference between the jugular vein and the carotid artery?"

"Yeah." Lucas raised the orange juice to his lips and took a sip. "That doesn't mean I killed those people."

"If you didn't, then you can at least point us in the right direction. You're going back to prison no matter what. If you help us, we'll take it easy on you."

Lucas sneered from over the juice can. "And what if I don't?"

"You'll be sentenced to life in prison."

Because he had said it so casually, it took Lucas a moment to comprehend Nick's words. When he did, he lowered the juice and started sputtering in panic. "But—but you can't do that."

"Then tell me how many people hired you to bury them like that."

"I don't know. Maybe a dozen."

"Would you be able to describe them? Any of them?"

"Possibly. The one before last night was some whiny chick and her boyfriend."

"I know about them," Nick said. "What about any of the others?"

Lucas rubbed his forehead. "I'm thinking."

Nick stood again, smiling as the grave digger tried to edge his chair as far away from the table as the ankle cuff would allow. Nick walked behind Lucas and clamped both hands on his shoulders. Lucas attempted to squirm out of his grip but was held firmly in place.

"Where did you get the coffin you used to bury those people?" Nick asked. "I'm sure it wasn't a souvenir from prison."

"I bought it."

"From where?"

"Does it really matter?"

"It might," Nick said. "You can't just run into Wal-Mart and buy one."

"I got it from some guy. He sold it to me really cheap if I promised to give him a cut of whatever money I made."

Nick added pressure to Lucas's shoulders, causing him to sink slowly in the chair. "Let's make a deal, Lucas. If you tell us who sold you that coffin, we'll let you go. We'll forget about your side job in the cemetery, granted you promise not to do it again. How does that sound?"

"The guy's name is Bob," Lucas said.

"Bob who?"

"Bob McNeil."

# TWENTY-SIX

Henry felt a pair of lips brush his earlobe.

"Wake up, sleepyhead," a voice whispered. "It's morning."

He rolled onto his side, trying in vain to delay the inevitable moment when he had to get out of bed.

"Just five more minutes."

"You said that five minutes ago." Deana climbed on top of him in an effort to rouse him. "This time you have to get up."

She was right. It was morning, and that meant getting ready for another day at the *Gazette*. Deana also had work obligations, in the form of Troy Gunzelman's wake. But even though Henry knew they had to get out of bed at some point, it didn't mean he had to like it.

"Fine," he said. "I'll get up."

Deana remained on top of him. "You have to kiss me first."

Henry pecked her lightly on both cheeks and her forehead. "Was that acceptable?"

"Not really," she replied teasingly.

"Then let's try this."

Wrapping his arms around Deana's lithe frame, Henry rolled until he was on top of her. His open mouth was instantly upon hers, kissing her so deeply that soft moans formed in the back of her throat. When they finally broke away, Henry was aroused and Deana was breathless.

"That was much better," she said.

"I'm glad you approve."

He approved, too. Five years was a long time to go without the touch of a woman, and Henry was surprised by how much he missed it. Deana awakened a desire he thought had vanished long ago. And when he finally did crawl out of bed, it was with extreme reluctance.

He got dressed quickly, knowing speed would be the only thing that propelled him from the safe confines of Deana's bedroom. If he lingered, he was likely to be drawn right back into bed, taking Deana with him. And that wouldn't be good for either of them.

Yet on his way out, Henry paused at a photograph hanging by the door. He hadn't noticed it during the night. There had been other things to focus on. But in the morning light he found himself fascinated by the picture. It depicted a little girl and a little boy standing with two adults in front of the very house he was now occupying.

"Is that you?" he asked, pointing to the girl.

Deana crept up behind him and wrapped her arms around his chest. "That's me. Little Deana. I think I was nine when that was taken."

Although clad in a frilly pink dress, the girl in the photograph was already showing signs of the woman she'd eventually become. Henry saw the same bright eyes, the kind smile.

Deana pointed to the boy. "And that's little Martin."

"And these are your parents?"

"They are. I think they would have liked you."

Mrs. Swan was pretty, with teased hair and a slim figure. She held the hand of Deana's father, a tall, powerfully built man with jet-black hair and pale skin. Although his facial features were strong, they were overshadowed by a scar that cut through the left side of his face.

"Was that from the first mill accident?" Henry asked.

Deana nodded as she reached out from behind him and touched the photograph.

"He was so self-conscious about it. The rest of us didn't care. We still thought he was the most handsome person in the world."

"Is that what drew you to me?" Henry turned around and kissed her. "My scar?"

"No," Deana said. "It's the way you deal with it. I know what people say about you. I know how mean they can be. But, as with my father, I can see past it, at the man you truly are."

They kissed again, more forcefully. But before it got too heated, Henry broke it off.

"I need to go."

Leaving Deana alone in her bedroom, Henry descended the stairs. When he reached the front door, he saw a small den just off the living room. Something else he had failed to notice during the night.

Henry craned his neck to peek inside. Like the rest of the house, the den looked warm and tidy. He glimpsed more books, more plants, and the edge of an antique desk that sat next to a window.

He stepped inside, the floorboards lightly creaking under his weight as the desk came into full view. Another framed family portrait sat on top of it, this time missing a father. Next to that was a telephone, also antique. And sitting beside it, quite unexpectedly, was a blue jay.

Startled by its presence, it took Henry a moment to realize the bird was stuffed and mounted onto a piece of bark. He saw another animal on the floor—a rabbit looking ready to nibble one of the houseplants. On the wall opposite the desk was a deer head. A single cobweb stretched between its antlers.

"I see you've met Bambi."

It was Deana, who had entered the den unnoticed.

"I call the bird Tweety," she said. "The rabbit is Thumper."

"Where did you get these?"

Deana looked more than a little chagrined as she said, "They're bizarre, I know. But they belonged to my father."

Henry knelt before the stuffed rabbit. It was so lifelike it was eerie. He didn't know if he wanted to pet it or run away from it.

"He was a hunter?"

"A big hunter," Deana said. "And he stuffed them himself, something the rest of us found barbaric. But I can't get rid of them. I tried once but just couldn't do it. As strange as it sounds, they remind me of him."

She held out her hand and Henry took it, allowing himself to be pulled to his feet and out of the den. In the foyer, they kissed again, just as passionately as they had upstairs. The kiss was so strong and the attraction between them so palpable that Henry found himself hoping with all his might that Deana was telling the truth.

When Kat reached the funeral home, she discovered that talking to Bob McNeil wasn't going to be easy. A crowd had gathered there. A huge one. Sheathed in black, they loitered on the lawn, weighed down the front porch, and filled the foyer to capacity.

Nick Donnelly would have had no problem parting the crowd. But Nick wasn't there. He had decided to stay with Lucas Hatcher until after they got Bob McNeil's side of the story. If it panned out, then Lucas was a free man. If it turned out he was lying, then the state police would be calling his parole officer.

The only problem was finding Bob McNeil. After squeezing through the cluster of people on the funeral home's porch, Kat had to push her way across the foyer. When she reached the viewing room, she at last understood the reason for the crowd—she had just crashed the viewing for Troy Gunzelman.

Laid out in a casket, hands folded over his chest, he looked better than when Kat last saw him, in another coffin in a far different location. His face had more color, and the black suit he had been dressed in covered up the gash in his neck. But he was just as dead as when she found him on Lake Squall, just as tragically lifeless.

Surrounding the casket, seated in rows of folding chairs, was a parade of familiar faces—Alma Winnick, Jasper Fox, Adrienne Wellington. Martin Swan hovered next to his sister, carrying his ubiquitous reporter's notebook. All of them wore the same expression. It was fear mixed with anger, worry tinged with disappointment.

Kat knew they were fearful and suspicious. She also knew they blamed her for not finding the killer yet. No one said this to her outright. Folks remained as polite as always. Some nodded in her direction. Others offered small waves. But Kat knew the way Perry Hollow worked, and as soon as she passed, the whispering started.

She received different reactions from the two women in

Troy's life. Amber Lefferts and Lisa Gunzelman seemed not to notice Kat at all.

Amber looked paler than usual, thanks to the black dress she was wearing. She also seemed inconsolable, weeping openly and loudly as she signed the condolence book by the door.

Kat felt sorry for the girl. She was young and had little experience with loss. She wore her grief on her sleeve.

Lisa Gunzelman was another story. Sitting next to the casket, she displayed no tears, no trembling lips. Nothing about her grief was showy. It was lodged in her gut so deep it could never be removed.

Kat was about to express her condolences when she saw Bob McNeil enter the viewing room. He paused in the doorway, looking bearlike in an ill-fitting brown suit. Kat was by his side in a flash and tugging on his sleeve.

"We need to talk."

"About what?"

"Coffins."

"What about them?"

"How much they cost," Kat said. "I'm guessing you know all about that sort of thing."

Bob stayed motionless at the threshold of the viewing room, squirming in his suit. He tugged at his collar, pulling it away from his thick neck. He seemed as uncomfortable in Kat's presence as she was in his. A welcome change. Usually Bob McNeil was the one doing the creeping out.

"Are you looking to buy a coffin?" he asked.

Kat shrugged. "Not really. I'm more interested in if there's a black market for them."

She thought back to the evening spent with him in the embalming room. There, he told her a black market existed for everything. She had no idea he was speaking from experience.

"I'm assuming there is," she said.

Bob yanked at his collar again before dropping his hands to his sides. Staring at Kat through his bug-eyed glasses, a grimace played across his lips.

"Am I being accused of something?"

"Should you be?" Kat asked. "I mean, couldn't you lose your license if it was revealed that you sold a coffin to someone for a purpose other than burial?"

She enjoyed the way Bob flinched ever so slightly, wordlessly admitting his guilt.

"Not here," he whispered, glancing at the mourners shuffling all around them. "Follow me."

He lumbered through the crowd, clearing a path for Kat. She followed him out of the foyer, through a side door and down the steps to the embalming room. Unlike her first visit, the stainless steel table was empty. The lights above them were shut off, making the room darker—and more unsettling—than before.

Bob stood in the center of the room, staring at Kat with those huge eyes, not blinking, forcing her to make the first move.

"I know about the coffin you sold to Lucas Hatcher," she said. "And I'm assuming your father doesn't. Think I should fill him in?"

"Please don't tell him." Desperation crept into Bob's voice. "I don't want him to find out about it."

"Then you better explain yourself."

Above them, the ceiling creaked, moaning under the weight of all those mourners. Kat heard footsteps, muffled voices, and the lone, inappropriate flutter of a laugh.

"I did it for a reason," Bob said.

"Which was?"

"Money, of course."

"You're the only funeral home in town," Kat said. "I doubt money's too tight for you and your father."

"I need money my father can't know about."

"For what purpose?"

Bob removed his glasses. He wiped them across the sleeve of his suit, using his thumb to swirl the fabric over the lenses. When he put them back on, there were tears in his eyes, the lenses making them look as big as raindrops.

"To get the hell out of here," he said. "Do you think I enjoy living with my father two floors above an embalming room? That I like seeing more people who are dead than alive? It's torture, Kat."

"Things can't be that bad."

"You have no idea what bad is," Bob said. "You don't have to live in the same house as that monster."

Kat couldn't believe what she was hearing. Arthur McNeil a monster? She doubted that. Art was as harmless as a puppy. Bob was the dangerous one, with his surly attitude and his shady dealings on the side.

"You should stop making excuses for yourself," she said, the harshness in her voice surprising even her. "And you should stop blaming your father."

"You don't know what kind of person he is."

"Then tell me."

"I already did. A monster."

Bob was red-faced now, the raindrop tears falling with increased frequency. When he wiped them away, Kat saw his hands were shaking. Bob was afraid—but not of getting caught. He was afraid of his father.

"Did he do something to you?" Kat asked. "When you were a boy?"

Bob sniffed. Then he nodded.

"Did he abuse you?"

Another sniff. Another nod.

"How?"

Bob McNeil remained surly in his pain. "How do you think?"

A shiver of horror entered Kat's body. She had never considered there was a reason behind Bob's attitude, a cause for his discomfort around people. She thought it was just part of his personality. But she was wrong. People didn't get that way on their own. Someone had to cause it.

"How old were you when it started?"

Bob looked away. "I don't want to talk about it."

Kat knew he didn't, but she needed him to. She approached him slowly and laid a hand on his shoulder. Bob shrugged it off with a grunt.

"Please tell me," she said gently. "I can help you."

"It started when I was eight. It ended when I was ten. After Mom killed herself."

Kat flashed back to her childhood, when she had stared at her dinner plate as her father talked about how Leota McNeil took her own life. She remembered hearing him mention the layers of clothing and the bricks that weighed Mrs. McNeil down. *Like a stone*, was how he had phrased it. Leota McNeil sank like a stone.

When she was a girl, she couldn't comprehend why an adult would do something like that. Especially a wife and mother. But now Kat knew the reason. Leota McNeil had discovered Art's dirty secret and opted to throw herself into Lake Squall instead of confronting her husband.

"Do you think your mother's death made him stop?"

"I know it did."

"Did Art tell you that?"

"Right here in this very room."

There was pain in Bob's eyes as he glanced around the embalming room. Kat couldn't imagine having to come down there every day, knowing there was such a terrible memory associated with the place. But Bob had done it. And he continued to do it.

He pointed to the embalming table. "My mother lay right there. They had just pulled her from the water. Her skin was still blue."

The shiver of horror had never left Kat's body. But listening to Bob, it grew until it became a quake.

"She was naked," he said. "The first naked woman I had ever seen. I was repelled and excited at the same time. Later on, I threw up thinking about it. Or it might have been the embalming that did it. It was my first."

Kat felt nauseated herself. Deep down, she wanted Bob to stop talking. It was a struggle to keep from holding her hands over her ears.

"Dad gave me the scalpel. He made me slice the neck. And then the arteries. He made me do it all. I didn't want to, but he said it was punishment for making her kill herself."

"But you weren't responsible," Kat blurted out.

"I didn't know that. I was ten, for Christ's sake."

Ten years old. The same age James was now. If Bob was telling the truth, then Art McNeil really was a monster.

"He also told me he'd stop," Bob said. "He'd stop if I helped embalm her. And I wanted that more than anything. So I did it. I embalmed my own mother. He made me sew the mouth shut. It wasn't the way I showed you. It was the old-fashioned way, a needle and thread through the lips. Dad said it was special. That it was important to do it that way. After that—"

Kat knew what he was going to say next. "You put pennies over her eyes."

Bob nodded. "And then we were done."

Kat's nausea increased, making her woozy. She had to steady herself on the wheeled tray next to the embalming table. Scattered across it were all the tools of the mortician's trade that she had learned about during her first visit there. Scalpel. Eye caps. Aneurysm hook. Trocar.

That night, Bob had explained the things someone would need to embalm a corpse. One was formaldehyde, which was locked in a cabinet on the far side of the room. Another was space, which the embalming room provided in spades. The third was drainage, and lots of it. Looking at her feet, Kat saw she was standing over the drain in the floor.

A bit of clarity cut through her dizziness. She thought of George Winnick and Troy Gunzelman. They both had been embalmed in that room. Not just once, after she had found them dead. But most likely another time—*before* they were found.

The second embalmings were done by Bob McNeil, in the professional way. But the first ones, occurring before anyone even knew they were dead, were more primitive. The results were so rough because the person doing it had ignored modern methods in favor of something more old-fashioned. And that person wasn't Lucas Hatcher or Bob McNeil.

It was Art.

"I need to talk to your father," Kat said.

Bob's expression changed into one of abject terror. The wide lenses of his glasses reflected what he saw—a figure standing just outside of the embalming room. The person moved inside, close enough that Kat could make out his face in the reflection.

"Talk to me about what?" Art McNeil asked.

Kat whirled around to face him. He was smiling, but it was cold and meaningless—a liar's grin.

"Art, I'm going to have to take you in for questioning."

"Have I done something wrong?"

*Oh, yes*, Kat thought. The list of things he had done wrong was so great she didn't know which one to address first.

"It's best if we talk about this down at the station. Is there a way we can leave without drawing attention?"

Art looked first to Kat, then to his son. "What am I being accused of? What has Robert been telling you?"

"Everything," Bob said. "I told her everything."

The frigid grin of Arthur McNeil's lips melted into a flat line. Calmly, he moved the wheeled tray out of the way until there was nothing between him and his son.

"I thought you had learned," he said. "I thought that after what happened to your mother, you would have learned."

"I had to tell her." Bob's voice was reedy and panicked. *He sounds like a boy*, Kat thought. *Like a ten-year-old boy.*

"Just like you had to tell your mother," Art said. "You told her and then she abandoned us. If you had just kept your goddamned mouth shut, she'd still be here. But you whined to her, just like you whined to Chief Campbell."

When he had finished berating his son, Art turned to Kat. His voice was almost gentlemanly as he said, "I sincerely apologize for all the trouble Robert has caused you. Now, I really must return to my guests."

With his back straight and head held high, Arthur McNeil exited the embalming room. Kat waited until she heard him start up the steps. Then she looked down at the tray. The tools were still there.

Except one.

Art had taken the scalpel with him.

Kat sprinted out of the embalming room. She hit the stairs running, taking them two at a time. When she reached the top one, a scream erupted from the viewing room.

She followed the sound, shoving her way inside. Everyone

there was motionless, their eyes locked on Arthur McNeil, who stood next to Troy's casket. The scalpel was in his hand.

"Don't do this, Art. Just come with me."

"You think I abused my child."

"I don't know," Kat said. "But I need to talk to you about that. Not here. Alone. Where you can be honest."

Art looked down at the corpse beside him. A tiny flame of pride ignited in his eyes as he admired the handiwork.

"My son did that," he said. "He's so much better at it than I ever was."

He raised the scalpel, prompting another scream from somewhere in the back of the viewing room. He placed the scalpel against his neck, blade perilously close to slicing his flesh.

"Put the scalpel down," Kat said, pleading. "Please don't do this."

"You think I'm a bad person," Art said.

When he spoke, the scalpel blade bit into his skin slightly. The result was a tiny smear of blood at his neck. It was a bright red, like a lipstick mark left by a secret lover.

"I think you need to leave everyone here alone and come with me."

Art made no attempt to move. "You think I killed them, don't you? George and Troy? You think I had something to do with their deaths."

"I don't know. Did you?"

"I think I did," he said. "I really think I did."

He increased the pressure on the scalpel until it sank into his neck. A thin line of blood leaked from the wound, rolling onto his knuckles and staining his hands. Then, assured that the blade was in deep enough, Arthur McNeil swiped the scalpel across his throat.

# OCTOBER

# TWENTY-SEVEN

The first drops of rain hit Nick's windshield as soon as he left Philadelphia. By the time he reached Perry Hollow, he found himself in a downpour. The drumming of the rain on the car roof was so loud it drowned out the Beatles song he was listening to: "Here Comes the Sun."

The irony wasn't lost on Nick as he drove down Main Street. It was Friday, and what should have been a perfect autumn evening was marred by the storm. The rain pelted the decorations that had been put up for the next day's Halloween festival. It soaked the orange lights and black bunting over the storefronts. The pumpkins that sat on nearly every doorstep were now slick with it. And the wind that accompanied the storm rustled the pots of mums in front of Big Joe's and skewed the ragged scarecrows standing outside Awesome Blossoms.

Standing in the deluge was Jasper Fox, trying to keep the scarecrows upright. Seeing Nick, he gave an exasperated wave. Nick returned the gesture. In the past four months, he had become well acquainted with many of Perry Hollow's residents. Spending as much time as he did there had bred a certain degree of familiarity, which became more apparent after each visit.

In the Shop and Save parking lot, for example, he spotted Carl Bauersox. They sprinted through the rain together, taking shelter beneath the wide awning that hung over the front door.

"Back again?" the deputy asked, talking loudly to be heard over the rain. "You can't seem to stay away."

"You could say that," Nick said.

Since July he had spent every other weekend in Perry Hollow. When people asked about his frequent visits, Nick told them he found the town quaint. That much was true. Perry Hollow's charms had grown on him. And that's what he told Carl as they parted ways inside the store. The real reason, however, was simple to understand but difficult to explain: he couldn't let go of the case. Just not yet. Too much uncertainty surrounded the events of July, and Arthur McNeil's confession was anything but conclusive.

A search of the funeral home after his suicide turned up nothing unusual. No dead animals stuffed with sawdust. No trace of the two other portable fax machines that had been purchased back in February. Even the formaldehyde was all accounted for, with purchase records provided by Bob McNeil to back it up.

Plus, Art didn't fit Cassie's profile. He was far older than most serial killers and much weaker. If he was the Grim Reaper, then he had help. But who was it? His son? Lucas Hatcher? The elusive Meg Parrier, who didn't seem to exist yet managed to activate fax numbers and rent post office boxes?

Then there were the more practical questions. How did he do it? And why? Those led to dead ends that had frustrated Nick for months.

The killer was smart enough to make sure no footprints, fingerprints, or transfer were left at the crime scene or on his victims. Yet he purposefully placed animals filled with sawdust at the abduction sites. And the Grim Reaper brazenly left the portable fax machines on Henry Goll's doorstep but had made sure there'd be no way to trace them back to him. He knew how to embalm corpses, knowing there was no way they could find out when he had picked up that particular skill.

Each trip to Perry Hollow was spent doing as much investigating as he could. He pored over police records, looking for something he might have missed. He went to the locations where the bodies were found, interviewed anyone willing to talk. His collection of newspaper clippings and handwritten notes had grown so large that they now crept across a second wall at the good old Sleepy Hollow Inn.

Nick knew it all made sense—somehow. He just needed to put it together in the right way. And when he did, it would become clear that either Art McNeil had indeed been the killer or that it was the work of someone else. Someone still out there.

That's why he kept investigating, even after the other members of the task force went their separate ways. Cassie Lieberfarb started her own private practice. Tony Vasquez was enjoying a recent promotion. And Rudy Taylor had joined the FBI, where he was no doubt the butt of many short jokes. Nick was now alone in his quest. And until he had all the answers, he intended to keep visiting Perry Hollow.

Inside the grocery store, Nick did his shopping in a hurry. He had promised to make lasagna for Kat and James. That meant grabbing the rest of his ingredients in a quick sweep of the store. Noodles. Cheese. Ground beef. Sauce.

At the checkout counter, the rain lashed the store's front windows. Through the streaked glass, Nick saw that the sky had darkened considerably since he first arrived. Zigzags of lightning occasionally cut through the gloom, bringing with it another roar of thunder. One boom was so loud it shook the floor beneath his feet.

"That was a close one," he said to the cashier, an amiable

woman named Pearl who seemed to be working every Friday evening.

"I hope it goes the hell away," she said. "This is a summer storm, only it's not summer. Something weird is happening out there."

Beyond the window, the gusts grew stronger. Trees in the distance were bent at unnatural angles, and a rogue shopping cart did pirouettes through the parking lot.

"I wouldn't worry," the man behind Nick said. "It's just remnants of that hurricane that hit North Carolina the other day. We should see some wind damage, maybe a little flash flooding."

Pearl puckered her lips in distaste. "That doesn't make me feel better."

The man chuckled. "I did the best I could. Right, Lieutenant?"

Lifting his grocery bags, Nick turned to see that it was Caleb Fisher standing behind him. He hadn't changed a bit—still large, friendly, strong.

"I'm surprised you remember me," Nick said.

"I'll never be able to forget. It's not every day that the state police comes to your door."

"Probably not."

Pearl eavesdropped on their conversation as she rang up Caleb's sole item: a roll of plumber's tape.

"Expecting a leaky roof?" Nick asked.

"Closing the house up for winter. I'll be heading back to Philadelphia after the weekend."

Caleb paid Pearl, wished her a safe drive home, and followed Nick out of the store. Beneath the overhang, both men surveyed the virtual monsoon falling over the parking lot. Every few seconds brought another flash of lightning and a gust of wind, although the shopping cart had finished its ballet and sat overturned next to a utility pole at the parking lot's entrance.

"I guess I need to make a run for it," Nick said.

Caleb raised an umbrella. "I'd be happy to share."

Under the shelter of the umbrella, they trudged to their vehicles, which luckily were parked next to each other. Nick tossed his bags in the trunk and extended a hand.

"Thanks for the assistance," he said.

A bolt of lightning cut him off. It streaked directly from the sky to the utility pole, striking the transformer on top of it. The contact first created a boom so loud it was like cannon fire. Next came a spray of sparks, shooting out of the transformer.

Nick averted his eyes, looking instead at Caleb Fisher's pickup truck. When the transformer exploded—as he knew it would—the flash brightened the sky, casting a blinding white glow on the rain-soaked asphalt. It was so bright, it allowed Nick to clearly see inside the truck.

And there, sitting discreetly on the passenger seat, was a pair of gloves, a white handkerchief, and enough rope to tie a man down.

Henry held the phone close to his ear, straining to hear the voice on the other line. Because his office was located directly under the eaves, even the smallest storms sounded loud there. But the downpour currently beating the roof was another story entirely. It was so loud and incessant that Henry felt like he was inside a snare drum.

"I'm sorry," he said. "I'm having a hard time hearing you."

Deana tried again, all but shouting into the phone. "I asked you where you were taking me tomorrow night."

She didn't normally call Henry at the office. After months of dating, she had learned he preferred to work in peace. When they did talk during work hours, it was because their jobs necessitated it, and even then they kept it mostly businesslike. But a special occasion was coming up, so Henry didn't mind the intrusion.

"I haven't given it much thought. I was thinking the Perry Hollow Diner."

"That's perfect," Deana said, voice thick with sarcasm. "I want nothing more than to celebrate my birthday at a diner."

In truth, Henry had reserved a table for two at Maison D'Avignon, the French restaurant that had spurred Perry Hollow's rebirth. After that, the two of them would move to the restaurant's balcony for their own private view of the Halloween parade. Henry knew she would love the entire night. He just wanted it to be a surprise.

But Deana wasn't giving up. "Seriously. Where are we going?"

"You'll have to wait until tomorrow night."

"Six o'clock, right?"

"On the dot. That is, if this rain ever lets up."

"Even if it doesn't, we're still going," Deana said. "I don't care if an ark is needed. We're going out on my birthday."

That was Henry's cue to end the call. "I guess I should hang up and check the phone book for ark rentals."

In reality, he needed to get to Awesome Blossoms and order flowers for the next day before the store closed. Only he wanted that to be a surprise, too. Deana made him appreciate life's little surprises. After all, she was one of them.

Despite their passionate night together, both of them agreed they needed to take things slowly. At least Henry needed to, and Deana grudgingly went along with it. He still thought of Gia often, although not as much as before, and the nightmare haunted him with less frequency. That, he guessed, was progress.

The only person not making progress was Deana's brother. Martin Swan still frowned upon the relationship, and he rebuffed every attempt Deana made to include him in their plans.

When Henry bumped into him at the *Gazette,* Martin acted like he was a stranger, not the person dating his sister.

To his credit, Martin never told Deana about Henry's past. Henry assumed it was for Deana's sake. But the threat remained, which Henry remembered every time he saw Martin at work.

On their last date, Deana had asked him if their relationship would ever progress into something more permanent. Henry couldn't answer. He had no expectations for the future. If he had learned anything in the past five years, it was that fate didn't give a damn about your expectations. Still, he was grateful for the time spent with Deana. And he wanted to thank her for teaching him that, hence the birthday dinner and the flowers.

Checking his watch, Henry saw it was almost six. Awesome Blossoms closed at six thirty, which didn't give him much time to pick out a bouquet. He had no choice but to leave work early.

Not that any late obituaries would show up in his absence. Business had slowed considerably for McNeil Funeral Home ever since its owner killed himself during a viewing. Bob McNeil was now running the show, with increased help from Deana. But most of Perry Hollow's bereaved now looked out of town for their mortuary needs. They didn't want to risk something similarly gruesome happening on their dime.

Just as he was heading for the door, Henry heard the fax machine start up, proving him wrong about a late obituary. At least he knew it wasn't from Deana. She would have given him a heads-up. That meant it was from one of McNeil's new rivals, who offered Henry no such courtesy.

Sighing, he plopped back down at his desk and waited for the transmission to finish. When it did, he grabbed the obituary and took a look.

As rain pounded the roof and thunder shook the building, Henry saw a name, a time, a date. And just as he realized what it all meant, the lights went out in his office, his building, and the entire town of Perry Hollow.

James was trying on his Halloween costume when the power went out. The costume itself wasn't difficult—just a white sheet with two holes for eyes and one for the mouth—but the trickle of dim light that came from the office window left him struggling.

"I can't see," he said, trying to align the holes cut into the sheet with his eyes. "What happened to the lights?"

Kat called out to Lou van Sickle, who was at her post down the hall. "Are the lights out where you are?"

"Yes," Lou yelled back. "And the phones are dead, too."

Kat tried her own phone and heard silence in place of a dial tone. James, meanwhile, continued to writhe under the sheet. The eyeholes were now at the side of his head, somewhere near his right ear.

"Let me help," Kat said, yanking the sheet. The movement caught James off guard, and he stumbled blindly toward her desk.

"I don't like this," he said.

Kat wasn't sure if James meant the costume or being stuck in her office for the afternoon. Not that it mattered. She couldn't do anything to change either.

The office situation was their normal Friday night routine now that Amber Lefferts was out of the picture. Troy's death had hit her hard, and she no longer wanted to babysit James. That meant James had to spend many of his after-school hours with Kat at the police station or at Lou van Sickle's house when Kat was busy.

As for James's ghost costume, well, it was mandatory. Everyone from his school would be draped in similar white sheets for the parade that kicked off the Halloween Festival. All students were welcome to march in the parade, provided they all wore the same easy but standard disguise. Kat didn't fully understand the rationale behind the decision—something about preventing some kids from upstaging others with elaborate costumes—but since it only cost her an old sheet, she didn't care. Plus, in the five years since it started, the March of the Ghosts, as it was called, had become the most popular part of the parade.

That the festival was taking place at all was something of a small miracle. After Troy's murder and Art's suicide, Kat wondered if Perry Hollow would ever fully recover. But as the weeks passed and residents emerged from their shocked numbness, it was generally acknowledged that the town had to put on a brave face, even if everything wasn't back to normal.

An uptick in visitors had a lot to do with that. What Perry Hollow lost in normalcy, it gained in notoriety. People flocked to the town more than ever before, eager to visit the site of such heinous acts. Stores along Main Street accepted them anyway. At least, they accepted their money. And since it had been a bad year for business, the Halloween Festival was the town's last chance to make a profit by wringing more cash out of the morbidly curious. Because of that, it had to go on.

If the storm ever stopped. When Nick arrived, he was soaked to the skin, looking to Kat like he had just showered with his clothes on.

"Lightning just struck a transformer outside the Shop and Save."

By that point in their friendship, Nick no longer bothered with actual greetings. He was in Kat's office so much that it sometimes felt like he was another one of her deputies. When he wasn't at the station or getting much-needed rest at the Sleepy Hollow Inn, he was at her house, cooking dinner, entertaining James, and watching whatever DVD Kat had picked out.

At the station, Lou and Carl ribbed her about the frequent

visits. Lou even went so far as to ask Kat if she'd be wearing an engagement ring soon. Other people in town talked, too. In Perry Hollow, gossip was considered a recreational sport, and the current talk was that Chief Campbell was getting cozy with that handsome state police lieutenant.

The rumors and innuendo didn't bother Kat, mostly because she knew they weren't true. She had absolutely no romantic interest in Nick Donnelly, and he showed no signs of attraction to her. And although he used investigating the Grim Reaper killings as an excuse, Kat knew the real reason Nick came to town. Quite simply, he wanted a family. Kat and James were the sister and nephew he could never have.

"How bad is it?" Kat asked.

"Bad. But Carl was already there," Nick said, his shoes squishing on the floor as he crossed the office. "And I saw a truck from the power company arriving as I was leaving."

Kat reached for the windbreaker hanging on her wall. "I should check it out."

"Before you go," Nick said, "we need to talk about our taxidermist friend."

"Caleb Fisher?"

"Yeah. I saw him at the grocery store and looked inside his pickup truck."

"Accidentally or on purpose?"

Nick rolled his eyes. "Accidentally. Sort of. And there was rope, gloves, and a handkerchief inside. Plus, he was buying duct tape at the Shop and Save."

"That's it? Just tape?"

"He said he was preparing to close up the house for the winter. I've never owned a summer home, but I'm not sure why it needs rope and gloves."

"You're being too suspicious," Kat said. "It's not illegal to keep rope in your truck. Or gloves."

"What about the handkerchief?"

Kat slipped into the windbreaker and zipped it to her chin. "We'll talk about it later."

On her way out the door, she stopped at Lou's desk and asked the dispatcher if she could keep an eye on both James and Nick until she returned.

"I'll be back soon. I promise."

"I've heard that one before," Lou said.

Kat moved steadily toward the door. Before opening it, she lifted the windbreaker's hood over her head. Then, taking a deep breath, she pushed through the door and stepped into the storm.

Sprinting across the parking lot, she made it all the way into the Crown Vic before seeing Henry Goll. She had already started the car and was rolling out of the lot when Henry suddenly emerged in the torrent of rain. Seeing him created a bubble of fear that rose in Kat's throat. Henry never visited unless he had a reason.

And on that evening, his reason for being there was a soggy piece of paper gripped in his hand. Kat rolled down her window as Henry approached and thrust the sheet at her.

"It's another one," he said.

Despite the page's sodden state, Kat clearly saw the lone sentence typed across it.

*Amber Lefferts, 16, of Perry Hollow, Pa., died at 6:30 P.M. on October 30.*

# TWENTY-EIGHT

Heart hammering in her chest, Kat again looked at Amber's name. Then she looked at the clock on the dashboard. It was ten after six. If she wanted to save Amber's life, she needed to hurry.

Flicking on the Crown Vic's siren, she started to pull away. Henry trotted beside the car, waiting for instructions.

"Nick is inside," Kat said. "Tell him what's going on. And hurry."

"Where are you going?"

Kat picked up speed, shaking Henry's pursuit. She yelled her destination out the open window.

"Amber's house. I can't let this happen again."

She was on her cell phone before she was even out of the parking lot. Steering with one hand, she dialed with the other. The result was a right turn so tight the Crown Vic scraped a fire hydrant on the way around the curb. Kat didn't care. She needed to reach Amber immediately.

Once around the corner, she increased the car's speed as the phone rang once.

"Pick up, Amber," Kat muttered as it rang a second time. "Please pick up."

She cut a sharp left and bumped down a narrow alley. For the sake of time, she wanted to avoid the town's main streets. Even though they were far from clogged, the rain made for slow driving, especially during a power outage.

The phone rang a third time, its buzz cut short as Amber Lefferts finally answered.

"Chief Campbell? Is that you?"

Kat answered with a question of her own. "Where are you?"

"Home. Although the power is out."

"It's out everywhere. Are you alone?"

Amber paused, an uneasy silence that made Kat clutch both the phone and steering wheel with worry.

"Amber?" she said. "Are you alone?"

The girl's response was a whisper. "I don't know."

"What do you mean?"

"Someone was just at the house," Amber said. "They rang the doorbell and left something on the doorstep."

"What did they leave?"

"A bird."

The answer made Kat's already racing heart speed up a few beats.

"It was dead," Amber continued. "Why would someone do that?"

Kat was speeding down a side street now. Up ahead, a Cadillac idled at the curb. Its brake lights flared a moment as the Caddy started to pull out in front of her. Kat punched the gas pedal to the floor, trying to speed past.

She almost made it.

The Cadillac edged into the street as Kat flew by. And although the vehicles themselves missed each other, their side mirrors did not. The force of the collision slammed the mirror on the Crown Vic against the passenger side window. The Caddy's twisted downward and dangled against the door.

Turning left again, Kat kept moving. She had to. Stopping was not an option.

"Are the doors locked?" she asked Amber.

"No."

"Do it now. Lock, deadbolt, and chain."

"Why?" Amber asked. "What's going on?"

Kat barked into the phone. "Just do it! And don't unlock it until I get there."

"Why are you coming—"

Amber let the rest of the question remain unspoken. Kat did the same with the answer. Instead, she listened to a series of snaps, creaks, and jangles as the girl locked the front door. Finally, she said, "It's him, isn't it? The same person who killed Troy."

"You're safe inside," Kat said. "That's all that matters."

She glanced at the speedometer. She was going fifty-five. She jacked up the speed, pushing sixty as she reached Main Street. The Crown Vic shot through traffic, crossing the thoroughfare at bullet speed. Vehicles in both directions came to a skidding, screeching halt. Her car clipped the rear bumper of a Volkswagen that couldn't get out of the way. The bumper tore off as the Volkswagen slid into the path of an SUV heading north.

Kat heard the collision—a symphony of shattering glass and metal scraping against metal—but didn't look back. She kept her eyes fixed on the road.

On the phone, Amber began to weep. Kat heard the girl's choked breathing and muffled sobs. "I don't want to die," she said. "Please don't let me die."

"Nothing is going to happen to you," Kat said. "I'm almost there. I'm a block away."

She peered out the window, squinting to try to see past the rain and windshield wipers and darkness. The Lefferts' house edged into view. Dark, just like every other home on the block.

"I'm here," she said. "Just hold tight until I get inside."

"Hurry," Amber said. "Please hurry."

Then she screamed.

"Amber? Tell me what's going on?"

The girl's response bordered on the hysterical, high-pitched and unintelligible. Kat could make out one word—*bird*.

"A bird?"

"I just found another one," Amber cried.

"Where? On the porch again?"

"No," Amber said. "Inside. It's *inside* the house."

Kat brought the Crown Vic to a screeching halt in front of the Lefferts' residence. Instead of parking at the curb, she steered the car over it, across the sidewalk and into the yard. Kat leaped from the car and bolted across the lawn. The phone was still gripped in her hand. Amber's terrified voice blasted out of it.

"There's more of them in the hallway. Oh God, they're everywhere!"

Halfway across the lawn, Kat dropped the phone, grabbed her Glock, and shouted directly at the house. "I'm coming, Amber! Get out of the house!"

She hit the porch at full speed, not stopping until she collided with the front door. At her feet was the dead bird Amber had mentioned. A cardinal, it had been stuffed so full that it looked like it had swallowed a baseball. When Kat kicked it aside, sawdust spilled from its abdomen.

"Amber?" She tried the door. It was still locked. "Are you in there?"

Kat didn't move. She didn't speak. She didn't breathe. Pressed tight against the door, she searched for the slightest noise from inside the house. It came a moment later.

"I'm here!" Amber yelled on the other side. "I'm still here!"

"The door is locked!" Kat yelled back. "I need you to open it!"

Through the barrier of the door, she heard Amber's frantic footsteps in the hallway. They were followed by a sharp click. It was the lock, sliding loose. Next was a louder, stronger click. The deadbolt.

The door opened a crack. Amber was just on the other side, pressing her face in the gap between door and frame. Her cheeks were streaked with tears and her body vibrated with fear.

"Thank God you're here," she said. "I think he's inside."

She gasped suddenly, her eyes widening in shock. And then, so quickly that Kat could barely comprehend what was going on, Amber Lefferts was yanked backward and out of sight.

Kat shoved the door. It opened another inch before coming to a jarring stop. The chain. It was still in place.

On the other side of the door, Amber screamed. It echoed from deep inside the house before quickly, eerily cutting off. The interrupted cry told Kat everything she needed to know.

The killer was inside.

And he had Amber.

Shoving the door open as far as the chain would allow, Kat shouted, "I'm coming! Don't worry!"

There was no response from Amber. Not even another scream. Rearing back on the porch, Kat rammed into the door, shoulder-first. She felt a momentary queasiness as pain pulsed through her body. Then the chain snapped free, letting the door fly open and smash against the wall behind it.

"Amber?" Kat yelled. "Where are you?"

The power came back on as soon as she entered the house. All the lights suddenly sprang into brightness, forcing Kat to squint. That's when she saw the birds. There were four of them, jumbled together in a heap on the hallway floor.

"Amber? Answer if you can hear me!"

In the kitchen, the back door slammed shut. Kat raced toward it.

She stepped on a bird in the hallway. Her feet slid forward, jerking her legs out from under her. When Kat fell, the birds on the floor cushioned the blow. Lumpy balls of feathers, sawdust, and bone crushed under her spine.

Kat pushed herself off the floor and ran to the kitchen,

not stopping until she reached the back door. Flinging it open, she scanned the back porch, seeing nothing. Beyond it was the backyard, a neighbor's house, and the street, where a white van idled at the curb.

Kat had seen the van before. The white Ford with the words Awesome Blossoms painted across its side had eluded her for the better part of a year. It was Jasper Fox's stolen delivery van, and now it sat just beyond the Lefferts' backyard.

Before she was able to piece together why the van was there, it jerked to a start. Kat took off across the lawn after it, but it was too late. The van roared away from the curb, moving so fast she couldn't get a glimpse of the driver through the rain-soaked windshield.

The killer was behind the wheel. Kat had no doubt about that. And Amber was inside the van, possibly dead already, being driven to a place where a homemade coffin waited just for her.

# TWENTY-NINE

Henry rode shotgun with Nick. Because Kat had left too fast for them to keep up, they found the Lefferts' residence by following the collateral damage left in her wake. A scrape of white paint on a fire hydrant guided them north. They turned left at the Cadillac askew in the road, missing a side mirror. The debris was worse on Main Street, where an SUV had collided with a Volkwagen. Three blocks later Henry spotted Kat's patrol car sitting in the Lefferts' front yard, still running.

Nick screeched to a stop at the curb on the other side of the street. Henry hopped out of the car and was immediately pummeled by the rain. It fell in huge, cold drops that stung when they hit his skin. Blinded by the deluge, he stumbled into the street.

He was halfway across when a white van appeared, careening around the corner. Caught in the van's path, Henry froze. It bore down on him quickly, its grille a sneering mouth, its headlights as bright as dragon's eyes.

"Henry, watch out!"

He heard a series of splashes on the asphalt, heavy and fast. Footsteps. A blur of darkness burst into view, coming from Henry's right. It was Nick, sprinting toward him. The lieutenant tackled him, knocking the breath out of his lungs as they both tumbled into a puddle on the asphalt. Hot air, exhaust fumes, and a spray of oily water rushed over them as the van roared by, missing Henry by inches.

Nick wasn't so lucky.

Scrambling to push Henry out of harm's way, his right leg jutted into the street. The van's tires bumped over it. It then increased its speed and shot through a stop sign at the end of the block.

In the road, Nick howled with pain. Struggling to sit up, he grabbed at his injured leg. His pants were torn at the knee, the shredded fabric revealing oozing blood littered with gravel and dirt.

More yells came from Amber's house, where Henry saw Kat burst onto the porch.

"He has Amber!" she shouted as she ran to her car.

"We can't lose it."

It was Nick answering her, pushing himself off the ground with an agonized grunt.

Henry helped him stand, Nick putting all his weight on his uninjured leg. He wasn't able to walk, so he lurched instead, dragging himself toward the car.

"We need to follow that van," he said through gritted teeth. Although he seemed to be on the verge of passing out, he didn't stop moving. He made it all the way to the car, every step causing a high-pitched wail.

"Henry," he said, gasping. "You need to drive."

Nick shoved him toward the driver's side door. Within seconds, Henry was behind the wheel, strapping the seat belt across his chest. Nick sat beside him, body shaking, as water slid off his flushed face.

"Step on it," he said.

Henry hadn't been behind the wheel of a car in five years. Not since that terrible night. But as soon as he gripped the steering wheel, it all came back to him. Shifting the car into gear, he did what Nick had instructed.

In the rearview mirror, he saw Kat jump into her patrol car. She fishtailed in the soggy lawn, struggling to get traction. Henry had no such problem. The car careened down the street, leaving Kat behind.

Blasting down the street, Henry had one thing on his mind—catching up with the van. The quickly descending nightfall made it difficult to see. So did the rain, which overwhelmed the wipers working at high speed.

"I don't see it," Henry said.

Nick seemed to have settled into his pain. His body trembled less as he craned his neck to search every side street they barreled past. He spoke in ragged breaths, forcing every word out of his mouth.

"Where were Troy and George found?"

"Old Mill Road and the lake, which is near it."

"Go there."

Henry steered the car through back alleys until they were at Oak Street.

"There it is!" Nick gripped Henry's arm. "To the left!"

Henry cut the wheel sharply to the left. The van was now just ahead of them, moving quickly northward. They followed it, rumbling past the cemetery.

Not slowing, the van suddenly swiped to the right, tires jumping the curb as it turned onto a side road. Henry followed suit, taking the corner tight. The car skidded on the wet pavement, and for a moment he thought they might spin out of control. But he corrected the steering, held the car steady, and they rounded the turn unscathed.

The van next made a sudden left. Henry did, too, fanning out widely to avoid an oncoming Jeep. When the van veered right one more time, Henry stayed on its tail, realizing they were now on Old Mill Road, the vast expanse of Lake Squall to their left.

The road was wider and smoother than the ones in the heart of town, allowing the van to pick up speed. Henry kept his foot pressed on the gas. The car shimmied as the engine opened up. He peeked at the speedometer. Seventy and rising.

Henry realized he had been going that fast the last time he drove a car. He tried not to think about it. He needed to focus on the van and not the past. But memories snuck in, coming at him in quick, blinding flashes. The rain. The speedometer inching forward. The jackknifed truck getting closer. Gia's screams.

*"Christ, Henry, look out!"*

At first, Henry thought it was his memory, sounding as loud as the present in his ears. Then he realized it was Nick, shouting in the here and now.

Henry's gaze shot to the road in front of them, seeing what Nick was yelling about. A deer stood on spindly legs just beyond the road's shoulder. Startled by the noise of the chase, it jumped out of the brush and into the van's path.

The van's brake lights flared and its tires screeched as the vehicle fishtailed. It did no good. The deer was in midleap, arched across the road as the van barreled forward. One second later, the inevitable happened—the van and the deer collided.

To Henry, everything unfolded in slow motion. When he hit the brakes, the uncontrollable skidding of the car seemed to wind down to a crawl, the seconds expanding into minutes. He saw the van lose control, the deer pinwheeling away from its shattered grille as the van veered off the road.

The van bounced down an embankment, three endless leaps in which the vehicle seemed unencumbered by gravity. It tipped onto its side in the weeds next to the lake. The van's back doors had been forced open, revealing spikes of shattered pine.

A homemade coffin. Overturned, it spilled out its contents, which in this case was a young girl, lifeless and still.

Henry turned his head forward again, facing the road, where the mangled deer, thriving on momentum, rolled toward them.

Time seemed to right itself when the animal connected with the windshield. Henry experienced a breathless speediness as the deer smashed into the glass. The windshield cracked as the animal's body fell away. It slipped off the hood, tumbling under them, lodging itself between the road and the front wheels.

The tires locked, bringing the car to a gut-tugging halt. The back of the vehicle kept on going, whipping it around until it faced the opposite direction.

Henry stomped on the brakes, which did nothing to stop them. The car spun wildly, smashing into a telephone pole before bouncing away like a pinball and shooting across the road. Henry closed his eyes, feeling bits of glass from the freshly shattered window bounce off his eyelids.

When he opened them again, the world was upside down. Earth and sky seemed to switch places briefly before returning to their normal positions. Then they reversed a second time, a sickening roll of horizons that happened again and again.

Henry had heard Nick screaming when the flipping began, but now he was silent and motionless, a limp rag doll being tossed by gravity. When they did another turnaround, Henry saw they were fast approaching a copse of pine trees. The car rolled into them, tires first, as if it could drive right up their trunks.

But it couldn't. The car tilted back violently. It rocked a moment before flipping onto the roof and staying that way.

Henry's seat belt snapped. He fell forward, smacking against the dashboard that no longer resembled a dashboard. Eyes closed, he was vaguely aware of Nick dangling upside down above him, held captive by his unbroken seat belt.

He heard the car's engine, clicking to a weary stop. The automotive equivalent of a death rattle.

Henry, too, began to wind down. His head hurt. His limbs felt heavy. His ears stopped hearing. Then, giving in to darkness and pain, he passed out.

# THIRTY

Nick hurt so bad he wanted to puke. The pain was in his chest. His head. His back. But he felt it most in his right leg, which was like a fist continually punching.

When he opened his eyes, he saw nothing but clouds. Dark, unruly ones that rolled across his field of vision.

Then a figure emerged from them, obscured by their grayness. It was a girl. Moving toward him, she stopped a few feet away. Her long, dark hair was parted in the center, an open curtain revealing tear-filled eyes, pale skin, and a sad smile.

It had been ages since Nick last saw her. Decades since she had waved to him as she left for work at the drugstore. But there she was, standing before him, smiling and crying at the same time.

Nick spoke her name. "Sarah."

"Nick?" she said. "Can you hear me?"

The pain made it difficult to nod, but somehow he managed.

"Yes," he murmured. "I can hear you."

"Amber Lefferts survived," Sarah said. "I thought you'd want to know that."

The clouds took over again, churning past Sarah, erasing her features. Her hair drifted away in the swirl. As did her face, her body. In their place was someone else Nick knew. She was much older than Sarah and taller. But she was still sad, still crying.

Kat Campbell.

"Did you hear me?" she asked.

The clouds evaporated, clearing Nick's vision. He saw gray walls and a white ceiling.

"Where am I?"

His question came out mangled. His mouth was parched.

Kat held a cup of water to his lips, tipping it gently. Nick savored the cool liquid that rushed into his mouth, soothing his throat. He swallowed before again asking, "Where am I?'

"The county hospital," Kat said. "In ICU."

Nick narrowed his eyes, looking down the length of his body. He was in bed, flat on his back. A cast covered his right leg from foot to thigh. It was elevated, held in place by a plastic sling hanging from a pole that had been attached to the bed.

His leg. He remembered how it had been run over in the

street. Pain like that was impossible to forget. Other memories flooded his head. The car. The chase. The deer.

And he remembered the van, running off the road and doing cartwheels next to the lake. Amber Lefferts had been inside, and now she was badly hurt. At least she wasn't dead. If that was the only good news to come out of the whole mess, it was fine by him.

"How bad is she?"

Kat wiped away her tears. "She'll live. But everything is just so—awful."

Covering her mouth to stifle a sob, Kat rushed out of Nick's view. In an instant, others took her place. One of them was Cassie Lieberfarb, who also had tears in her eyes. Rudy Taylor was there, too. And Tony Vasquez. Nick's old team, re-united once again.

None of them spoke, which Nick found odd. They had always been a talkative bunch. But then he saw that someone else was with them—Gloria Ambrose. Even in his pain and confusion, Nick knew her presence spelled trouble. If she had come all that way, then he was in deep shit.

"Lieutenant Donnelly," she said in a clipped voice. "Before we begin, I need to be certain that you can fully comprehend what I'm saying. Can you?"

Nick answered yes, although he had no idea just what it was they were about to start.

Satisfied he was of sound mind and half-sound body, Gloria asked, "Were you the person behind the wheel of your car when today's accident occurred?"

Nick shook his head wearily. "No."

"Was the person driving your car named Henry Goll?"

*Henry.* Kat had said nothing about him. She only mentioned Amber. Worry flooded Nick's body, temporarily erasing the pain.

"Is he okay?" he asked, throat again parched. "Tell me he's all right."

Gloria handed him the cup of water. As Nick gulped, she said, "Mr. Goll is fine. He suffered only minor scrapes and bruises. You bore the brunt of the injuries."

Nick was okay with that. Since Amber was still alive and Henry escaped unscathed, he was happy to be the injured one.

"Did Mr. Goll get behind the wheel of his own accord?"

"No."

"So you're saying Mr. Goll only got behind the wheel because you encouraged him?"

Yes, Nick definitely did that. Driven mad by pain and a desire to stop the killer, he had pushed Henry into the driver's seat and told him to chase the van. Now he was badly hurt, Amber was, too, and the whole situation was coming back to bite him in the ass. Hard.

"This is a serious matter, Nick," Gloria told him, as if he didn't already know that. "There will be an official inquiry into today's events once you're fully healed. Until that time, you are suspended from the state police without pay. Is that understood?"

Loud and clear. So loud that Nick silently begged for the pain to increase, only so it could drown out Gloria's voice. He didn't want to hear any more. It only made him feel worse.

But the pain humming through his body was no match for Gloria's vocal cords. Her voice continued to penetrate his ears, saying, "You also will have nothing to do with the investigation into the Perry Hollow killings. I have officially taken control of it. All Perry Hollow law enforcement officials have been instructed to not speak to you regarding the case."

"Is Kat in trouble?" Nick asked.

"No. I've spoken with her. She knew nothing about your attempt to chase the van. Not getting her tangled up in this is the only smart thing you've done all day."

"And what about Henry? Is he in the clear?"

Knowing Gloria, Nick assumed she thought Henry definitely deserved a legal smackdown. He couldn't let that happen.

"For the record," he said. "I take full responsibility for what happened. Henry had nothing to do with it. He was only following my orders."

Nick was digging his own grave. Not that it mattered. He was already a goner as far as the state police was concerned. The inquiry was just a formality, to make people like Gloria feel important. Since his days at the BCI were clearly over, Nick wanted to spare Henry as much trouble as possible.

"I'll pass that on to the local authorities," Gloria said. "Before I do, I need to ask you a few questions."

Giving a feeble wave, Nick said, "Shoot."

"Did you get a good look at the van's driver?"

Thinking back to the moments before the crash, Nick realized he hadn't. The van had been going too fast and the pain had been too extreme. All he remembered was the van itself and not the person driving it.

"I didn't," he replied. "Did Kat and Henry?"

Gloria's silence was enough of an answer. They hadn't.

"If Amber Lefferts was hurt in the van crash, does that mean the Grim Reaper was, too?" Nick asked.

"You're off this case, Nick. You're no longer privy to such information."

Gloria was playing hardball, punishing him with the thing she knew would hurt the most—an unanswered question. But Nick needed to know. If the Grim Reaper had been caught, it would make things easier for him. He could accept being booted from the BCI if he knew this particular psycho was off the streets.

"Please," he said. His throat grew dry again, as if he had just swallowed a bucket of sand. "I have to know."

Gloria once again helped him take a drink. And when she spoke, her voice was softer. Both the gesture and her tone made it obvious to Nick that she was taking pity on him.

"The van was registered to a flower shop called Awesome Blossoms," she said. "It was stolen back in March. Chief Campbell found it next to the lake about ten minutes after the crash."

She told Nick the first thing Kat did was find out if he and Henry were alive. When she saw that they were, she rushed to the van, where she found Amber Lefferts in the back, unconscious.

"Chief Campbell then looked inside the front of the van," Gloria continued. "Guess what she found?"

Nick managed a shrug. "No idea."

"Nothing," Gloria said. "There was nothing there. In the ten minutes between the crash and Chief Campbell's arrival, whoever was behind the wheel of that van managed to get out and run away."

The hospital's cafeteria was a sad little box painted in shades of mauve and gray. Other than a bored volunteer manning the cash register, Henry was the only person there. He sat by the wall, next to a framed poster of purple wildflowers spreading across a meadow. Henry assumed the picture's intent was to make those who saw it feel better. If so, it wasn't working. He was in the throes of a dark and dangerous mood, and no piece of cheap art could change that.

A cup of lukewarm coffee sat in front of him. Looking like mud, it tasted that way, too. But the caffeine helped. It was just enough to chase the numbness from his limbs and the pain from his joints.

"Nick is awake."

Henry looked up to see Kat leaving the cash register, stirring her own cup of mud.

"How bad is he?"

"He's pretty banged up," she said, taking a seat at Henry's table. "But he'll live."

Henry thought of his own minor injuries. A square of gauze covered a stitched-up cut on his forearm, and his forehead still stung from the antiseptic dabbed onto a small scrape there. Other than that, he was fine. Miraculously so.

Yet Henry felt anything but lucky. He felt downright awful.

"I'll understand," he said, "if you want to press charges. It's only fair."

A girl was badly injured, a state police lieutenant was in intensive care, and a killer was still at large. All because of him. He couldn't blame Kat if she threw the book at him and sent him immediately to jail. He deserved it.

But Kat showed no intention of locking him up. She reached across the table, taking his hands into hers.

"Nick claimed all responsibility for what happened. He made it very clear you were only doing what he told you to do."

"But I was the one behind the wheel," Henry said. "I could have avoided the crash."

"How? It wasn't your fault that deer jumped in front of the van. I know others might disagree with me, but you couldn't have prevented any of this."

Kat was right. Others *would* disagree with her. Henry imagined the rest of Perry Hollow demanding justice for what he had done. People were unforgiving. Experience had taught him that.

"This has happened before," he said.

"What has?"

"What took place today. It happened five years ago, in almost exactly the same way."

In the years since the accident, Henry had never felt

compelled to discuss it. But facing Kat, he felt like he needed to say something. The situation that day had opened up a flood-gate of emotions, and the more he tried to contain them, the faster they flowed. Anger, sadness, regret—all of them gnawed at him.

He began slowly, starting with the basics. "It was during the worst storm I had ever seen."

They had planned to spend the night inside, curled up with pizza and a DVD. But when Henry got home from work, he found Gia restless and irritable. She had cabin fever in a big way. The pregnancy didn't help. It was the tail end of her ninth month, and she was ready to be done with the whole thing.

"I love this baby," she told him, hands supporting her extended stomach, "but I just want it out of me."

So instead of staying indoors that rainy Friday, she had convinced Henry to take her to their favorite Thai place outside the city. The restaurant itself was nothing special, just a plain, family-run joint in the suburbs. But the food was delectable and among the spiciest Henry had ever tasted.

As a reason for going, Gia jokingly mentioned a *Newsweek* article that said eating spicy food was a way to induce labor. Even though she spoke in jest, Henry knew she was secretly hopeful it might work. She was ready to be a mother. He was ready to be a dad.

It was raining when they took Interstate 279 out of the city. The forecast had called for it, so Henry wasn't concerned.

The dinner of extra-spicy pad thai was excellent, as usual. To wash away the heat, Henry drank Singha beer. Four bottles of it. His rationale was that Gia could drive if he couldn't. Being pregnant made her the ideal designated driver.

The rain was still falling when dinner was over, only

harder than before. And Gia said she wasn't feeling well. Heartburn, she said. From the spicy food.

So Henry got behind the wheel. He wasn't drunk. Just pleasantly buzzed. He could drive them home safely if he took it easy and really concentrated.

But merging onto I-279 again, they found themselves in the middle of an unexpected deluge. Nothing in the forecast had prepared them for the harsh conditions. The rain covered the windshield in seconds. When Henry swiped it away with a flick of the wipers, more water arrived to replace it.

He drove cautiously, traveling well below the speed limit. Visibility was next to nothing, but there were no other cars on the road to worry about. All he had to do was drive slowly and stay on the road. If he managed that, everything would be fine.

Then Gia's water broke.

Because he was keeping his eyes on the road, Henry didn't see it. Instead, he heard a hiccup of shock from Gia, followed by a muffled splashing as fluid spilled onto the passenger seat.

"I think it's happening," she said.

Henry remained calm. They had prepared for this. It was a different scenario than the one they expected, but there was no need to lose their cool. They would simply drive to the nearest hospital. But Henry had no idea where that was. They were a half hour from home, with rain blotting out all useful highway signs.

When the first contraction hit, Henry was driving thirty-five miles an hour. By the time the second one arrived, he was going forty. He applied pressure on the gas pedal every time Gia gripped the dashboard and grunted in pain.

"I don't think it wants to stay in," she said, gritting her teeth as another wave of contractions took over.

By then, Henry was pushing fifty and not letting up on the gas. The rain was like a wall in front of them, but he couldn't slow down. The woman he loved was in pain and his first child was about to be born. Slowing down was not an option.

The car was sailing at seventy when a contraction caused Gia so much agony she screamed. Henry took his eyes off the road to see if she was okay. Gia had removed her seat belt to give herself more room. Clutching her stomach with one hand and grabbing the edge of her seat with the other, she stared straight out the windshield.

Her eyes widened in horror.

"Christ, Henry, look out!"

That's when Henry saw the truck. Within seconds, the driver was sprinting into the road. Before he knew it, their car was sliding toward both truck and driver, unstoppable.

The last thing Henry remembered was the airbag deploying an instant before impact. It exploded, like a parachute opening, and engulfed him.

Then, nothing.

Amazingly, Henry didn't shed a tear during his recounting of the accident. He had never spoken about it before. Never intended to. But he always assumed that if he did, it would be through sobs of grief.

They were still present, only not from him. Kat was the one crying, and she continued to weep as Henry resumed the story at the point where he had regained consciousness.

"I woke up three weeks later in the burn unit at Mercy Hospital. They had put me into an induced coma, knowing it was the only way my body would be able to heal itself."

He had emerged from the coma surrounded by a horde of doctors, all gray-faced and serious. They told him about the car catching on fire and burning part of his face. They told him about the chunk of glass that sliced him from ear to lip.

"Then they told me about Gia," Henry said numbly. "She

died upon impact. The baby died with her. The funeral was held a few days after the crash, while I was still unconscious. I closed my eyes and when I opened them again, twenty-one days had passed. My wife was two weeks in the ground, my child was dead before it was even born, and my entire life was gone."

Although Gia's death was the worst of it, there was more trauma to come, playing out while Henry remained a prisoner in the cold, sterile burn unit.

"The truck driver survived," he said. "While I was under, he told police I had been speeding and driving out of control. When I was healthy enough to answer their questions, the police asked me for details of the crash. I told them everything. Mostly."

In his fear and confusion, he had left out the part about the beer. But the police already knew about that. They had talked to the restaurant's owners, who showed them a copy of the bill.

"I thought they would arrest me," he said. "I wanted them to. I deserved it."

But there was no evidence he actually drank all four beers. No proof he had been drunk while driving. The arrest never happened and he eventually healed.

But the scars remained.

In the five years since the accident, Henry had never considered plastic surgery to correct his deformity. He wanted the scars. He needed them. Every time he looked in a mirror, he wanted to be reminded of what he had done and all that he had lost.

# THIRTY-ONE

In the morning, Kat returned to the hospital bearing flowers and two cards handmade by James. The one for Amber boasted flowers scrawled in every conceivable Crayola color. Nick's featured a Magic Marker puppy. Both had glitter.

Amber, surrounded by her bleary-eyed parents, oohed and aahed over both the card and the bouquet. Her mother and father were less touched. They gave Kat the stink-eye as soon as she walked through the door.

It was a look she had grown accustomed to since the previous night. She noticed it everywhere—walking down the street, buying bread at the Shop and Save. Everyone at Awesome Blossoms was so cold to her that she was surprised the store didn't freeze over.

She knew everyone blamed her. Not for the actual crimes, of course, but for failing to stop them.

Amber, on the other hand, didn't seem to blame anyone for what happened to her. It didn't matter that her right eye was swollen shut, her left arm was broken, and two of her ribs were fractured. She knew she was lucky to be alive.

When the requisite small talk about itchy casts and bad hospital food was over, Kat got down to business.

"You know I need to ask you about last night," she said. "Is there anything you remember that might help us identify who tried to kill you?"

"You mean, did I see him?"

Yep. That would do the trick. Just a hint of description

about Amber's attacker would be more than what they presently had.

"Anything," Kat said. "Height. Hair color. Anything you might have seen."

"He came at me from behind. So I didn't get a look at him. The lights were out, so his clothes looked black, but they could have been any color."

"Did he say anything? Make any sort of sound?"

Amber shook her head. "It all happened so fast. And then I passed out."

That was because of the handkerchief doused with chloroform, which was found in the wrecked van. Also inside were a wheeled handcart, which the killer likely used to transport the coffins, and a shattered fax machine with a missing serial number. No doubt used to send Amber's premature death notice.

What they didn't find in the van was the gun that Jasper Fox had kept in the glove compartment. Nor were there any fingerprints, fibers, or blood. That last one amazed Kat. The killer was able to run away from a van wreck and not even bleed. It was the only time in her career that she wished the airbags had failed.

Kat was about to ask if Amber was conscious during the crash, but she was interrupted by Gloria Ambrose, who entered the room with three state troopers. Dressed in matching uniforms, they formed a silent wall behind her.

"I hate to bust in on you like this," she said in the quick, efficient tones of a schoolmarm. "But we can take over from here."

"Why?" Kat asked.

The way Gloria Ambrose explained it, the state police investigators were more accomplished at coaxing accurate information out of traumatized witnesses. But Kat knew the score. After two murders and one near miss, they were taking control of the case.

Kat didn't argue. She didn't even put up a fight. Turf wars weren't her style. If the state's Bureau of Criminal Investigation wanted to take over, she'd let them. Just as long as they caught the Grim Reaper and dragged his ass out of her town and into jail.

Before leaving, she hugged Amber and got more cold looks from her parents. Then it was up to the third floor, where Nick was located.

It was quieter there. Also more empty. The only person Kat saw was a burly man posted at the nurse's station. He sported a buzz cut and a tattooed band around his left bicep.

"Are you family?" he asked Kat when she started to enter Nick's room.

Kat halted, her hand on the door handle. "No. I'm a friend."

"Then you can't go in there."

"Why not?"

"ICU," the man said. "No visitors except for family."

"He doesn't have any family."

The nurse shrugged. "That's not my problem."

Kat stepped closer, hoping her uniform and badge would intimidate him. They didn't.

"What's your name?" she asked.

"Gary."

"Well, Gary. I just wanted to give Lieutenant Donnelly a card my son made for him. Please see that he gets it."

The nurse, who definitely needed to work on his bedside manner, took the card and immediately opened it to read the message James had written inside.

"I'll try," he said. "No guarantees."

On her way out of the hospital, Kat was stopped by Martin Swan, who was on his way in. He carried his ever-present pen

262 | TODD RITTER

and notebook, which were at the ready before Kat had a chance
to make a quick escape.

"Just a few questions, Chief," Martin said, already scrib-
bling. Since she hadn't said a word, Kat assumed he was describ-
ing the way she looked as detail for his article. She imagined him
writing that she looked haggard. Also tired, defeated, and not
allowed to investigate murders that took place in her own town.
Or maybe she was just projecting.

"About what?"

"Were you here to see Amber Lefferts?" he asked.

"I was."

"How'd she look?"

"Like she almost died."

Not catching her sarcasm, Martin jotted down the response.

"In light of last night's events, do you know if the Halloween Festival is still on?"

"I don't know. You'd have to ask the mayor."

"I did. He said it is."

Kat already knew that. She had met with the mayor and
the town council late in the night to discuss the pros and cons
of continuing the Halloween Festival. The main pro, espoused
by the town officials, was that businesses needed the event if
they wanted to break even for the year. Also, many visitors had
already arrived, and most of the vendors had their booths set
up downtown.

The officials had listened politely as Kat shared the only
con—there was a killer on the loose. But, as usual, commerce
won out over safety, and the festival would go on as planned.

"Are you worried about the residents during such a large
event?" Martin asked.

Kat was, but it was out of her hands. She and Carl and a
few sheriff's officers were scheduled to be there for crowd con-

trol. But she had a feeling it would turn into crowd surveillance. If someone started to act suspicious, she wouldn't hesitate to arrest him.

"There's safety in numbers," she said, pushing out the door as Martin scribbled every single word.

From the hospital, it was off to Oak Knoll Cemetery. Although Kat no longer had a role in the investigation, she didn't see the harm in poking around a little. And she knew exactly which person she was going to poke.

Pulling into the cemetery parking lot, Kat saw she wasn't the only person visiting that morning. There were a half-dozen other cars there, all with out-of-state plates. About twenty visitors roamed the graveyard itself. Most of them were in their late teens or early twenties, and many were draped in black. Trudging through the cemetery, Kat saw three girls with pancake makeup and blue streaks in their hair pause at Troy Gunzelman's grave. Two of them smiled in front of it as the third took a picture with her cell phone.

*Vultures,* Kat thought. That's what Perry Hollow had become since the murders began—a perch for vultures. She expected to see more of them later that night, when the festival kicked into high gear. She wasn't looking forward to it.

Lucas Hatcher stood away from the tourists, raking leaves between the graves. He wore his usual uniform—dirt-smeared jeans, dirt-smeared jacket, dirt-smeared gloves. The only new addition to his ensemble was a pair of sunglasses that obscured his eyes.

"What's with the specs, Lucas?" Kat asked as she approached.

The grave digger dropped the rake and leaned on the nearest tombstone. "Just keeping the sun out of my eyes."

Kat lifted her eyes to the sky. It was chilly and overcast, with the sun nowhere to be found.

"I can see just fine," she said. "What's the real reason?"

"Haven't you harassed me enough?" he asked. "I've been keeping my nose clean, just like I told that state police asshole I would."

Lucas was being honest in that regard. The hole he had used to bury people alive had been covered up in July, and the coffin Bob McNeil sold him was destroyed. Every week, Kat sent Carl to the cemetery to make sure he wasn't reopened for business. So far, he wasn't.

"I'm not harassing. I just want to know where you were last night."

"That's none of your business."

But it *was* Kat's business, despite what Gloria Ambrose said. Something terrible was happening in her town, and she had an inkling Lucas had something to do with it. She didn't regret keeping his shady graveyard activities a secret from his parole officer. Nick had promised Lucas they would keep silent, and that promise is what led them to Art McNeil. But the grave digger was up to something, and she wasn't going to wait around for the BCI to figure it out.

"Were you at the Jigsaw again? That's your usual excuse."

"It's not an excuse," Lucas said. "It's the God's honest truth."

"So if I walked over there and asked, I'd be told that you were there?"

"Yup. Just like the last time you thought I was the Grim Reaper."

Kat decided to give up for the time being. She was exhausted, and going around in circles with Lucas Hatcher wasn't making her feel any better.

But as she started to make her way out of the cemetery, she saw Lucas bend down to pick up the rake. The sunglasses slid from his nose and fell off. He tried to catch them, but it was too late. With the glasses gone, Kat could clearly see a gigantic bruise around his left eye, still raw and throbbing.

# THIRTY-TWO

*Christ, Henry, look out!*

Henry had experienced the dream so many times that he knew exactly how it would unfold. First, there would be a scream, followed by the jackknifed truck appearing like an apparition through the rain. Then the driver, sprinting into the road. The car would skid, both truck and driver getting closer. The driver would bounce over the windshield and then—the inevitable.

Only this time, the dream was different. After Gia's scream of warning, her voice grew normal. It lowered in volume and worry, becoming conversational as she turned to give him a bittersweet smile.

"Henry," she said, hands cradling her rounded stomach, "you know I'm not going to survive this."

On the edge of his vision, he saw the faint outlines of the truck emerge through the rain. Henry ignored it.

"I know," he said. "I don't want this to happen."

The truck was fully visible now, stretched across the entire highway. A blur appeared on the side of the road. The truck driver, running in front of them.

"We can't stop it," Gia said. "It's inevitable."

The truck driver hit the windshield. As he bounced up the glass and over the car, Henry kept his eyes locked on Gia. She looked back at him with so much love and tenderness that Henry wished they could remain that way, frozen forever.

A tear stuck to Henry's eyelashes, balancing there until it dropped onto his unblemished cheek. Gia reached out and brushed it away with her hand. Henry leaned in slightly, relishing the way her soft skin felt against his.

Through the windshield smeared with the truck driver's blood, Henry saw the truck getting inexorably closer. It wouldn't be long before impact. Seconds, maybe. The last seconds he would ever spend with his beloved wife.

Another tear fell from Henry's eyes, dripping onto Gia's fingers, rolling over her knuckles.

"I'm going to miss you so much."

"I know you will," Gia said. "You need to say good-bye, and then you need to move on."

The truck loomed large in front of them, a solid wall they couldn't avoid. This was it. This was the end.

Henry grabbed Gia's hand and kissed her palm. "I love you."

They were upon the truck now, mere inches away. Gia was about to be snatched from him forever. Somehow he knew he would never again gaze upon her face, not even in his dreams. Because he knew this, Henry pressed Gia's palm against his lips and held it there.

The car smashed into the truck. Glass rained down upon them as steel twisted around their bodies.

Henry felt Gia's hand pull away from his face. He reached out, catching two of her fingers. Gripping them tightly, he made sure the feel of her was seared into his brain. That way he would never forget her.

Then, only because he had to, Henry let her go.

When he woke up, Henry knew he would never have the dream again. There had been a finality to it that was both freeing and sad. He wondered if he would see his wife again in other, happier dreams. He certainly hoped so.

Standing and stretching, Henry knew what he needed to do next. He had to follow the instructions Gia had given him in the dream. He had to say good-bye.

He shaved and showered quickly. Once dressed, he made a few phone calls to book train tickets and reserve a hotel room in Pittsburgh. He packed. He typed up his resignation letter and delivered it to the publisher of the *Perry Hollow Gazette*.

When all that was taken care of, he walked to Deana's house. The door was unlocked, so he let himself inside. He heard Deana upstairs in her bedroom, preparing for the birthday dinner that would never happen.

"Is someone there?" she called.

Henry started to climb the stairs. "It's me."

He had reached the second floor by the time Deana emerged from her room. Although she was wrapped in a bathrobe, her hair and makeup were perfect.

"You're early," she said. "Or am I running late?"

Her face sank when Henry said, "We need to talk."

Silently, Deana took his hand and led him to the bedroom. Sitting on the edge of her bed, facing the photograph of her shattered family, Henry started to tell her about his own broken life.

"Five years ago, my wife died in a car accident. I was badly hurt. During the time of the crash, she was nine months pregnant. Paramedics couldn't save her or the baby."

Henry waited for a response. It came in the form of a gentle caress at his temples. Deana's silent way of telling him to continue. He did, detailing what happened before, during, and after the crash, leaving nothing out. It was his second confession in as many days.

Once he had finished, Deana leaned on his shoulder and said, "I knew all about that, Henry. My brother told me long ago."

Surprise didn't begin to describe Henry's reaction. Deana had known all this time yet never mentioned it.

"Why didn't you tell me you knew?"

"I didn't see the point." She reached up and stroked his face, her fingers smoothing lightly over the mottled skin at his temples. "We've all done bad things in our lives. All trying to escape our pain. That's why you came to Perry Hollow, isn't it?"

"Yes. I thought I could escape everything. Now I know I can't."

Deana's caresses stopped. Her hand fell away.

"You're leaving, aren't you?"

"I'm sorry," Henry said, nodding slowly. "I have to."

"Will you come back?"

"Hopefully someday. But for now, I need to go back to Pittsburgh."

And once there, he needed to visit Gia's grave for the very first time. It would be hard, he knew. But it was necessary.

"If it's what you need to do," Deana said, "then I support your decision. Just try not to forget about me."

"I won't. I couldn't."

Both of them descended into silence, choosing instead to let their hands do the talking. Deana lightly touched Henry's chest, her fingers running down his stomach. Henry responded in turn, delicately palming her breasts. With rising desire, he rolled on top of her.

"When are you leaving?" she asked.

"Tonight."

"If this is good-bye," she said, "let's make it memorable."

They made love for the last time in her dusk-shrouded bedroom. When it was over, Henry got dressed, kissed her quickly, and departed. As he descended the stairs, he heard Deana rise from the bed. Her footfalls crossed the room. He heard a click as she picked up the phone.

On his way out the door, he heard her speak.

"Henry's leaving town. I hope you're happy."

An hour before the parade's start, Kat paid another visit to the Jigsaw. The place was packed—more crowded than she had ever seen it. None of the regulars were there. Instead, the bar was filled with strangers in costumes, ordering drinks with themed names like the Hallowtini and the Mummy Mohito. It seemed that not even the Jigsaw was immune from the invasion.

Chuck Budman surveyed the crowd from behind the bar. He looked a little chagrined when he spotted Kat, like a kid caught with his hand in the cookie jar.

"Where's your normal crowd?"

"Staying far away from this place," Chuck said. "The upside is that these suckers are making me twice as much money as my regulars."

It was his excuse for turning his normally seedy bar into a happening nightspot, even if it was just for one night. Kat couldn't blame him. Every business on Main Street was doing the same thing.

"Do you think Lucas Hatcher will be in tonight?" she asked.

"Maybe. But I'm not expecting him to. Not after last night."

"What happened last night? Was he here?"

"Unfortunately," Chuck said with a huff. "He started a fight with a tourist. Got himself punched right in the face. I bet he has one hell of a shiner."

Kat knew that he did and that he was now wearing sunglasses to cover it up.

"What time did it happen?"

"Early," Chuck said. "Lucas didn't even have any liquor in him at that point. I guess it was about five thirty."

That was all Kat needed to know. She thanked Chuck and

made her way out of the bar and into Main Street, which was just as crowded. Again, she saw no familiar faces. Everyone strolling Main with their caramel apples and hot cider was an outsider.

Or maybe that was because of the costumes. Everyone was wearing one, kids and adults alike. Kat saw people dressed as witches and devils, pirates and surgeons. The whole crowd was a jumble of pointed black hats and plastic pitchforks. There were about a dozen pirates, all of them sporting eye patches and fake swords. The surgeons were numerous, too, their bodies swimming in sea-blue scrubs, their faces half covered by masks.

Stuck in the crowd, Kat thought about Lucas Hatcher. Once again, he had told her the truth. He was at the Jigsaw the previous night. He even had a black eye to prove it. So much for her theory that the wound was the result of a crashed van, which he had been driving.

In the distance, the sound of a marching band rose in the crisp air. It was the Perry Hollow High School band, warming up for the start of the parade. The crowd on Main Street cheered, enlivened by the rapid beat of the band's percussionists. The devils raised their pitchforks. The pirates lifted their swords. The witches and surgeons clapped.

Kat found herself surrounded by more arriving revelers. They stood behind her and on both sides, boxing her in. Trapped between a witch and a pirate, something occurred to Kat.

The bar fight was at five thirty. Amber was dragged from her house at quarter after six. That left an entire forty-five minutes in which Lucas was unaccounted for.

# THIRTY-THREE

After saying good-bye to Deana, Henry returned to the *Gazette* newsroom one last time to collect the few personal belongings he had there. Sneaking up the back stairs to the third floor, he heard the high school marching band tuning up in the parking lot next door. The parade would be starting soon. When it did, Henry could sneak out unseen by anyone. Considering his nickname, it was an appropriate way to leave.

Inside his office, Henry switched on the lamp at the desk. Although everything looked the same, the room felt different. Soon, nothing there would be his anymore. Not the desk. Not the chair behind it. Not even the operas saved on what had once been his computer. The only items that truly belonged to him were a few reference books on the shelf, a thermos in a bottom desk drawer, and a rarely used sport coat hanging in the corner.

Gathering them in his arms, Henry prepared to leave the office behind. Standing in the center of the room, he rotated slowly, giving the place one long, last look. The room was small. It was dingy. It was barely a step above an attic. Yet Henry had loved working there and would miss it. It was the only thing about the *Gazette* he would miss.

He was halfway out the door when an unmistakable noise rose from the desk.

The fax machine. It was awakening with an agitated hum.

Frozen in the doorway, Henry watched as a single sheet of paper rolled out of the machine.

A now-familiar dread-filled chill ran up his back. Dropping his belongings, he moved to the desk on unsteady legs. He reached out toward the page, his hand cautious and fearful.

Using a thumb and forefinger, he picked up a corner of the page. As he lifted it, Henry closed his eyes. He didn't want to look. He didn't want the responsibility looking would bring.

But he had to. The fax could contain a single name. If so, that person was now marked for death. He had to tell Kat about it. He had to help.

Henry opened his eyes, first the left, then the right. It took a second for them to work in unison. There was a brief blur, followed by the page coming into focus, the words typed across it clear and unmistakable.

When he saw the name printed on the death notice, Henry half gasped, half sobbed. The sound reverberated through the office as he dropped the fax. He heard the echo, the noise sticking in his ears as he sprinted out the door and down the stairs.

Out on the street, he picked up his pace. The sidewalk was packed with costumed revelers, making it hard to move. When the marching band fired up in earnest at the southern end of the street, signaling the beginning of the parade, the crowd surged forward, taking Henry with it.

He elbowed his way out of the cresting wave of humanity, shoving through them. He dodged bystanders, weaved past them, bowled them over.

A young couple pushing a stroller moved into his path. He jumped out of their way, crashing instead into a large man holding a cup of coffee. They blindsided each other, the cup flying, the coffee arching in the air. Henry then reeled into the couple. The stroller flipped, the baby tumbling onto the pavement.

Henry climbed to his feet while the couple gathered the child, cursing at him. Bystanders joined them, shouting at his back. Moving forward, Henry ignored them. Someone dressed in a clown costume tried to stop him by grabbing his shirt. Henry jerked his arm away, the shirt tearing, and continued running.

Propelling himself up Main Street, Henry scanned the crowd, searching frantically for Kat. He strained to catch a view of her uniform, a glimpse of her hair. But it was too crowded. All he saw was a moving tapestry of bobbing heads that filled the sidewalk.

Stopping for a moment, he cupped his hands around his mouth and shouted her name. "Kat!"

The people standing closest to him whirled around, either annoyed, startled, or both. Henry paid them no attention, shouting even louder.

*"Kat!"*

His voice was drowned out by the band, which was now in the street, marching parallel to him. The blare of trumpets mixed with the *rat-a-tat-tat* of snare drums to stifle his calls.

Henry looked across the street. He was tall enough to see over the heads of the people standing at the curb, getting a clear view of the opposite sidewalk. There, enmeshed in the crowd, was Kat Campbell.

A sense of urgency tugged at Henry, pulling him through the crowd lining the sidewalk.

He had to reach Kat.

He had to warn her.

Henry nudged his way to the curb. With no small amount of force, the crowd parted, letting him leap off the sidewalk. He darted into the street, the band marching on, trying to ignore him. He shuffled between flute players and dodged around the drums until he was on the other side of the street, screaming Kat's name, rushing toward her.

When he finally reached her, he gripped her in an urgent embrace.

"I just got another death notice," he said. "It's for James."

All the air evaporated from Kat's lungs when Henry told her the news. She staggered a moment, gripping his arm for support.

"What did it say?" Speaking was a struggle, accomplished only through sheer force of will.

"It had his name," Henry said. "It had today's date."

Kat's mind raced, rolling over a thousand different thoughts and scenarios. What Henry was telling her didn't seem possible. It couldn't be. Things like that happened to other people. To Alma Winnick. To Lisa Gunzelman.

Not to her.

But she knew Henry wasn't lying. His face was flushed and anxious, with a streak of crimson following the path of his scar. She saw fear in his eyes—the dark, quaking fear that overcame people when they encountered something unspeakable.

It was happening, all right. It was happening to her.

"When?" she whispered. "What time did it say he'd die?"

The fear didn't leave Henry's eyes as they roamed up and down Main Street.

"Now," he said. "Right now."

Kat bolted into the street, stumbling into the middle of the parade. The marching band was still there, members of it scattering out of her way. The song they were playing fell apart, a lopsided chorus of sour notes and skipped beats. As the song wound down, Kat raised her voice, screaming her son's name in the middle of Main Street.

"James!"

Behind the band was the March of the Ghosts—dozens of children dressed in exactly the same way. They walked in a hodgepodge of white sheets, some waving, others skipping.

James was among them. At least he was supposed to be.

Kat prayed he was there, secure in his costume, blending in with all the others.

She sprinted into the fray, shrieking his name like a woman possessed.

"James! Where are you?"

She paused, hoping to hear him return her call. When no response came, she reached out to the nearest child and yanked the costume away. It uncovered a young boy who wasn't James, and who was startled to be so suddenly unmasked.

"Do you know James Campbell?" Kat asked him. "Have you seen him?"

She didn't give the boy a chance to reply, moving instead to the next ghost, ripping the sheet away. She continued that way down the street, running against the tide of ghosts, grabbing whomever she could reach. She tugged off their costumes, letting them fall when she saw that the child beneath wasn't her son.

None of them were.

Kat stumbled through the group, panic paralyzing her body. Her arms and legs were weak, no stronger than toothpicks, brittle and ready to snap. Her breath was ragged and unsteady, interrupted by sobs that bubbled up from her chest.

"James!" she yelled. "Talk to me, Little Bear!"

Many of the children had started to scurry away from her, moving up the street as Kat stormed down it. She still grabbed at them, missing some, catching others. She snagged one child by the edge of his costume, jerking him backward until he bumped up against her. When the sheet came off, she saw it was Jeremy, eyeglasses askew on his nose.

Kat dropped to her knees in front of him. "Have you seen James?"

Jeremy shook his head, frightened. She tried to speak calmly.

"Honey, do you know if he's in the parade?"

The boy's response was a shake of the head and a timid murmur. "I don't know."

"When was the last time you saw him?"

"When we were putting our costumes on."

A parade float now ran along beside them. It was a flatbed truck decorated to look like a cemetery, complete with plywood tombstones and zombies tossing candy to the crowd.

Kat grabbed Jeremy's shoulders, shaking him in desperation. "Where was that?"

"Down the street," he said.

"You didn't see him after that?"

Another scared shake of the head. Another "I don't know."

Kat released the boy. She stood. Whirling in the street, she studied the crowd, hoping to see her son tucked somewhere within it. Her despairing gaze ran across the bystanders at the curb, beseeching them for help.

"Has anyone seen my son?" she called. "Please tell me if you've seen him."

She turned to face the other side of the street. The float was still there, proceeding at a crawl, blocking her view. The zombies on board had stopped their dancing and candy tossing. They stared at Kat, perplexed. She stared back, eyes moving from them to the fake cemetery they stood in. She saw the graves, wobbling from the movement of the truck. She saw a gnarled tree made out of cardboard.

And she saw a coffin.

A small rectangle, it sat at the back of the float, resting on a bed of crepe-paper grass. The coffin was made of untreated wood.

Kat had seen that type of coffin before. Twice.

She ran to the edge of the float, reaching out to the people riding it.

"Help me!" she said. "I need to get up there!"

Two of the zombies bent down and, holding Kat by the arms, lifted her onto the float. She moved across it, stumbling slightly as the truck lurched to a stop.

When Kat reached the coffin, she fell in front of it, her palms flattened against the lid. She made no sound as her hands ran over the rough wood. When a splinter of pine sunk into the flesh of her palm, she didn't react. She was too numb to feel it and too weak to make a sound even if she had.

Slowly, she moved her hands to each side of the lid. It had been nailed down in the center and at each corner, just like the other coffins. Kat had become an expert at loosening them, knowing the right places to apply pressure and pull. But when she slid her hands into position, they froze, refusing to move any further.

Kat knew she needed to open the coffin. There was a strong possibility that James was inside, maybe dead. With the Grim Reaper's other victims—Troy Gunzelman, for example— she hadn't been afraid to tear off the lid. But now it was her son she would be exposing. Her only son. Her only source of happiness. That fact left her paralyzed, unable to lift the box's lid.

She thought about what Lisa Gunzelman had said after Troy's death. This was the feeling she was talking about. At that moment, Kat was still a mother, and for all she knew, James was still alive. But if she opened that coffin and found her son lying dead inside, it would all be over. She would instantly be ripped in half, shredded into another person entirely.

Everyone around her had become surreally quiet. The men on the float. The people lined up at the curb. Even the marching band. All of them were mute with fear and anxiety. Kat felt the tension radiating from the crowd. They wanted her to open the coffin. It was brutal human nature. They wanted to see what was inside.

Kat did, too, even if it meant devastating news. Even if it meant that life as she knew it was over.

She held her breath.

She lifted the lid.

She looked inside.

The coffin was empty, a fact that made Kat almost weep with joy. She shoved a hand inside and moved it around, feeling the rough bottom, the interior walls. She had become so convinced James was inside that when it turned out he wasn't, she immediately assumed her eyes were playing tricks on her.

But they weren't. Her son wasn't there. Yet Kat's relief was tempered by a gnawing fear. Because if James wasn't in the coffin—and clearly he wasn't—then where was he?

# THIRTY-FOUR

Henry raced down Main Street, his arms and legs pumping so hard he thought they'd fall off. The parade had come to a complete stop, its participants parting to get out of his way. Those who didn't were bulldozed aside without discrimination.

He shouted James's name as he ran, screaming it until his throat ached from the strain.

"James Campbell! Say something if you can hear me!"

At the bottom of Main Street, Henry spotted the Jigsaw, its neon sign working overtime. He paused beneath it, lungs aching from a breathlessness he hadn't experienced since his ordeal in the cemetery. Getting his bearings, he saw he was at the end of the street. Still no sign of James. Beyond Main, he had no idea where to look. He was about to start north again to make a second pass when he heard a noise coming from just around the corner.

It was a boy. And he was crying.

Henry sprinted around the corner, finding himself on a deserted side street that ran between the Jigsaw and the back of a hardware store. More of an alley than a street, it was lit only by the distant lamps on Main and the residual glow of the bar's neon sign.

James was there, standing alone. His ghost costume had been pushed off his head and was now draped over his shoulders. Tears streaked his face.

"James? What are you doing here?"

It took a second for the boy to register who he was. When recognition hit, he ran toward Henry and wrapped his arms around his legs.

"I got lost," he said, sobbing. "I was waiting for the parade to start. Then someone grabbed me."

Henry's eyes darted back and forth across the alley, searching for signs of anyone else. He detected nothing.

"Who grabbed you?"

James shook his head. He didn't know.

"I couldn't see," he said. "He pulled me here and left me."

"How long ago was this?"

James shrugged. Once again, he didn't know.

"You're safe now," Henry told him. "Let's find your mother. She's worried sick."

They turned toward the street just as someone else rounded the corner and stepped into the alleyway. It was a hulk of a man, cloaked in shadow. Still, Henry recognized him instantly.

Lucas Hatcher.

Henry raced toward him. "Did you bring him here?"

"Him?" Lucas pointed at James. "Never saw him before."

"Don't lie to me," Henry said, circling Lucas warily. "The boy said someone led him here. And there's no one else here but you."

"I don't know what you're talking about," Lucas said. "I just got here. Was heading into the bar when I heard you two talking."

Henry didn't believe him. The grave digger looked as guilty as sin. He was physically capable of doing all the things the Grim Reaper was accused of. With his bulky frame, he certainly could have overpowered George Winnick and Troy Gunzelman. Amber Lefferts had probably been a snap. All he had needed to do was wrap his tree-trunk arms around her waist and yank her from her house.

He scanned the alley again, noticing a narrow passageway running behind the Jigsaw. By day, it was probably used for deliveries and taking out the trash. At night, however, it was a pitch-black corridor. The perfect place to hide—and wait.

"Is that where your van is waiting? Were you going to grab him just like you did George and Troy and Amber?"

Lucas wrinkled his forehead. "What are you talking about?"

"Why did you do it?" Henry asked. "Just tell me why."

"Do what?"

"You killed them. Without remorse, without reason."

"You think I'm the Grim Reaper?"

"I do," Henry said.

"Well, I'm not."

Lucas's denial opened a set of floodgates deep within Henry, letting loose a wave of primal rage. For months, the town had been frozen in terror as more people died. And Henry had been in the middle of it, the unwitting link between the killer and everyone else. Now he wanted to know why.

"Why did you send me those death notices?" he asked,

clenching his fists as he moved toward Lucas. He needed an explanation, and he was prepared to beat it out of him if necessary. "Why did you give me those fax machines?"

This time Lucas didn't back away. He was angry, too. His shifty eyes grew wild, and his face was so flushed it almost hid his massive birthmark.

"I'm not the killer," he yelled. "Most people say you—"

A gunshot cut him off.

It erupted behind Henry's back, coming from the dark corridor by the bar. He felt the bullet whiz past him, stinging hot air that brushed his head before embedding itself into Lucas Hatcher.

The bullet entered above the bridge of his nose, forming a small red dot as it passed through his flesh. The back of his head, however, exploded, raining blood and brains onto the street. Henry felt a dollop of it splatter him as fragments of skull ricocheted off his face.

James screamed when Lucas hit the ground. An earsplitting shriek, it continued as he stared wide-eyed at the corpse, watching blood gush from Lucas's head and wash over Henry's shoes.

Grabbing James's arm, Henry tried to drag him in the direction of Main Street. When James didn't budge, he pulled harder, jerking him out of his horrified trance.

"We need to go. Right now."

Henry heard footsteps behind him, loud and quick on the pavement. Someone jumped onto his back, throwing a hand over his face. Whoever it was held a handkerchief, pressing it against his nose and mouth.

Twisting his body, he tried to buck the person off, without success. The hand kept the handkerchief in place, cutting off all air.

Henry's right arm was pinned at his side. His left grasped

at the person on his back. He managed to push the handkerchief away from his mouth long enough to shout at James.

"Run, James!" he shouted. "Get out of here!"

Then the hand was upon him again, palm spread wide, flattening the handkerchief against his face. Henry gasped, feeling cotton on his tongue. His vision blurred, everything turning a fearsome shade of white.

He shut his eyelids, unable to stop their descent. His head followed, bobbing uncontrollably as a deep, bone-weakening weariness took control.

Kat was still on the float when she heard the gunshot. The noise came from the lower end of Main Street. Hearing it, the crowd erupted into full-blown panic. They pushed into the street, mixing with the halted parade and rushing north.

The float rocked as people shoved past it. Standing unsteadily, Kat surveyed the length of the street, seeing nothing but shouting people and fear-stricken faces. Only one of them was familiar.

It belonged to James.

He was in the middle of the street, oblivious to the surging crowd while he ran north as fast as his little legs could carry him.

Kat jumped off the float and rushed toward him. When they met, she swept him into her arms, lifting him into an embrace tighter and longer than the one she had given him on the day he was born.

"James, honey, where were you?"

Tears of happiness formed at her eyes. Kat decided that instead of holding them back, she'd let them flow. The son she thought was dead was instead alive, safe and sound in her arms. If that wasn't cause for weeping with joy, then she didn't know what was.

Finally, setting James down, Kat saw he was also crying, though not from happiness. Teardrops soaked his face and his body heaved with sobs.

"Are you okay?" she asked, dropping to her knees so she could be at eye level with him. "Are you hurt?"

James gazed up at her, blank-eyed. Kat had seen that look before, in the faces of abuse victims, in the stares of crash victims who had survived while their loved ones hadn't. It was shock, and her son was now stunned by it.

"Little Bear, please tell me what happened."

The shock had left James mute. His mouth opened and closed, but no words came out. Only a horrified murmur—the sound made during nightmares.

He wiped away his tears with one hand. The other was bunched into a fist, which he thrust outward, fingers unfurling. Stuck to his sweat-dampened palm was a strip of paper no larger than a gum wrapper.

"Who gave this to you? Henry?"

When James didn't answer, Kat grabbed the paper and pulled it taut. Handwriting stretched across it, running from one side to the other. The words were cramped, bordering on the illegible. But by holding the paper close to her face, Kat was able to make out what had been scrawled across it.

*Henry Goll, 39, of Perry Hollow, Pa., died at 7:30 P.M. on October 31.*

# THIRTY-FIVE

The painkillers were starting to kick in. Nick knew it from the sense of calm that infiltrated his aching body. It started at his right leg, so restless in its plaster cage, soothing it into numbness. The feeling moved through his torso and chest, extending out to his arms. Soon it was at his neck, rising into his head.

He'd be asleep soon, his pain-riddled body overtaken by a pleasurable numbness, and all the anger and guilt and hurt he felt would be chased away until morning.

Sitting in his lap was the scrapbook of clippings about his sister. It and the rest of Nick's belongings had been salvaged from his wrecked car and placed in his room. When Nick first opened the scrapbook, he found not only the clippings about Sarah but his notes on the Grim Reaper killings as well. The photos and headlines were enough to disturb anyone else, but to Nick they were a balm. He felt better having them with him. It fooled him into thinking he was still part of the investigation.

Gazing at the clippings through drug-glazed eyes, he heard a now-familiar voice outside his door.

"Sorry, ma'am. You can't go in there."

It was Harry—or was it Gary?—the Nazi nurse situated outside his room. Although he had been in and out of consciousness all day, Nick had heard him turn away at least three visitors. Now Harry-Gary was trying to make it four. Only this visitor was putting up a fight.

"This is a life-or-death situation. I have to see him."

"I'm sorry," Harry-Gary said. "The answer is still no."

"I'm with the police and I'm going in there."

A bit of haze emptied out of Nick's brain. Not a lot. Just enough to allow him to recognize that the visitor's voice belonged to Kat Campbell.

"I'm going to get in trouble if you do," Harry-Gary said.

"That's not my problem."

A second later, Kat burst inside. Locking the door behind her, she raced to the bed and gripped Nick's shoulders, shaking him.

"Nick?" she said. "Wake up."

The shaking dislodged more of the drug's effects from his head. Nick estimated half of his brain was working by that point.

"I'm awake," he said. "What's going on? You shouldn't be here."

Kat continued to jostle him awake. "It's the Grim Reaper."

"What about him?"

"He has Henry."

Henry woke up slowly, consciousness seeping into his brain at a glacial pace. Although he was awake, he couldn't open his eyes. That required strength he didn't possess.

Lying in the darkness, he was vaguely aware of motion. It came from beneath him, a subtle rocking that shook his body. He concentrated on it, ears alert to the noises the movement produced. He heard tires humming along pavement and the steady roar of an engine.

He was in a vehicle, being transported somewhere. What that destination was, he had no idea.

Despite now knowing he was in a vehicle, he still felt strange. His surroundings were too small, too enclosed. Something hard pressed against his sides. Too weak to move his arms, he explored with his fingers. They skated along something flat and rough.

Wood, he realized. He was lying on something wooden.

He raised his fingers, running them up and down whatever was against his body. That, too, was wood.

He moaned, the sound of it stopping just above his face and bouncing back toward him. The noise was trapped, just as he was.

He grew tired again. Just that small amount of thinking and moving had sapped his body, leaving him exhausted. Consciousness left his skull, floating away as slowly as it had entered.

Although he was fading fast, he summoned up a thought. It was weak, like everything else about him, pushing intermittently through the haze that filled his skull.

*Where*—

The haze continued to roll in.

*—am*—

It took hold of him, squeezing out the remaining word.

*—I?*

As sleep draped itself over him, he realized where he was. It should have been obvious, but his addled brain prevented him from seeing it until that moment. Now it was clear.

Somehow, for reasons unknown, Henry Goll was once again in a coffin.

Nick inched higher on the bed, barely able to support himself with his elbows. His dilated pupils made it clear he was heavily drugged. Kat hoped he was as alert as he claimed to be, alert enough to help her. Because she desperately needed his help.

"When was he taken?" Nick asked.

"Ten minutes ago."

His eyes drifted to the clock at his bedside. "That means he has about—"

Twenty minutes. Kat knew that. Twenty goddamn minutes to figure out who took him and where.

"How do we figure out where he is?" she said. "Tell me where to start."

"We need to put ourselves in the Grim Reaper's shoes. Remember when I told you how serial killers pick their victims?"

Kat had been terrified to discover a mere glimpse could spur a madman to strike. Now she needed to know where in Perry Hollow those glimpses occurred. If they could do that—which was a very big if—perhaps then they could identify the killer.

"He saw them," she said. "He saw George Winnick and Troy Gunzelman and Amber Lefferts."

And James. She couldn't forget about that, no matter how much she wanted to. Although he was alive, thank God, and now safe at Lou van Sickle's house, she knew the killer had seen him, too. Somewhere. At some point.

"I need to know where he saw them. And why he picked them."

"Let's think through the possibilities. Name all the places in Perry Hollow with heavy traffic."

Nick seemed more awake than when Kat had entered the room, more vibrant. He even managed to sit up, although the movement knocked the photo album that had been in his lap onto the floor.

Kat bent down to retrieve it as she listed the possibilities. "Main Street, obviously. Big Joe's. The diner. The Shop and Save."

She put the scrapbook back onto the bed, its contents spilling across Nick's lap. Kat saw scrawled notes, photographs, and newspaper clippings. She scanned the headlines, all of them from the *Gazette*. There was the one about her finding George

Winnick's body on Old Mill Road, followed by coverage of his funeral.

Beneath it was an article about Art McNeil's suicide during Troy Gunzelman's viewing. It was accompanied by a large photograph of the funeral home, the blue sky highlighting its Victorian architecture.

"McNeil Funeral Home," she murmured.

That was another busy place. It had seen more foot traffic than normal in the past year. So many grisly deaths. So many burials.

"What about the funerals?" Kat asked. "For George and Troy? Do you think the killer could have gone to them?"

"It's possible," Nick said. "Serial killers have been known to enjoy seeing their victims being buried."

Kat thought back to both funerals. Each one had been packed, with practically the entire town turning out to pay their respects.

"I'm not talking about seeing the victims after they died," she said. "I'm thinking the killer saw them there *before* they died."

Nick shook his head, confounded. "I don't understand."

"Alma Winnick's brother died a month before her husband did. She said that at her brother's funeral, George was the first person to sign the condolence book."

"And wasn't Troy Gunzelman a pallbearer at George's funeral?" Nick asked.

"The lead pallbearer."

"I bet he signed the condolence book, too."

"Amber Lefferts did the same at Troy's viewing," Kat added. "I watched her do it."

As she pieced the facts together, a clearer picture began to form.

"That's where it began," she said. "That's where the killer saw them."

If the killer hadn't known who George and Troy were, he could easily have learned their names once they signed the condolence book. Then he most likely watched them. For months. Seeing George work in the barn. Spying on Troy as he went to the gym. Passing the Lefferts' house, where Amber was locked inside. There must have been waiting involved, too. Waiting for the perfect moment to attack. For George, it was at night in the barn, away from his wife. For Troy, it was the Fourth of July, when no one else would be in the locker room. And for Amber, it was when she was home alone.

Only one question remained unanswered, and Nick asked it.

"But who could have gone to all of those funerals?"

Art McNeil had. But he was dead himself, meaning he wasn't the one who abducted Amber and now had Henry. But two other funeral home employees were alive and well.

"Bob McNeil and Deana Swan," Kat said.

She turned her attention to the clippings again, scattering them to search for articles specifically about the funerals. Perhaps one of them contained a list of attendees or a photograph in which mourners were visible.

Sliding them around, she found the infamous GRIM REAPER STRIKES AGAIN headline. Another clipping sat on top of it, obscuring the last two words, so all Kat saw was the GRIM REAPER part. It was so big—and the letters so bold—that she couldn't keep from staring at it.

"What are you looking at?" Nick asked.

Kat raised an index finger to shush him. She then placed the still-extended finger over the headline, covering the first R in *reaper*. The two words merged, forming a new one—M EAPER.

Quickly, she slapped her right hand over the last four letters of the word. Now it spelled M E.

"Sweet Jesus," she muttered. "How did we miss this?"

She began to tear up the headline, creating one piece for

each letter. When she was finished, ten scraps of paper lay on the bed. She rearranged the letters until they spelled out a name— MEG PARRIER.

They had known all along it was a fake. But all of them had failed to see the significance behind it.

Nick read the name with astonishment. "It's an anagram?"

"Yes," Kat said. "For Grim Reaper."

And knowing that was the key to understanding everything else. It was a jolt of realization that left Kat feeling stupid for not seeing it sooner.

"I know," she said. "I know who the killer is."

At some point between bouts of consciousness, Henry had been removed from the coffin. He woke up free of its walls. When he moved his fingers, he still felt wood, but it was now smoother.

Why he was lifted from the coffin, Henry didn't know. His current location also remained a mystery. Had he been able to open his eyes, he could have looked for himself. But each eyelid was still heavy and unwieldy.

Once again, he relied on his other senses, hoping they could tell him where he was and, more important, what was going to happen to him.

His ears no longer detected the sound of a vehicle; nor did Henry experience the insistent motion he felt earlier. He was no longer traveling. He had reached his final destination.

To his right, Henry heard the clomping of shoes on wood. Footsteps. Coming closer.

Soon, someone stood next to him, breathing lightly. Although his own eyes were closed, Henry sensed the other person's probing gaze. It left him feeling exposed and violated. The person was studying him.

Henry tried to speak but discovered it was impossible. His jaws felt rusted shut and just as heavy as his eyelids. His tongue was a parched fish flopping in his mouth. He managed only a meager grunt before giving up.

"You're awake," the person said. "Excellent."

Whoever it was bent over him and placed a length of rope across his chest. It tightened, forcing his arms against his sides. Henry attempted to move them but couldn't. The rope was taut, knotted, unbreakable. The person did the same thing to Henry's waist, then to his legs, binding them together just above the knees.

Henry's heart quickened as panic weaseled into his brain, burning away the haze that lingered there. His mind rolled into action again, his thoughts coming into focus.

*I'm trapped,* was his first thought. It was followed closely by, *I'm about to die.*

Henry's renewed mental capability soon spread to the rest of his body. His strength increased, allowing him to buck uselessly against the wooden flat he lay upon. The rust fell away from his jaws. His tongue stopped flopping. He could speak.

And the word he chose to say was "No."

Some of the weight lifted from his eyelids. Using complete concentration, he was able to open them, the strain causing his lashes to flutter. He pushed on, willing his eyes to open completely.

When they did, he saw a figure wearing surgical scrubs and latex gloves. A mask sheathed his face, covering his nose and mouth. A paper cap covered his head. Wrapped around his waist and chest was a black rubber apron.

Seeing Henry's open eyes, the figure yanked the mask down and gave him a bemused smile.

It was Martin Swan.

"Hello, Henry," he said. "Glad I could catch you before you left town."

# THIRTY-SIX

Kat and Nick made half a dozen calls between them. To Gloria Ambrose. To Tony Vasquez. To the state police and the county sheriff and Carl.

"Go to Martin Swan's house," Kat told her deputy. "Go there now."

It was the same thing she and Nick had told everyone they reached. Carl was the only one to ask questions.

"What about crowd control?" he said. "People are still going crazy down here."

He was talking to her on his cell phone in the middle of Main Street. The confusion in his voice was clear even through the spotty reception and panicked background noise.

"This is more important," Kat said. "Just go. Now."

"You haven't told me why."

"Because Martin Swan is the Grim Reaper."

Kat was certain of it. The proof was spread across Nick's bed. Martin had written about George's and Troy's funerals, which meant he had attended both. Alma Winnick mentioned her brother's funeral had also been in the *Gazette*. Martin covered that one, too.

But more damning than his byline was the nickname he had given the killer in print. Grim Reaper, which when scrambled spelled Meg Parrier. Only Kat had come across that name after George's murder, before the Grim Reaper nickname was coined in the paper. That meant Martin Swan had it in mind long before he made his first kill.

"What about you?" Carl asked. "Where will you be?"

"I'm at the hospital. I'll be there as soon as I can."

When Kat hung up, she caught Nick staring at her.

"You shouldn't go to Martin's house," he said.

"But I have to. He has Henry."

"Then Gloria and the rest will find him there."

There was a distance in his voice, the result of more than just medication. He was still thinking. Kat saw it in his eyes.

"You don't think he's there, do you?"

Nick shook his head. "He needs more seclusion than that. Think of the space required. And the noise it would make. He used a different location."

"Then where?" Desperation had seeped into her voice. The clock was ticking and time was running out for Henry Goll. "Help me figure out where it is."

"I am," Nick said. "Again, we need to think like him and look at the clues."

"He barely left any clues," Kat said, exasperated.

Her entire body twitched, yearning to escape the hospital room and join the others at Martin's house. But Nick insisted on being methodical.

"He left animals at the scene," he said. "What were they stuffed with?"

Kat thought back to Caleb Fisher's basement. He used prefabricated molds on his animals. The ones Martin left behind had been stuffed the old-fashioned way.

"Sawdust."

"Which begs the question why. Why not rags? Or hay? Or paper?"

"Because it was the only thing readily available."

"Very good," Nick said. "But where could he have found that much sawdust lying around?"

Kat remembered examining the squirrel in Troy Gunzelman's locker. She had pushed a finger through the hole in the squirrel's stomach, finding sawdust. But not just any sawdust. It had smelled of pine. The same wood used to build George Winnick's coffin.

She mentally listed everything she knew about the crimes. The homemade coffins, built of plain pine planks. The vehicle Caleb Fisher heard on Squall Lane. The seclusion and space the killer needed to enact such heinous deeds. And now the sawdust.

It all connected, leading Kat to only one possible location.

She gasped. "Henry's at the sawmill."

Henry couldn't summon more than the one word he had previously uttered. His brain produced a torrent of them inside his head, rising and falling in half-completed thoughts. But a disconnect remained between brain and mouth, causing him to repeat that one word over and over.

"No," he moaned as his captor contemplated his weakened state. "No."

Martin slipped the surgical mask over his face again and walked away. Henry rolled his head to follow him, but he was lost in the darkness.

The whole place was dark, a bubble of blackness surrounding him. Henry tried to get an idea of where he could be. He sensed walls and a ceiling, but they were far away. The scent of pine and damp wood tickled his nostrils. Somewhere, he heard a pipe drip.

Then footsteps. Martin. Coming toward him again.

This time he brought light with him. It was a kerosene lantern, which he placed on the table next to Henry.

The glow from the lantern allowed Henry to finally see his surroundings. He was in a barn of some sort. An old one, vast and abandoned. Exposed beams hovered high above. The distant walls were paneled with uneven wooden planks.

Martin planted a hand on Henry's skull, holding his head in place. Henry felt a length of rope slide across his forehead, just below the hairline. It tightened, trapping his head in place, forcing his eyes to face upward.

"Keep still," Martin said, leaning over him. "This is going to hurt."

On the edge of his vision, Henry saw a needle. It was about two inches in length and looped with thick, black thread. When Martin moved the needle to his other hand, it passed before Henry's eyes, catching the lantern glow and reflecting it briefly. Soon it was gone, and all he saw were Martin's knuckles moving just beneath his nose.

The needle pierced Henry's bottom lip. Then pain. Worse than he expected.

It started at the needle's entry point, concentrated there. But when Martin pushed the entire needle through the flesh of Henry's lip, the pain spread, pulsing outward in a circle of agony.

On its way out, the needle's eye snagged on the exit wound, pulling Henry's lip away from his teeth—a hook refusing to let go of a fish.

The pain forced him to speak again.

"No."

Martin didn't stop. He drove the needle directly into Henry's upper lip, where it repeated the same steps of push, pain, pulse, pull.

Beads of blood sprouted on Henry's lips. Some clung to the thread. Others rolled down his chin, tickling their way onto his neck. Still more moved back toward his lips, slipping between them and into his mouth. Henry tasted the blood, bitter on his tongue.

He spoke again. "Martin."

At last, a new word. The pain ignited Henry's mind. More words formed in his head and managed to escape his lips.

"Why?" he asked. "Tell me why."

Needle in hand, Martin stretched his arm, tightening the thread inside both lips. It created a slithery feeling, like a maggot burrowing just beneath the surface of Henry's skin.

"Why?" he persisted.

"Does it really matter, Henry?" Martin's voice was distracted as he concentrated on the task at hand. "What's important now is that you stop talking."

Henry didn't. Talking meant his lips were still moving. Which made them harder to pin down. Which meant they wouldn't be sewn shut. Which meant Martin couldn't continue with whatever else he had planned. If that's what it took to stop him, then Henry was prepared to talk all day.

"Tell me."

Martin didn't wait for his lips to stop moving before shoving the needle into them. It was the bottom lip again. Push, pain, pulse, pull.

"It's a long story," he said.

He moved to the upper lip. When he yanked the thread taut, it hurt worse than the first time he'd done it. Instead of one slithering probe inside him, Henry felt two, tightening in unison.

"I want to know."

"I suspect," Martin said, "that you already do."

He continued to sew Henry's mouth, creating new points of pain in his lips, all of them connected by the sliding thread. He also continued to talk, practically chatting as Henry squirmed beneath his needle and thread.

"I know you've been in my sister's bedroom. So I know you saw the picture of my father. That's why Deana was drawn to you, you know. Not because you're actually worthy of her. Because of Dad and how much you looked like him, scars and all. The resemblance was—"

He stabbed Henry's bottom lip.

"Uncanny. That's the word for it. I noticed it, of course. It was like seeing his ghost. And you know what they say about ghosts, right? They have to be put to rest."

Martin stabbed his upper lip.

"But I couldn't just do it outright. That would have been disastrous. I needed practice first."

Bottom lip.

"That's why George was the first. So tall, you two. Both about the same height. I noticed it when I was covering his brother-in-law's funeral. That's when it dawned on me that if I practiced on people who had the same qualities you did, I'd be an expert at preservation when your time came."

Upper lip.

"Troy was the second. He was younger and, let's face it, Henry, far better looking. But he was the only person in Perry Hollow who had your build. All those muscles. All that strength."

Bottom lip.

"Then there was Amber Lefferts. Such pale skin. Exactly the same shade as yours. Only I never got the chance to see what it was like to preserve it. A pity, really. I hope you don't turn out badly because of my lack of practice in that regard."

Upper lip.

By that point, half of Henry's mouth had been sewn shut. When he spoke, it was out of the unobstructed side of his mouth. The words came slowly, thick and slurred.

"You . . . don't . . . need . . . to . . . kill . . . me."

Martin shook his head, clucking in disapproval. "But I do. It's not over until I do that. It's not over until I preserve you, just like I preserved Daddy."

He resumed his sewing, plunging the needle once more into Henry's bottom lip.

"But you were a hard man to get to. Always alone. Always locked in your office. That's why I had to send you those faxes. It was the only way to flush you out. It's why I faxed you the Campbell boy's name tonight. When Deana called to tell me you were leaving town, I had to act fast. I needed a decoy. And I knew that when you saw his name, you wouldn't leave. You'd try to save him, just like the others. And you did."

Martin finished his task with alarming speed.

Bottom lip.

Upper lip.

Push, pain, pulse, pull.

Finished, he tied off the thread and took the needle away.

Henry's mouth was now entirely sewn shut. He screamed behind the unnatural seal, trying in vain to make his voice connect with the air outside of his mouth.

Martin ignored him as he walked away from the table. Henry felt his presence recede in the darkness. A moment later, he returned. Henry heard a small clunk on the table next to his head, followed by the light scraping sound of fabric being opened. It was a pouch of some sort, filled with something heavy.

"I've got my tools," Martin said brightly. "It's amazing what you can buy on the Internet. Formaldehyde. Chloroform. Aneurysm hooks. It's all there for the taking."

Henry was mute and terrified, his eyes widening as Martin leaned over him again. He held up something sharp and metallic, giving Henry a good look.

It was a scalpel, glinting in the lantern light.

"I have a feeling," Martin said, "that you know what's going to come next."

# THIRTY-SEVEN

It should have taken Kat fifteen minutes to get from the hospital to Perry Mill. She made it in six.

Swerving onto the gravel road that led to the mill, she cut the car's headlights. When she was within a hundred yards of the mill's sole remaining structure, she shut off the engine and jumped out of the car.

Rising against Lake Squall, the mill towered over her, blotting out the stars in the night sky. The way it stood next to the water made Kat think of a graveyard. The mill was the tombstone. The lake was the grave. With a nervous shudder, she realized it could already be marking the spot of Henry's death. And in a few minutes, maybe her own.

She'd find out soon enough.

She sprinted toward the mill, a flashlight her guide. When she reached it, she saw Martin Swan's pickup truck parked next to a wide-open rectangle on the southern side of the building.

Kat reached for her Glock. She held the gun and flashlight together in her outstretched arms, one on top of the other. Before being swallowed into the mill's darkness, she paused.

In the car, she had tried to radio Carl, with no luck. She suspected he was with the others at Martin's house, searching the empty premises. She knew she needed backup. It was downright irresponsible to go into that mill alone. But she also knew Henry was inside, and the prospect of finding him alive dimmed with each passing second. Waiting to reach her deputy would take time she didn't have to spare.

She had to risk it.

As she crept into the building, Kat's nose was immediately filled with the smell of dust, decay, and pine. Everywhere, pine. Rising off the floor. Drifting down from above. Closing in at her sides.

*This,* Kat thought, *is what it smelled like inside one of those homemade coffins.*

The thought disturbed her. So did the darkness, which had joined the pine scent in surrounding her.

Sweeping the flashlight back and forth, Kat saw she was in a warehouse of sorts. Stacks of pine planks dotted the room, forgotten relics of the mill's heyday. Moving through the piles of rotting wood, she spotted a small door on the other side of the room. Chipped paint across the front designated it as AC-COUNTING.

Kat reached the door in five long strides and burst inside.

It was an office. At least it had been long ago. A desk still sat in a corner, overtaken by rust. A filing cabinet lay overturned on the floor. A calendar hung on the wall, its mold-streaked pages forever insisting it was March 1990.

Kat spotted several large jars sitting on the dilapidated desk, each filled with coins. She pointed the flashlight into one of the jars. A copper glow reflected back at her.

Pennies. Hundreds of them.

She moved on, pushing out of the office and into a short hallway littered with feathers, used condoms, and rodent shit. Kat stepped over all of it as she peeked into the three rooms that lined the hall.

The first one was mostly bare, its floor containing the same detritus found in the hallway. The only object inside was a wood-handled hatchet. Its blade was sunk deep into the floor, the handle rising from it like a petrified sapling.

Kat kicked at the handle and the hatchet toppled onto its side, the blade digging up a chunk of the floor with it.

She turned her attention to the second room, aiming both the gun and the flashlight into its dark recesses. The light latched onto a pair of eyes, which reflected it back in an ominous glow. Seeing them, Kat gasped.

The noise startled the eyes' owner, which in this case was a deer. Standing in the center of the room, it raised its antlered head and looked at her. When Kat took a step backward, the deer charged toward the door, an angry snort puffing from its snout.

Kat jumped out of the way, flipping into the next room as the buck burst into the hallway. It turned, hindquarters skidding into the wall, and clomped down the hall. Kat watched it leave, white tail bounding into the office she had just vacated.

She stayed hidden in the third room, trying to calm the pounding of her heart. When her pulse slowed to an acceptable rate, she scanned the room. It contained more wood. But instead of planks of pine, it was filled with boxes made of it.

Coffins.

A dozen of them sat evenly spaced on the floor. A matching lid covered each one. Unlike the coffins Kat had found George and Troy in, the lids weren't nailed shut.

These were empty and unused and waiting to be filled.

As she backed away, Kat knocked into one of the coffins. She tumbled over it, taking the lid with her. It flipped off and clattered on top of her legs. Kat kicked it away while swinging the light in front of her until the beam stopped at the now-open coffin.

Someone was inside it.

Kat held back a yelp. Crawling to her knees, she shuffled to the coffin's edge and peered inside.

It was Lucas Hatcher. His arms were crossed at his chest. Two pennies covered his eyes. In the middle of his forehead was a bullet hole.

Kat looked for, but couldn't find, stitches in his lips or a gash at his neck. That mutilation, she realized with horror, had been reserved for Henry.

Nick clamped a hand over his mouth to keep from yelling. The pain was bad when he slid out of bed but manageable. Now, when he was forced to actually walk, it was excruciating.

He edged across the room, supporting himself with the metal pole his broken leg had hung from. His entire body silently screamed for him to stop. And his mouth would have screamed out loud if it wasn't for his hand, which remained over his lips.

He finally removed his hand when he reached the door. Counting to three, he threw the door open. Harry-Gary stood a few feet away, his back turned. Nick didn't waste a moment. He hobbled up to the nurse until he was right behind him.

"Harry?" he asked.

The nurse spun around, surprised.

"It's Gary."

"My mistake."

While he spoke, Nick raised his right leg. His bones creaked inside the plaster cast. Pain spiked at the knee and shot through his entire body. Nick tried to ignore it. There'd be more pain to come in a second. Worse pain.

The cast was heavy, which made it hard to lift. But the pros outweighed the cons, especially when Nick slammed its weight into Gary's groin.

Nick knew it hurt him more than it did Gary. But he was prepared for it. The nurse wasn't, and the pain made him double over. Nick raised the cast again, striking Gary in the head. That was enough to knock him out for a little bit. Hopefully long enough for Nick to get out of that shithole they called a hospital.

Before doing that, Nick grabbed the pole. Still attached to it was the plastic sling, which he slipped over the nurse's head until it was around his neck. Nick pushed the pole just inside the door, leaving the plastic band outside. When he closed the door, it held the sling in place, tightening it like a noose around Gary's neck. Even if the nurse did wake up soon, he wouldn't be able to move.

With Gary secured, Nick rifled through his pockets, finding a set of car keys.

"Thanks, Gary," he said, patting him on the cheek. "I owe you a beer."

Nick shuffled down the hall, exhilaration halving his pain. Determination dulled the rest. He needed to get to the exit at the end of the hall without anyone seeing him. After that, it was off to the parking lot, then the mill.

He hoped he wasn't too late. He hoped that when he got there, Henry—and Kat herself—would still be alive.

Seeing the scalpel, Henry tried to scream behind his closed mouth. The vibration it created caused the pain to erupt once again across his lips, making him scream even more. Martin ignored the sound as he swiped the flat side of the scalpel across his scrubs, cleaning it.

He then placed it against the right side of Henry's neck. Its razor-sharp blade scraped along his skin. Henry closed his eyes, waiting to feel it slice into his flesh.

That didn't happen. Instead, Martin pulled the blade away.

"This is going to be tough on Deana," he said. "I tried to warn you, Henry. I told you to stay away. But you didn't, and now you're going to break my sister's heart."

Martin pressed the scalpel to his neck again. This time it stayed there.

Henry cried out—a terrified whimper that rattled around

in his mouth. He attempted another scream, hoping the force of it would separate his lips. When that didn't work, he tried opening his mouth. The jaws parted, straining against the thread coiled inside his lips. The thread tugged his skin—two dozen pinpoints of sheer agony.

Martin applied pressure to the scalpel. The blade began its descent into Henry's flesh.

He opened his mouth wider, hoping he could part it enough to snap the thread that trembled inside his lips.

The scalpel broke through the barrier of Henry's skin, sinking deeper into his neck. There was a flash of coldness as the blade entered his body. It was followed by a stomach-roiling tickle as Martin slid the scalpel down his neck, slicing it open.

Henry opened his mouth wider. The thread in his lips trembled like a plucked guitar string, the tension wearing it down, making it weak.

He closed his eyes. Summoning every ounce of energy left in his violated body, he screamed again.

Instead of breaking, the thread acted as its own scalpel, cutting through the rubbery flesh of his lips. It ripped through the bottom lip in a gush of blood and skin until his mouth parted.

The scream burst out, blasting into the open and echoing through the darkness. Meanwhile, blood gushed from his neck, spilling out of him in a crimson waterfall. It soaked the table and collected in puddles around his head and shoulders.

Henry grew dizzy. Whether it was from loss of blood or basic primal terror, he didn't know. Weakness settled over his body. His vision clouded and his mind grew hazy. He could open his mouth again, but he knew that whatever words came out wouldn't stop the inevitable. They wouldn't clot the blood rushing from his neck.

"No," he mumbled through lips that also bled. "No."

Martin chastised him. "You shouldn't have done that, Henry. It'll only make it worse."

He had released the scalpel and now held another tool. Henry strained to see what it was. When he did, he immediately regretted it.

It was a metal hook, which Martin placed next to Henry's neck.

As blood still flowed out of the cut, Martin poked the hook into it. The feeling it produced was worse than the scalpel, worse than the needle and thread. It was an outright invasion of his body, causing Henry to shake violently as the hook dug around in his neck, searching for something to latch onto.

"I want the jugular vein first," Martin said as he manipulated the hook. "I got that wrong the first time. But I think George still came out okay in the end."

He increased the speed of his digging, the hook swiping blindly inside Henry's neck. Each movement of it caused his head to jerk in a seizure of helplessness. He had no control over his body anymore. No control over anything. He was just a living cadaver, being raped by cold, hard steel.

When Martin snagged an artery, Henry felt it in his entire body. His head stopped twitching. His neck tightened. His throat constricted.

Martin tugged slightly and the artery tightened within Henry's body. He couldn't breathe. He couldn't swallow. He tried, but his muscles were under attack, refusing to function. A croaking sound formed in the back of his throat, unable to be stopped. It gurgled up past his tongue and through his shredded lips.

"No," he gasped.

As Martin continued to pull on the vein, Henry knew he

was going to die. His body was preparing for it, getting ready for the inevitable end. That's what caused the twitching and the croaking. It was a rehearsal of the death rattle that was certain to come.

The vein was outside his body now. It exited with a slimy sucking noise that reminded Henry of earthworms in rain-soaked dirt.

Its exposure sent his body into shock. His heart, which had been pumping at warp speed for so long, suddenly slowed. His eyes went blank. Although Henry still had them open, he saw nothing but a cottony haze covering his pupils.

The croak burped out of his throat again, gradually extending itself until it was a guttural hiss.

His ears felt plugged. He barely heard Martin mumbling to himself.

"Now I cut the artery."

Henry's body revved up again in one last flash of energy before fading forever. His heart thrummed again. His hearing cleared. His eyes could suddenly see. He shifted them to Martin, who hovered over him. The hook was in his left hand. The scalpel was in his right. They were about to connect at his artery. When they did, he would be dead.

Martin took a deep breath as he placed the scalpel blade to his artery.

Henry understood with crystalline clarity that he had mere seconds left to try to save his life. Using his body, which was tied up and worn down, wasn't possible. All he had were his wits—and his voice.

"No."

When Henry spoke, he felt the artery moving through the gash in his neck. Each word made it bend like a plastic straw.

"Please. No."

"I'm sorry," Martin said. "I have to."

"No, you don't."

The voice wasn't Henry's. It came from a darkened corner of the room. When it spoke again, Henry knew who it belonged to.

"You don't have to do it, Martin," Kat Campbell said. "You can stop this right now."

# THIRTY-EIGHT

Kat had followed the scream. That blast of noise, a bansheelike wail that cut through the darkness, led her to back into the hallway, down a precarious set of steps, and into the bowels of the mill. Rounding a corner, she saw Martin immediately.

His entire body was covered in the same type of scrubs she had worn in the embalming room. Gown. Apron. Gloves. Cap concealing the hair. Paper coverings over the shoes. It explained why they had never been able to lift a print or hair sample from anything he had contact with. There was nothing exposed that could have left any.

He stood in front of a table, blocking Kat's view. To Martin's right, she saw a pair of legs stretched out and tied up. Henry's legs.

Martin held the scalpel in his right hand, guiding it toward an area of Henry's body that Kat couldn't see. That's when she raised her Glock, pointed it at the back of Martin's head and spoke.

When he didn't move, Kat spoke again.

"I'm going to count to three. If you don't put the scalpel down and back away, I'm going to kill you."

She meant it. Arms outstretched, she felt the Glock heavy

in her grip. Her finger twitched against the trigger. She wasn't a violent woman. Not by any means. But Martin's actions had torn the town apart and haunted her dreams for months. He had gone after her son, and James would likely be scarred for the rest of his life because of it. So nothing would have pleased her more than to gun Martin down right then and there.

"One," she said.

Martin raised his hands.

"Two."

He placed the scalpel flat on the table.

"Three."

He finally backed away, giving Kat a good look at Henry. Shirtless and bound to a plank of pine in four places, he was bleeding profusely but still alive.

With the gun still trained on Martin, she edged into the room.

"Keep your hands in the air and take ten steps away from him," she said. "If you run, I will shoot you. If you take only nine steps, I will shoot you. Start moving."

Martin moved backward while Kat counted his steps. For each one he took away from the table, she took one toward it. As she drew close to Henry, she saw that his neck had been sliced open. A wormlike vein stuck out of the wound. She reached the table and, without thinking, poked it back into his neck before clamping a hand over the gash. Blood squeezed between her fingers.

"You're going to be okay," she said, not knowing if that was the truth. "I'm going to get you out of here."

Henry stared at her helplessly. There was gratefulness in his eyes. Panic, too. He knew it could be too late to save his life. He opened his mouth and Kat saw that his lips had been reduced to shreds of flesh. Thread slithered throughout the skin.

He managed to choke out a few words. "Stitch. Neck."

Kat shushed him. She knew what had to be done. Henry was bleeding to death. She needed to close the wound in his neck immediately, even if it meant turning her back on the man who called himself the Grim Reaper. It was a risk, but one she was forced to take if Henry was going to survive.

"Say something, Martin," she barked. "I need to know you're still standing far away."

"What do you want me to say?"

Kat noted the volume in his voice and judged his distance. If he got any louder, then it meant he was getting closer. Which meant she would kill him.

"Tell me about Arthur McNeil," she said. "I know what he did to you."

"Then I guess I don't need to talk about it."

A needle already looped with thread sat next to the scalpel on the table. Wasting no time, Kat lowered the gun, picked up the needle and shoved it into Henry's neck. Blood squished between her trembling fingers, but she didn't stop. She couldn't.

"When did it start? Before your father died?"

"Yes," Martin said, his voice maintaining the same volume. "I was eleven."

"It took place in the embalming room, right?"

"Yes."

"While your mother worked upstairs?"

"Yes."

Kat continued the stitching at Henry's neck. So far, she had managed to loop the thread through the wound twice.

"I know that when your dad died, Art told you he'd stop if you did something for him. What was that?"

"You seem to be the expert," Martin said sarcastically. "You tell me."

"He made you embalm your father. He made you cut the neck and the arteries. He made you pour in the embalming fluid."

And after that was the sewing of the lips and the coins over the eyes. Exactly like what had happened to Bob. Kat couldn't begin to comprehend what it must have been like. Martin's father was lying dead in front of him and a trusted family friend was forcing him to do things no kid could ever understand.

"Am I right?" she asked.

Kat slipped the needle through Henry's neck one last time before tying off the thread. It was a horrible stitch job. The thread was crooked and knotted in parts. Huge gaps remained where she should have made another pass with the needle. But it was good enough. Henry's bleeding had slowed considerably.

"Martin, is that what happened?"

"Yes."

Kat's spine stiffened when she heard Martin's voice.

It was closer.

Much closer.

She reached for the Glock before whirling around to face him.

Martin stood only five feet away, and he had his own gun. Kat knew it was the same one that had been in the delivery van, the same one used to kill Lucas Hatcher.

Without saying a word, Martin fired twice.

The bullets punched into Kat's chest. She screamed, flying backward next to the table. The last thing she saw was Henry. On the table itself. Surrounded by blood. Mouthing her name.

Her back struck the floor, a collision of bone and wood that sent shock waves up her spine. Pain squeezed her body. Air rushed out of her lungs.

Then, with one last gasp, Kat Campbell's world went dark.

It took only an instant for Kat to fall. One second she stood at Henry's side. The next she was on the floor. When it was over, Henry strained against the ropes, trying to shout her name.

Only he couldn't shout. He could barely speak. But his thoughts were so loud in his head that it felt like he was screaming at full volume.

*Kat! Dear God, no!*

Grunting with exertion, he tried to sit up, pushing himself against the ropes that held him down. He needed to see her. He needed to know if she was still alive. If she was, he needed to help her, just as she had helped him. But the binds refused to budge, the rope digging into him.

*Kat! Can you hear me? Answer me!*

He turned his head as far as the rope and the pain would allow, catching a glimpse of Kat's legs splayed on the floor. Tears burned their way down his cheeks as he managed to croak out her name.

"Kat."

His thoughts screamed the rest.

*Don't die! Please don't die!*

Martin took a few steps toward Kat's body and kicked her in the ribs. Satisfied she was dead, he shoved his gun into a deep pocket of his apron, where it had been hidden the entire time. He then bent forward and picked up Kat's gun. Wordlessly, he opened the chamber and let the bullets slide into his palm. Then he threw them into the darkness, where they bounced and scattered. Next, he tossed the gun away. It hit the wall before clunking to the floor.

With the guns out of the way, Martin vanished to a corner of the room. He returned a moment later, dragging a metal pail behind him. As he reached the table, he removed a plastic bottle and a funnel attached to a thin rubber tube.

Henry's thoughts grew silent when Martin opened the bottle. The odor of chemicals assaulted his nose.

Formaldehyde. It filled the air around him.

The odor meant one thing—Martin still intended to embalm him.

Glancing between Henry and the bottle, Martin poured the formaldehyde into the pail. When the bottle was empty, he returned to the table and held Henry's head in place. His hand fumbled along the wood next to him, finding the scalpel exactly where he had left it.

Picking it up, he held the blade to Henry's neck.

"This time," he said, "I'm not going to hesitate to kill you."

Pain.

That's all Kat felt.

Horrible pain. Deep in her chest, it pulsed at the spot where the two bullets had hit, feeling like twin holes in her sternum.

But Kat knew there'd be no holes there. Bruises, yes. Maybe marks worse than the ones on Henry's face. But no bullet holes. At least not on that day.

With her eyes still closed, she slid a hand across her chest. Her fingers snaked past the buttons of her uniform and ran over the Kevlar vest she had taken from the trunk of her patrol car. The two bullets were embedded deep inside it, squished into still-hot studs of metal.

Sitting up, Kat opened her eyes.

Martin was next to Henry again, lantern light glinting off the scalpel in his hand.

Kat climbed to her feet. She shot across the room, the pain in her chest flaring as she tackled Martin from behind.

He dropped the scalpel as he fell forward onto Henry's chest. Pushing himself away from the table, he nudged Kat backward until her feet hit the pail on the floor.

The pail rattled between her ankles. Kat tried to keep it

upright with her feet but couldn't. The pail fell over. Formaldehyde sloshed out, splashing her shoes before washing across the floor.

She moved out of the puddle the formaldehyde created and tried to push Martin against the table again. Martin's arms flailed, fighting back. He reached back to grab Kat's hair with one hand. The other stretched out, reaching for the scalpel.

Kat tugged Martin's arm. His fingers pulled away from the scalpel, grabbing the kerosene lantern instead. The lamp toppled over in a crush of glass and fire. Kerosene rushed over the table, soaking Henry before dripping onto the floor.

Fanned by Martin's flapping hands, the flame spread. It caught the trail of kerosene and leaped to life in a menacing *whoosh* that rushed past Henry's ear. A second later, it was everywhere. Flames streaked across the table and ignited his clothes. The fire spread to his shoulder and right arm, eating the fabric of his shirt.

The fire reached the rope that tied Henry down. As flames chewed through it, he pushed his arms away from his side. The rope snapped in a burst of sparks and fell away, trailing smoke.

When she saw that Henry was almost free, Kat yanked Martin's arm again. The force of the tug whirled him around until he faced her. Not wasting a golden opportunity, Kat punched him in the jaw.

Stunned, Martin twisted away, taking Kat with him. Both of them fell backward, smashing into the table. It lurched under their weight and listed to the left. A table leg snapped beneath them. Kat could see Henry trying to hold on, even as the table itself, creaking and groaning, tipped over.

Henry slipped off the table, riding a slide of kerosene, blood, and fire. Then Kat was next, tumbling with Martin. They crashed next to Henry, landing on the overturned table, breaking it apart.

The table's contents spilled to the floor.

The scalpel skittered away, blade up.

The fire grew larger.

Fueled by the kerosene, it spread fast. Flames rushed over what remained of the table before roaring across the floor.

Kat and Martin rolled away from the blaze, tumbling over, then under, each other. First, Kat was on top. Then Martin. Then Kat again. In the tumult, she managed to stick out a foot to halt their trajectory. When they stopped, Martin was on his back with Kat practically sitting on top of him.

Beneath her was the gun he had shot her with. The handle poked out of his apron pocket, begging to be grabbed. When Kat reached for it, Martin lifted his knee, nudging her off balance and onto her back.

The gun receded into the pocket again as Martin lunged forward and jumped on top of her.

Straddling Kat's waist, he punched all over. Her head. Her face. Her gut. A fist connected with her jaw, causing a flash of blue lights to dot her vision.

The blue continued as Martin wrapped his hands around her neck, squeezing tight. Struggling for breath, Kat tried to pry him from her neck with one hand. The other flailed over her head, knuckles scraping the floor.

Martin lifted Kat's head off the floor and slammed it down again. He did it two more times—lift, slam, lift, slam.

The pain of the blows created even more blue lights. They grew until she could barely see.

She could barely breathe.

She could barely think.

Her free hand continued to scrape across the floor. Sawdust raked her fingers. A splinter jabbed into her palm. Then steel brushed her knuckles.

The scalpel. Right at her fingertips.

Martin saw it, too, and swatted Kat's hand away.

On the other side of the room, a vaporous hiss rose off the floor. The fire had reached the overturned pail and puddle of formaldehyde. Even in the chaos, Kat recalled Bob McNeil's warning about formaldehyde. It was flammable. It was explosive.

He was right on both counts.

The hiss mutated into a roar that sent a ball of flame leaping off the floor. Kat watched wide-eyed as the tower of fire rose to the rafters. The flames lit the ceiling, sending tendrils of fire across it. They spread outward swiftly, moving to the walls and back down to the floor.

Still on top of her, Martin Swan didn't notice the flames overhead. But Kat did. And she knew what he didn't—that the mill was now completely engulfed.

# THIRTY-NINE

Kat knew how this scenario would play out. The fire would eventually chew through the roof, sending it falling onto them. The walls would follow, crushing whatever was left.

She had only minutes to escape. Minutes to take Henry with her.

But she had to get Martin off of her first. And the only way to do that would be with the scalpel.

Kat twisted her arm, hand flexing. She scraped her fingers along the floor again, seeking the scalpel.

It wasn't there.

Her hand searched the floor, desperately trying to find it. Instead, Kat felt hot wood, simmering blood, and pinpricks of fire.

Martin's hands tightened around her neck. Kat could no longer breathe. All air was gone, blocked by Martin's steely grip.

Her vision was also blocked. By her fluttering eyelids. By the flashes of blue. By an encroaching darkness.

She barely saw Henry as he crawled behind Martin, his face streaked with blood and smoke.

In his hand was the scalpel.

Henry lifted it. The blade glinted orange, reflecting the fire that surrounded them. It became a blur as Henry's hand swiped across Martin's throat. The scalpel created a thin, red line from one side of his neck to the other. Martin's eyes widened when he realized what had happened.

Then he swallowed.

The gash in Martin's neck opened up. Blood spewed out of it, pouring down his chest. He clutched his throat, gasping, but the blood flowed unabated in thick rivulets.

Kat crawled backward as Martin slumped forward. Face down on the floor, he flopped morbidly, hands useless against the tide of blood. After one last flop and a pained, rattling gasp, Martin Swan grew still.

Every part of Henry's body was weak, worn down by trauma, blood loss, and the still-unreal fact that he had just killed someone.

He needed rest. And a hospital. Both would have to wait. With the fire growing, he and Kat were still in harm's way.

"How do we get out of here?" Kat asked.

"Don't. Know."

He could barely speak. Each word was agony. Every syllable tugged at the stitches in his neck and inflamed his mutilated lips.

They rose together, clutching each other for support until

both of them were on their feet. Henry was more unsteady than Kat, threatening to tip over at any moment. But Kat kept hold of him.

"This way," she said, scanning the room with mounting desperation. "I think it's this way."

The fire had spread across the floor in red-hot tentacles, grabbing whatever it could reach. The table, Henry noted, was now a charred lump, having been consumed—then discarded—by the flames.

They stumbled past it, groping blindly in the thick smoke. Their destination was the door where Kat had entered. Only they couldn't find it. The smoke was so overwhelming that they lost all sense of direction.

He and Kat shuffled back to their original spot. On their way there, Henry saw the fire had reached Martin. His scrubs smoldered a moment before bursting into flames. The fire danced across his body, ripping across his back and igniting his hair.

That would be them soon, he realized. The smoke would overpower them, and the fire would close in on them until they, too, succumbed to the flames.

He and Kat still stumbled backward, edging to a far wall—the place where there seemed to be the least smoke.

"What are we going to do?" Kat asked.

Henry coughed out his answer. "Pray."

He could no longer see Kat. The smoke was too heavy. It moved between them in roiling clouds, cramming his eyes, his nose, his mouth. The searing heat of the encroaching fire forced them to back up even farther until there was no place left to move.

"We're trapped," he heard Kat say. "Goddamn it, we're trapped."

The smoke blinded Henry, forcing his eyes shut. When he felt something hard bump against his back, he knew what Kat was talking about. It was the wall, trapping them from behind. In front of them, the smoke created another wall. Beyond that was a third barrier of flames that burned steadily toward them.

Henry turned to the wall. His hands tripped across it. Kat's did the same. She choked out words through the smoke.

"Our Father, who art in Heaven, hallowed be thy name."

It was the Lord's Prayer. She was literally praying for her life.

Henry mentally joined in.

*Thy Kingdom come, thy will be done.*

Their hands never left the wall. Their scraped and bloody fingers moved across the wood, hoping against hope to find some opening, some way out of the inferno.

*On Earth, as it is in Heaven.*

One of Henry's fingers suddenly slipped forward, feeling nothing. It had dipped into a crack that divided one panel of wood from another.

He pushed his face toward the crack and smelled fresh air. Clean, cool, blessed air. And water. Just beyond the wall.

"Lake," he gasped to Kat. "The. Lake."

Backing up as far as the fire would allow, Kat rammed herself against the wall. When it didn't budge, she tried it again. Then again, her body a hammer of desperation beating against the unbending wood.

Henry faced the fire again. It was closer now, about knee-high, turning the gray smoke orange. He saw movement within the smoke—a person, rushing toward them. Then Nick Donnelly burst into view. His blackened face twisted in pain as he hobbled on his right leg, which was wrapped in a cast. Fire tripped over the plaster.

Gripped in Nick's hands was a wood-handled hatchet, which he hoisted over his shoulder and thrust into the wall. The panel splintered from the force, opening slightly. Nick removed the hatchet and assaulted the wall again. The hatchet connected with the wood a second time, a whole panel of the wall breaking loose.

The three of them shoved their bodies against it until the wall gave way. Then they tumbled out of the fiery mill, falling into the lake beside it.

The cool water embraced Henry as he broke through its surface. The lake surrounded him, enveloped him, soothed him. As he sank to the bottom, the water took away the soot the smoke had left on his face and hands. It washed the wounds at his neck and mouth.

When he reached the lake floor, Henry pushed upward. The shimmering surface was just a few yards away. Swimming toward it, he couldn't wait to get there. Once he broke through it, he'd be cleansed. Free of the fire. Free of the smoke. Free of the blood.

Free of his past.

Free of his guilt.

Free.

# EPILOGUE

On New Year's Day, Kat awoke to the sound of shrieks and cheerful barking coming from the living room. Lifting her head, she glanced at the clock on the nightstand. It was barely eight. James and his new friend were up early and, most likely, needing to be fed.

The noise grew louder when Kat headed downstairs. It was accompanied by a few bumps of furniture and the pitter-patter of paws on the floor. She found James in the living room, rolling on the carpet. A rambunctious beagle hopped around him, tail wagging with abandon. James reached for the dog, pulling it into a wriggling hug.

"We're playing tag," he said when he saw Kat. "Wanna play?"

Kat declined. "Mommy needs coffee first."

The beagle followed her down the hall to the kitchen, where it made a beeline to its personalized food bowl. Kat poured kibble into the bowl, which was marked with the name Scooby.

The beagle came from Caleb Fisher, whose own dogs had produced a litter of puppies. Upon seeing them, James begged to keep one and Kat relented. He deserved it after all he had gone through.

That was another reason Kat gave in on the puppy front—therapy. Although James's shock wore off a few days after Halloween, remnants of stress remained. Nightmares. Irrational fears. He was plagued by it all. Kat took him to therapy once a week. She didn't know if he'd fully recover from what he saw that night. But his therapist had hope. Kat did, too.

Having the dog helped. James was devoted to it. And Scooby made him happy, which was good enough for her.

After taking care of the dog, Kat fed James, pouring him a bowl of Cheerios and a glass of orange juice. Then came coffee, which Kat brewed up extra-strength.

The phone rang as she poured the steaming java into the largest mug she could find. Answering it, she heard a familiar voice.

"Turn on CNN," Nick Donnelly said.

Kat stifled a yawn. "Happy New Year to you, too."

"Just turn on the TV."

Carrying both phone and coffee, Kat returned to the living room and flicked on the television. She was immediately greeted by an image of Nick, looking as sharp as ever while giving an interview in the CNN studios.

A cane leaned against his chair. Kat knew he couldn't walk without it. His right leg was so busted that it never healed properly. There had been surgeries and physical therapy sessions, but the prognosis was always the same—a permanent limp.

"Do you see me?" he asked.

"I do. But how are you talking to me and to CNN at the same time? Don't tell me you cloned yourself in order to catch more bad guys."

Her sarcasm wasn't lost on Nick, who said, "That's very amusing. And although cloning is a great idea, the interview was taped two weeks ago."

On the TV, Kat watched him say, "The case was fascinating. Martin Swan was so warped by his own trauma that he didn't care if he caused other people pain."

Kat muted the television. She knew the details intimately. She didn't need to hear them rehashed on TV, even if the rehashing was coming from a friend.

"So how many interviews has this been?" Kat asked Nick as she stared at the silent television.

"Too many to count. I wasn't going to do this one, but it was for their special on the top ten biggest news stories of the year. We're ranked number seven, if you care."

Kat didn't. Ever since the night the mill burned down, she had been bombarded with interview requests. Magazines wanted her story. TV news programs wanted to devote whole episodes to her. A publishing house specializing in true crime stories had even offered a book deal.

She understood the fascination. It was a compelling case. Martin, having been forced to embalm his own father as a boy, tried it again on innocent victims, including someone who looked so much like his father it was eerie.

Although Kat could never be sure, she suspected that Art McNeil knew Martin was the killer. He also probably knew that his abuse had spurred the crimes. That's why he made his cryptic confession just before killing himself. He was trying to absolve himself of his guilt.

What Art did was monstrous, but the blame still fell on Martin alone. He must have enjoyed some aspect of his deeds because he spent a lot of time planning them. The embalming tools, chloroform, formaldehyde, and surgical scrubs were all ordered off multiple sites on the Internet. A search of Martin's home computer yielded records of purchases from dozens of different sites. All of it had been sent to various post office boxes registered under his pseudonym—Meg Parrier.

The only thing Martin didn't buy himself were the portable fax machines used to send the obituaries. Those were purchased by Deana, who was the woman the clerk had seen at the Best Buy.

The day after his death, Deana admitted her brother had asked her to buy the machines. When she asked him why, he told her they would be used by *Gazette* staff members. He said the newspaper was paying for them and handed her the large amount of cash necessary for the purchase. After buying the machines, she gave them to Martin, who activated the fax numbers under the name Meg Parrier.

Deana swore she didn't know what Martin was really using them for. Kat believed her. Her dismay at what had happened was too great to be faked. And the fact that she had played a role in the murders only compounded Deana's stress. Her brother was a killer. Her former boyfriend had been a target. And now both of them were out of her life forever.

Ironically, the only media outlet not begging for her attention was the *Perry Hollow Gazette*. The paper never printed another issue after Halloween. That was the aftermath of having your crime reporter being outed as a serial killer.

Even if the *Gazette* still existed, Kat wouldn't have given them an interview. She turned down every offer that came her way—from *The New York Times* to *Good Morning America*.

Her reasons for doing so were simple.

First, the incident was still too horrible to reflect upon. She had almost died that night. So had her son. She wanted to forget Martin Swan, not talk about him endlessly to strangers who could never truly know how terrifying the experience had been.

Second, the story wasn't hers alone. Henry was really the main character of that particular tale. Although Kat was the police chief and Nick the one who saved the day, Henry had seen—and suffered—the most.

And he wasn't talking.

The night of the fire was the last time Kat saw him. His injuries were too extreme to be treated at the county hospital, so he was whisked away in a helicopter to one in Philadelphia. When Kat was released from the hospital herself, she made an attempt to visit him. But he was gone.

As for Nick Donnelly, he accepted every offer Kat turned down, including the true crime book. He called her regularly, regaling her with tales of all the rich and famous people he had met during the media blitz surrounding the murders. Kat listened patiently, assuring him she was happy for his good fortune.

"So how did you spend New Year's Eve?" he asked.

"On the couch. Watching the ball drop with James. You?"

"In Philadelphia. There was a gala fundraiser for the foundation. I never got your RSVP."

"Sorry about that," Kat said. "I'm not a gala kind of gal."

Nick was fired from the state police after an investigation found him responsible for the crash that injured Amber Lefferts. Then there was the matter of the nurse he assaulted outside his hospital room. That had sealed the deal, and the state police now wanted nothing to do with him. The only thing keeping him from criminal charges was his former boss, Gloria Ambrose. She told anyone who would listen that firing Nick was punishment enough.

Free of his state police ties, Nick had founded the Sarah Donnelly Foundation, which was devoted to investigating unsolved crimes. He used all the publicity gained from the Perry Hollow murders—not to mention the money that came with it—to tout the foundation.

Glancing at the TV, Kat saw the foundation's name and phone number running across the bottom of the screen. She turned the sound back up, hearing Nick say, "Using private re-sources, the foundation vows to look into unsolved cases that authorities have given up on."

Hearing his own voice over the phone, Nick said, "Ah, my spiel. How does it sound?"

"Intense."

"Good. That's what I was aiming for."

"Have you had any takers yet?"

"Not yet," Nick said. "But I have an opening for an investigator, if you ever get tired of Hicksville."

It wasn't the first time he had asked her to work for the foundation. It wasn't even the third. Every time they spoke, the topic invariably came up. And each time, she gave the same response.

"I'll think about it," she said.

And she did. She thought about it quite a bit, always deciding that Perry Hollow was where she needed to be. It was her home. It was James's home. It was all they had, and all they needed.

"Tell me when you change your mind," Nick said. "I know you will someday."

When the call ended, Kat carried her coffee back to the kitchen. Scooby had finished his breakfast. So had James. While they resumed their game of tag on the floor, Kat sorted through the stack of mail that had piled up during the holidays.

She perused the usual sea of Christmas greetings, bills, and credit card offers until one postcard caught her eye. On the front was a picture of La Scala, Milan's famous opera house. On the back was a six-word message.

"More scars," it read. "But I'll be okay."

Henry Goll didn't leave a return address or wish her and James a happy new year. He didn't thank her for saving his life. He didn't even sign the postcard. But Kat knew it wasn't an insult on his part. It was just his way, and she understood completely.

Besides, the card was more precious without the addition of sentiment. It was a perfect summation of what life was all about. Everyone had scars. Henry obviously did. Nick also had them. Kat did, too, in the form of two circles on her chest where the Kevlar vest had stopped Martin Swan's bullets.

Even if she didn't have physical scars, the mental ones would have been enough. The events of the past year would stay with her for a long time.

But she had her son. She had her health. She had her town. And, scars and all, she knew they would all be okay.

# ACKNOWLEDGMENTS

It's unfair that only my name appears on the cover of this book when, in reality, so many people helped make it happen. Chief among them are my agent, Michelle Brower, who took a chance and said yes when it probably would have been easier to say no, and my editor, Kelley Ragland, whose advice and suggestions helped polish this chunk of coal until it was a diamond.

My family inspired me in ways they can't imagine. So I need to thank my mother, Linda Ritter, for the books, my sister, Stephanie Ritter, for the music, and my father, Raymond Ritter, for the taxidermy.

For their opinions, information, and general support, I'm indebted to Edward Aycock, Mike Beltranena, Adrian Blain, Sarah Dutton, Leeza Hernandez, Sam Livio, Susan Livio, Barbara Poelle, Brooke Sample, Mike Scott, Felecia Wellington, and all my newspaper friends scattered throughout New Jersey.

Finally, the person who deserves the most credit—and the biggest thanks—is Michael Livio, who read every draft, listened to every idea, whim, and complaint, and, most important, never, ever stopped believing in me. I could thank you for eternity and it still wouldn't be enough.